"You Gotta Have Heart"

"You Gotta Have Heart"

AN AUTOBIOGRAPHY BY

Richard Adler

With

LEE DAVIS

DONALD I. FINE, INC.
New York

Library of Congress Cataloging-in-Publication Data

Adler, Richard, 1921–
You gotta have heart / by Richard Adler with Lee Davis.
p.   cm.
ISBN 1-55611-201-7 (alk. paper)
1. Adler, Richard, 1921–   . 2. Composers—United States-
-Biography.   I. Davis, Lee.   II. Title.
ML410.A235A3 1989
782.1'4'092—dc20
[B]   89-46032
CIP
MN

Manufactured in the United States of America
10 9 8 7 6 5 4 3 2 1

BOOK DESIGN BY BARBARA M. BACHMAN

To Gurumayi,
who showed me
how to find my heart.

PREFACE

Richard Adler is a good looking man. He is what we used to call tall, dark and handsome. Those of you who know him don't have to be told that but for those of you who have never seen Richard Adler it should be stated. Such is the look of the man who is telling you about himself.

I have always called Richard Dick. He prefers Richard but we—Hal Prince, Bobby Griffiths and I—in the days of our working together (and no matter how many shows you do, struggling together) always called him Dick. And so it has a certain warmness for me.

We worked untold hours in our mutual struggle to make a hit of *Pajama Game*. Only those who have co-worked in that fashion know what a bond it creates. We get to know each other. An intimacy develops which is hard to describe. You fight, of course . . . 'tho that is too harsh a word for the arguments that take place. You learn to trust your fellow worker. Underneath all that shouting is a common goal . . . improve it, make it better, make it perfect.

So I shall read Richard's story about himself with great interest . . . and I shall see him shouting his opinions with a passionate voice and blazing eyes and think . . . that it is as it should be.

George Abbott
April 30, 1990

CONTENTS

INTRODUCTION

Writing this story—this book—this life of mine was interesting to me. Interesting the way it all came back to me piece by piece—incident by incident—episode by episode—the people—the anecdotes—the drama of my life—all returned, flowing upstream—and yet I never kept one, single note to which I could refer. I simply dictated my story into tapes, on and off, over a five-year period. It had never once entered my mind that I would ever write my autobiography—and it certainly never occurred to me that my life story could ever capture the imagination of a publisher, and as I read the galleys now, I am awed and sometimes even dismayed that this life of mine was really lived this way. It has been, as you will soon note, a roller coaster ride through life—full of peaks and lots of valleys—some plateaus too, though few.

I have few regrets, however, about the mistakes I have heretofore made. I *now* know, that in order to get from where I was to where I am today, spiritually, that I had to encounter the obstacles—the challenges that were placed in my path. It's been a great but sometimes rough journey and I pray that from here on in, the waters I span will be more placid. Let dissonance be limited to musical expression. And may consonant harmony reign supreme in the years to follow.

Everybody who crossed my path, who wrote a syllable I read, who did something I admired or disdained, who taught me, nudged me, loved me, hated me, helped me, should rightfully be thanked, for they contributed to this book.

So, to my friends and associates who directly or indirectly aided in the preparation of *You Gotta Have Heart*—let me offer appreciation, and again, to all of you whose faith, forebearance, and fortitude got me through the seemingly endless hours, days, months, and years of its birth and blossoming: If I have forgotten to express my gratitude to some of you, please forgive me.

There are certain undeniable, constant helpers whom I would like to thank. First, there are those who shared their memories with me, expanding and correcting my own. George Abbott, Hal Prince, Gwen Verdon, and particularly Judy Coulter, Jerry's widow, reawakened and made indelible the early theatre years, and my longtime, close, and loyal friend, U.S. Senator Terry Sanford helped me to revisit my college years.

Then, there are the unsung toilers who checked the facts and expanded the research: Mary Lou Barber who worked endless hours collecting and cataloguing reviews, pictures and show information; Dorothy Swerdlove of the Billy Rose Collection of the New York Public Library, who facilitated the use of some of the pictures in the book.

To Sureshwar Schweid, who fine-tuned my Sanskrit; to my agent Rollene Saal, who had the faith in my life to carry it through to publication; to Sharon Powers who helped with corrections; and finally, to Mary Adler, who read manuscript and offered valuable suggestions and whose love and loyalty to me and my sons are unforgettable; and to Susan Ivory, who not only took the photograph that is the centerpiece of the cover, but whose faith and love and encouragement and judgment made the final fruition of this project possible—my boundless and heartfelt thanks.

To my beloved friends who are alphabetically listed below, do not be offended that you are not a part of this autobiography. The omission of your name does not in any degree indicate that you have not been an important part of my life, nor is it an inference that I do not love you. I promise you I still do and always shall:

Joan Benny, Joanne and Ken Bilby, Gill Cell, Gail Coverdale, Dr. Richard Dolins, Barbara and Chris Fordham, Ida and Bill Friday, Anne and Jim Fuchs, Lib and Bob Gersten, Elly and Randy Guggenheimer, Irene and Guzzie Guzewicz, Kenza and Foulath Hadid, Barbara and Paul Hardin, Lee and Richard Lisman, Lynne Manger, Betty and Herb Maranz, Kitty and Bill McKnight, Jeannie Nicholas, Jerri and Butch Nunn, Pat and Ambassador Nid Pibulsonggram, Morris Pliskow, Hope Preminger, Paul Pritchard, Bill Rosensohn, Mike Shapiro, Jan and Admiral Taze Shepard, Merriam and Mike

Siegel, Susan and Bob Summer, Peggy and Alan Tishman, Marilyn and Andy Weiss.

Richard Adler
New York, N.Y.
April, 1990

PROLOGUE

I was lost.

Jesus I was lost. Here we were, on top, scraping the stars, as they say. A Tony last year and maybe a Tony this year. *Pajama Game* and *Damn Yankees,* music and lyrics by Richard Adler and Jerry Ross. Both running. Both selling out. A movie contract. A pile of offers for new shows. No more wondering how we were going to pay the rent. No more being afraid that we weren't good enough to write for Broadway.

And then suddenly, there was nothing to worry about, and nothing to write about, and nothing to hope for, and nothing to accomplish. None of it meant a damned thing, because my partner, my best friend, the brother I never had, was dead.

Just like that. Here today, dead tomorrow. Twenty-nine years old, and the finest friend, the finest *person* I'd ever met. The *only* person, man or woman, for whom I could really turn my heart inside out, and know it wouldn't be stepped on. We'd been like two ends of a thought, the beginning and the end of a musical phrase.

I stood at the corner of Park Avenue and 71st Street and I couldn't make up my mind which direction to walk. It was the middle of November, and the sky looked new, like it had been painted and polished. Compared to it, the city was scuffed, and crowded. And there's nothing like crowds to make you feel lonely.

Okay. Cut it out, I said, as I started across 71st Street, stop feeling sorry for yourself. Stop hanging on to it.

And then a wave of grief broke somewhere inside of me and I began to cry again. I didn't give a damn if the people I passed looked at me oddly. I just kept on crying, because it was all there was left to do.

Maybe I ought to call Judy, I thought. Two lost souls. Jerry's friend and Jerry's wife. She and I had been on the phone every day since Jerry died.

And then I stopped again. My God, I thought, looking at my watch. I'd forgotten. Cole Porter had called yesterday. He was coming in, from his eastern digs in Williamstown, Massachusetts, and he wanted to talk to me.

And I'd been so involved with my own troubles I was going to miss him.

I took off at a fast clip, up Park Avenue, around the corner, past the doorman, and into the lobby of my apartment house. Nobody had arrived, asking for me, he answered, to my shouted question. Good, I thought. *Something's* working for me, anyway.

In the apartment, I splashed water on my face, smoothed down my hair, changed my shirt, and was just knotting my tie when the buzzer rang from downstairs. "Mr. Porter," said the doorman.

"Send him up," I shouted, as nervous as the first time I'd met him, for dinner, at Michael's Pub, after he'd phoned me—virtually unknown me—while I was having a haircut in DiZemler's barbershop, under Rockefeller Center.

"Call for you," my barber Rocco had said then, passing me the phone.

"Richard Adler?" a soft, high-pitched voice had asked.

"Yes."

"This is Cole Porter."

"And this is Irving Berlin," I'd wise-guyed him, thinking it was one of my friends putting me on.

"No no no. Really." The voice on the phone had continued, excitedly, while I sank more deeply into the barber chair, "This *is* Cole Porter, and I admire your work. I've seen *Damn Yankees* four times and I'm seeing it again tonight, with some friends. I'd like you to meet me for dinner, after—"

I answered the door, and there he was, this short and distinguished and legendary man, immaculately dressed, with a fresh flower in the buttonhole of his camel's hair topcoat, his body faintly bowed, his cane a jauntily angled and necessary support.

He put his free hand on my arm. "I'm sorry," he said, simply. "There's nothing anybody can say except that." He sat down on the sofa in my small apartment and very gently led me out of myself, step by step, moment by moment.

"It's going to take a while, but you'll heal," he said, and I was aware of the scores of operations he'd had on his legs, and how little physical healing he'd been allowed. But what a hell of a strong spirit he had. What an example he was.

"When are you going to start writing again?" he finally asked me.

I didn't know what to say. Working? Writing music? It was unthinkable. Jerry and I hadn't set a note of music or a word of lyric to paper without each other since we'd met.

"It's only been—" I floundered. "I haven't thought about it," I finished, aimlessly.

"You should."

"I don't have a partner—"

"Then why not do both? Lyrics and music. Do it all. Write by yourself."

"Oh, I couldn't do that," I protested, waving him off. "I always—"

He smiled, not unkindly. "I do it," he said. "It's easy."

I looked at him and tried to smile. It might be easy for him, I thought. But it sure as hell isn't going to be easy for me.

Still, Cole Porter looked at me, challenging me from across the living room, in the same way Jerry had, across a sidewalk, five short, monumental years ago.

I

JERRY

I.

I M A G I N E being alive and part of Broadway when it was at its peak. Imagine being young and full of ideas. Imagine the summer of 1950, in front of the Brill Building, in New York, on Broadway, between 49th and 50th Streets.

It's a sunny afternoon, and the sidewalk's full of songwriters. They're talking about—what else?—songs. Maybe they're buzzing about Frank Loesser's score for his new show, Guys and Dolls. *Or how Irving Berlin pulled a 1914 song called "Simple Melody" out of his trunk and republished it and how, thirty-six years later, it's climbing toward the top of the Hit Parade. Or maybe they're wondering why there are so many Cake Songs this year: Bob Merrill's "Candy and Cake," and Burke and Van Heusen's "Sunshine Cake," and Bob Merrill, Clem Watts, and Al Hoffman's "If I Knew You Were Comin' I'd 'Ave Baked a Cake."*

In 1950, Al Hoffman and I were pretty good friends and sometime collaborators, and if it was summer, and if the day was nice, we'd be on the sidewalk with the other songwriters, gabbing, arguing, keeping up on the latest news, trading quips, griping about which one of the publishers and managers in the Brill Building didn't appreciate us enough.

Because, in those days, the Brill Building was Tin Pan Alley. *It was the hub of the music business. If you were in the business, that's where you camped out. When you had something to peddle, you went from floor to floor, and you knocked on doors, and if they'd open, you'd say, "I've got something great to show you!" And if you were lucky, they listened. And if it was a normal day, and you were unknown, they didn't.*

Anyway, picture this sunny summer day. The sidewalk's full of songwriters, and standing across from me is this short, dark-haired guy with energy shooting out of him like little lightning bolts. He's in motion, even though he's standing still.

7

"Who is he?" I ask Al Hoffman.

"Young kid. Jerry Ross," answers Al. "Wanta meet him?"

I'm five years older than this peanut. I've been knocking around, writing copy for a plastics company, turning out a lot of poems, trying to set them to music, publishing a couple of songs. But on Tin Pan Alley, I'm a cipher.

Al introduces me to Jerry Ross. Together, we look kind of like a modern Mutt and Jeff.

And together, we're going to make wonderful music.

Only, we don't know it at the time. What we do know is that we like each other, on sight. There's no jockeying around, no b.s. We shake hands, we talk a little, we feel a link. We know we're at ease with each other. It seems good, but you never can tell, especially on the sidewalk in front of the Brill Building, where most business deals last about as long as forced flowers.

Still, if you don't try, you can't tell. So, on that sunny day, on the streets of New York, we decide, what the hell. We both need a boost up and we're willing to try anything, even collaborating.

And so it begins.

"How come, if you're Jewish, you look Irish?" I asked Jerry, the first day we sat down to work. He did look Irish. With his minimal height, his small, turned-up nose and mouth, a twinkle in his eye and a soft, crystal clear, melodious voice, he was the portrait of a slightly overage choirboy. And more. Much more. A moment in Jerry Ross's presence was like a month with somebody else. He was a direct, altogether engaging, sweet, disarming man, whose approach to both his life and a new relationship was a swan dive into the middle of it.

As for me: In those days, I was tall and skinny and energetic, and a nervous wreck. I wanted everything to happen. Now. But underneath all of that drive was a small voice that kept saying, "Careful. Organize it. Don't rush. Be sure before you take the next step."

Some combination. It would help me and hinder me all of my life, and I had the keystone in the structure of my life, my father, the great and respected pianist and teacher, Clarence Adler, to thank for it. He'd taught me that caution and stability come first, even before inspiration.

So, now, in that all-important autumn of 1950, when Jerry Ross and I settled down to work, I was, in spite of my first, wild enthusiasm, the careful one.

Jerry'd been working with Buddy Kaye, an eclectic songscribe and musician, who had to his credit such songs as "Till the End of Time," "Thoughtless," "Full Moon and Empty Arms," and "A, You're Adorable."

Within a very short time, Jerry'd ended his partnership with Buddy and turned his full attention to me. But I still hung on to Al Hoffman. He was my safety net and I wasn't used to working without a net in those days. So, for a while, we were a trio, a sort of poor man's, 1950 version of De Sylva, Brown, and Henderson, the team that wrote "Bye Bye Blackbird," "Birth of the Blues," and "The Best Things in Life Are Free."

Jerry didn't say anything about it. He just let me make up my mind in my own time, which I did.

"I like Al," I said, one afternoon when the two of us were working at my parents' place on the West Side. "But I don't think we need him."

Jerry nodded his head. He'd known it all along, the son of a gun, but he also knew that the decision had to come from me, and that simple and perceptive gesture made me more certain than ever that this was the partner with whom I could most comfortably and tirelessly—maybe endlessly—work.

Now, at the time, we had no aspirations to write theatre music. It never even occurred to us. It was too far away. Completely out of the question.

All either of us cared about in the autumn of 1950 was getting our names on a piece of printed sheet music—together.

And that's what we set out to do, with a carload of Jerry's confidence.

Jerry was a good pianist, and we did all of our composing at the piano, which was something new for me. Before I met Jerry, while I was trying to develop myself as a lyricist and a composer, I'd work out my ideas in a rather unique way. You see, I neither played the piano nor read music—a consequence of an early act of rebellion against my father, who did both, magnificently.

In those days, I composed with a toy xylophone. I'd gotten the idea from Bob Merrill, who was a well known and highly successful writer of popular songs, and who would later compose the scores of *New Girl in Town, Carnival,* and *Funny Girl (lyrics only).* One day, I mentioned to him that I neither played nor read music, and I felt sort of like a musical cripple. Ironically, he admitted to the same affliction.

Bob traveled a lot from coast to coast. He'd solved the problem of not being able to carry a piano onto an airplane by packing a toy xylophone. He'd written numbers in indelible ink on the keys. Middle C would be 4; C sharp would be 5, etc. When he was composing, he'd jot down the numbers, and thus, he'd have the tune for always. Terrific idea, I thought, and I went out and bought a xylophone. From then on, I worked out melodies and harmonies by the numbers.

Compulsively, I'd set challenges for myself—to write a song about the rain, about hands, about the distance between two people, etc. One day, I worked out what I figured would be the ultimate. I took my toy xylophone and some paper and a pencil into the bathroom and told myself I wouldn't leave until I'd written a song about something in that bathroom.

Good idea. Excruciating experience.

Time ached by. Nothing suggested itself to me. I felt like I was in a cell.

I looked around for the fiftieth time. There certainly wasn't much softness in a bathroom, I thought. There was the john, but Jesus, you can't write about a lover on the john. Or brushing teeth. Or squirting deodorant.

I stopped looking and started listening. The faucet was dripping. Ah hah, I thought. A little rhythm there.

And then I dropped that idea as quickly as I'd picked it up. Frank Loesser had written a tune called "Bloop Bleep / The faucet's dripping / And I just can't sleep." So that was out.

I looked around the room one more time. Against the far wall, there was an old radiator, and it was hissing like a snake. F-s-s-s-s-s it went.

And I had it.

First the words:

> *F-S-S-S-Steam heat—*
> *I got f-s-s-steam heat—*
> *But I need your love*
> *To keep away the cold—*

I began to beat out a rhythm while I looked for a rhyme for cold: bold, hold, mold—

Then, behind the words, the melody began to take shape. I banged out a sequence of notes on the xylophone, and wrote down the numbers.

When I left the bathroom, I had a song:

I got (clang, clang!) f-s-s-s-steam heat;
I got (clang, clang!) f-s-s-s-steam heat;
I got (clang, clang!) f-s-s-s-steam heat;
But I need your love,
  to keep away the cold.
I got (clang, clang!!) f-s-s-s-steam heat;
I got (clang, clang!!) f-s-s-s-steam heat;
I got (clang, clang!!) f-s-s-s-steam heat;
But I can't get warm,
  without your hand to hold.
The radiator's hissin',
Still I need your kissin',
To keep me from freezin' each night—
I got a hot water bottle,
But nothin' I got'll
  take the place of your holding me tight . . .

Well, it'll never be immortal, I thought, but it might be worth trying out on Jerry.

The next day, I brought in my songlet, and we developed it, modifying the melody, sharpening the lyrics, throwing out whole sections and building new ones. Within a week, I'd gotten an appointment with Mitch Miller, who was then A&R (Artists and Repertory) chief for Mercury Records.

He listened patiently enough to our song, and then brushed it and us aside. "Save it for a show," he said.

Sure, I thought. That's your way of saying it's crap.

And so, "Steam Heat" was stashed away.

Every so often, the time comes, if you pay attention to it, for a break. And now was the time for a break for us. And it, like most strokes of what we sometimes mistake as good luck, was the climax of a string of preparatory events. A few years earlier, I'd written "Teasin'," with Phil Springer, and it had become a minor hit in America and a major hit in England. Connie Haines had recorded it here and the Beverly Sisters had recorded it in England, and it had been chosen as a command performance song, sung at the Night of a Hundred Stars Gala, which was held at the London Palladium in honor of His Majesty, King George VI.

On the strength of this, and at about the same time Jerry and I met, Lou Levy introduced me to Manny Sachs, the A&R chief at Columbia Records. Manny liked my stuff a lot, and he called Frank Loesser.

Now, Frank Loesser was not only the composer-lyricist of *Guys and Dolls,* the biggest hit on Broadway, and the owner of his own music publishing company, he was also known in the business as a man who was always on the lookout for creative talent.

So, I went to him, with Manny Sachs' introduction in one hand and a sheaf of my lyrics in the other. At first sight, Frank was unimpressive. He was a small, gravel-voiced man with thinning, sandy hair, dancing eyes, a broad nose, a lantern jaw, and a mind like a bear trap—a sort of Runyonesque, Mafioso sprite. But one minute in his presence, and you felt his greatness. He knew more about everything than anybody I've ever known. He was a better copyright lawyer than the lawyers who worked for him. He was a skilled astronomer. A master carpenter and cabinet maker. A terrific cartoonist.

And like all really great men, he carried this enormous talent as if it were weightless. He was well educated, but he purposely talked like Damon Runyon had written his dialogue. In fact, if you heard him speaking in the next room, you'd swear he was a streetcorner bookie. But I was in the same room that afternoon, and I saw the twinkle in his eye when he barked, "Lotta stuff I read don't mean nothin'! Nothin' to most of it. But yours—it's good."

Talk about music to your ears! Here was this enormously influential, important man, and he *liked* what I *did*!

"Don't you have somebody you write music with?" he asked, and I hesitated for a moment, but only a moment. There was really only one person I wanted to work with right now.

"Yes," I answered. "Jerry Ross."

"Good," he said, and invited us both back the next day to play our songs for him.

We were there, ahead of the agreed-upon time. Frank was as kind and gruff and ungrammatical with Jerry as he'd been with me.

"Okay," he said, "Begin." And he settled back in his chair.

We started with an uptempo tune that I sold as hard as I could. In those days, my voice was better suited to fast songs and calling taxis than the long, sustained notes of ballads. These, Jerry did, with a clarity and a kind of controlled feeling that illuminated the very essence of the song.

I thought to myself as I looked across the office at Frank Loesser, sitting silently in his chair, listening to Jerry sing one of our ballads, that this was a man with the kind of attributes I admired. He was tough, but he was talented. He knew music well. But he knew the *business* of music *equally* well. And that's quite a combination.

You had to be both in those days. I remembered, while we were selling our songs to Frank Loesser, my first days in Tin Pan Alley, at Mills Music, when Phil Springer and I were making probably the smallest royalties paid in the industry, and how veteran publisher Jack Mills had thrown his arm around me one day and said, "Adler—If you ever wanta get ahead in this game, you gotta sing your own songs—no matter how bad you sing, you gotta learn to sing your own stuff, because no one can sell it like the songwriter can."

And he was right, I realized later, in the hall outside of his office, when I ran into Roy Brodsky and Sid Tepper. If anyone knew how to sell their songs, it was Brodsky and Tepper. Roy would sing and Sid would cup his hands together and imitate a trumpet. One day, they'd stopped me in the hall, and said, "Hey listen. Whataya think of this?" They got into their selling pose, and Roy started to sing, "I've got some red roses, for a blue lady . . ."

I thought, gee, what a lovely and simple idea. What a beautiful way to say something musically. And here were these guys, singing and imitating a trumpet in a crowded hallway in a busy building. And even though the song would eventually become number one all over the world, it would probably never sound more sincere than it did that afternoon.

Jerry finished the song, and we waited.

Frank didn't believe in dramatic nonsense. He came right to the point. "Good," he said, "Good but not good enough. You have to keep writing more and more and more."

Our spirits dove to our shoes.

"But I *did* like that country song," he went on. " 'The Strange Little Girl.' Good story. Good tune."

It was a song *we* liked too—eerie, and a little weird, with a story to match.

"Yeah," he went on. "I like that song, and I think it could be a hit. And I'm gonna try to make it one."

Our spirits rose. "Look," he said, "I wantya to have a contract with this house. I wantya to be one of my family. You'll be our writers, and we'll get ya work. Now"—and he pulled out a check book and began to write—"Here's a five hundred dollar advance for 'Strange Little Girl.' And on toppa that, we'll pay ya fifty a week against future earnings."

We waited till we'd shut the door of his office behind us before we went crazy. It was probably the best news either of us had ever had. As far as we were concerned, the check and the deal could have been for a million bucks.

Jerry called his wife Judy, a petite, quiet, intelligent, and buxom blonde whom Jerry adored, and whom I liked almost as much as I did Jerry. The three of us hit the town. Life was going to be good forever. We were young enough and eager enough and blind enough to believe that.

What Frank said he'd do, he did. He not only published "The Strange Little Girl," he pushed it with all of the top record companies, and got nine records. Red Foley, Cowboy Copas, Hank Williams, and all the rest—their names might as well have been Russian to me. I didn't know any of them, but I had faith in Frank.

The records were released, the disc jockeys began to play them, and the song began to appear on the trade charts. And very slowly, it took off. First in the South. Then in the West. Then in New York.

And then disaster struck.

Patti Page recorded a country folk number called "The Tennessee Waltz."

And that was that for "The Strange Little Girl."

At first, we were flummoxed. It was a setback, but setbacks didn't faze us forever. And so, our collaboration started to settle in again. Every day, we'd get together, either at my parents' place on the West Side, or miles and miles up the river at Jerry and Judy's apartment, on stratospheric upper Broadway. "Who the hell lives at 5000 Broadway?" I asked him when he told me where he lived.

"Listen Quimby," he said—he nicknamed me Quimby, after his favorite movie cartoonist, Fred Quimby—"It could be worse. I could live in Montreal."

And we were off on an idea for a tune about two long distance lovers. That's the way it would go. We'd reach into a situation, or a sentence, or a scene, and for a reason we neither understood nor questioned, we'd start thinking as if we shared one brain. It was miraculous. We had the same feeling for ideas, words, sounds, notes, phrases, melodic lines—it was weird. And very wonderful.

Before long, we stumbled on a kind of process that we felt would be the key to our success together. We reduced it to three words: "The Negative rules"—which meant that if either of us didn't like what the other was doing or suggesting, it was out. If I rushed into a writing session—and I did that a lot—and slammed down my hat and said, "God, have I got something great! Listen to this!" and I sang Jerry a song, or a title, or a line, or a melody, and he didn't like it, that was the end of it.

And the same applied for Jerry.

This didn't mean we couldn't electioneer. If I *really* thought my idea was wonderful, I'd try to sell it.

"Listen, Jerry," I'd say. "Maybe I didn't sing it well enough. Suppose—"

And he'd sit at the piano, with his head to one side, and concentrate while I argued, really giving it a try. And then, if it wasn't right, he'd straighten up and look at me, and say, "No. I don't think that's right." And it would *really* be out.

I don't think we could have worked this way if we hadn't, from the beginning to the end of our collaboration, cared about each other as much as we did for ourselves. We never let our own shadow steal the other's sunlight. And I think that came from the fact that we'd learned our "street smarts" early. We knew how to defend ourselves, but we also knew the value of our own and somebody else's territory.

In a few weeks, we had another batch of tunes ready for Frank Loesser. We took the subway to his publishing office on West 54th Street and played them while he listened intently, this little man with a big effect upon us. When we'd finished, he leaned forward and said, " 'Pretty Bird, Don't Fly Away.' That's a good song. A very good song. I like it a lot."

"Pretty Bird" was destined to become one of the slower starters in the Sweepstakes of The Popular American Song. But that afternoon, in our minds, it was already nose to nose with "White Christmas."

"Tell you what. I'm going to take this out to Hollywood and sell it to a picture company," said Frank. He looked at his watch. "Gotta go. Gotta meet Lynne," and he winked.

Sure, he had to meet his wife. Like I had to swim the East River.

Lynne Loesser was large and domineering and not too popular. Around Broadway, they called her the evil of two Loessers.

Not that Frank was perfect. I'd already become slightly aware of a few of his human failings. If Lynne was domineering, he was bewitching. And very careful about the money he spent. After all, with a few choice words, hadn't he snared our complete faith and absolute loyalty? And wasn't he giving us a truly Picayune stipend? Little did I know that our work would eventually make him millions of dollars. And that in the end, he'd make more on us than *we* ever made on us.

But none of this seriously concerned Jerry and me then. We were getting far more than money from him, and we knew it, and we appreciated it. He was our mentor, our guide, our inspiration, the object of our ceaseless admiration, and a genius—which gave him a lot of rights. So, when he disappeared with our song under his arm, we felt like a couple of kids whose exam grades were A's.

But the euphoria didn't last. It took a long, long time for the grades to be posted. So long, in fact, that, away from his powerful presence, we began to give up on Frank Loesser.

And so long, in fact, that I had time, in the late winter of 1951, to meet the woman who would become my first wife.

It all began on a miserable day in early March. Freddy Bienstock, who was then a song plugger for Chappell Music, Inc., called me and asked if I wanted to write with a young woman who composed music.

"Is she pretty?" I asked.

"Very," he said.

"Send her over."

I was twenty-nine, and single, and I'd just moved into a new apartment at 222 East 61st Street. I'm sure that my interest at that moment in this young woman who happened to be a songwriter had very little to do with her musical talents and more to do with the fact that Freddy had told me she was pretty.

For, from an age so early I can no longer remember it, I was obsessed with women. They were an apparently incurable addiction. I loved to be in their presence. To talk to them. To listen to them. To watch them. To touch them. To make love to them.

In those early years, women were my abiding reason to rise in the morning and to go to bed—usually with one of them—at night. I did my work, but like Bernard in Truffaut's film *The Man Who Loved Women,* I lived for women.

Other men had trouble with money, with ethics, with a fear of dying—I had trouble with my insatiable appetite for the opposite sex. To have desire and not fulfill it, to have fantasies and not act them out was unthinkable to me.

It would be my personal joy and my personal anguish for most of my life, for when I was most in love with one woman, I was most aware of every other beautiful woman who crossed my path. And when I was young and my supply of sexual scruples was meager, I would, even in my most married moments, set out to conquer any woman I found desirable.

Maybe it was a way of showing my father I was better than he— because perhaps, in some Oedipal way, I was jealous of his ability to snare and hold such a beautiful woman as my mother. Maybe it was a way of showing myself I was better than I suspected I was.

For whatever reason, through most of my adult life, the cock wagged the man. I was an unabashed and unregenerate but benevolent womanizer.

Now, I'm not very happy about it. Then, I was gloriously proud of it, as I opened the door to my apartment and welcomed into my life one of the most beautiful women I had, until that moment, met.

Freddy had been conservative in his description of her. She was a knockout. Tall, and brunette, and curvy. She more than slightly resembled Ava Gardner, with her long dark hair and flashing brown eyes, I thought to myself, "Adler, this is going to be one of your luckier days!"

We didn't write music that rainy afternoon. We spent it in bed together. And before long, I was head over heels in love with Marion Hart, an exciting, intelligent, strong-willed woman who, at the age of eleven, had left Germany with her nine-year-old sister on a children's refugee ship bound for England. Between them, they had one satchel of clothing, and two German marks of money.

That afternoon, while we lay in my bed and marveled about coincidence and luck and how easy it was to be together, she told me about growing up in Germany, in a large house, with servants and comforts and no worries at all, and how suddenly it had all disappeared.

She went on to tell me about how she and a group of other refugee children had finally, after a grueling journey, arrived at London's Victoria Station. She and her sister, too dazzled by the adventure of being away from home and speaking not one word of English, had gotten on the wrong train in the London underground, and had become separated from the rest.

But in the same kind of miraculous coincidence that had brought us together, they found the others, and the headquarters where they should have been, all along.

But the reunion didn't last long. She and her sister were separated. Her sister remained in London, and Marion was shipped off to a life in Scotland, where the miserly family with whom she lived even forced her to wash out her sanitary napkins and reuse them.

Before the war ended, her parents arrived in England with only a bolt of fabric they'd managed to save or scavenge, and an enormous will to reconstruct their lives.

Her mother and father wasted no time. On a rented sewing machine, Mrs. Hart started making blouses out of the fabric they'd brought with them, her father began to sell them, and within a few years, this tiny, door-to-door peddling business grew into an international corporation.

Marion had become determined to write music and succeed at it. That she wouldn't succeed, would torture her—and, eventually—us. But at the time we met, it was only a background annoyance, one we convinced ourselves would soon be eliminated.

She was making forty dollars a week then as a tour guide at Rockefeller Center. And she was married, to a singer named Frank Rogier, who was on the road with Menotti's *The Medium* and *The Telephone.*

As our relationship grew, the threats to it seemed to shrink. Marion was used to solving problems when and where they occurred. When I was with her, we didn't mention her husband, and the problem of our mutual poverty was going to be solved as soon as the world got wind of our talent. But, when, a couple of months later, she decided to take a trip to England to visit her parents, I sank into a black, immobilizing depression.

How could we begin to build a life? I thought. I was so poor, I couldn't even afford to phone her. I was still getting a few bucks in royalties from "Teasin'," and from a novelty number I'd written with John Jacob Loeb—a reply to an obnoxious but enormously popular song called "Goodnight Irene." We'd titled ours "Please Say Goodnight to the Guy, Irene, and Let Me Get Some Sleep." It had sold 750,000 records, but it certainly wasn't destined for immortality.

Finally, I called Frank Loesser, and said, as casually as I could without my voice breaking, "What's happening with 'Pretty Bird'?"

"Look," he said. "I'm doin' what I can. I wanna get a good deal for ya. Just leave it to me. Go back to writing. Don't worry about business."

Another month went by, and I called him again. "I'm doin' what I can," he said. "I wanna get a good deal for ya. Just—"

"I know I know I know," I raved, a little out of control from frustration, or deprivation, or both. "Go back to writing. You're doing what you can. But Frank, you're so rich," I wailed. "You're so powerful, and successful. You've got so much money. We're just poor people who have to pay bills."

Boy, was I upset. "Listen, Frank," I went on, "I have a girl who's in Europe, and I want to bring her back here and marry her."

"I thought she was already married?"

"What's that got to do with the price of eggs?" I shouted. "I have an apartment. I have rent to pay—"

"Keep your sense of humor," he said, "I'm going to bring George Abbott around when I get back to New York. Keep that in mind."

George Abbott!

When I told him, Jerry fairly flew to the piano. We worked like crazy, forgiving Frank for everything. Maybe he was tough, we thought, but so what—he was on our side.

And, true to his word, he showed up a month later with the most imposing, patrician-looking man I'd ever seen. Erect and aristocratic, as tall as a basketball center, with thinning, blonde hair, and perfect features—a straight nose and penetrating blue eyes—George Abbott looked like a combination of a matinee idol and a New England school-teacher. He was sixty-three years old then, and he'd been at the very top for over thirty-five years as a writer, director, producer and actor.

On that summer afternoon, I got to know what being in the presence of two gods of the theatre was like.

But the gods didn't smile on us. Mr. Abbott didn't say much, but you knew immediately that he wasn't going to offer us a contract to write a show for him. "Keep working," he said. "You're not ready yet, but you will be."

He unfolded himself from the sofa, where he'd been sitting, and he and Frank headed for the door. "Oh, by the way," said Frank, turning, "about 'Pretty Bird.' I heard from Metro today about it."

We both leaped to our feet.

He shook his head. "The cheap bastards would only give me twenty-five hundred for it—" He paused. We held our breath. "I turned them down." He put on his hat.

"Twenty-five hundred!?" we yelled, like a couple of Andy Hardys. "That's a fortune!"

He stopped again, and looked at George Abbott. "Fortune? That's not a fortune, boys. That's not *nearly* a fortune." And they left.

Two days later, a letter arrived from Marion. It had all the simplicity and impact of an avalanche. Marion was pregnant.

Now I *really* went crazy. I called on Uncle Ben, my father's brother from Wall Street, the only member of the family I knew who was rich and could keep a secret, and borrowed five hundred dollars to go to England, meet Marion's parents, and ask her to marry me.

She was waiting for me at London's Heathrow Airport, and she didn't need much convincing. She was as much in love with me as I was with her. All we needed to do was tell her parents that she should divorce her husband and marry me.

They lived at 2 Templewood Avenue, in Hampstead, about a half hour from central London, on a magnificent estate, which was carpeted with rolling, constantly surprising gardens, punctuated with well-ordered clarity by imposing, possibly ancient trees, and all of this overseen by a formal brick house, decorated exquisitely with glorious, incredibly valuable antiques and paintings. The rooms overflowed with inlaid marble-topped tables, Italian Renaissance furniture, and a sense of quiet good taste.

Marion's father Eric was a very tall, very lean man whose face, with its high forehead, aquiline nose, and angular features, seemed to have been chiseled out of the same marble as the table tops he and his wife collected. But that was all that seemed stony about Eric Hart. He was a soft-spoken, good-natured, hard-working man who nevertheless had a wistful, almost poetic side to him, a softness and a sweetness that was immensely touching, and in sharp contrast to his wife Edith, who was an attractive, intelligent, domineering, and tough woman. She was, you felt, the real force in the family, the one who kept the business on Oxford Street profitable and the household running. She seemed to be devoted to her family, although I found out later that she was carrying on an intense affair with a smooth and equally intelligent Austrian musicologist and author named Bernard Grun, and when Eric Hart suddenly died of a heart attack a few years later, she married Biba (as she called Bernard Grun) almost before the last shovelful of dirt had rained down on her husband's coffin.

Edith and Biba were well suited to each other. I wasn't kidding when, later on, I called them the Jewish Little Foxes. They were intent upon becoming as rich as they could, no matter what it cost the rest of the world. And, years later, I would almost become one of their victims.

But in 1952, I was dealing only with Marion and her parents, and, looking back on it, I suppose that, being as poor as I was in those days, I gathered in a false sense of security from all of this tasteful opulence. It was an atmosphere and a state of life I liked. The estate at 2 Templewood Avenue gave me a sense of where I wanted to go, and stay, some day. And now, being in it, basking in it, I felt as if I were almost there already.

So, the days we spent together were pleasant ones, a time of reasonable meetings of reasonable minds, and a warm joining of emotions. At the end, I was accepted, and by extension, so was the relationship between Marion and me.

The trip back to New York was a joyful one. The fact that I didn't have enough money to support us, and that she'd have to divorce Frank Rogier in a hurry didn't seem to bother her at all. She was, as I said, used to meeting obstacles head on.

Her parents had slipped her some money before we left, and she figured we could live on it for a while. And we did, but not very well.

It was time for Marion to break the news of our plans to her husband.

That, it turned out, was a lot more difficult than writing music. And it didn't happen at all the way we'd expected. When she went to Frank Rogier and told him the story, he didn't believe her. She insisted. He brushed it aside.

Back at my apartment, she broke the news to me. "*You* have to tell him," she said. "He won't believe me."

"*Me?*" I asked, with visions of mayhem dancing in my head. He was a big man. A muscular man. And I was still just a skinny kid. He could do a lot of damage to me. Men, I thought, who face their wive's lovers have been known to shoot them, or at least disfigure them. What good would I be to Marion and our child dead or disabled?

"Look, Marion," I continued. "That's just going to complicate things. Why don't you—"

"It's the only way," she insisted. "He just won't believe me."

So, after taking a deep breath, I figured, what the hell. Maybe he'll be reasonable. Maybe he'll only break my nose.

And so I went to him. And when I'd made him understand that every word that Marion had told him was absolutely true, I saw a stricken look on his face. I felt like putting my arm comfortingly around him. It was possibly as shattering an experience for me as it was for him, because, instead of punching me in the nose, he took it all very graciously, and, with compassion and kindness, wished us luck. I felt horrible. And relieved.

Within a week, Marion flew to Alabama, and got a one-day divorce.

The waiting was over, I figured. We'd get married right away.

But Marion had other ideas. "No. I want to be absolutely sure," she said. "I'm going away for four days. By myself. I have to be certain."

And she did, and I went crazy, again. I was nuts about her. I couldn't live without her. Why the hell was she putting us through this? I asked myself. Was there another guy? Was she getting an abortion? What in hell was going on? I didn't get much sleep and neither did Judy and Jerry. I was on the phone with them constantly.

At the end of the four days, Marion reappeared, still pregnant, and still, thank God, ready to get married, which we did, on September 4, 1951. The wedding was a simple, generic one, before a justice of the peace. The wedding party and the guests consisted of Judy, Jerry, Marion and me. And, out of sight, but not beyond our thoughts, our soon to be son, Andrew.

Andrew was a marvelous child, a bright happiness that glowed at the center of our lives, and made the fact that we were living on very little seem secondary.

Meanwhile, Jerry and I kept on writing, turning out special material for whomever we could. We did an opening number for Jan Murray's nightclub act. A song for Jimmy Durante. A piece of material for Joel Grey.

But these jobs, while they paid well, came along infrequently. Our chief source of income was Frank Loesser, who, in 1952, raised our advances to one hundred dollars a week. It was an improvement, but nothing to sing about.

What to do to better our situation?

I knew, as I know now, that contacts were almost as important as talent in the music business. But some of my experiences with contacts up till then had been pretty grim.

Take, for instance, the encounter I had had with my father's friend Phil Spitalny, the popular radio conductor of the All Girl Orchestra, featuring Evelyn and her Magic Violin. It had happened years before, but the memory of it still rankled.

It was when I first decided that I wanted to be a lyricist, and give up the corporate life at Celanese Corporation of America, where I was writing advertising copy. I'd gone to my father and asked him if he knew anybody in show business or the music business who could help me get started. He thought a moment. "Yes," he finally said, "I know one. Phil Spitalny."

I pleaded with him to set up an appointment, and so he did, a lunch at Lindy's on Broadway and 52nd Street. The three of us met, ate well, and then, after dessert, I laid a sheaf of lyrics in front of Spitalny. He took them in both hands, read them over silently, set them down on the white linen of the table, and then asked me, in stentorian tones that could be heard by half the diners in the room, "Do you have a job?"

"Yes," I replied.

"Keep it," he barked, and shoved the lyrics toward me.

This memory, for all its distance in time, was still fresh in my mind, as, sometime in the fall of 1951, I picked up the phone and called another friend of my father's, Harry Salter. Salter had created a very popular radio program called "Stop the Music," and at that time, he was producing it as a television show with Mark Goodson and Bill Todman.

He was, thank God, sympathetic, and agreed to see Jerry and me. He liked us, and introduced us to the show's director, Don Appel, who concurred with him that we were bright and energetic, and that our work was original and promising. He set up an appointment at the Goodson-Todman offices.

We arrived.

Things didn't get off to a very promising start. Although today he's one of my friends, Mark Goodson seemed at that first meeting to have the warmth of a glacier. But Don Appel, talking calmly and convincingly about us, melted Goodson down enough to get us a job as idea men, to evolve the visual packaging of the songs on the show.

Television was an infant in 1951, after all. It still hadn't covered its first national political convention. But people like Don Appel knew that it was basically a visual medium. And he also knew it was a *greedy* medium that ate up ideas by the mile. It needed more concept men than it had, and he probably figured we were worth the gamble.

We proved we were, and for the next year, we collected $125 apiece for working one day a week, coming up with visual frameworks for songs like "How Much Is That Doggie in the Window?" "Rag Mop" and "Trying."

In 1951, that was a hell of a salary for one day's work, especially for a couple of fledgling songwriters.

So, bolstered by small successes, Jerry and I kept on writing songs, and the quality of our work steadily improved. We were settling in, getting to know more about each other, and feeling more comfortable about working together.

But everything I got to know about Jerry that year didn't make me happy.

To the world, and to me at first, he was the picture of robustness—a bright eyed, tireless guy who consumed and gave off life with the eagerness and generosity of a guileless but very alert kid.

And that was the way he truly was, most of the time. And except for a kind of nagging cough, in that first year, he never seemed to be ill. I figured that keeping a mountain of Kleenex at his elbow when he worked was a quirk, an inheritance from an over-indulgent mother, or a habit he'd had so long he didn't notice it anymore.

But then, as the weeks we worked together ran into months and the months turned into a year, and more, I realized that the cough he had didn't really get any better. It would increase and decrease, but it would always be there, like some disquieting insinuation.

He would, after coughing into a Kleenex, examine it, closely. I again chalked it up to habit, and thought nothing of it. It was only the persistence of the coughing that concerned me.

"God, that's a lousy cold," I kept saying, and he would nod enigmatically, and we'd keep on working.

But nobody has a cold that long. And so, sometime during the end of our first year together, Jerry came clean with me. One day, during a truly horrendous coughing spell, after he'd spit into a Kleenex and looked at it for a long time, he told me why he coughed constantly, and why he kept the Kleenex near, and why he examined them so thoroughly. "The reason I didn't bother you with this was because I thought I had it licked," he said. "But I don't know. It doesn't seem to be improving."

I felt an odd uneasiness in the pit of my stomach.

He sat back, wearily, and explained to me that, as a youngster, he not only went to school faithfully and studied hard, but, every night, he'd take a subway down from the Bronx to lower Second Avenue, where he'd perform as an actor in the Yiddish Art Theatre. At midnight, he'd drag himself back home, fall into bed, get up, go to school, and repeat the whole routine, over and over, for months and months.

A year or two of this, and his health gave out. He developed TB, and, because of his acting experiences, he qualified for care at the Will Rogers Memorial Home for Actors at Saranac Lake.

"Good time there," he said, with a smile. "More women than a *healthy* man could handle. In fact, the heat of passion was so intense, they could have done without a furnace in my ward. Trouble is—" He sighed. "They got rid of my virginity but not my TB. So, I developed an abnormal dilation of the bronchial tubes. Bronchiectasis, they call it. Had it ever since."

The problem for Jerry was that the infection had descended so deeply into his lungs that blood capillaries had been eroded, and every once in a while, he'd spit up blood. That, he explained to me, was why he was a walking Kleenex warehouse.

"One thing I'm afraid of, Rich. And it really bothers me," he said to me that afternoon. "Hemorrhaging. And drowning in my own blood."

My God. I felt like I'd been hit by a bus. It just couldn't be possible. He seemed so healthy, except for a cough. And hell, everybody coughs.

There was a long silence. Then, I blurted out, lamely, "You look pretty good." I was trying to deal with the vertigo I was feeling. "Maybe if you saw another doctor—"

Jerry shook his head. "I've seen the best of them and the worst of them," he said, "and I haven't found two that agree yet. Or one who can give me the kind of hope I need."

Then, as quickly as his face had clouded, it cleared. He walked over to the piano bench. "Come on, Rich," he said, "quit goofing off."

One day, a year after our first meeting with George Abbott, Frank called us again. He was bringing him around on another visit, to hear our new songs. Mr. Abbott came in with Frank, nodded to us, sat down, listened, got up and said, "Good. Still not ready. But getting there."

It didn't bother us, because now, the special material assignments had begun to increase. Eddie Fisher was red hot. Jimmy Durante was opening in Vegas. They needed material. We delivered it. Joel Grey was paralleling Eddie Fisher, in different nightclubs. He asked for a new song for his act. We wrote it for him, and he was interested enough to climb into my car one morning and drive with me up to Jerry's place, to hear the number, which we'd called "The Elephant Boy."

He listened, loved it, and was in the middle of writing us a check for fifteen hundred dollars, when the phone rang. Jerry answered it in high spirits.

I was feeling pretty good myself. Fifteen hundred dollars in 1952 was a comfortable amount of money.

I glanced over at Jerry. He'd turned white. He was talking intensely into the phone, practically climbing into the mouthpiece. "It'll be all right," he was saying, urgently. "I'll take care of it, Pop. Just wait there. You gonna be okay? Get somebody to stay with you. All right then, just stay there. I'll call you back as soon as I can!"

He slammed down the telephone.

"What's the matter?" I asked.

"That was Judy's father," he said. "She's dead. Judy's *dead*!"

"Dead?" I gasped. "That's not possible."

"I know. I know." Jerry staggered into a seat. He was sweating. He reached for a Kleenex. "Heart attack. He said she had a heart attack at school." His voice was barely audible. And then, suddenly he was on his feet again. "Jesus *Christ*!" He started pacing. "How could she have a heart attack? How could that happen?" He was shaking now, and waving his arms hysterically.

"Come on," I said, "Let's go."

Joel and I each took one of Jerry's arms, and the three of us got into my car. I slid behind the wheel, and, ignoring traffic lights, common sense and cars hurtling at us from side streets, flew, at nearly one hundred miles per hour, down to 145th Street and St. Nicholas Avenue, to the school where Judy taught seventh grade.

The twenty minute ride was like an eternity. The closer we got to the school, the more dread I felt. What's going to happen to Jerry, I thought, when we finally get there? What's going to happen to this frail little guy who was coming apart in front of our eyes? It was all Joel and I could do to keep him from falling to pieces completely.

I'd barely stopped the car when Jerry leaped out and dashed ahead of us into the dilapidated stone building. We caught up to him in the principal's office. He was babbling incoherently, and the principal was looking at him in bewildered disbelief.

"We got a call!" Jerry was screaming. "Where is she? Where's Judy?"

"Mrs. *Ross*?" asked the principal. "Seventh grade?"

"*Of course*, Mrs. Ross!" Jerry shouted. "Where *is* she? What did—"

"Wait a minute," said the principal, and, more calmly than any of us thought he had a right to be, he motioned for us to follow him out of his office and down the corridor of the school. He stopped in front of a classroom door and motioned to Jerry to follow his gaze.

And there, on the other side of the glass-windowed door, was Judy, teaching a class, and looking a hundred times healthier at that moment than either Jerry, Joel, or I.

Jerry practically tore the door down. He burst into the room with Joel and me at his heels. He was crying, and singing out at the same time, "Thank God! Thank God! Thank God! You're alive!" He grabbed Judy in his arms, and hugged her so hard she must have *really* stopped breathing for a moment.

When Jerry had loosened up on Judy, I hugged her, just as hard, while Joel danced around us and the kids in the classroom rioted.

"You're alive!" Jerry shouted. "You're alive!"

Judy disentangled herself from us. "Of course I'm alive," she said, "and you're disrupting my class. What do you think you're doing?"

We explained the whole incident to her in the hallway, while the principal tried to tame the class. "This must be a joke," she said. "Let's call Pop."

We dashed to the faculty room and waited while Judy phoned her father. She talked for a long time, obviously calming him, too. Mrs. Ross, it seemed, *had* died, but it was her father's elderly sister, coincidentally married to a man named Ross, and out for a walk that morning, who had decided to take a shortcut through her neighborhood schoolyard, and there had succumbed to a heart attack. Somebody had called Judy's father and said, simply, "Mrs. Ross died in the schoolyard," and he'd naturally thought it was the apple of his eye, his daughter who was a schoolteacher.

It was a time to relax and enjoy being together, and Judy, Jerry, Marion and I did just that, at Joel Grey's opening at the Rainbow Room. At one point in his act, he paused for a moment, and then said, with a twinkle, "I'd like to dedicate this song to Judy Ross, in honor of her being alive." Nobody else in the Rainbow Room knew what he was talking about, or why the four of us were wildly applauding such an enigmatic dedication.

I remember looking at Jerry that night, his face glowing with happiness, and then thinking back at how distraught and directionless he had been just a few hours ago. How fragile he was under that lovely, bright exterior.

We'd served our apprenticeship together now. We knew each other. We loved each other. We respected each other. And it was about time for us to take all this shared talent and joy and focus it on one concentrated endeavor.

I was the one who came up with it.

Ever since I'd been a small boy, going to theatre matinees, ever since college, when I'd sat in the playwriting classes of the great Paul Green, ever since my days in the Navy during World War II, when I'd first read Harold Clurman's absorbing and reportorial account of the history of The Group Theatre, *The Fervent Years,* I'd felt an undeniable, uneraseable identification with the theatre.

At first, as a small boy, it was the glamour and the beauty and the fun viewed from the audience. Then, in college, because of Paul Green, it was the discovery that this was a particular and unique kind of expression, as valid as a novel, as involving as a painting. But it wasn't until I read Harold Clurman's book that I really began to *understand* the theatre, and why my fascination with it flickered like some insistent flame in the darkness of my indecision about the direction of my life.

From reading the book, I realized that there was an intensity about the theatre, a dedication and a shared feeling that this was a medium where not one, but a group of creative minds could gather together to unite, in one work, all of their dissimilar creative energies. The theatre was like the collection point on a prism, where several colors were transformed into one intensely bright and articulated pattern, and even now, I'm certain that The Group Theatre was the supreme expression of this. And that there's never been a more important movement in the American theatre than this one.

And so, in 1952, I wasn't unaware that part of my immense respect for Frank Loesser had to do with his position as one of the theatre's greatest and most respected composers and lyricists, nor that he was bringing the great Mr. Abbott around to listen to our songs with the idea that we might be potential composers and lyricists for a theatre project.

Besides, the time was right. A big musical seemed to be opening on Broadway every other week that year. Broadway, in 1952-3, was one of the busiest, most competitive places in the world. Rodgers and Hammerstein's *The King and I* was still running, as was *Guys and Dolls* and Irving Berlin and George Abbot's *Call Me Madam.* Cole Porter's *Can-Can* was casting; Leonard Bernstein's *Wonderful Town* had just opened; and one of the most exciting showcases for new talent ever mounted on Broadway, Leonard Sillman's *New Faces of 1952,* was introducing Ronny Graham, Carol Lawrence, Paul Lynde, Eartha Kitt, Alice Ghostley, and Robert Clary to the world.

And there, I suggested to Jerry one day, was where we should be directing our energies.

He was agreeable; writing special material came naturally to both of us, and the leap to the stage couldn't be that great. Besides, Jerry had the same kind of boyhood memories I had. His times on the stage of the Yiddish Theatre had been happy, treasurable ones. And so, it was only a matter of weeks before we signed with David Hocker at MCA, and a mere two months later that we signed to do *Six on a Honeymoon,* a new, mini-musical that was being written, directed and choreographed by a young guy who was as unknown and ambitious as we: Herbert Ross—whose film direction, decades later, of *The Turning Point* and *The Odd Couple* would make him a Hollywood celebrity.

Honeymoon was set to open in six weeks in Chicago, at the Black Hawk, a terrific combination steakhouse and nightclub. Jerry and I would each get fifteen hundred dollars plus fifty dollars a week royalty, and my wife Marion, who was, among many things, a fine seamstress and dress designer, was hired to do the costumes, for a one thousand dollar fee.

We auditioned in New York, and signed up our six young singer-dancer-actors, all unknowns. Two of whom—Pat Carroll and Barbara Cook—would be heard from a lot, in the future.

We went into rehearsal, and from the first moment, Herb's talent established itself. We felt good about the show when we started working on it; we felt better about it when we took it to Springfield, Illinois to try it out.

Opening night, the kids sang their hearts out, the music and the lyrics sounded okay, the costumes were fine, the show looked good. The audience responded. And to make it complete, Governor Adlai Stevenson was there in the audience, laughing and applauding as if he were having the time of his life.

A week later, we opened in Chicago. Don Roth, the owner of the Black Hawk, and a hell of a sweet guy, walked around like Ziegfeld. The first night audience applauded generously. The next day, the reviews were good.

That's more like it, we thought. Fame and fortune never hurt the deserving. Let's see, we figured, fifty dollars a week royalty times forever—

And then, three weeks later, the bad news arrived. Don Roth, that hell of a nice guy, had been hauled up before the Chicago Board of Health. The restaurant had been shut down. No restaurant; no show. Those great steaks that had made the Black Hawk such a terrific eating place were horsemeat.

Shortly after the Black Hawk fiasco, I broke my leg skiing, and while I was convalescing, and tossing song ideas around in my head, some of the conversations we'd had with Eddie Fisher crept into my mind. He'd told me about the truly tough boyhood he'd had in a Philadelphia ghetto. He'd grown up in a poor immigrant Jewish family, working and scratching for everything he got, until the night at Grossingers, that immense and star-studded resort in the Catskills, when he attracted the attention of Eddie Cantor. Cantor, Fisher told me, had taken him on as a protégé. And from then on, he never had to look back. It was a miraculous rise from obscurity and poverty to worldwide recognition as one of the big recording stars of the fifties, an inspiring climb from rags to riches.

Not a bad title, I thought. I called up Jerry. A couple of days of back and forth collaboration, and we had a sort of Neopolitan ballad, lush and romantic and nostalgic, and just right, we figured, for Eddie.

The next week, we showed it to him.

He didn't go for it. "Not for me," he said.

I was crushed. "How is that possible?" I asked. "It's your story!"

He looked at me for a long moment. "Maybe that's why it's not for me," he said, quietly. He paused. "It's still a good song," he added, putting an arm around my shoulder.

We agreed on that, at least, and a couple of days later, Jerry and I showed "Rags to Riches" to Mitch Miller, who'd succeeded Mannie Sachs as A&R chief of Columbia Records.

He liked it and accepted it, with the change of a couple of chords—something that didn't bother us much, because we knew that Mitch suggested a change in almost every song he took.

Three weeks later, Mitch called and asked us to stop by to hear something. Jerry wasn't feeling well that day, so I went alone, to the Columbia Records Studios on 7th Avenue and 52nd Street. Mitch sat me down and played me "Rags to Riches," sung by Tony Bennett with a driving, full-blooded, brass choir arrangement by Percy Faith.

I hated it, and I told him so. In fact, I got down on my hands and knees and begged Mitch not to release it.

He laughed, and said, "Adler, get out of here."

"Rags to Riches" was released in July. By the end of August, after respectable disc jockey play, it was buried.

But by that time, I'd learned to love the record. I went back to Mitch and said, "Give me five hundred dollars and I'll take the song around to all the disc jockeys in Pittsburgh, Detroit, Washington, Boston, Cleveland—I'll make it into a hit!"

He okayed the five hundred dollars.

I hit Boston first, and there I tracked down Norm Prescott and Bob Clayton, who were the two leading disc jockeys in Boston.

"Look," I said, in my carefully rehearsed pitch, "I know you gave the song a fair hearing, but how about giving it a second chance? Just try it, and if you get a response, play it again. It can't hurt."

They agreed, and the record again got respectable treatment.

So I traveled to Pittsburgh, St. Louis, Detroit—Finally, I reached Cleveland, and met Bill Randle, that town's number one DJ. I sat in his two-by-four studio and we shot the breeze for a while, and then he turned the program over to his engineer.

"Come on," he said, "Let's go down and have a cup of coffee."

And over that cup of coffee, I got a new idea. A truly crazy, wonderful idea. "What if you played 'Rags to Riches' *six times in a row*?" I asked him.

"They might think I fell asleep," he said. Then, without batting an eyelash, he added, "What the hell. Let's try it."

And we went back upstairs, and he played Tony Bennett's "Rags to Riches" six times in a row.

No telephones rang, so I figured it was a good idea the public just didn't accept. I went back to the Y, where I could afford to stay on the remains of Mitch's five hundred dollars. There'd been a phone call from Bill Randle. I returned it. "You want to feel good?" he asked.

"What do you mean?" I answered.

"Find a record store, and treat yourself," he said. "The phone's been ringing off the hook ever since you left."

I tracked down a record store, and sure enough, they'd sold out "Rags to Riches" an hour before. All the record stores had been stampeded. That weekend, the song went from nothing to number one in Cleveland.

Three weeks later, it made the Hit Parade at number two. It went on to sell almost two million copies. Adler and Ross had their first blockbuster hit. It stayed on the Hit Parade for five months.

And then, just when Jerry and I began to think that maybe we should forget about the theatre and concentrate on writing pop songs for the juke boxes, our agent, David Hocker, called.

John Murray Anderson, *the* John Murray Anderson, the director/producer who'd staged everything from the Ringling Brothers and Barnum and Bailey Circus to *Life Begins at 8:40*; from *The Ziegfeld Follies* to *The Greenwich Village Follies*, who'd pioneered all sorts of stage ideas like treadmills and turntables and young talent, wanted *us* for a new Broadway-bound revue!

Big revues were still popular then, and Anderson had just directed two. One—*Two's Company*, starring Bette Davis, with music by Vernon Duke and lyrics and sketches by Ogden Nash—had been a ninety performance flop, but the other—*New Faces of 1952*—looked like it was sure to run forever.

Now, he was going to revive a format and a title he'd had a huge success with in 1929—*John Murray Anderson's Almanac.* That show had had sketches by Noel Coward, Rube Goldberg, and Peter Arno; a show curtain created by Reginald Marsh; a score by Milton Ager and Henry Sullivan that included "I May Be Wrong (But I Think You're Wonderful)"; and a starring role by a very young Jimmy Savvo.

Anderson was going to star Harry Belafonte, who was on his way as a calypso singer, and feature Orson Bean and Polly Bergen, who were fairly well known around the nightclub circuit. In the clowning department, he was going to rely on Billy De Wolfe, a name in the movies but not on Broadway, and Hermione Gingold, an English revue star who had never appeared in America. (In the show, she'd marvel over the fact that we had a statue of Judith Anderson in New York Harbor.) Cyril Ritchard, who had never directed in America, was going to direct the sketches. Jean Kerr, who had yet to write *Mary, Mary* and *King of Hearts,* was going to write the sketches.

And for music: Cy Coleman, whose chief credentials were as a supper club pianist, and Sheldon Harnick, who'd just written some very clever lyrics for *New Faces,* including the hilarious "Boston Beguine," for Alice Ghostley.

But the *bulk* of the score was going to be written by a couple of young guys who already had a horsemeat musical behind them.

We were going to Broadway.

2.

F O U R months after we first shook hands with that sixty-six-year-old pixie, John Murray Anderson, the lunacy that I'd always remember about our first Broadway production began.

Murray, as everybody called him, was British, adorable, sweet, and absolutely untrustworthy. There he stood, that first day, in the middle of a rehearsal hall, in the middle of his created cosmos, waiting to take on the world. He was totally bald and had a face dominated by two sunken cheeks, a receding jaw, and buck teeth. Not exactly a matinee idol, but his power was palpable. With a sly, wicked, disarming smile, he could skewer you with his wit, and the next moment be your greatest, most eloquent champion.

Somewhere in the middle of the first week of rehearsals, he saw to it that everybody lost their real names. Mischievous to a fault, he pronounced, in his polished, singsong British accent, that henceforth, Hermione would be "Miss Binki," that Jerry would be known as "Boss Ross." And, since I seemed to be the dominant personality of the duo, I'd be known as "Boss Ross's Boss."

When rehearsals started heating up, this got to be too much of a mouthful to shout across a theatre, so "Boss Ross" was shortened to "The Pup" and "Boss Ross's Boss" went from "BRB" to "Bahbee." I can hear Murray now. "Pup?!" he'd shout, "Bahbee, come heah! Bahbee?! Wheah *are* those two idiots?" He could say anything and still make you love him.

Maybe because of the time he'd spent with Ringling Brothers, or maybe because the inner muse that set his rehearsal rhythms had a short attention span, John Murray Anderson turned the putting together of a show into a six ring circus.

Now we had a spot for a song, now we didn't. Now the song was Polly

Bergen's, now it wasn't. If he said on Tuesday he needed a ballad by Thursday, he was sure to change his mind on Wednesday.

The scenery was complicated and monumental. The costumes were numerous enough to fill a warehouse—and eventually did.

All of this stayed with me and skated through my mind three weeks into rehearsal, as I sat in a hall on downtown Second Avenue, where we were going through our fourth four-hour run-through. The unmistakable aroma of turkey was in the air.

At least it was to me. I had a wonderfully inaccurate theatrical sense in those days, seeing disaster where it wasn't, sensing doom where it didn't exist, waxing lyrical over numbers that would be thrown out at the next rehearsal.

But I learned. In that nuthouse of a show, where genius and dross intermingled like the threads in a fabric, my eye and ear sharpened. I was particularly laid in the aisles, for instance, by De Wolfe and Gingold's devastatingly funny performance in an old Bobby Howes (Sally Ann's father—the number one musical star of the London stage in the 30's and 40's) sketch called "Dinner for One," in which Hermione, as a deliciously demented grand dame, sat at a long table set for an army of her former lovers, all of whom were dead. Billy, playing her butler, joined her in toasting them and feeding them, and before the sketch had run its course, they were both sozzled and the stage was a shambles.

And Sheldon Harnick had, to my mind, written a wonderfully clever number called "Merry Little Minuet." It was a madrigal about the woes of the world ("They're rioting in Africa, tra la la la la la . . ."), set to his own music, and it both dazzled and delighted me every time it was performed.

But by the time we got to Boston, where we were beginning our tryout tour, I'd even stopped laughing at Miss Binki and Billy. The show was too confusing to be funny. I didn't know what was in or what was out. The running order changed more often than a downtown traffic light. At the last minute, before we left New York, Murray decided to resurrect one of his ballet ballads from the old *Greenwich Village Follies*, complete with old songs and white feathers.

Was *this* Broadway?

Still, Jerry and I wrote at least a couple of songs we both loved, one of which would have a numbing significance later in my life. The first was a ballad, sung by Polly Bergen, in a song sketch called "La Loge," based on the Renoir painting. Its title was "Fini," and it would have a less than moderate lifespan in a beautiful but old-fashioned record made by Edie Gorme:

> Fini, Fini,
> *They say that our love is* fini,
> *Your eyes, your roving eyes agree . . .*

The other was a ballad, too, written for Harry Belafonte. It was a gentle, pastoral song called "Acorn in the Meadow." The first time he stood, alone in the rehearsal hall, and sang our song will always remain rooted in my mind, a moment I'll always remember. It flowed perfectly from him, as if he'd been inside our minds when we wrote it:

> *Acorn in the meadow,*
> *Meadow filled with sun,*
> *Sun a' shinin' warm on the meadow,*
> *Tree begun.*
> *Baby in the cradle,*
> *Cradle filled with love,*
> *Mama smilin',*
> *Warm on the cradle from above.*
> *Some day my baby be a working man,*
> *Tree be mighty big and strong,*
> *Me, I'll sit in the shade of it,*
> *Just sit and relax all day long,*
> *Lord, I pray you help me*
> *Help me make him good.*
> *Help me make him gentle when he be grown.*
> *I can see it—*
> *Me in the shade of the acorn tree,*
> *He and his woman sittin' 'side 'a me*
> *And maybe my baby with an acorn of his own . . .*

It was a simple and touching moment, and everyone at the rehearsal either cried or cheered.

And Harry was never able to capture the same delivery or the mood again. All of us had to be satisfied with that moment.

Finally, we opened, at the Colonial Theatre, in Boston. It was a cold, blustery November night.

Jerry and I settled into our seats, trying to seem as inconspicuous as we could—which was easy for Jerry. He was a little guy. I had to fold myself up twice to sink out of sight.

By the time the final curtain came down, it was 12:15, and there were a lot of empty seats at the Colonial. We sneaked out into the lobby, and walked through it as quickly as we could.

We didn't want to go to the large and foolish opening night party that was held onstage after the performance, but felt we should at least put in an appearance. Everyone was smiling, a little too broadly, I thought, and talking, a little too loudly, it seemed to me.

I sipped a glass of champagne near an exit, and plotted my escape. As I was turning to go, a tall young man on crutches, with a lovely, dark-haired lady at his side, blocked my way. He smiled, an engaging, compelling, knowing smile. He didn't request, he *commanded* my attention.

"Heard you're one of the composahs," he said, in an accent that couldn't have come from anywhere but Boston. "Always honahd to meet composahs." He extended his hand. His grip was firm and strong, an undeniable affirmation. "Kennedy. Jack Kennedy," he said, "and this is my bride, Jackie."

"Hello," she said, breathily. There was a calm beauty about her, I thought, and a sort of distractedness, too. But they were real people, the first I'd talked to besides Jerry, it seemed, since the beginning of rehearsals. I abandoned my retreat, and spent most of the rest of the party talking with this out-of-the-ordinary couple.

Now, under the weight of several tons of scenery and costumes and hope, we staggered into New York. And I won't deny it. It was one hell of a thrill walking up 46th Street and seeing our names on the marquee of the Imperial Theatre.

"Jesus," I said to Jerry, after we'd made our twentieth tour up and down the block, "We're here."

We were young enough to see the majority of our lifetimes spread ahead of us. There was a lot to accomplish, and we were just beginning.

"Here we go," I said to Jerry and Judy the next night. "December 10, 1953. The night Adler and Ross hit Broadway."

It was one of the longest nights of my life, as the rehearsal period had been one of the longest rehearsal periods I'd ever go through.

The trouble was, I thought, as *John Murray Anderson's Almanac* unfolded before us, I'd never really felt that I was part of the show. With *Six on a Honeymoon,* we'd all been intensely *involved.* We'd been a six-week family. Herb had suggested changes in the songs. We'd suggested changes in the staging. I'd trained the singers. We'd all had a stake in each other.

With this show, Jerry and I had manufactured the material and somebody had put it on, like an overcoat. If this was Broadway, I thought, maybe even the Black Hawk was a better place to be. Maybe.

The curtain came down to tumultuous applause. "Never trust a first night audience," muttered Jerry as we walked toward the street. "They're all either crazy or friends of the producer."

We really didn't have to wait for the reviews, but we did, and that way, went to bed depressed instead of waking up that way.

Even our songs were minimized. Brooks Atkinson, in the *Times,* said that "the songs by Adler and Ross were routine." That was his entire review of our part of the score.

It stung. I went to my dictionary and looked up the word "routine" to see if it had a second meaning.

It didn't.

The show ran for 229 performances, a respectable run, but not good enough to pay off its backers.

Still, we had our yearly appointment with Frank Loesser and George Abbott a week from Tuesday. Maybe, we thought, now that we have a track record of sorts, our music will sound better to him.

A week from Tuesday didn't begin very fortuitously. First of all, it rained—a fine, depressing sort of mist.

Mr. Abbott and Frank Loesser entered into their yearly routine with a comforting kind of sameness. We performed and Mr. Abbott registered nothing.

And then, in one instant, everything changed.

The expression on Mr. Abbott's face softened. "Good," he said, with just the slightest hint of enthusiasm. "I think you're ready."

Jerry and I looked at each other, numb.

Mr. Abbott sauntered into the silence. "Freddie Brisson, Bobby Griffith and Hal Prince have a property," he said. "Bobby's my general stage manager. I'm going to direct, and write the libretto. It's going to be based on a book called *Seven and a Half Cents,* by Richard Bissell. It's about a strike in a pajama factory."

Mr. Abbott smiled at the bewilderment on our faces. "I know," he sighed, "It doesn't sound like Rodgers and Hammerstein, which is why they're not writing the score."

Mr. Abbott scribbled an address on a piece of paper. "Stop by the office and pick up two copies. Read it, and write us four songs. When you're ready, we'll listen."

We picked up the two copies of the book the same day and consumed them in a few hours. That night, we sat down and began hammering out the four songs.

For the past few months, Jerry and I had been working in a studio at 18 West 55th Street. It was about the size of a broom closet, but it only cost us sixty dollars a month, and it was private. There were no disturbances; there was no world but the one we controlled. When we closed the doors of our studio, we went to work immediately. We knew that we had no time to waste.

Within two days, we had four songs. And they were good.

We called up the producers and told them we were ready.

"Fine," said Mr. Abbott when he came on the line, and then, as if he'd been expecting us all along to consume this assignment as greedily as if it were our last meal, he added, "If I can get the others together, we'll be there at three o'clock tomorrow."

And for the first time in two days, my stomach lurched.

"By the way," he said, "did you like the book?"

I did. I could honestly answer him and say that I thought it was great fun. What I *didn't* tell him was that if it'd been *The Scott Tissue Gazette*, I would have liked it. I was that desperate to do a book musical. Christopher, my second son, was on the way, and my marriage was beginning to show faint signs of wear and tear. More than ever, I needed the work.

Three o'clock tomorrow came, and the production staff arrived. And arrived. And arrived.

Squeezed into our rabbit hutch of a studio that afternoon were Frank Loesser; George Abbott; the producers Brisson, Griffith and Prince; the musical director Hal Hastings; the set and costume designer Lem Ayers; Jerome Robbins, who was assisting George Abbott; and a young, quiet choreographer, whose first show this was going to be: Bob Fosse.

The place looked like a clown car in a circus, and to add to the fun, Bob Fosse chain smoked. Jerry started to turn green.

We began, and before we'd finished the third song, we knew we were in. The expressions on all those smiling faces added up to one three-letter word: Yes.

So, in less than a year, we'd gone from horsemeat to Broadway.

—Or, at least to the edge of Broadway. We still had some proving to do, we realized, particularly when we noticed that our contract included an interpolation clause. That meant that, at any time during the rehearsal period or out-of-town tryout, the producers could bring in another composer-lyricist.

Well, we reasoned, you can't blame them for being cautious. And besides, we weren't the only ones getting that kind of treatment. Although Jerry Robbins' official title was co-librettist with Mr. Abbott, the real reason he'd been brought in was insurance in case Bob Fosse flunked his first Broadway assignment.

Nor did it bother us when we learned, later on, that the score to the show had been turned down not only by Rodgers and Hammerstein, but by Frank Loesser, Jule Styne, Comden and Green, Harold Rome, Burton Lane and Cole Porter.

Nor, finally, were we distressed when we found out that Mr. Abbott hadn't *really* been willing to take a chance on us until Freddy Brisson's wife, Rosalind Russell, who was currently wowing them down the street in Mr. Abbott, Comden and Green, and Leonard Bernstein's *Wonderful Town,* had urged him to give us a try.

We were just glad for the chance to show him that we were better than the material we'd been given until now, and good enough to write for Broadway.

This was the big time at last. This was the big opportunity we had been working toward. This was *The Pajama Game.*

3.

W E wrote like a hurricane. We finished the score of *The Pajama Game* in five weeks. That's fast.

Casting started at various Shubert theatres, and it went on for three months.

At the same time, we began backers' auditions: thirty of them at least, evening after evening of trooping into some of the most elegant living rooms in Manhattan, gathering at the piano, and trying to sell the show. Jerry would play; Hal Prince would encapsulate the book; Edie Adams (who was blonde and buxom and terrific), Sheldon's brother, Jay Harnick (who had a rich, legit type voice), Jerry, and I would sing for people like Mrs. Vivian Coleman, Frank McMahon, Alfred Gwynne, and Jeanne Vanderbilt. And by the end of two months, we had the money.

From the beginning, we'd been absorbed into the life of the show. It was a new and consuming experience. *Almanac* had been a revue. This was a book musical, and a book musical, we found, was like a chain. One weak link could turn the whole chain into a pile of scrap metal. Every day, we sat down with Jerry Robbins, Bob Fosse, Mr. Abbott, Bobby Griffith, and Hal Prince, and made decisions with them. In *Almanac,* we'd come into a production that had already been cast. This time, we were operating strictly under the provisions of the Dramatists' Guild Contract, which meant that we had our say in all of the casting.

Janis Paige, who was an established and popular movie star, was a possibility for the heroine, Babe. And the first time she auditioned, I knew why. Although she wasn't a singer, her projection was convincing; although she didn't always sing in tune, she made a song work. The morning she sang and read for us the first time, she stood, erect and confident, under a bright rehearsal light, wearing a black leather jacket, her chin jutting out in a smart, affirmative way. She brought a strength, a kind of self-assurance with her that was absolutely right for the part.

And she was damned good looking besides—an arresting, traffic-stopping redhead with a fine body that she knew how to use.

"Jesus, she's wonderful!" I whispered to Jerry when she finished.

"Careful, Quimby," he said. He was on to me.

We had other Hollywood stars who tried out for the leads, too. Van Johnson wanted the part of Sid Sorokin, the superintendent of the pajama factory, very badly. He'd started on Broadway with Mr. Abbott as a chorus dancer, and he knew his way around a stage as well as he did around a sound stage. But, as good as his acting was, his voice wasn't strong enough for the kind of singers' songs we'd written. And those were the days before they wired Broadway theatres for sound. You either projected to the balcony or you didn't get the job. So, we had to pass on him.

The natural choice for the role, as Jerry and I saw it, was John Raitt. We'd seen him, a few months before, in a City Center revival of *Carousel*, and we suggested him to Mr. Abbott. Raitt auditioned, and, as we thought, his projection and his intonation were perfect for the Sorokin role. He was big, handsome, powerful, and a little on the square side—which wasn't wrong for the part. And if his vocal delivery was too operatic, so what, I thought. I can work with it.

But Mr. Abbott didn't like him. He was, in Mr. Abbott's opinion and words, a stiff actor. Jerry and I had to agree on that last point, but, being songwriters, we wanted our songs sung well. And we thought the other stuff could be overcome.

No dice. Mr. Abbott kept John Raitt's name on the callback list, but he also kept on searching for somebody else for the part.

It didn't take long to fill the comedy lead of Heinzie, the jealous suitor of Gladys. Eddie Foy, Jr., who'd been a star in vaudeville and on Broadway for several generations, and was another Abbott alumnus, had a shy, distracted quality and a great way with a number that sold him to us the moment he stepped onstage. He was our Heinzie from his first entrance.

As for the dance lead: Here, we took a chance with an unknown, Carol Haney, just as the producers had taken a chance with Bob Fosse and us. She was part Scandinavian, part Tibetan. Her eyes were slanted. She had a large mouth and a broad, beguiling smile that traveled from ear to ear and right into you. She wore her hair in a Dutch bob with spiked bangs, and forever after that, anyone who played the role would wear her hair that way too.

Bob Fosse brought her in; he was the only one who had seen her work, but five minutes after she began her audition, we knew that Bob had a fabulous eye.

It wouldn't be until two days before the beginning of rehearsals that Mr. Abbott would finally give in and hire John Raitt, and it would be with some reluctance. "We'll have our work cut out for us," he would mutter, when John's name was finally added to the cast list.

The first reading wasn't one of those magical times you see in backstage movies. Nobody gasped. Our songs weren't met with wild applause or soulful sighs. There was a junkpile of songs and dialogue that would be tossed out in the next six weeks, and there were songs and lines—lots of them—still to be written before we'd dare a run-through. In fact, when we went into rehearsal, the script resembled Swiss cheese. Still, the show was in the hands of George Abbott and we trusted him like a white water rafter trusts his guide.

He was a hard, fair, skilled taskmaster, and he whipped me into line the morning of the first rehearsal. A ten o'clock call had been given at the 54th Street Theatre—which is now, appropriately enough, the George Abbott Theatre. I arrived ten minutes late, and marched down the aisle to my seat. Suddenly, I was aware that the rehearsal had stopped dead.

Mr. Abbott had turned from his spot on the stage apron and was looking directly at me. And then he spoke, in no uncertain terms. "Time is money," he said, furiously, "and money is scarce. And who the hell do you think you are coming late for your own rehearsals? Everybody else was here on time. Everybody but you."

"I got caught in traffic," I stammered. "The taxi—There was a lot of traffic."

He looked at me with what seemed to be contempt. "Then you should have left earlier," he said, and turned back to the rehearsal.

I felt humiliated, squelched, ashamed, and remorseful. And from that moment on, I don't think I've ever been late for an appointment.

At first, shaping the show was a matter of moving scenes and songs around. Then, it was the larger task of filling in the holes.

"Write me a song about a kind of spooky nightclub, a sort of *rundown* nightclub, with a furtive look to it," Mr. Abbott said to us, one morning. "We need to set the scene and I want to do it musically.

Something very dark, a kind of speakeasy. Maybe Spanish."

Spanish. That was a good idea, I thought, when we got back to the studio. My mother's ancestors were Spanish, and I spoke the language fluently. I'd spent a lot of time in Central and South America during the war, and a Spanish approach appealed to me.

" 'Ernando," I said to Jerry, as we shrugged out of our coats.

"What's that?" he asked.

"A Spanish name, The kind of Spaniard who might run a place with a furtive look to it."

"A dark and spooky place called—"

" 'Ernando's 'Ideaway!"

"Okay!" enthused Jerry.

"*Ole!* you mean," I corrected him, and we were off.

I sang. "I know—a dark—secluded place—" It was already a tango.

We both rushed to the piano and simultaneously began to sing, in a whisper.

And "Hernando's Hideaway" was completed, in less than an hour.

Mr. Abbott liked it. Frank Loesser liked it. In fact, Frank seemed to like just about everything we wrote, and he only intruded on our ideas once.

There was a tender scene in the first act in which Sid Sorokin first realized he was in love with Babe. Mr. Abbott had conceived it as a solo turn. Sid, alone in his office after confronting Babe, would sing a love ballad into a dictaphone. A nice touch.

We wrote a really lousy song called "Dear Babe," or something like that. It was a letter set to music, and it was truly terrible. Mr. Abbott didn't like it, and neither did we.

So, we went back to work, and pretty soon, the idea of turning away from the direct approach of a letter and toward the indirect approach of an inner dialogue occurred to me.

The new idea did what a letter couldn't begin to accomplish. Not only would it be consistent with the tone of the scene, it would advance the plot and give the audience some insight into Sid's character. It could actually tune into a man fighting with himself.

Once we'd agreed upon the approach, the song almost wrote itself. As we wrote, we kept the scene surrounding the song constantly in mind, laying it out as we went along.

The door slams. Sid stands stock still for a moment, then begins to walk around the room. He's angry and, although he won't admit it, a little humiliated:

Hey There
You with the stars in your eyes—

he says, mocking himself. Then, he builds himself up:

Love never made a fool of you,
You used to be too wise.

More mocking:

Hey There,
You on that high flying cloud,

Then, some insight:

Though she won't throw a crumb to you,
You think some day she'll come to you.

He decides to walk away:

Better forget her—
Her with her nose in the air.

And he knows the logical reason:

She has you dancing on a string.
Break it, and she won't care!

But sexual impulse knocks logic out of the box:

Won't you take this advice I hand you like a brother—
Or, are you not seeing things too clear?
Are you too much in love to hear?
Is it all going in one ear—
—And out the other?

We brought "Hey There" in the next day. Mr. Abbott listened silently. "That's good work, boys," he said, and went back into rehearsal.

Translation: He loved it. He was a man of few words and much concentration, and we'd already learned how to read his verbal short-hand.

There was only one change that he demanded, the next day. " 'Are you too much in love to hear?' It embarrasses me," he said. "Write something else."

We thought it was right, for the character and the moment and the song, but we also knew that when Mr. Abbott wanted a change, you made it. "Are you just too far gone to hear," Sid Sorokin sang from then on, but after the show opened, and it was recorded separately from the cast album, we restored the original line to the song.

A few days later, when we played "Hey There" for Frank in his office, he, as usual, liked it, but he had a small suggestion.

"Boys," he said, "if you wanta make a song work, sell the title."

We looked at him uncomprehendingly.

"Don't get me wrong," he went on. "I love the number. I just don't think you sell the title enough. You only use it twice. But I have an idea."

He was the old pro. I leaned on his advice.

"Put the title in again, at the end," he said.

"The end?" I asked.

"Sure. Like this: *You* end it 'Is it all going in one ear and out the other.' No good. What you *have* to do, so people will remember it is, end it *this* way: 'Is it all going in one ear and out the other. Hey There, you with the stars in your eyes.' That'll make it more sellable."

And he winked.

Jerry turned to me. "That's not a bad idea. Easy to fix," he said.

I didn't know what to do. I nodded, but my gut feeling was that it was really a terrible way to end the song.

We left Frank's office, and in the elevator, I turned to Jerry. "The Negative rules," I said. "That's a lousy idea. I mean, how cheap do we have to get?"

"You really feel that way?" asked Jerry, not challenging me, just asking for an explanation.

"You bet I do," I said, as we headed toward the rehearsal hall. "I love Frank. I respect him. But let's leave it the way it is and take our chances."

"Okay, partner," said Jerry, cheerfully, and that was that as far as he was concerned.

I wish it had been for me. Frank had sowed the seed of doubt in my own insecurity that afternoon; maybe it had been there all along. The more I heard the song, the less I believed it would work in the show. Every day, when Jerry and I met in the studio, I'd come in with a replacement for "Hey There." Jerry went along with my crusade. We must have written five other songs for that spot. From then until we opened, I kept pestering Mr. Abbott, trying to get him to take "Hey There" out of the show and put in one of our supposedly more accessible songs.

He'd listen, quietly, and then say "No good." And leave. Every time. Thank God he did.

Jerry didn't have a great deal of interest in rehearsing the singers. Most of that fell to me, and I learned a lot.

Janis Paige's musical problem was her intonation. She sang flat. I had to work with her intensely. "Think sharp," I said. "Think *above* the note. Concentrate." She did, and so did I, and pretty soon, a small romance began to blossom.

With John Raitt, both Mr. Abbott and I had—as the director had prophesied—our work cut out for us. I didn't have any trouble with his stiffness in the role, because I felt that Sid Sorokin was a square anyway. It was his musical approach that bothered me. The first day we worked together, I pointed it out to him, "Look, John," I said. "When you're the pajama factory superintendent, and you're speaking dialogue, you sound like a factory superintendent. But when you're singing a song, you sound like an opera star, making with the round, pearly tones. Why not sound like a superintendent when you're singing, too?"

He began:

> *Hey Theah—*
> *Yaw with the stahs in—*

"John," I interrupted. "It isn't *yaw*. It's *you*. '*You* with the stars in your eyes.' "

He laughed. And he got it, but slowly. Very slowly. Years of operatic training and very legit theatre singing got in the way. Finally, after a solid month of individual work, he found that ideal combination of rich sound and sustained character that gave his role unity and life onstage, and I think he was as happy the day he found it as I was.

Eddie Foy, Jr., was a worrier, like me. The difference was that my worries drove me into action. His tied his memory in knots. After three weeks, he was still "going up"—forgetting—some of his lyrics. Well,

I thought, he's a pro, like the rest. He'll come around.

And as soon as I'd set that problem to rest in my mind, another one popped up. There was a waltz, called "I'm Not at All in Love," that Janis sang, with the girls. It was a "Methinks [she] doth protest too much" sort of song, in which she denied her true feelings.

Jerry Robbins was staging it like a kind of mock Agnes de Mille girl talk number, with Janis and a stage full of female singers and dancers.

One day in rehearsal, he came over to me and said, "Look, Richard, you've got to do some writing on this."

"Where?" I asked. It looked fine to me. Whimsical, funny, full of movement.

"It needs action. The lyrics stop while the band is playing pickup notes. The singers are standing around with their mouths closed. Give them lyrics in the pick-up notes."

It was a revelation. Of course! To me, the pick-ups had just been a phrase leading into the next phrase. To a master like Jerry Robbins, they were dead air that had to be brought to life.

The pick-up notes/lyrics we added were:

> It's easy to see that
> *Her daffy grin*
> *Is the grin she always wears . . .*

Just five little words. But they made a big difference.

I never forgot the lesson, as I never forgot Jerry Robbins. Frank Loesser had said, at the beginning, that "Black Jerry" (as he was known in those days because of his jet black hair) and I would inevitably cross swords during rehearsals, because we had similar temperaments. It never happened. Jerry Robbins, as far as I could see, never made a wrong move when he was staging a number. My admiration for him grew to be boundless.

Only nine days into rehearsal, Mr. Abbott called the first run-through, minus the dances. Everyone was there, including Frank Loesser.

In my enthusiasm and optimism and inexperience, I guess I was looking forward to a finished product. I settled into my seat, ready for the miracle.

But the run-through was, to me, a shambles. A disappointment. A disaster area. All those bright hopes. That new car I was going to buy.

All those people who were going to know my name. Wiped out in one afternoon in a crummy rehearsal hall over Al and Dick's Steakhouse on 54th Street.

Frank Loesser, buoyant as usual, came over to Jerry and me. "Well, what did you think?" he asked.

"I thought it was terrible. It was embarrassing," I said, sinking even further into a black funk.

"Whaddaya mean? It's *great*! You got a big hit," he said, and walked away.

I looked after him in disbelief. "He must be crazy," I said to Jerry, as we joined the circle of production people gathered around Mr. Abbott for an impromptu meeting.

Mr. Abbott's first words injected some reality into the afternoon. He had a perplexed scowl on his face—a mirror, I figured, of my own plummeting feelings. But it was no mirror. It was the face of an experienced pro making some hard decisions.

"Well," he said, in a soft, determined voice, "I see a lot of changes that have to be made. I've been wrong. I thought we needed more of a subplot. We don't. It has to be changed."

The subplot had to do with a rivalry for Heinzie between a girl named Poopsie, played by Charlotte Rae, a then little known actress, and Gladys. But Carol Haney had such star quality, it was apparent to Mr. Abbott that Poopsie had to go—and with her, the very talented Charlotte Rae. Her part would be absorbed into Carol's, building it up and balancing it with the major story. Such were the sometimes cruel realities of the professional theatre.

This also meant moving some songs around. Poopsie had sung "There Once Was a Man." It went to Babe and Sid, and eventually evolved into a show stopper. But then, to do this, a scene had to be written before and after it.

So it went. In the sometimes frantic days and nights to come, more scenes and songs were moved, deleted, added, trimmed, and tightened. The show was like a cloud that changed its shape over and over. Some changes were thrown out as quickly as they appeared. Others remained, strong and solidly right.

And that, essentially, was the show with which we opened, four weeks later, in New Haven.

The Shubert in New Haven was a wonderful, old, and ugly theatre. The show was rough. Janis was being difficult. At the first dress parade, she pronounced the costumes that Lem Ayres had executed for her absolutely unacceptable. She wouldn't go on in them.

There were shouts and pleadings and a stormy scene, into the middle of which Roz Russell calmly walked. Taking Janis on one arm and motioning to Hal Prince, Bobby Griffith, and her husband Fred Brisson to come along, she steered the disgruntled entourage through the lobby of the theatre and out to a long limousine, parked in front.

She opened the doors of the limo, got into the chauffeur's seat, and drove the entire group off on a shopping spree. When they got back, two hours later, they had a trunk full of clothes and a happy leading lady.

But no simple tour of the stores in New Haven could have calmed my terror. I was so insecure that, when Mr. and Mrs. J. Horace Block, two friends of mine from New York, showed up in front of the theater for a Saturday matinee, I intercepted them.

"You can't go in," I said, frantically, standing between them and the box office.

"What do you mean?" asked Mrs. Block.

I waved my arms like a demented scarecrow. "It's not ready. Go back to New York. I'll tell you when to come. Please," I pleaded.

They probably figured it was easier to placate me than to put up with my madness. So, they didn't go into the theatre. At least, I didn't see them go in. I was sure I was right in sending them away. When I went inside, I saw Mary Martin and Leland Hayward sitting toward the back of the orchestra. They'd come up to see Jerry Robbins' latest work. Latest mess, I thought, dying of embarrassment and moving as far away from them as I could get.

The show began. Eddie Foy, Jr., still didn't know his lyrics. A piece of scenery careened off a pipe, nearly wiping out Janis Paige. "There Once Was a Man" didn't cause a ripple.

The first review I read in New Haven was one written by the critic for the Yale paper. He hated everything about the show. And because I was now as much a part of *Pajama Game* as if I were married to it, I hated everything about *him*.

"Take it easy, Richard," Jerry said, when I poured out my anger. "It probably won't be the last bad review we'll get."

Ironically, it was, but how could we have known that? I was furious, and upset, about a lot of things, not the least of which was my marriage.

Marion had scarcely spoken to me when I'd packed to leave for New

Haven. I wasn't overly unhappy about that. Whenever we'd spoken lately, it had been in anger. We both had explosive tempers, we were both feeling the tension that happens when two creative people are close, and one of them is succeeding and the other isn't.

If I'd been more mature then, if I'd carried my small success a little more gracefully, if I'd realized then as I do now that she must have been painfully aware that her talents weren't powerful enough to push her over the hurdle of "getting there," I would have been more considerate of her feelings.

But I wasn't. I was too immature to see that the most serene kind of success is large enough to include more than just yourself.

"You're more married to Jerry than you are to me," she'd said, tearfully, before we left for New Haven. And she was right. Collaboration *is* a kind of marriage. And Jerry to me was, besides the brother I'd never had, the ideal, undemanding, non-combative wife no husband will *ever* have, but wishes for, especially when the rest of the world is making impossible demands upon him.

At the time, I put it out of my mind. I figured I needed the company of men and undemanding women, so I could concentrate on the show. And every minute I thought that way, my marriage disintegrated a little bit more.

Janis and I had promised ourselves that we'd spend our first night in New Haven together. After the rehearsal, the cast and the production staff went to Kasey's, a restaurant across the street from the Taft Hotel, where we were staying. My mind wasn't on my food or the conversation, and as soon as Janis and I could gracefully excuse ourselves, we did.

We walked across the street to the hotel. "Yours or mine?" I asked, as we got into the elevator.

"How about—" Janis said, and stopped.

I turned around. Mr. Abbott was entering the elevator. He nodded pleasantly to the two of us, probably wondering why Janis was giggling.

Sure, I thought, as I got off the elevator with Mr. Abbott at our floor and saw the doors close on a smiling Janis, that just about makes the evening perfect.

Fifteen minutes later, the phone rang. It was Janis. "How about my place?" she said.

I was there in two minutes. She opened the door, and she was dressed the way she was in the finale of the show: Pajama tops and high heels, and nothing else. And she was still smiling. But differently.

At the theatre the next day, Bob Fosse was caught in the middle of a large problem. He'd staged a fancy ballet to open the second act, and Mr. Abbott had decided that it had to go.

"The boss feels it doesn't work," Bob said to me. "He thinks we ought to do an entertainment. An amateur entertainment. A show the union is putting on for its members. Sort of a cabaret." Bob lit up another cigarette, and turned to me. "You guys have anything like that?"

We thought for a while. Amateur night. A one-person song. A two-person song. A three-person song.

"Something with a strong beat," he suggested.

We tossed some suggestions back and forth, and then, it occurred to me.

"We wrote something I'm ashamed of," I said. "Something that began in a bathroom."

"In a *bathroom?*" Bob asked.

"Yeah, but you don't want to hear this one," I backtracked.

"Play it for me," he demanded.

"It's—" we both began.

"Just try it," he urged.

And we did "Steam Heat" for him.

> *I got (clang clang!) f-s-s-s-s-steam heat;*

I sang, in my best vaudeville counterfeit.

> *I got (clang clang!) f-s-s-s-s-steam heat;*

echoed Jerry, thumping out the rhythm on the pit piano.

> *I got (clang clang!) f-s-s-s-s-steam heat:*

we sang, together, then I stepped out, selling it:

> *But I need your love,*
> *to keep away the cold . . .*

Frankly, it was embarrassing, and neither one of us could believe Bob's reaction.

"That's it!" He smiled.

"You're kidding," I said. "That piece of junk?"

"Give me a couple of days," he said. "I might change my mind."

"How can he change his mind when he's lost it?" I asked Jerry, as we left the theatre.

Jerry shrugged. "Maybe he knows something we don't."

Two days later, Bob had worked out a rough sketch of the number. It needed more music than we'd originally written. We worked with him, and came up with an added section in the middle:

> *They told me to shovel more coal in the boiler;*
> *They told me to shovel more coal in the boiler;*
> *They told me to shovel more coal in the boiler;*

and then, in perfect Frank Loesser grammar:

> *But that don't do no good!*

Then, just to spread the heat around:

> *They told me to pour some more oil in the burner;*
> *They told me to pour some more oil in the burner;*
> *They told me to pour some more oil in the burner;*
> *But* that *don't do no good!*

And *that* was that.

Boston, our next stop, was a friendly and understanding town—if you had a smash.

But opening night there looked to me like a replay of New Haven. Whatever could go wrong on an opening night went wrong. Cues were late. Scenery didn't work. Eddie Foy, Jr., still didn't know his lyrics.

And, to top it off, the tape went crazy during Raitt's performance of "Hey There." The routine was something I'd dreamed up when Mr. Abbott first gave us the idea of having John sing the song into a dictaphone. Why not, I said, play it back, and then add a sung obligato against it? Of course, for the trick to come off, the timing had to be precise, so that the orchestra plays a live accompaniment under the recording.

But none of us were prepared for what happened in Boston that night. For some reason, the tape was played back at a different speed than the one at which it was recorded. It came over the system about a third of a tone *higher* than both Raitt and the orchestra.

I was standing at the back of the theatre, and what I heard sounded like a Charles Ives piece. "Jesus," I said to myself, "this is awful. We're going to get killed."

I could hardly wait to see the death notices in the local papers. The reviews would have to be assassination attempts.

But they were terrific. Everyone loved it, went crazy over it, predicted it would run forever—except Eliot Norton, the great critic of the *Boston Post,* who really didn't care for the show too much. But he did like one moment. "Adler and Ross have written a very beautiful song called 'Hey There,'" he wrote, "and it's performed in lovely style—" Jesus, I thought, he must have the worst tin ear that ever was. And he's reviewing *musicals*—?

So, the Boston run was a success, but the big hurdle, the one that counted, the New York opening, was still ahead. And we were in trouble. The show had been underfinanced. Even in 1954, $250,000 wasn't much to spend on a first class musical, and by the time we'd closed in Boston, the coffers were empty.

We sneaked into New York. There was a paltry $15,000 advance sale at the box office. There was no money to properly advertise the show. We were living very dangerously indeed. What we needed, to survive, were across-the-board raves. And in 1954, there were nine newspapers in New York. If we didn't get them, we'd close. Right away.

Still, we weren't exactly gloomy. We'd had the audiences hysterical the last few nights in Boston. Everything had started to come together. "There Once Was a Man" finally clicked. "I'll Never Be Jealous Again" stopped the show. So did "Steam Heat." And Eddie Foy, Jr., had learned all his song lyrics except one.

We could make it. If the fates were with us. If the audience was with us. And if—and this was the biggest if of all, because they could sink us with a sentence—the critics were with us.

About three months before we'd gone out of town with the show, I'd spent a weekend as Eddie Fisher's guest at Grossingers in the Catskills. Because of his celebrity, he practically owned the place. Sometime late Sunday, just before we left, he'd introduced me to Marlene Dietrich. I'd been flabbergasted—at her beauty, at her warmth, at the seeming simplicity of this exotic international star, who was currently knocking them dead in Las Vegas. And for a salary I couldn't even imagine in those days.

A couple of weeks later, the phone had rung. It was Dietrich, who just happened to be in town and just happened to be lunching at Sardi's with Michele Morgan, the French film beauty for whom a thousand men would gladly die. Would I come?

Would I!

When I arrived at Sardi's and made my way to their table, I was practically—but not altogether—speechless. It was every young man's fantasy come true: Marlene Dietrich, in a marvelously tailored, stunning blue suit, on one side of me; Michele Morgan, on the other side, in another clinging blue suit and a white blouse, drowning me in her soft blue eyes.

I don't remember what we talked about that afternoon. I only remember dropping my napkin a lot and sneaking looks at two pairs of gorgeous legs. And feeling like the cock of the walk, a totally unknown composer, and today the filling in one of the most gorgeous sandwiches you could imagine.

Marlene, I later learned, always knew exactly what she was doing, and I believe she reveled in the fact that she was wrapping me up in glamour and gorgeousness that afternoon.

Now, just before the opening of *Pajama Game*, I called her. "I can't have lunch, darling, and I'm busy for dinner," she said, "but why don't you come up to my place for a cocktail?"

We sat in her living room and talked—about her career, about mine, about our lives and the people in them, about her relationship with Hemingway, about the theatre and the world in general. When she showed me her bedroom, it was for information, not passion.

"I believe in comfort, darling," she said, as she brought me into a sensual setting that rightfully belonged in a Somerset Maugham novel. The carpet was as thick as uncut grass. Heavy, luxurious drapes and impeccable, tasteful art decorated the walls. The room was dominated by a gigantic, tufted bed.

Her sense of the theatrical was absolute. She sat on the edge of the mattress. "Now it's milady's bedroom," she said, and reached under the bed. The overhead lights dimmed. "And now," she purred, "It's *Marlene's* bedroom." A light glowed subtly from beneath the bed, turning the room into an erotic playpen. "That's so my darling lover doesn't have to throw his shirt over the lamp."

Later, at the door, as she kissed me lightly on both cheeks, I thought to myself, maybe I should have concentrated on something else besides her fascinating conversation, for historical reasons, if nothing else.

"Break a leg, darling," said Marlene, running her fingers up and down my arm, "I'll be there."

And so May 13, 1954, a balmy, still, spring evening arrived. I dressed in a daze. Marion was soft, and affectionate, and supportive. I felt sick with fear, but hopeful. When this is over, if it's a hit, I'll make it up to her, I thought. We'll go away, and it'll be all right.

The crowd in front of the St. James was huge and glittering. There was electricity in the air. Anticipation. Terror. Jerry and Judy met us, and we found our seats. What a life, I thought. Every opening an agony. How did I ever get mixed up in this?

The overture started. The curtain went up. There was a contented murmur, a sort of settling in.

I looked around me. Faces swam in and out of the darkness. Marion. Jerry. Judy. And two rows away, my mother and father. What were they thinking, I thought.

My father's face was immobile, and strong. He'd become famous and respected by *earning* fame and respect. It had been a long, hard process, and it had consumed him, but it hadn't wearied him. He was concentrating on the stage as single-mindedly as I remembered him concentrating on a Chopin prelude.

My mother's face was glowing. I knew she'd think it was the most wonderful work since The Creation. As intelligent and tasteful as she was in everything else, she had absolutely no judgment about the worth of what *I* did. As long as it was my doing, she adored it.

And there was Marion. Her face was tense and unfathomable. It wasn't the face of a happy woman. Would it ever be, I wondered, as long as we were together?

The lights were coming up. It was intermission, and somehow, the first act had flown by without my even knowing it. It was as if I'd been drugged.

Eddie Fisher was sitting two rows ahead of us, with Mike Todd, who was then one of the most successful motion picture and theatre producers in the world. Eddie turned around and smiled, and held up one hand, with the forefinger and thumb joined in a circle of assurance.

Sure, I thought, as I got up and headed for the lobby, fleeing from everybody I knew. He's a good friend.

The sidewalk in front of the theatre was a sea of people. I tried to listen in on their conversations, tried to get some sense of how it was going. Most of them were talking about how wonderful it was. There was something wrong about that, too, I thought, with galloping paranoia. It all sounded too damned good. Nobody was negative. Maybe I was imagining what they were saying. Maybe they were all drunk.

Maybe I should go back and sit down next to Marion, I thought. At least I know she'll be realistic.

And then, I heard a deep, familiar voice, calling my name. "Richard!" The voice reached out and snared me from the far side of the St. James marquee.

The sea of people parted, and Marlene Dietrich pushed her way toward me. "Darling," she said, "it's brilliant," and threw her arms around me. And there, on a sidewalk full of people, she gave me a tremendous, affirmative kiss, right on the mouth. And with that kiss, from that lady who really knew, I finally began to lift the curtain of fear that I'd closed around one of the brightest, greatest nights of my life. Maybe, I thought, as I walked back into the theatre, maybe we might just possibly have a hit.

The second act streaked by, but the haze I was in was a warm one. This time, the laughs, and the applause began to get through to me. And maybe it was my cranked up mood, but suddenly, Marion's face had relaxed, and my father seemed to be enjoying himself, and my mother—well—

"Okay, you three," said Jerry, to Marion, Judy, and me, after the final curtain had come down to what seemed to be a thousand curtain calls, and my mother had cried, and my father had said, as he shook my hand, "I don't understand this sort of thing very well, but I know when something succeeds," and we'd been slapped on the back by a dozen exuberant friends, and had shaken hands with more and been embraced by still more, and had gone backstage and shared some of the delirium there, "Let's do something very ordinary," Jerry went on. "Let's go to Sardi's, and buy ourselves a drink. We deserve it."

So we did, because we *did* deserve it. We'd made the trip from nowhere to somewhere in a few short years. We'd learned well—that the way to the summit was one of unremitting hard work and continuous attention not only to our mentors, but to every experience we had, even the bad ones.

We toasted all of this, I think. Or maybe we didn't. Maybe it was all too glorious and wonderful to analyze, and we just drank to that monumental moment when we were past the treeline, and headed for the top.

By the time we got to the first of a series of parties, the reviews had started to come in. There was a black tie shindig at Roz Russell's sister's house on East 72nd Street. In the living room, Mr. Abbott was reading the notices.

They were raves. Across-the-board raves.

Ironically, the review he was reading aloud at that moment was the one by the dean of American drama critics, Brooks Atkinson of the *New York Times*—the same Brooks Atkinson who'd dismissed our songs as "routine" a few months earlier.

"The last new musical of the season is the best," he began, and the room erupted in cheers. Mr. Abbott held up his hand in his best directorial manner, and read on. "Like the customers who are now going to pour into the St. James, Mr. Abbott is really interested in the color, humor and revelry of a first-rate musical rumpus . . .

"John Raitt, with the deep voice and the romantic manner . . . Janis Paige, whose voice is almost as exhilarating as her shape . . . Eddie Foy, Jr., a true clown who can strut standing still . . . staged by Mr. Abbott and Jerome Robbins, both of whom like motion on the stage. That may account for the lightness and friskiness of the performance. And that may also help to explain why Bob Fosse's ballets and improvised—"

"Improvised?!" Bob shouted.

"—dance turns seem to come so spontaneously out of the story. This is the place to express considerable gratitude to Carol Haney . . . a comic dancer of extraordinary versatility . . .

"*Richard Adler and Jerry Ross*"—and here, Mr. Abbott looked at us, owl-like, from over the top of his glasses—"have written an exuberant score in any number of good American idioms without self-consciousness. Beginning with an amusing satire of the work tempo in a factory, they produce love songs with more fever than is usual this year; and they manage to get through a long evening enthusiastically in other respects also . . . 'There Once Was a Man' takes the goo out of love expertly. Mr. Adler and Mr. Ross write like musicians with a sense of humor . . ."

The following Sunday, Atkinson would pronounce us "folk heroes of the future."

Well, I thought, happily, there was nothing routine about the dean of critics' change of heart. And later, there would be nothing in the rest of the reviews that would even begin to contradict it.

So there it was—a hit, a solid hit, and we were a major part of it. Each one of us—Bob Fosse, Carol Haney, Jerry, and I—had crossed the border into fame that May evening, and life would never be quite the same for any of us, ever again.

Hal Prince, that sweet, articulate, talented man, who, with Bobby Griffith, had run the show that night—both of them in their tuxedos, with flashlights in their back pockets, the two best-dressed stage managers on Broadway—came over to us and took both of our hands.

"Think about it," he said, beaming. "This morning we had $15,000 in the box office. That was enough to run the show for three days. And look at what happened." He shook his head, slowly. "Isn't it a wonder?" he finally said, softly. "Isn't it a limitless wonder?"

The rest of the night swam by. We bounced from party to party, never tiring of the slaps on the back, or the handshakes, or the hugs. This was the other side of the mountain from the times when the songs didn't work, the production numbers failed, and the whole house of cards that is a show in rehearsal seemed to be collapsing. It was the final result of what happened when the right people came together at the right time, and made the right decisions.

"Come on, let's go to Lindy's and get something to eat," Jerry said at five in the morning. He looked terrible. His cherub face was drawn and pasty, and he was gasping for breath.

"Hey, why don't we go home," I said, worried for him.

"Just some scrambled eggs," Judy said, and squeezed my arm. "Just that."

She wanted him to be able to play out the evening the way he wanted it, I realized. His sickness had given him so many dark days, he deserved whatever brightness he got. And so we wound up that memorable night, those last few steps on the climb to the heights, at Lindy's, eating bacon and eggs.

It was six o'clock now, and a balmy morning, and Marion and I walked back to our little apartment on Riverside Drive, stopping on the way to pick up copies of all of the morning dailies.

We opened the door to the apartment quietly.

The two babies—Andrew and Christopher—were sound asleep. Marion turned out the light. "Coming to bed?" she asked.

"In a minute," I answered, and went into the bathroom. I was too wound up to sleep. This had been too important a time to end just yet.

I sat on the john and started to read the notices aloud to myself.

And then, in the middle of them, I heard Marion crying. Hell, I thought, I should keep on sharing this with her. I could cry for joy myself.

I got up and went into the bedroom. And then I stopped. The tears in her eyes were tears of infinite, inconsolable sadness.

"Now I've *really* lost you to the world," she said.

I took her in my arms, and I tried to comfort her. And so began a pattern that would run through the rest of my life: a sadness that would hang around the edges of some of my brightest moments of success, shading the triumphs with despair.

Tonight, I knew my career had begun. Tonight, I knew our marriage had ended.

4.

F A M E can be a nourishing tonic, and when it comes early and overnight, it's like first love—a sudden rush, a high fever, and a lot of joy. That's the way it was with Jerry and me in the spring of 1954. The weeklies and then the monthlies added their rave reviews of *Pajama Game* to those in the daily papers. "Hey There" joined "Hernando's Hideaway" on the Hit Parade, where our rundown nightclub number had resided since before the show opened. And from then on, every Saturday night for months, the two songs would alternate at the top. First, "Hey There" would be number one, and "Hernando's Hideaway" number two. Then, they'd reverse. And the next week, they'd reverse again.

We were creating theatrical and musical history. It was the first and last time that two songs by one team would ever share the two top spots on the Hit Parade. Even Richard Rodgers and Oscar Hammerstein, whom I revered, had had to settle for numbers one and five for "Some Enchanted Evening" and "Bali Ha'i." And here we were, a couple of kids from the streets of New York, and our songs were number one and number two in the country, and our show was selling out, and producers were calling *us*—

In fact, just a couple of weeks after the opening, Frank Loesser phoned.

"Couple guys wanta see you," he barked. "Wanta offer you a show."

"Which two guys?" I asked, trying to sound as casual as I could.

"Cy Feuer. Ernie Martin. They produced my show."

I covered the mouthpiece and whispered to Jerry. "Feuer and Martin. They did *Guys and Dolls*. They want us to do a show for them!"

What neither of us knew then, in the first year of our professional lives in the theatre, was that even successful producers sometimes had

6 0

bad ideas. When the script, which was called *Hold 'Em Joe*, arrived the next day by messenger, we tore open the envelope, eager to get a glimpse of our second success.

But by the time the day had passed, and we'd both read the script, which was a laughless, nearly insulting story about an American Indian and his comic escapades in a saloon on the edge of a reservation, we knew we weren't going to do it.

"Well, I guess we're really successful now," said Jerry, as we packed up the script. "We've actually turned down somebody who offered us work."

"I hope this isn't what it's like all the time," I muttered, but I had to admit that we'd learned a lot. We knew workable from unworkable now, and when, four years later, *Hold 'Em Joe* turned up on Broadway as *Whoop-Up,* and closed, fifty-six performances later, I had the satisfaction of knowing that our instincts had been right—though we really didn't like to see *anybody's* show fail.

The scripts kept coming in. But nothing seemed right. Nothing clicked in our heads. The Negative ruled.

And then, one afternoon in early August, a messenger appeared.

He was carrying an envelope from Mr. Abbott's office. Inside was a copy of another book. It was *The Year the Yankees Lost the Pennant,* by Douglas Wallop. Attached to it was a note in Mr. Abbott's neat handwriting. "Interested?" it said, economically, as always.

The story was about a guy who sells his soul to the Devil so he can lead his favorite baseball team, the Washington Senators, from the cellar to victory over the New York Yankees.

We read it enthusiastically, and by the end of the week, we knew we'd do it. It would be the old production team together again, only on slightly different terms. First of all, Jerome Robbins wouldn't be there in case Bob Fosse didn't come through. And, this time, the contract for Jerry and me offered a bigger royalty and had no interpolation clause.

In our wild and naive enthusiasm, we were blissfully unaware that the project violated, in every way, an age-old and revered show business tradition. Nobody had ever, in the entire history of the theatre, written a successful piece about baseball.

Meanwhile, like the dying nerve in a tooth, my marriage was coming to a painful, agonizing conclusion. I was learning, as I suppose everybody must, that just as there are no easy answers, there are no easy endings in life. It was a terrible, heartrending time, not only for Marion and me, but for Andrew and Christopher, our two lovely and bewildered babies. And it was also, I imagine, an inevitable moment, the end of a logical equation. We were so young, and we knew so little about ourselves. We'd shared the tough times. How could we have known at the beginning that we wouldn't be able to share the good ones?

Even my relationship with Jerry contributed, in a kind of perverse way, to the downfall of my marriage. The more Jerry and I worked together, the more time we spent together, the more we flourished, the closer I felt to him. The accusation that Marion had flung at me months ago, that I was more married to Jerry than to her was even truer now than it had been before. We were each other's best friend. We complemented each other like nobody else we knew. Jerry was the one person in my life for whom I felt the kind of open-handed, generous, nonbinding affection I could no longer feel for Marion, or her for me.

But beyond that. I admired Jerry, and I think I'd ceased to admire either Marion or myself for the way we were concluding our marriage. And what I discovered was that admiration is as necessary to a relationship or a collaboration as a rudder is to a ship. I respected much about Jerry. But his courage, particularly in those days, was one of his most admirable and abiding qualities. His illness and its implications were terrifying. There was something inexorable and dark about it all, but he spent no more time with the terror than he did with anything else that was negative.

It was always business as usual for him, even after a particularly wracking session of coughing, during which I would have to prop him up with a pillow. When it was over—if no blood had appeared—it was over, and time to present that pixyish face to the world and that large talent to the piano.

Late in the spring, we got a unique kind of phone call. It was from Warner Brothers, and they wanted to talk to us about a movie musical. An Adler and Ross vehicle, the voice on the other end of the line said. Hop a plane to L.A., and we'll talk, it continued.

Why not? I thought. If you're on a roll, keep on rolling. I talked it over with Jerry, who was as enthusiastic as I was about everything but the trip to L.A.

"You go," he said.

"But this is a great opportunity. For both of us," I insisted.

"I'm just going to take it easy, Rich," he countered. "Put my feet up. Get acquainted with my family."

I felt a twinge of pain. Judy and Jerry had a new daughter, Janie Beth, and her arrival had made a good marriage better. I had two children and my marriage was getting rancid. Life at home, in fact, was like life around a negotiating table when the negotiators don't trust each other.

So, I was happy to accept the airline ticket, and relieved to be able to put three thousand miles between myself and my troubles.

I was met at the airport by a chauffeured limousine, which sped me effortlessly through a maze of crazy freeway traffic, onto Beverly Drive, past a pastel army of elegant and—to me at the time—mysterious mansions, and on to my destination, the Beverly Hills Hotel.

And there, painted on a banner spanning its posh and sweeping driveway, and flipping in the shimmering California sunlight were two words, in letters ten feet high:

HERNANDO'S HIDEAWAY

What a tribute! I said to myself. What a great greeting! What next? A band? A couple of blonde and nubile majorettes twirling me in?

Easy, Richard, I said, under my breath, as a liveried bellboy picked up my luggage, and I was politely but quietly welcomed at the desk. That would be overdoing it. Still—

It was "Mr. Adler this" and "Mr. Adler that" as I was ushered to the suite that Warner Brothers had reserved for me. It was muted, sunny, serene, and gigantic, and on a glass-topped coffee table fronting a pink sofa sat an enormous basket of fruit. To the right of it was a silver bucket holding an iced bottle of champagne, and nestled before that was a little bowl of ice, supporting an arrangement of lemons, chopped onions, chopped eggs, toast points, and caviar.

I tipped the bellboy jauntily. I popped the champagne and poured myself a glass. Who said California didn't pay attention to the theatre? I mused. Who said a kid from New York—

And then I picked up the neat white card that was planted perfectly between an orange and a banana in the basket. It was one of those all-purpose notes, with a space in the salutation to drop in the guest's name.

"Dear Mr. Adler," it said. "Welcome to the Beverly Hills Hotel. Hope you enjoy your stay."

And it was signed, *Hernando* Courtwright, Manager.

Oh well, I thought, as the wind left my sails and I set down the champagne glass, a little humility never hurt anyone.

The next night, through Frank Loesser's good offices, I went to a party upstairs at Mike Romanoff's restaurant. I knew, as anyone who read the gossip columns did, that everyone who was anyone went to Romanoff's. And *only* everyone who was anyone. Mike may have been phony royalty, but he had authentic ways of endearing himself to the stars. They knew they wouldn't be bothered at Romanoff's, because you had to be a star to get past the maître d'.

What I wasn't prepared for was the lineup of movie greats at the party. My whole boyhood of Saturday afternoons came to life that night. Gary Cooper was in one corner. Harpo Marx was in another. Hedy Lamarr, Myrna Loy, Gregory Peck, Clark Gable—they were there, and in 3-D.

The first celebrity I headed for was Gene Kelly. I felt I had a special link with him, from the show. I introduced myself, and he smiled, and was tremendously congenial. "I've heard so many wonderful things about you from Carol," I gushed.

A small frown flicked across his face. "Carol?" he asked.

"Yes, Carol," I repeated.

"Carol who?"

"Carol Haney."

He looked as blank as an unpainted wall, so I rushed on, "You know," I laughed, "Your former assistant. The star of *The Pajama Game.*"

The blank look was replaced by something a little colder. "Excuse me," he said, and walked away.

Oh my God, I thought. Two gaffs in twenty-four hours. I hadn't been talking to Gene Kelly at all. I'd mistaken the great Fred Astaire for the great Gene Kelly. What a clumsy way to begin an important trip!

As it turned out, the trip was anything but auspicious. There wasn't any movie, nor was there a prospect of one in the near future. Four days of shuffling from one plush office to another convinced me that all Warner Brothers wanted to do was to tie us up for a couple of years, as an investment. And even at this early point, I knew that it was the wrong time for Jerry and me to sign anything that might keep us from flying free.

So, I came back home, to a couple of major projects. To the show, which was now called *Damn Yankees,* and to one final, futile attempt to save my marriage.

Mark Twain said that our consciences take up more room and are more useless to us than anything else we possess. I suppose he was right, but heeding our useless and tricky consciences, Marion and I had decided that maybe a change of environment might toss our marriage a life line. New place, new perspective, we thought. So, we'd rented a nondescript beach house that gave on to the ocean and that gathered in the breezes from the Bay on Fire Island. Of course it was foolish. Of course it only proved to both of us that there was no hope for us as man and wife.

The summer began happily enough. Fire Island is an entirely self-contained island, isolated from the scurry of civilization after the last ferry for the mainland leaves at 10:00 P.M. I loved the sound of the ocean at night, loved getting up early, watching the sunrise over the ocean, and fishing every day with *New Yorker* drama critic Wolcott Gibbs.

We had a few guests on weekends. Jacob and Marion Javits spent a week with us in early August. He was Attorney General for the State of New York then, and it was his way of getting out from under the Gibraltar of responsibilities he was carrying. We had a fine, abundant seven days. I taught Marion Javits waterskiing, and Jack Javits taught me politics.

And after they left, there were other good times with Chris and Andrew on the beach, and there was a warmth about that. But later, after the guests had gone back to the mainland, and the kids had gone to bed, and just Marion and I were left to relate to each other, we'd run out of words. Or, at least, civil words.

Marion was a wonderful woman, but I was restless, and she knew it, and so did I, and it wouldn't be the first or the last time I'd have trouble maintaining a close relationship with a woman. I was terrific at meeting women. I was lousy at staying with them. I think it was the *mainte-nance* of intimacy that escaped me. You have to *maintain* a relationship, and work at it, and the only partnership I was having any success in maintaining those days was the one I had with Jerry. At the end of the summer, Marion and I parted company for good, she to get a legal separation, and I to begin work on *Damn Yankees.*

I was happy and relieved to lose myself in the pre-production bustle of the show. The search for Lola, the witch-temptress the Devil uses to keep the hero of the piece true to his pact, was a concentrated and intense one. Marilyn Monroe heard about it, and wanted to audition, and did, but I don't believe Mr. Abbott ever seriously considered her for the part. He *did* search out Mitzi Gaynor, but she turned him down. Zizi Jeanmaire, who looked a little like a French Carol Haney, and who had danced a very sexy Carmen in her husband Roland Petit's ballet of the same name, was also offered the part. She refused it, too.

Bob Fosse was campaigning for Gwen Verdon, whom he'd first met in 1950 in Los Angeles, when both of them were auditioning for a revue called *Alive and Kicking* (she'd gotten the part; he hadn't). Since then, she'd created a sensation in a body stocking, playing Eve in the Adam and Eve ballet in Cole Porter's *Can-Can*.

The trouble was, she was on her way home from working in a movie in Europe, and there was a dock strike in New York. This didn't deter Mr. Abbott. When he finally made up his mind to audition her, he placed a shore-to-ship call to inform her that when she docked, he wanted her to read for the lead in *Damn Yankees*.

She arrived in New York a day later, and spent two days becalmed in New York harbor, while they settled the strike. Even George Abbott couldn't hurry up the International Longshoreman's Union.

The next morning, she appeared for her audition on the stage of the Majestic Theatre. She had the same, gamin-like quality that Carol Haney had, a shock of wildly red hair, a great pair of legs, and something else that was particularly and uniquely hers: It was, I think, a finely tuned sense of whimsy, combined with a touching, affecting vulnerability. The evil role hadn't been written that would make an audience lose its sympathy for Gwen. Jerry and I were sold on her as a singer and as an actress, and everybody knew what a great dancer she was. We were ready to hire her on the spot.

But Mr. Abbott said nothing. In the dark of a theatre during an audition, silence is thunderous. This was deafening. Finally, he spoke to Gwen, who was waiting nervously onstage. "Can you do a Spanish accent?" he asked. "A pseudo-Spanish accent?"

"Yes," she answered, almost before the question reached her.

"We'll call you," he said.

Well, we thought, Mr. Abbott had disagreed with us before, and he'd usually—no, *always*—been right. Still, one look at Bob's face and I knew there'd be a battle if Mr. Abbott decided against Gwen.

Later on, she told me that she spent the next two days on Ninth and Tenth avenues, picking up a combination European and Spanish accent—and also, a couple of pounds around the hips. She figured the terrific Spanish food was part of her research.

Finally, Mr. Abbott told Hal Prince to call Gwen and ask her to join them at Roseland. "He loves to dance, and he'd like to get to know you," Hal explained, hastily, to the long silence on the other end of the line.

Gwen, of course, wasn't fooled for a second. She knew she was still being auditioned, especially when she and Mr. Abbott danced every rhumba and mambo and merengue the orchestra played.

"I almost blew it," she confessed to me, later. "Halfway through the evening I told Mr. Abbott he was on the wrong beat. And he stopped right there, and he made me sit down. And then he hired one of the hostesses to dance with him for the rest of the night, while Hal held my hand. I figured that was that for me."

It wasn't. We had our Lola.

Getting *Damn Yankees* ready for Broadway was different from *Pajama Game* in lots of ways: There were no backers' auditions, for instance, no more standup routines in Edie Adams' living room, no more capsule run-throughs for potential shareholders. On the strength of *Pajama Game,* Hal was able to raise the money for *Damn Yankees* over the telephone.

I only wish that the tryout period had been that easy. Not that the show seemed to be in difficulty during its early rehearsals. Jerry and I worked hard and fast, starting from the top of the show, and completing the opening chorus with no difficulties.

Mr. Abbott didn't like everything we wrote, but we didn't expect that he would. We knew, from *Pajama Game,* that his standards were high and strict, built solidly upon long years of experience and an almost flawless instinct about what would or wouldn't work on a stage.

We'd both learned, largely from him, but also from our own slowly accumulating experience, that the single most essential quality that every piece of theatre music must possess is its usefulness in the show. A song can be pretty, or tragic, or stirring enough to set you on fire, but if it doesn't help the show, if it doesn't move it forward, or establish a mood or sustain a feeling or deepen a character or define a relationship, it has no business being written in the first place.

And that was the compass setting Jerry and I used when we sat down to work. All of our theatre songs were cemented into particular moments in their shows. That some of the songs stood on their own and became standards was our good luck. But when we wrote them, we were writing for a character in a scene, and whatever we did was designed to help that character move the show forward.

In *Damn Yankees*, the simple love songs for the middle-aged couple had an almost folklike straightforwardness. "The Game" and "You Gotta Have Heart" were raucous outbursts, the interior spirit of the ballplayers made exterior. "Whatever Lola Wants" was written for Gwen's particular brand of insouciance and sexiness, for Lola's way of life and the living of it, and for the scene.

It came as the climactic moment of a comic seduction, The seduction had been coming on for a while, and just about all that could have been said had been said. It was time to turn up the heat and the intensity. So, we picked—what else?—a tango, for its sinuousness.

A short vamp, a repetition of notes in a rhythm pattern under the dialogue, raised the temperature a notch, enough for Lola to marshall her many forces. She then moved down an absolutely straightforward path she'd travelled before, as she purred:

> *Whatever Lola wants,*
> *Lola gets . . .*

There was an economy of melody, and an economy of motion. She was a woman who knew how to get from point to point with no wasted steps. She knew what sounds to make, how to wrap herself around the letter *L,* which is very sexy:

> *. . . And leetle man*
> *Leetle Lola*
> *wants you!*

By the time she'd flung herself through the final two words, "Give in!" Lola had, very succinctly, demolished all the arguments, smashed all the barriers, and done what had to be done. With style, which was her way.

It's one talent to write a song, and another to write *and* sell a song, as Jerry and I had learned in the Brill Building. Every team has to have a businessman to sell their work, and I was not only half of the creative part of the partnership, but the business end as well. It was up to me to deliver the songs to Mr. Abbott at rehearsal, and I'd do it, with great belief and enthusiasm, because that was what I felt about everything we wrote.

"This is terrific," I'd say. "You'll love it. It's just right for the spot," and hope he'd agree.

If he nodded affirmatively, I was delighted. If he said, flatly, "Write something else," it was all right, too. I had to prepare myself equally for either answer, and if it was negative, I'd roll up the song and say, "We'll have it tomorrow." Because I knew he was right, and I knew we'd *get* it right—if not tomorrow, then the third or fourth time. And the final choice would be the best choice.

That we would compose more music for *Damn Yankees* than we had for *Pajama Game,* and that there would be more changes and more trouble ahead than we could dream of, didn't occur to any of us during the first rehearsals. We had a good show, we felt, and we were ready to risk it in front of the public.

And that's when our troubles with *Damn Yankees* would really begin.

But that, too, was unknown and ahead of us on the night of March 27, 1955, when the *Pajama Game* leads and production staff sat at several adjacent tables in the Plaza Hotel ballroom, waiting for the Ninth Annual Tony Awards Ceremony to begin. In those days, the Tonys were handed out on a Sunday evening, in a hotel. It was a sort of friendly, fraternal gathering together of people in the business, honoring each other, and only the Mutual Radio network carried this private party beyond the ballroom.

The Pajama Game was up for a slew of awards in a season that was, by any standards, a stellar one. Alfred Lunt was up for best actor that year in *Quadrille.* So was Frederic March, for *Desperate Hours.* The musical segment of the awards was full of formidable entries. There was Harold Arlen's great score for Truman Capote's *House of Flowers.* There was Harold Rome's for *Fanny,* based on the Pagnol trilogy, which was packing them in at the Majestic. There was *Peter Pan,* with all those musical theatre heavyweights—Leonard Bernstein, Jule Styne, Comden and Green, Mary Martin, and Cyril Ritchard. There was even an opera, for God's sake: Gian Carlo Menotti's *The Saint of Bleeker Street.* In those days, the Broadway theatre was imaginative and healthy enough to support everything from burlesque to grand opera.

So, on the night of March 27, while Judy held on to Jerry's arm and I tried to keep my hands still and occupied, we replayed the numbing nervousness of opening night of *Pajama Game.* Bob Fosse was just as unstrung as we were, and Carol Haney looked like she'd been rescued from a cave. Only Mr. Abbott maintained the kind of aplomb that comes from long experience with just about everything your profession can pitch at you. He was as cool and collected as the Lunts.

I haven't the foggiest recollection of what happened before the musical awards began. I know our hearts sank when Thomas Schippers won the musical director award for *The Saint of Bleeker Street.* It was the first musical honor and it didn't bode well, I thought.

But again, I was wrong. Suddenly, with a little warning rumble, the avalanche began. Mr. Abbott and Richard Bissell were announced as winners of the Tony for writers of the best book of a musical. Then, Freddy Brisson, Bobby Griffith, and Hal Prince won as producers.

A momentary hush. A pause. Cyril Ritchard took the supporting actor's award for his role as Captain Hook in *Peter Pan.*

Then, Walter Slezak won as best actor in a musical, for *Fanny,* and Mary Martin won as best actress for *Peter Pan.*

But from then on, it was pure *Pajama Game.* We swept the board. Carol Haney won as best supporting actress, Bob Fosse as best choreographer, the show won as best musical, and Jerry and I, floating again, won for the best score.

It was a monumental evening. We'd succeeded with the audiences long ago. And that was lovely and good. But to win in this place, among your peers, was quite another, sweeter victory. We'd crossed a boundary, now, and we knew it.

The next morning, we were back in the studio, working. As rehearsals progressed, Jerry reduced his presence in the theatre or the rehearsal hall. When he did go, he'd sit in a seat near the front of the orchestra or on a bench by the wall, the stub of an unsmoked cigar tucked into a corner of his mouth.

Gwen loved to kid him about it. "The only other man I know who puts a cigar in his mouth and doesn't smoke it is Red Skelton," she said. "He has a lighter that doesn't light, too. Do you?"

And Jerry would chuckle. He loved Gwen and he loved being in the theatre, and I'm sure he was upset at the fact that he couldn't take a more active role in the day-to-day musical evolution of the production. But that fell to me, and as it did, I noticed a slight change in the wind, a small shift in the way people talked to me and treated me. Up till now, I'd been considered the business side of the collaboration, presenting the songs. Now I was the decision side of it, too. Once the number went into the show, I had to stand up for what I thought were our best interests and exercise the sort of judgment I thought we both would have made, had Jerry been there. So, like the message carrier to the king, I became the bastard member of the collaboration, and Jerry the sweetheart. Well, I figured, it's worth it, and I really don't mind all that much. Besides, one of these days, after Jerry has that damned operation, it'll even out. And he can be the bastard for a while.

Damn Yankees wound up rehearsals in New York on a high note. The last afternoon before we were to leave for New Haven we gave the customary matinee run-through for show folk. Of course, it was a little rough. There were still holes, and the fine polish that out of town would give to the show hadn't been applied.

But the show biz audience ate it up. Number after number stopped the show cold. There were cheers, laughter, a standing ovation during the curtain calls. We were in, we felt, as we packed for the road. It was another *Pajama Game,* another smooth sail into the harbor of hits.

By the time we arrived in New Haven, reality had begun to temper our high spirits. Though audiences and critics here had gone for *Pajama Game,* how would they treat *Damn Yankees*? We were schooled enough in the theatre by now to know that the public was unpredictable, and that its response might not be as favorable as that of the crazed-with-enthusiasm audience of our fellow actors the last afternoon in New York.

And for the first few minutes of the opening performance of the show, our spirits were high. What had happened in New York happened again in New Haven. The opening chorus, with its counterpoint between the male baseball fans and the disgruntled wives, complaining about the "Six Months Out of Every Year" of the baseball season, got a big hand. The first love song was greeted warmly. There was laughter and applause and acceptance.

The baseball quartet ambled on, and sang "You Gotta Have Heart," and the number stopped the show. It brought down the house, just as it had a week ago in New York. Jerry and I could have cried for joy. We had it, all right. A hit in our hands. One more time, as Count Basie would say.

And then, very slowly, but with a relentlessness you could feel in your nerve ends, it all began to unravel. Imperceptibly, then perceptibly, the laughs started to space themselves out, with great deserts of silence in between. The applause drifted from wild to polite. The coughs that signal wandering attention began, little islands of dissatisfaction in the darkness.

Gwen, who could charm suicides down from a ledge, was having no luck with this audience. In fact, like thin smoke, a cloud of resentment was beginning to rise, and not only against the Devil and his helper. It was directed at the show itself. The bond that links the audience to the performance, which was so palpable during the first few moments, was hanging in two separate pieces. The audience didn't care anymore. They just didn't care. And when an audience stops caring, you're dead onstage.

When the curtain fell, that night in New Haven, we were dead. Oh, were we dead. I didn't dare look at the faces of the audience members as they began to plod up the aisles. The atmosphere in the theatre, as heavy as an overcoat and as oppressive as the fourth day of a rainstorm, told it all.

"They're confused," Mr. Abbott said, at the wakelike production meeting after the show. "I think that's what it is. They don't know which story line to follow, the baseball story, the love story, or the Faust story. The stories keep getting in the way of each other, and they hate us for it." He paused, and sighed. "Now," he continued, "the problem is to find the one they'll follow most easily, and still keep the other two in perspective."

The rest of us remained silent. We knew that this was a problem that Mr. Abbott, Doug Wallop, and Dick Bissell, who'd been called in to punch up some of the comedy lines, would have to face, that night. And we also knew, that once they had, it would be time to write new songs, move them around, stage new numbers—who knew, eliminate characters, the way we had in *Pajama Game*?

We were back where we started, only now the pressure was on. Hard.

The atmosphere out of town for any show is as charged as a lightning bolt. Nobody ever mistook being in the theatre for working in a library. But during our out-of-town agonies with *Damn Yankees*, the voltage was extraordinary, and it took its particular toll on the performers. They had to come out of the craziness of daily rewrites and repositionings and throwouts, and face the audience like they'd been doing the new business for weeks, not moments.

The way "A Little Brains, a Little Talent" found its way is an example. Today, it's an integral part of *Damn Yankees*: Lola's first number. Foreshadowing. Character exposition, done in song, the way it should be in the musical theatre.

But in New Haven, the song didn't even exist. There was something else in the spot—I don't remember exactly what—but it didn't work, and so, after an all-night session one Tuesday in New Haven, we handed Gwen the new song. She had to learn the lyrics that day, because Mr. Abbott was determined to put it into the show at the next matinee.

It was written so quickly, in fact, that there wasn't time for an orchestration to be made, so Jerry and I sketched out a piano part, and Don Walker, the orchestrator, added drum, bass, and clarinet parts for rhythm and the fills.

At noon, Gwen came to me on the verge of tears. "I can't learn these lyrics," she said. "They don't rhyme. I can't remember what comes next, because nothing rhymes."

"Of course it rhymes," I said.

"No it doesn't," she insisted. "Look," and she thrust the manuscript at me. " 'I took the zing out of the King of Siam/I took the starch out of the sails of the Prince of Wales.' Don't tell me that Siam and Wales rhyme, because they don't. Not in English, anyway."

I was dumbfounded. We'd been up three quarters of the night, writing a new tune and a new lyric that set up a relationship, set out character exposition, and was in the right spirit for that scene and that time in the show.

And which contained some of our favorite interior rhymes.

"The rhymes are on the inside," I said.

"Inside? Inside of what?"

"They're interior rhymes," I explained. "Inside the sentence. Zing and king and sails and Wales. See what I mean?"

Of course Gwen did. She's one of the brightest performers in the theatre, but that afternoon, fatigue and nervousness, and the almost inhuman chore of forgetting one set of lyrics and music and learning another in a matter of minutes, and then going out in front of an audience and convincing them that this is something you've been rehearsing ever since you left New York, had downshifted her mind.

We went out to the lobby and worked with her on the old, beat-up piano that had been rolled into a corner:

It's no great art gettin' the heart of a man on a silver platter—
  A little brains
  A little talent
  With an emphasis on the latter . . .

I made mince meat out of a sweet young farmer
I knocked the fight out of a knight when I pierced his armor;
And I'll bet I can upset every male in a Yale regatta . . .

Jerry and I loved the rhyme scheme, which hadn't come easily, and we were willing to do anything to get it through to Gwen. But she was having a hell of a time, and the closer the clock got to matinee time, the worse her memory got.

The release was easy enough for her:

You've gotta know just what to say and how to say it,
You've gotta know what game to play and how to play it . . .

But then she'd start to break down again with:

You've gotta stack those decks with a couple of extra aces,
And this queen has her aces in all the right places . . .

And the next line absolutely buffaloed her:

I've done much more than that old bore, Delilah.
I took the curl out of the hair of a millionaire.
There is no trick gettin' some hick who is cool
Just a little warmer . . .
*   A little brains, a little talent,*
*   with an emphasis on the former.*

By now, Mr. Abbott and Bob Fosse were hovering around the edges of what looked like an imminent disaster. Finally, Bob grabbed Gwen by the arm, and hauled her out of the lobby and onstage. The number was being done "in one," that is, on the apron, with the show curtain closed behind it. Bob gave Gwen and Ray Walston, our Devil, some simple movements, and then, he said, "Okay, go!"

And she did it perfectly, without dropping a syllable.

"How the hell did you do that?" I whispered to Bob, who had slumped into a seat alongside of me.

"Stage manager behind the curtain," he said, as tight lipped as he could without biting off the end of his eternally present cigarette.

And that was the way Gwen did the number that afternoon and evening, with the stage manager throwing her lyrics from behind the curtain.

The song worked, and as soon as Gwen was convinced that it did, the interior rhyme sprang magically into her head and stayed there for good.

Ray Walston, on the other hand, seemed like he was never going to get the meter of "Those Were the Good Old Days." It was a simple, slow rhythm number in which the Devil recollects some of the bloodiest disasters in history, which he regards with sentimental, nostalgic bliss. Ray had no trouble learning the lyrics. He just couldn't keep time. Words kept ending on the wrong notes, or else between the notes. The song got some laughs every night, but Hal Hastings, the conductor, was having apoplexy in the pit trying to keep up with Ray's strange twists and turns and skips.

Finally, things got so bad, Mr. Abbott and Bob put Gwen in the number. They'd let Ray do his thing with the rhythm at the beginning of the line, and then they'd bring Gwen in to paste it back together at the end. "Antoinette, dainty queen," Ray would sing, and Gwen would come in, "with her quaint guillotine." Or, "In the aisles I would lay 'em," Ray would sing, and Gwen would add, "with arsenic and mayhem."

And there'd be no laugh. Nothing. Just stony silence.

We tried it a couple of more days. Bob changed the staging, and put in some clever sight bits, but the number still bombed.

And then, all of a sudden, the reason occurred to me.

"It'll never work with Gwen in it," I told Bob at the end of the second week in Boston.

"Why not?" he asked, from the other side of a fog bank of cigarette smoke.

"Because the Devil can say those horrible things about people, and have that irreverent attitude, but Gwen can't. The audience is out there hating her for the terrible things she's saying."

And I was right. That time. Other times, I wasn't, like the time I tried to modify some staging Bob had given Gwen in "A Little Brains, a Little Talent." He'd given her a tiny, subtle hitch of the hip on the word "talent," and it was a cute little touch, but I thought it could be made bigger, so I shouted out to Gwen during a rehearsal in one of our early days in New Haven, "Gwen, I think when you do that bump, it should be much bigger, because my friends don't know what you're doing."

She stopped. Silence clouded the theatre like an approaching storm. She threw me a look that could melt brass.

And then she spoke. "First of all," she said, in deliberately measured tones, "it's not a bump. And second of all, *my* friends think it's terrific!"

It was in Boston, later, that our worst crisis occurred. Gwen decided to leave the show. She said it was because the part wasn't right for her. But obviously it wasn't the rightness of the part but the wrongness of the show at that point that was discouraging her.

It was a tense, nail-biting moment. Replacing a star that close to an opening would have meant delays and expenses that we just couldn't meet. Besides, we all loved Gwen, in person and in the part, and we knew—we felt—we hoped—it was just a collision of overwhelming work and frayed nerves that had led her to this decision. A little common sense, some quiet, and some well-placed, persuasive talk might fix it all.

Still, we paced the hallway, one grim morning, wondering what was going on behind the closed doors of the suite at the Ritz Hotel, where the producers and Mr. Abbott were closeted with Gwen.

When the doors opened, and she emerged, smiling at us and asking, "Got a new song for me today?" we felt the way a truck driver must feel when he's just avoided a fatal accident.

We plunged back into the reconstruction of the show. The story had improved, but it still didn't work. Baseball and love and Faust made an unpalatable stew, it seemed, and the book writers still hadn't found the magic balance that would make it delectable.

By the last couple of weeks of the Boston run, we were all getting a little tired and testy. Numbers kept flying in and flying out. A huge, second act baseball ballet, in which the dancers were costumed like the animals or birds or objects after which the teams were named, was one of the most spectacular and expensive casualties. There were cardinals, orioles, white sox, red sox, and Bosox. Gwen was dressed like a senator, representing Washington, and some dancer in a gorilla suit stood for the Yankees. It was a lot of fun, but it just didn't work, and, while the producers went quietly crazy over the amount of money they'd spent on the costumes, Mr. Abbott pulled it—two weeks before we were to open in New York.

"You'll have to come up with a smaller piece, a song for Gwen and a dancer to do," he said. "Maybe a Latin number." Just like he'd thrown the assignment of "Hernando's Hideaway" at us a year ago, we thought. Or maybe it was all those nights at Roseland that made him think Latin in a pinch.

Again, while Jerry got paler and I got skinnier, we wrote "Who's Got the Pain (When They Do the Mambo)?" The Mambo was big on the resort circuit that year, and Perry Como had just recorded "Papa Loves Mambo," so we wrote a takeoff:

> *Who's got the pain when they do the Mambo?*
> *Who's got the pain when they go 'uhh!'?*
> *Who's got the pain when they do the Mambo?*
> *I dunno who; do you?*

Gwen and Bob worked on it together, and who knows? It might have been then that they decided to get married. There's nothing like a little panic collaboration to get people together.

So, on and on we went, for what seemed an eternity, while rewrites and repositionings took place every day. Nothing seemed to be solid enough to stay except one number, which always worked, and which brought down the house every night. We had to keep adding verses to keep up with the calls for encores, and every time we needed our spirits raised, we went into the wings and watched while those crazy, lovable ballplayers, or, in the reprise, Jean Stapleton—in a voice that, many years hence, television audiences would identify with "All in the Family," but which then just sounded like ten penny nails being pried out of wood—wowed the crowd with "You Gotta Have Heart."

For those few minutes, everyone in the audience seemed to love the show, without question. And if they loved the show, that meant they loved us, too, right? Right, we kept telling ourselves, as Mr. Abbott tore still another song out of the show and demanded another one by tomorrow morning.

Finally, the road came to an end, and we were back in New York, almost a year to the day from the time we first strode into town with *The Pajama Game*. Only, this time, we didn't stride, we sneaked. The advance sale, though better than *Pajama Game* before opening, was nothing to publicize.

If I'd been scared before the opening of *Pajama Game*, I was a basket case before the opening of *Damn Yankees*. My hands were cold and clammy as I slammed through drawers, trying to find the shirt studs that Marion had once carefully counted and laid out for me.

And then I stopped. Okay, I told myself, maybe it *is* like walking the plank every time there's an opening night. But it's that way for everybody. And besides, I thought, as I tied my black tie, you can't fix it now.

I hailed a cab, picked up my parents and an old friend, Dr. Richard Winter, and we made our painful way, inching toward the 46th Street Theatre. Next time, I thought, after Jerry has the operation, he'll be able to do more. It'll be like it was, only better, because we've learned something since *Pajama Game*. Something invaluable. We've learned trouble.

I walked around to the stage door, and looked in on Shannon Bolin, who was playing Meg, Joe Hardy's wife; and Bob Shafer, the big tenor who'd been so great in *Song of Norway*, and who'd been so touching on the road as the middle-aged Joe Hardy. And Rae Allen, who played the brassy reporter, Gloria. And Jean Stapleton, who had such a refined, dulcet voice and personality when she wasn't in character. And Ray Walston, who was nervously going through "Good Old Days," unnecessarily. Like Eddie Foy, Jr., a year ago, he was a trouper. He'd gotten past his problems, long before we'd left Boston. The only person whose dressing room I steered clear of was Gwen's. Opening night in Boston, I'd stuck my head in and wished her good luck, and she'd cursed me out with words I hadn't heard since my Navy days. It was a good lesson. I found out early that some of the nicest people in the world turn into their opposites under the stress of opening nights.

The corridors backstage were as hot as the back burners in a busy restaurant. Bob Fosse was pouring sweat, his cigarette making it even hotter around him. We hugged each other nevertheless. Jerry looked gray, and old, and horrendously tired. But his spirits were higher than mine. "Come on Quimby," he said, slapping me on the back, as he took my arm. "It's an opening night, not a wake. They don't throw things at the stage in New York."

So, once more, we settled into our seats, just before the overture. This time, Eddie Fisher and Mike Todd weren't there to signal encouragement. This time, directly in front of us, were—Oh God, I thought, as my heart sank below my knees—Richard Rodgers and Oscar Hammerstein. My idols.

The overture began.

There *are* longer nights in our lives than opening nights, I know. But I haven't experienced any yet, so I can only conclude that I never will. And this one lasted at least a month.

At first, I tried to read the faces around me. I leaned forward, tracing, with my mind, the expressions on the faces of Rodgers and Hammerstein. They were cigar store Indians. I looked around me, at less famous people. Enigmas again. All of them.

Then, I turned my attention to the stage, and tried to see it clearly, in the present. But the last six months shouted at me, drowning out what was happening at the moment. All those experiences we hadn't had in *Pajama Game.* All those question marks. All the troubles, the baseball jinx, the three stories that were incompatible with each other.

And now we had a good show. That's what we'd told ourselves yesterday.

I was jolted out of my thoughts by applause. "Six Months Out of Every Year" was getting a big hand. The ballads followed, and they were appreciated. "You Gotta Have Heart" stopped the show. The encore stopped the show.

It was working. Everything was working, and yet I was terrified. It was crazy. The undeniable evidence that we had a good show was unfolding in front of my eyes, but to protect myself from a major disappointment, I wasn't allowing myself to think we had a hit.

Finally, I couldn't take it any longer. I got out of my seat, which was fortunately on the aisle, and headed for the rear of the orchestra. At least nobody would notice my nervousness there I thought. I could be by myself.

But when I reached the last row I was met with a crowd of frantically pacing, black-tied professionals. Hal was there. Mr. Abbott was there. And Bobby Griffith, and Bob Fosse. They didn't even look up when I joined in their silent and singleminded dance of discomfort.

I must have paced a mile before I was aware of heavy breathing at my shoulder. I looked over. Jerry had joined us. He looked up at me as we both executed a tight turn, and shrugged. "Okay," he whispered. "I could have been wrong. Maybe they do throw things at the stage in New York."

And then, the curtain came down. The first act was over. As silently as if we were in an early Chaplin movie, we all headed for the lobby and positioned ourselves so that we could check the expressions on the faces of the audience.

We waited. I watched the crowd surging toward us.

And then I knew. I didn't need Marlene Dietrich to tell me this time. We had a hit. Even with all the trouble, we had a hit.

There were the customary opening night parties, again. This time, the big one was at the apartment of Dr. Albert Cinelli, a friend of Hal Prince. There were more well-wishers than there had been last year, it seemed. Roz Russell was at the center of activity. Richard Rodgers wasn't, but his daughter Mary was. And there was a young, talented friend of Hal's, standing at the edge of the party, who was just beginning to learn the ropes about breaking onto Broadway. His name was Stephen Sondheim.

Now, the reviews came in, and once again, Mr. Abbott donned his glasses to read them aloud. And like last year, they were raves. Across the board. Brooks Atkinson was on vacation, but Lewis Funke, writing for him in the *Times*, loved the show. He called it "as shiny as a new baseball and almost as smooth" and concluded that "as far as this umpire is concerned, you can count it among the healthy clouts of the campaign."

"Campaign? What campaign?" asked Jerry. "Did I miss something? Did we write a political show?"

"Shh," I said. They were reading about us. "Richard Adler and Jerry Ross have contributed a thoroughly robust score . . . the lyrics are appropriate and smart . . . 'Heart' is a humorous ode to the need for courage on the athletic field, and it is done splendidly . . . In 'Whatever Lola Wants,' there is a first-class gem in which music, lyrics and dance combine to make a memorable episode of the femme fatale operating on the hapless male . . ."

Everybody got cheers. Gwen was a certifiable star; Bob Fosse's choreography established him once and for all as a major force in theatre dance; the musical direction, the sets, and most of all, Mr. Abbott were praised like a sunny summer day after a rain.

And oh, had it rained! "All that trouble," I muttered, to Jerry after the reviews had been put away, and the party slowly began to break up.

"Yeah. Goes to show how much we know, doesn't it?"

But our troubles with *Damn Yankees* weren't over yet. Nor was the rewriting. At 8:30 the next morning, my phone rang. It was Hal Prince. "Mr. Abbott wants a production meeting. He's been up all night. The show's too long, and the final curtain isn't right. How about meeting us for coffee at Dinty Moore's, in an hour?"

Sure, I said. Why not? I'd become so used to rewriting the show, it would have felt uncomfortable *not* to have a crisis meeting.

We all looked a little haggard. Bobby Griffith hadn't shaved, Hal had deep pockets under his eyes, and I'd lost so much weight during the

5.

O N E   day in early June, Jerry broke the news. "I'm going to have the operation, Rich," he said, simply and absolutely.

I was relieved. And scared. "When?" I asked him.

"After London."

Pajama Game was opening in London in October. "That's a hell of a long time from now," I said. "Don't you think—"

"After London," he repeated, and I knew that tone. His mind was made up and nobody, not even his closest friend, was going to change it.

He and Judy disappeared upstate for the summer, and I settled into a sublet at 750 Park Avenue, at 72nd Street. Leonard Lyons, the syndicated columnist, had taken charge of my social life now, and he'd fixed me up with a couple of fabulous ladies. One was Margaret Truman; the other was Marilyn Monroe, and they were two terrific reasons to stay in New York. But I was restless, and unhappy; I was physically drained from what I'd done for *Damn Yankees*, and emotionally exhausted from the dissolution of my marriage.

Casting in London for *Pajama Game* was slated for early July. So, I decided to combine business and pleasure and spend the rest of the summer touring Europe. I'd stop in London first, participate in the casting of the show, fly down to the French Riviera, explore Rome, and get back to London in time to begin rehearsals.

"You're going to the South of France?" Leonard Lyons asked, as I told him my plans one Sunday night in Sardi's. "Then, you'll have to look up Willie Maugham," he went on, smiling. "I'll write him a letter and tell him you're coming. I know he'll be pleased to meet you."

And so began one of the wildest junkets of my life.

My first stop was London, where the casting call had already been posted for *Pajama Game*. Bobby Griffith was recreating Mr. Abbott's staging, and Zoya Leporska was recreating Bob Fosse's dances.

Hundreds of hopeful and talented youngsters read and sang and danced for us, and by the end of the week, we had a super cast, with Max Wall in the part of Hines, Joy Nichols as Babe, and Edmund Hockridge as Sid. Each of them was a proven star and a big talent.

But the girl who eventually became our greatest performer, the one who would invest the Carol Haney role with a kind of personal magic that only Carol herself could better, almost escaped us.

Like much good fortune, Elizabeth Seal appeared unexpectedly. She was just an anonymous number in a routine chorus call for dancers. And like Carol, and her understudy, Shirley MacLaine, the impact of her unique talent hit me like a torpedo. She was about five feet five, with an olive complexion, striking black eyes, and a mouth that seemed disproportionately large for her face. She wasn't plump and she wasn't thin, but she had a sort of seething sexiness about her, a way of asserting her personality and her individuality that—in my excited mind that afternoon—no one else in that chorus call could even approach.

I was sold on her the first moment I saw her.

But nobody, absolutely nobody else was. Bobby wasn't impressed, nor was Zoya Leporska. Nor was Jerry White, who was representing Rodgers and Hammerstein, the co-producers of the London production.

I wouldn't be put off. I persisted. I lobbied for a callback for her. Finally, they agreed, reluctantly, and when she danced and sang and read for us a second time, they again rejected her.

But I refused to give up. It became a campaign with me. I pleaded. I cajoled. I demanded. I knew she had something special, and I wasn't going to let her get away. While Elizabeth waited backstage, we argued. We reasoned. We reviewed the possibilities. And finally, maybe out of sheer exhaustion, maybe because they knew I was determined to have my way on this one, Bobby and Zoya and Jerry gave in.

I went backstage. She was pacing nervously back and forth in the hallway. She looked up expectantly as I came up to her and took both of her shoulders in my hands.

"Elizabeth," I said, "you're going to have to almost kill yourself when we start rehearsing. I've put my neck on the block for you. And you've *got* to be great. And in order to be great, you're going to have to work your ass off."

She blinked, and a small suggestion of tears formed at the corners of her eyes. And then, that big, ear-to-ear slice-of-watermelon smile divided her face. "I will," she said, eagerly but softly.

Once the show had been cast, I packed my bags and left London. A day of winding up business, and I was off to the South of France, to meet Danny Kaye, who was in Monaco.

And to fulfill my appointment, arranged by Leonard Lyons, with Somerset Maugham.

I checked into La Réserve, a small, luxury hotel on the Boulevard Marachel Leclerc in Beaulieu, and phoned the Villa Mauresque, Maugham's residence in nearby Cap Ferrat. Alan Searle, his private secretary, answered.

Yes, Mr. Maugham had received Mr. Lyon's letter. Yes, he wanted to see me. Would three o'clock day after tomorrow be convenient? It would.

So, on that day after tomorrow, I hopped into my little rented *Quatre Chevaux,* and took off. The winding approach from Beaulieu to Cap Ferrat was a sweet prelude to the serenity of Maugham's Villa Mauresque, a magnificent stone villa on the mountainous lip of the Mediterranean, surrounded by terraces and gardens and palm trees and quiet. It was a unique and tasteful journey's end, a kind of stone statement of supreme achievement.

Punctually at 3:30, Maugham shambled onto the sun porch, where Alan Searle had installed me. He wore a straw hat pulled down over his forehead, and had a light jacket thrown, capelike, over his shoulders. His pants showed some evidence of what he'd eaten that noon, and his sandals were expensive and well worn. He was eighty-five then, and spoke with a pronounced stammer.

"P-p-p-pleasant to m-m-meet you," he said, offering his hand. "Leonard. H-h-how is he?"

I allowed that he was well and active, and our conversation drifted easily forward, while Maugham downed three martinis, in dazzling rapidity. And then, with what seemed to me greater agility than he'd shown when he came into the room, he asked me if I'd like to see his studio. I of course said yes, and followed him as he nimbly bounded up three flights of stairs.

The sun was setting, a great red ball poised slightly over the sea, which was shimmering now, like a showgirl's sequined cape.

"Here. N-n-n-now what do you think of that?"

I was blinded. There, with the sun pouring through it, was a painted window, pinioned to the glass of the greater window of Maugham's studio.

"F-from G-G-Gauguin's hut. In Tahiti. B-b-b-bought it th-th-there in 1902 for t-t-two p-p-pounds."

It stunned me. I have no recollection of anything else in that room in which Maugham worked. The colors of the window consumed the entirety of it, and me. And I wondered how he could concentrate. And then, I realized that he probably only worked in the morning, when the sun was on the *other* side of the studio.

He entered my reverie. "Y-you g-g-g-go down, and have another d-d-drink," he said. "I'll join you. Have to take a n-n-nap."

I descended to the first floor. The sunlight softened. Time passed, and I began to feel out of place, for the first time that day. Finally, Alan Searle, in his own quiet, distant way, slipped into the room. "Mr. Maugham wants you to have lunch with him here, at one o'clock next Wednesday," he said, gently, as he cleared the cocktail shakers and glasses.

"Is he all right?" I asked. "He said he was going to take a nap."

"He always says that," answered the secretary, "but he won't be down. Had a large pipe today."

"Pipe?"

"Opium," he explained, matter-of-factly. "Will we see you Wednesday?"

I nodded. Of course I'd be back, just to see how this venerable writer managed to stay alive.

On Wednesday, as agile, as bouncy, and as halting in his speech as ever, Maugham met me on the sun porch. Only this time, with drinks in hand, he guided me through his gardens. They were almost as magnificent as his studio. Rock terraces gave on to slate steppes, bursting with all manner and color of flowers, gathered like clusters of Van Gogh paintings. Punctuating these were pear trees, apple trees, and, in one elevated place, set off from the others, as if it were enshrined, was an avocado tree.

Maugham smiled, noticing my slack jaw. "Yes. R-r-rather odd, having that here, what? Took a c-c-c-cutting from a t-t-tree in P-P-Palm B-B-Beach. B-b-b-brought it b-b-b-back. We'll have avocado f-f-f-foule for dessert."

"Foule?"

"P-p-pudding," and he drained his third martini.

The taste of avocado pudding failed to take shape in my imagination, and anyway, it would have been wiped away immediately by the sight that now greeted me as Maugham ushered us into his baronial dining room. The walls were resplendent with an absolutely incredible collection of masterpieces.

"Magnificent," I finally said.

"Yes. Q-q-quite," agreed Maugham, obviously enjoying the effect this must have had upon every first time visitor.

I walked up to one of the works—a charcoal of a man working in a field. It was unsigned. "Whose is this?" I asked.

"You you you g-g-g-guess it, I'll g-g-g-give it to you," whispered my host, smiling wickedly.

I began to sweat. I wanted to impress him. I had a funny feeling he was toying with me, but that if I could rise to the occasion, he'd respect me more than he did at this moment. I looked. And looked. And then, I began to get a feeling. I waited until I was almost sure the feeling wouldn't leave, and then I said, "It's an early Lautrec."

He blanched. "My G-G-G-God," he gasped. "You're right. Y-y-y-you're the f-f-first one to g-g-g-guess it."

We sat down at the table. We ate a hearty lunch.

And he never gave me the picture.

But he *did* open up that afternoon, and become expansive, and thoroughly charming. He launched into a string of memorable, well-told anecdotes. He was a winning, winsome, ribald, free soul, who lived his life as he pleased, where he pleased, and with whom he pleased. We would become friends, that afternoon, enough so that I was able to forgive him for not having honored his word and presenting me with the Lautrec. I almost brought it up a couple of times. He was, after all, the one who'd made the offer, and fair is fair. But then, I forgot it until after his death, when the charcoal I'd identified was sold for $350,000.

When it was time to leave, I felt comfortable enough to invite Maugham to the London opening of *The Pajama Game.*

He thought for a moment, and then accepted, with enthusiasm. It would be the first opening he'd attended in twenty-five years.

It was time to trade British reserve and the quiet of Beaulieu for the comic relief of Danny Kaye. I looked forward to meeting him again. Though I barely knew him, Danny was a performer I admired enormously. Back in New York, shortly after *Damn Yankees* had opened, Jerry, Howard Lindsay, Russell Crouse, and I had talked eagerly with him about putting together a musical version of the Alec Guiness film, *The Captain's Paradise,* and the deal had only fallen through when it became obvious that Danny just didn't feel comfortable about uprooting himself from California and committing himself to New York for a long run. It was a shame, because it could have been a hell of a show.

While we were discussing the deal, Danny and I would double-date in New York. He'd take Gwen Verdon, and I'd take Hildegarde Neff—who was then starring in Cole Porter's *Silk Stockings*—to El Morocco, the Copa, and '21,' and the evenings would almost inevitably become wild and marvelous circuses. Offstage, Danny was usually *onstage*—but charmingly, inventively so. He'd bewilder waiters with double-talk orders, convulse nearby tables with outrageous routines, and send me home with my sides aching from nonstop laughter.

So, as I climbed into my rented car and headed up the coastline to Monaco, where I was to meet him, I was ready to mine two contrasting riches—Monte Carlo's casinos and a few comical days with Danny Kaye.

I checked into the Hotel de Paris in Monte Carlo, where Danny was staying, and phoned him immediately. He was his usual, high-spirited self, and told me to lay out my black tie. We were going to the Sporting Palace that night, to take in the show, to gamble, to gambol.

The Sporting Palace *Spectacle* was the usual European floorshow: showgirls, a dog act, a mime, "comedy," some acrobats, a dance team, and this night, a magnificent display of fireworks over the Mediterranean, since tomorrow would be *Quatorze Juillet*—Bastille Day. At midnight, the bandleader called for a drum roll and a spotlight, and announced that the great American comedian Mr. Danny Kaye was in the audience. And that, if this gathering applauded long enough and loudly enough, he might, just might perform for them.

Tumultuous applause crackled through the room. Danny rose, smiled, waved, and sat down. Once again the bandleader repeated his invitation. Once again, Danny demurred. Thrice did Caesar refuse the crown. But on the fourth coronation attempt, he gave in, strolled up to the bandstand, and began to undo his tie. It was a gesture and a routine that Frank Sinatra and a lot of other entertainers were using at the time to suggest informality and chumminess.

But Danny didn't stop there. He began to unbutton his shirt, at the same time ordering the bandleader to remove *his* shirt—an ornate, red, ruffled affair that made the conductor look like a middle-aged bouquet of roses. And there they stood—formal, but barechested. Danny whipped the bandleader's red ruffled shirt from his hand, banished him from the stage, shrugged into the shirt, and proceeded to do an hour of some of the most boffola material I've ever heard. By the end of it, he had the audience crying with laughter and cheering for more.

It had been just the sort of evening I'd expected, but now it was one in the morning, and I was exhausted. During the applause, Danny had disappeared into the crowd. I made my way to the lobby. There was an enormous crush of people heading in various directions, to the bar, to the gaming rooms, to the exit. By the time I'd oriented myself, Danny'd reappeared, at the far side of the lobby. He was still glowing with energy, and talking earnestly with a short, swarthy, attractive man with a receding hairline, a straight, prominent nose, and a calm, gentle air. Danny waved to me, and when I drew closer, he introduced me to his friend, somebody named Kahn.

"Pleased to meet you, Mr. Kahn," I mumbled, shaking hands wearily, and thinking, where did Danny find this guy? I'd already met ten other cloakees in the South of France.

"See you tomorrow," I said, slapping Danny on the back. "I'm bushed." And I went back to my room.

The next morning, at 7:30, the phone rang. It was Danny, sounding as cheerful and wide awake as he had six hours ago.

"Don't you ever sleep?" I asked him.

"Waste of time," he shouted. "Get dressed. Your Mister Kahn has invited us to take a cruise on his yacht to St. Tropez."

"Rich American, huh?" I sighed, stretching.

"You really don't know who that was?" asked Danny, incredulously.

"What do you mean?"

"That, Richard, was no mister. That was Prince Aly Kahn."

It was a slightly chastened composer who climbed aboard Aly Kahn's elegant and understated yacht in the harbor of Monaco later that July morning. It was Bastille Day, after all, and the cafes along the quay were crowded with celebrants, munching croissants and drinking coffee and admiring the sleek lines of the Prince's yacht and the Prince's guests.

My royal host couldn't have been more gracious, or more forgiving of my social gaff. In fact, later that afternoon, in a quiet moment on the flying bridge, I would try to apologize for calling him Mr. Kahn.

He would laugh, expansively. "Oh Deek, don't be stupeed," he would say. "It doesn't matter. Call me anytheeng. Call me son of a beech, eef you like."

But now, he occupied himself with introducing Danny and me to

a group of distinguished people and beautiful women. I had no trouble
gravitating toward the beautiful women. Barbara Warner was aboard,
and the Princess Domatilia Sforza-Ruspoli, and Martine de Wavrin,
one of the most ravishing redheads I'd ever met.

Martine, it turned out, was also one of the most *heartbroken* women
I'd ever met. After the first amenities, for most of the trip down the
coast to St. Tropez, she cried on my shoulder. It seemed that she'd been
having a consuming affair with Aly for the past year. But that was
rapidly becoming past history. Bettina, a Jacques Fath model, had
entered Aly's life, and that, she realized, was *"finita la commedia."*
Martine was, even as we cruised slowly to St. Tropez, fading into the
prince's past. And becoming part of my present, however fleetingly. I
was smitten enough with her, on that windswept, sunswept morning
on the Mediterranean to later write an instrumental piece called "Martine," which I would, years afterward, use in another longer work.

The morning unfolded effortlessly, as we drifted slowly westward
along the coast. Amin and Karim, Aly's two sons, the two young
princes, both of them high-spirited and handsome teenagers, paced us
in their speedboat, water skiing, waving at us, bouncing crazily back
and forth over the watery ridges of our wake.

When we docked, they came aboard and joined us while we swam
from the boat and then disembarked for lunch in a sun-drenched
restaurant on the quay, where we were served a succulent, bottomless
bouillabaisse, mountains of bread, gallons of wine, all of it seasoned
with Danny's madcap antics.

Three hours later, when lunch was finally modulating to a soft and
exhausted conclusion, I gathered up my camera and clambered into the
two young princes' speedboat, to photograph them. They clowned; I
snapped, and the day was done. I climbed ashore and began to walk
back to the yacht.

Suddenly, there was a horrendous, ear-shattering explosion. The
force of it slammed into my back, pitching me forward. I whirled
around. The speedboat was a sickening tower of flames, already sinking.
The boys had been blown into the water, and were struggling toward
the dock. Both of them were obviously dazed and in a lot of pain.

I shouted to the folks on the yacht, and dashed to the edge of the
dock, flattening myself on my stomach and reaching over the side to
grab Amin's flailing hands. Within seconds, Aly was there, helping us
to wrap the two badly burned boys in blankets, tenderly soothing them
with words while they were gently lifted and carried aboard the yacht.

We rifled through the first aid supplies. There wasn't nearly enough salve to relieve the boys' pain. Their burns were beginning to blister.

Aly motioned to Danny and me. "Come on," he said. "We need more ointments."

"They need a doctor," I said, as we sprinted down the gangplank and into St. Tropez.

"It's Bastille Day," replied Aly, grimly. "There won't be any doctors. The pharmacies will all be closed."

And so, the three of us went from house to house, pleading for salves and ointments to keep the boys comfortable until we could get back to Cannes, and Aly's doctor, who, Bastille Day or not, would tend to them.

The boys recovered. And I was invited back, many times that July and early August, to Aly's Château de l'Horizon, on the sea near Cannes. Those few terrible moments that afternoon had opened a door of friendship for us that would remain open until Aly's premature death in an automobile accident, five years later. When the two boys would go to Harvard, he would ask me to serve as their unofficial guardian. And I would do it, willingly.

He was a good, thoughtful, articulate, and highly communicative friend, a collector of art and horses and women, yes. And his playboy image wasn't without a foundation. It would haunt him, follow him, as the memory of his marriage to Rita Hayworth probably did. And later, his father would pass him over and Karim would become the Aga Kahn. But there was a deeper dimension to Aly, an underlying understanding and intelligence that only in the last years of his life, when he became Pakistan's permanent envoy to the United Nations, would he allow the rest of the world to see. It was undeniable and obvious to me that summer on the French Riviera, when he invited Danny and me to most of a glittering string of cocktail parties that constantly filled the Château de l'Horizon with fascinating people—most of whom spoke French to each other, and practically no English.

And that, alas, was a drawback for me. I spoke very little French, and it was frustrating, particularly if, as was frequently the case, the speaker of French was a beautiful woman.

Aly, who characteristically seemed to be boundlessly aware of every need and each wish and most of the troubles of his guests, noticed this. One evening, at the end of July, he came up to me and said, "You should learn to speak French, Deek. You never know when it will come in handy."

I dismissed it. I'd get by.

At the beginning of August, Danny, Marvin Safir (who was a friend of mine from New York), and I took off in a rented car for a one-day trip through Provence, a quick tour of that green and sunwashed countryside, via poplar-lined country roads that wound past lush vineyards with stone storerooms that smelled like the Dark Ages, where we stopped and drank wine in unlabeled bottles and loaded up the back of the car with the same, glorious stuff.

That night, tired and anxious to get back to our hotel, we found ourselves in the middle of a small, whitewashed village, which was in the midst of one of those unexpected but pervasive French street fairs. It was Saturday, and the streets, the sidewalks, the cafes, the doorways were choked with good-natured people who were in no hurry to move out of our way. It was fun, but frustrating.

"Looks like we're stuck for the night," muttered Marvin.

"Not at all, not at all," said Danny, and he ripped Marvin's pith helmet—which he'd worn to protect himself from the hot sun of the afternoon—from his head. Slamming the hat on his own head, Danny flung open the car door, nearly flattening a couple of revelers.

Now, he was a French policeman, gesturing wildly and shouting to the crowd, Danny Kaye-like, in rapid-fire, fractured French, delivered with such energy and such authority, it almost—but not quite—sounded real.

The revelers froze in their tracks. Danny raved on, moving ahead of us, and into the square. And then slowly, smiles began to light the faces of the villagers. As if he were on a stage or in a nightclub, Danny built a rapt and loving audience. Nobody knew what he was saying, but it didn't matter. They would follow his gibberish over a cliff, if necessary.

And within five minutes, he'd cleared a path for us, through the village, and back to Monte Carlo, and the exhausted remnants of my last night on the French Riviera.

The next day, I was on my way to Rome, which I'd never seen, and to which I was looking forward immensely. But before I left, I wanted to express my appreciation to Aly for his kindness and our newfound friendship. I'd brought a few copies of the Random House editions of

The Pajama Game and *Damn Yankees* with me, and I had one of each delivered from the hotel to the Château de l'Horizon. Inside the cover of one of them, I wrote,

> *To* Mister *Aly Khan—*
> *—a* Prince *of a guy.*
> *(signed) Richard Adler*

Rome was all I'd ever hoped or read it would be. It was a bouquet for my senses—Bernini's baroque and thickly populated fountains, the Divine Comedy of the Via Veneto, with its paparazzi-haunted celebrities, the ruins that jutted up, ghostlike, in the middle of modern Rome, collapsing time as if it were as fragile and meaningless as a whim.

I stayed in luxury and leisure at the Excelsior, reveling in the wealth that had been almost unimaginable a short eighteen months ago. Next to the hotel was a small shop selling exquisite Italian silks and wools. I bought a sumptuous black stole for Judy Ross, and two bolts of silk shantung for Jerry. He loved nice clothes, and he also loved the ability we both now had to buy them and wear them. It would be the best and most personal present I could think of to bring to him.

When I got back to the hotel, there was a message waiting for me, from Aly Khan. It thanked me for the books, and invited me to spend the *Grande Semaine* of racing in September at Deauville, at his Villa Gorizia.

Europe had suddenly become familiar and neighborly. All that was missing was a beautiful woman, and later that same night, on the Via Veneto, in one of the cafes strung like bright beads along that wild thoroughfare, I met her. She was dark and voluptuous and Italian, and her name was—so help me—Silvana Mangani—a mere letter removed from the movie star Gwen had feared she resembled in the *Damn Yankees* publicity. Her body was a copy of her near namesake, and she was more beautiful, but different enough not to interest the paparazzi. Which was fine with me, because I was certainly interested in her. She was earthy and bright, and endlessly amused by teaching me elementary Italian eating techniques, like rolling spaghetti on a fork and recognizing a proper *pasta carbonara*.

One night before I left, when the moon was so bright it seemed that the Eternal City was lit by an eternal twilight, we strolled down the Via dei Fori Imperiali, to the Roman Forum. "Here," she said, taking my hand and drawing me into the moonswept ruins. "Here are the most beautiful parts of the past. But only if you see them at night, with me."

It was strangely still. The whines of the Vespas and the intense honking of horns in the tangled traffic of the city seemed to be a hundred miles away. Stark exclamations of pillars, fragments of temples, overturned boulders seemed to burst into life. Maybe it was the moon, or the wine, or my proximity to Silvana Mangani, or my own fertile and unsated imagination, but I swear to this day that two thousand years fell away that night, and a ghostly, ancient Rome rose silently and affirmatively out of those ruins. The senate was in session. The senators' white togas caught the moonlight and flung it back at me. Roman soldiers, the plumes of their helmets shifting in the slight breeze, their flat swords gleaming like mirrors, stood silently at each ruined pillar.

An hour, a shake of the head and an ordering of the senses, and it was the present again. And the next morning, I was off to London, to begin rehearsals of *The Pajama Game.* It had been a memorable vacation, but now it was time to resume work. I looked forward to getting back into a theatre again, and seeing Jerry. I was itching for a new project. Maybe, I thought to myself on the plane, one of Maugham's novels. Maybe meeting the author had been fortuitous. Maybe fate was taking a hand.

When I got to the hotel, there was a cable from Jerry. "UNABLE TO COME TO LONDON. WILL PHONE AND EXPLAIN."

I called him, immediately. His voice was as cheerful and upbeat as usual. "Sorry I can't make it, Rich," he said. "Got to take some tests and take it easy." His operation was scheduled for the end of September, he went on, and after it was over, he'd race me around the stage of the 46th Street Theatre.

Before rehearsals began, I had one tag end of vacation time to knot. I'd never been to Deauville, and I was looking forward to seeing Aly again.

I was met at the airport by a faultlessly dressed, meticulously manicured man who looked like he'd stepped out of a Bond Street window. One of Aly's wealthy friends, I thought.

"Your bags, sir?" the sartorial regent asked, in perfect, public school English, brushed by the faintest French accent.

His name was Jacques, and he was not only a splendid, enviable dresser, but also the man who'd just won first prize as France's best bartender—a capacity he was filling for Aly when he wasn't chauffeuring guests to the Villa Gorizia.

I sneaked a look at myself in the rear view mirror as Jacques drove me to the villa. If bartenders dressed like this, I mused, what did their customers wear? Gold lamé?

I soon found out, as we swept up the circular driveway to the villa's front entrance. Aly, with a three-day growth of beard, decked out in a shirt and pair of pants that he might have slept in, greeted me warmly and disarmingly.

"Forgeeve me, Deek, I have had the flu," he said. "But that does not mean that my guests have to look like me."

He flung his arm around my shoulder as if we'd been through much together as good friends—which we had—and led me into the grand hallway of the villa.

"Have you learned French yet?" he asked me.

I confessed that I hadn't.

"Good," he answered, steering me down the hall. "Now, I will show you to your room."

I could hear the faint murmur of guests echoing upward from an endless succession of unseen corridors.

We paused before a huge, carved oak door. Aly opened it, and motioned for me to precede him into the room.

I did. And stopped dead in my tracks. There, propped up in a very large, very elegant bed, was a breathtakingly beautiful blonde.

"*Bon jour,*" she said, in a voice with the soft resonance of a lightly struck bell.

"Now, Deek," said Aly, as he left, gently closing the door behind him, "you learn French."

Besides being a knockout, the young girl was intelligent, playful, and—most of all—fun to be with. She was the daughter of the Air Minister of France, and she'd made a pact with Aly when he'd proposed his little plan: If she were happy with the arrangement, if she liked me, she'd stay. If not, they'd both pass it off as a practical joke.

She stayed, and didn't tell me about the arrangement until the end of the week.

So, we spent delicious times together, at the villa, and in the fields beyond Deauville, where Aly kept his horses, It was, in fact, fitting that she was with me, because Aly was not nearly as accessible to his guests as he had been at the Château de l'Horizon in the South of France at the beginning of the summer.

The difference was the presence of Bettina. She was now solidly and certainly at the center of his life, and he'd focused his entire concentration upon her. When she was with him—which was most of the time—the rest of the world simply fell away for him. He would speak politely but impersonally to you. He wanted you to feel comfortable and cared for under his roof. But there was, you understood, nothing of himself left over to give to you. That was totally taken by Bettina. He doted upon her, worshipped her, deferred to her. And she blossomed, she grew under this attention. Each day, she looked fifty times lovelier than she had the day before. And I thought to myself, "Now *that* is the way to woo and win and hold a woman."

And so, left to their own devices at night, the rest of his guests spent a lot of time in the Salon d'Été, Deauville's posh gambling casino. And it was there that I ran into an English industrialist I'd first met in London at the beginning of the summer. He'd been pleasant enough, and friendly enough then, but I'd never, for an instant, been able to understand a word he was saying. His mouth seemed to be constantly filled with hot potatoes.

So, when I ran into him once again, one night in the Salon d'Été in Deauville, I had mixed expectations.

He greeted me with military properness, and was as stolid, stiff-upper-lipped and incomprehensible as he'd been in London.

"Mxmfgpm," he said, warmly.

"I beg your pardon?"

"Mxmfgpm?" he repeated, with a slightly different inflection.

I raised my arms, with the palms of my hands flattened and facing upward. I still didn't understand one word he said. He was the most British Brit I'd ever met, and I was determined to be polite.

He nodded joyfully, and took my arm, propelling me to the ten thousand franc *chemin de fer* table.

A heavy roller, I thought, as he chatted cheerily on. He placed some chips on the table, received the deck of cards, and set them neatly on the green cloth.

"Ct," he said.

I looked at him blankly.

"Ct," he repeated, more insistently, and motioned to the deck of cards.

"Cut?" I asked. "You want me to cut the cards?"

He nodded.

I followed his instructions, he mumbled something in incomprehensible French to the croupier, made a few motions with the cards, and suddenly announced, "Banco!"

The croupier nodded and shoved an armful of chips at the man, which he neatly divided into two piles.

"Yours," he said, indicating one of them, and then, shaking my hand and biting out, "Thank y'very mch," he disappeared into the crowd.

I was dumfounded, flabbergasted, and holding a pile of valuable chips. I went to the window and cashed them in. They were worth three thousand dollars. Today, that would be the approximate equivalent of forty-five thousand dollars!

I pocketed the money and broke out in a cold sweat. What if he'd lost? I thought. He would have asked me for three thousand dollars—when he'd finally made me understand what had happened.

The very next day, early in the morning, Aly asked me if I'd like to accompany him to a horse farm in the interior of Brittany. He was a skilled horsetrader, and he was going out to a farm near Deauville to look at a horse named Rose à la Bonheur. He'd be grateful if I could come with him.

It was a clear, end-of-summer morning, and the hour drive to the farm was a lovely, sweet-smelling one. Aly was his amiable, and open self, and we discussed art and literature and women—three subjects he knew surpassing well.

The horse, a chestnut mare, was magnificent. A trainer ran her around the track, and as she scudded past, like a wind-driven cloud, I could feel the positive vibrations pulsating from Aly.

But to the horse's owner, he was reserved and cagey. He betrayed little enthusiasm as he bargained. When the deal was finally consummated, he'd bought Rose à la Bonheur for very little money.

I waited until we'd rejoined Jacques in the car before I let my own eagerness loose. "It's a good horse." I said.

Aly nodded and smiled. "It's a good horse," he agreed.

"A *great* horse!"

Aly held up a restraining hand. "We'll see at La Toques," he said.

It was the last race of the Grand Week, the climactic event, and I was determined to turn it into a flush finale.

"Look. I feel lucky," I said. "I won a lot of money last night, and I'm going to put it all on the nose of Rose à la Bonheur."

Aly turned to me in alarm. "Don't" he warned, emphatically. "Don't be stupeed. We don't know this horse. She could lose very badly."

"But—"

"Didn't I geev you good advice before?"

He had. I'd wanted to bet on him in the Gentlemen's Race that had begun the meet, and he'd forbidden it. And he'd finished last.

"Relax, Deek," he said. "Enjoy yourself and your money. I'll tell you when to bet on me."

So, I kept my money in my pocket. And the next day, Rose à la Bonheur came in first, and paid thirty to one.

The dizzying week in Deauville had finally come to an end. Except for that one morning at the horse farm, I'd spoken very little to Aly. But then, neither had anyone else, except Bettina.

Still, I'd received such abundance from him that summer, such largesse of friendship, I felt rich in a multitude of ways, not the least of which was my newfound adequacy in French.

It was time to get back to London and down to work on *The Pajama Game*. Bobby Griffith and I worked feverishly, trying to recapture as much of the brashness and speed of the New York production as we could, without taking it beyond the reach of London audiences.

My parents arrived right after the first of October. My mother was, as usual, ebullient and excited, and full of compliments even before the show opened. She appreciated everything. She loved everything.

My father was, as usual, quiet. Congenial and dignified, he kept his feelings as under control as a skilled horseman. This, his first trip back to London in years and years, must have been a gala occasion for him. But he accepted it all with careful equanimity, self-contained to a fault.

Maugham, on the other hand, was effusiveness personified. "F-f-f-first opening I've been to in twenty-five years," he gurgled again, over the phone, after he'd settled in at his usual hotel, Brown's, on Half Moon Street.

On October 11, a small package arrived at my flat at 1 Curzon Place, Inside, was a lovely note, and a piece of carved jade the size of an arrowhead. The note was from Maugham, as was the gift, and it said that in 1902, when he was first in China, this piece of jade had been given to him by a venerable Chinese philosopher, for good luck. He was giving it to me now, for good luck.

I cherished it for years, until, unhappily, it was lifted by an ex-housekeeper. To this day, I'd give anything to get it back.

On opening night, the show was greeted with even more wild enthusiasm than it had received in New York. Number after number stopped the show. This time, I was able to enjoy most of it, except for one, gnawing bit of knowledge that I'd been given and that nibbled at my well-being: The importance of the gallery.

The English gallery, Jerry White, the producers' representative told me, was noted for its mercilessness. If the patrons up there disliked you, they could bury you. No matter how far removed those upper reaches of the last rows were from the stage—and in the London Coliseum, where we were playing, they were practically in the clouds. But the gallery could and would be heard. They could stamp their feet, drowning out dialogue, and singing. They could hoot, whistle, sing other songs, or throw garbage. But if they liked you, you were home free.

So I listened with one ear cocked toward the gallery. And as the show settled in, as one number followed another, I could feel the rising tide of noise from the "heaven" atop the back of the house.

And when, at the curtain calls, Elizabeth Seal, our Gladys, and the object of my crusade at the beginning of the summer, stepped forward, the entire gallery leaped to its feet and shrieked, in joyous unison: "Seal! Seal! Seal! Seal!" It became a mantra.

Bobby Griffith, with George Abbott, who had come over to rehearse the company in the final week of rehearsals, turned and smiled at me.

It was great—and a great relief—to have been right.

There was an opening night party, but no reviews. The London papers didn't appear until the following morning.

"You were very, very good," I said to Elizabeth Seal at the party.

"Thank you, Richard," she said, shyly and disbelievingly. I was struck by her absolute lack of ego.

The next morning, I bought as many papers as I could. They were more than an echo of New York: The notices, instead of being in the theatre section, were on the front page. And they were mostly about our smiling Gladys, extolling her, raving about her, beatifying her.

At noon, I phoned Elizabeth, and asked her if she'd seen the papers.

"Not yet," she said.

"What do you think the reviews say?" I asked her.

"I suspect they're very good."

"Why do you say that?"

"Because," she continued, with a small laugh, "as I'm speaking to you, there are fifty reporters outside the front door."

The ecstatic reviews would win the show hundreds of performances and the British equivalent of the Tony, the *Evening Standard Award.*

It was a phenomenal success story, particularly for an American show. Broadway musicals, in 1955, simply didn't win such awards in London.

So, we'd done it again, and I was exhausted and rundown. I'd developed a horrendous cold. I was anxious to get back to New York and Jerry, but not with the flu. I wanted to see him, not infect him, so I headed south again, this time to Majorca, to recuperate in the sun.

Jerry had had the operation, and it had been a long, complex, ten-hour ordeal, during which some ribs and the deteriorated lung had been removed. I'd been on the phone constantly with Judy, who assured me that he'd come through it beautifully, and that the doctors were highly optimistic and talking about a complete recovery.

So, I relaxed for a week, and then caught a plane for home.

Jerry looked like he'd been through a lot. Nobody seems wonderful in a hospital, but I remember he appeared smaller to me, and more frail than before. Still, his humor was intact, and his spirit was flying.

The operation had been a success; he was on the mend, and anxious for all the inside news from London. The cast of the London *Pajama Game* had sent him a wallet and a pair of pajamas, and he had them displayed on the windowsill, between several plants.

I gave Judy the wool stole from Rome, and Jerry the bolts of silk shantung. She gasped, and Jerry glowed. "God, Rich, I'll put George Jessel to shame," he said, running his hands caressingly over the fabric.

"Just get better soon," I said. "If you lose any more weight, there'll be enough for three suits instead of two."

Later, outside of his room, I asked Judy how he really was. "Fine," she said. "The doctors say he's coming along fine." She sighed. "He doesn't think so. He's worried. You know how he worries."

"Well, it takes time," I said, and hugged her.

I had to fly out to the Twin Cities, and pick up the touring company of *Pajama Game,* which was going to open in Chicago at the end of the month. The company, headed by Fran Warren, was in need of coaching.

"I'll be back in a couple of weeks," I said, and left.

I met Bobby Griffith and Hal Prince at the Twin Cities Airport. It was snowing, even though it was the first week in November. We set out by train across the Rockies.

The higher we climbed, the heavier the snow fell. By nightfall, we were in the middle of an undeniable blizzard. Whiteness, encompassing whiteness flew past the train windows. We were enclosed in a deepening, darkening universe of snow as the train chugged and snorted up the mountain. Nobody thought much about what was happening outside. Inside, it was snug and warm and self-contained, as if we were aboard a miniature ocean liner.

By eleven o'clock we'd reached a high pass at a place called Whitefish, Montana.

The train shuddered, groaned, and stopped. A few minutes later, the conductor strolled into the car and gave us the news: There'd been a small avalanche of snow onto the tracks ahead of us. It would be several hours before a plow could be dispatched to get us loose, but there wasn't any cause for worry. We had plenty of heat and light and food, and Whitefish wasn't a bad place to spend a few hours.

Most of the rest of the passengers settled down to the warmth and insulation of the train. I was restless, as usual. I put on my overcoat and stepped off the train, into the storm.

Whitefish was a tiny whistle stop with a short main street and a handful of stores, all of them shuttered up tightly against the snow and the cold. It was barely discernible beyond the whipping whiteness of the storm. But even in the dark, even with the snow stinging my eyes and cloaking everything as if trees and grounds and houses were furniture in a summer room, shrouded in sheets for the winter, there was something overwhelming and right about the majesty of nature that surrounded and overlooked this miniscule village. The snow was scurrying wildly around me, and I had to turn my back to it in order to see. There was a low roar as the wind rounded hidden walls of invisible canyons, pummelling the tops of huge pines and spruces, setting them in rhythmical motion.

That was the outer layer, the cover of the storm. But as I plowed further into it, as I listened carefully, I realized that there was some-

thing more profound at work. Underlying it, there was an immense and
strangely comforting silence that, once you became aware of it, diminished the violence of the wind, reducing it to an insinuation, as natural
and vital and irremovable as the sound of breathing. I was neither
worried nor frightened. For some reason that became more apparent
to me as the storm slowly subsided after midnight, and the moon lit
the peaks of looming mountains rising up out of the crystalline cloak
of pervasive, peaceful quiet that had settled like a truce over everything,
I felt more connected to this nature in this place than to any one person
in my life, even Jerry. It was like it had been when I was a boy in Lake
Placid, New York. There was a significance, a realization, and a bond
that was forged that night that would take forty years and a lifetime
of looking to finally, fully manifest itself.

Early in the morning, we set out again for Seattle, arriving later that
afternoon. The show needed lots of work. I did some preliminary
digging with the chorus and with Fran, and spent the rest of the time
walking around the city.

Back at the hotel, I called Judy and asked her how Jerry was doing.

"Good," she answered. "Sitting up in bed, teasing the nurses. Don't
worry."

"Listen," I said, making up my mind on the spot, "I have the
weekend off. Don't tell him I'm coming. I'll fly in."

"You don't have to," she said.

"I know," I countered. "I just want to see my partner."

So, I caught a plane to New York that Friday night, with Hal Prince,
who was leaving the show to Bobby and me. And Saturday morning,
early, I appeared at the door of Jerry's hospital room.

He looked all right. He'd gained some weight and some color since
I'd last seen him. But he still had a hospital pallor. And he was quiet,
much quieter than Jerry usually was.

We talked for a long time, about what we'd done, about what we'd
gone through, about what there was ahead for us. Jerry and Judy and
I drew very close that day. I went out and had some lunch, and came
back, and we took up again as if we'd only paused to breathe. It was
a soft, simple day, the sort that love makes memorable.

Finally, it was time to go. I had to catch a plane that night to be
back in time for a Sunday afternoon rehearsal in St. Louis, where the
show was opening on Tuesday.

I picked up my coat. "Come here, you two," said Jerry. He held out both of his hands.

I put my coat down and walked over to the bed. Judy took one hand and I took the other, and we stayed that way for a long time, not speaking, just looking at each other, appreciating each other, appreciating this moment, when we were together and close and in touch with the love that flowed quietly and eloquently through us.

Then, we released our hands, and Jerry and I held each other, like the brothers we were.

I shrugged into my coat, and got as far as the door, when Jerry's voice stopped me.

"Quimby," he said.

I turned. He was smiling. "Quimby," and he paused. "You look great."

Tears rushed into my eyes. I couldn't speak. I just waved. The words hadn't been created to say what I was feeling at that instant.

St. Louis was a more colorful city than Seattle. At least, it seemed that way to me. We were rehearsing hard, there, before Chicago, where the critics were really tough, where we'd be opening in a week. Fran was coming along fine. Everything was fine. The world was my oyster.

And then, late in the afternoon of November 11, 1955, the backstage phone rang. It was for me, the stage manager said. I told him to tell them to call me back, after rehearsal. "You better take it," he said. "It's Mr. Prince."

Hal's voice was quiet and flat. "Richard," he said. "You'd better get the next plane to New York. Jerry's dead."

I don't remember anything about the trip, how I got the tickets, how I packed, if I packed. I only remember the quiet, familiar faces of Hal Prince and my agent David Hocker, waiting for me when I landed in New York. They didn't say anything. They just hugged me and picked up my luggage and guided me toward a taxi.

"The bronchus blew," David finally said, in the taxi, after I asked him how it happened. "All those years, I guess. I don't know. It was all going so well."

I pulled myself into a tight knot. It had happened. What Jerry had feared most. He'd drowned. And there hadn't been a thing anyone could do to prevent it.

"I figured I'd better show you this first," said Hal, unfolding the *New*

York Post. There, in the obituary section, was the account of Jerry's passing and his accomplishments. And there, above the obituary, captioned *Jerry Ross,* was a picture of *me.*

"Jesus," I said, crumpling up the paper. The symbolism of it hadn't escaped me.

As soon as we got into town, and Hal and David had left off my luggage, I headed uptown, to Jerry and Judy's apartment.

The families were gathered. Judy met me at the door. Her eyes, large anyway, seemed larger than ever, and swollen from crying. Her nose was red, her hair was disarranged. She looked like she hadn't slept in days. She took the mangled handkerchief she was holding against her face away from it and threw her arms around me.

We held each other for a long time, as if by doing it, we were somehow holding Jerry, too. Then we slowly let go.

"What are we going to do without him?" she whispered to me.

"I don't know," I answered. And I honestly didn't. My insides were churning. I was as lost and as empty as I had ever been in my life or ever would be again. Nothing, absolutely nothing seemed to make sense, not Jerry's death, not Judy's tears, not the wild, stricken face of his father, who was absolutely inconsolable, who moaned, and threw his arms in the air, and beat at his chest, in the way that old Jews had vented their anguish for centuries.

Grief can use up the very air in a place, and at the moment, I was having trouble breathing. I had to leave, and be with the only person who had ever been able to set things right, even in the most bizarre situations: Jerry. I kissed Judy goodbye and she thanked me, and then withdrew into her own envelope of sorrow.

I ran down the stairs to the street. It was a sunny, clear, November day. The sidewalks were full. I headed for the nearest telephone booth. My mind simply wouldn't focus on any one scene, any solitary impulse. I figured I couldn't trust myself to accomplish the simplest, most straightforward task, and so I called Eddie Fisher.

His voice shattered when he heard mine.

"Jesus," he said. "What a hell of day, huh?"

"Yeah," I said. "Look. I gotta see him. Will you come with me?"

"Sure. Of course I will."

The funeral home had a tasteful, festive, flower-framed air to it. We were directed, by a quiet, dark-suited young man to the tiny room where Jerry's body lay in state. We stayed very close to each other as we approached the coffin. Neither of us really wanted to be there, and yet both of us wanted, more than anything in the world, to be there. In our own, lonely ways, we felt that somehow, there was something that hadn't been said yet, some word or gesture that we could still make, something appropriate and final that would end the story the way it should end. And we had to be near Jerry's body to say it. It was an obligation that went beyond my terrible, terminal fear of being in the same room with the cold, mute evidence of death.

And then we stopped, frozen in our tracks. Something horrible had happened. Something had apparently gone wrong with the embalming process. Jerry's face was *purple*. Black, blood purple.

We were struck dumb. For what seemed like an endless interval, we stared, open-mouthed, at this grim and degrading spectacle.

"What've they *done* to him?" I finally croaked at Eddie.

"I don't know, but they're going to *un*do it right away," he said, and he turned on his heel and went to find the funeral director.

I was left alone with Jerry, very much the way we'd spent most of the last four years of our lives. Two ends of a single thought. Two men who were closer than brothers. And now the Negative was really ruling, for the last time.

Suddenly, a huge bubble of fury rose in me, like a high speed elevator. I felt it reach my throat, stay there for a moment, and then burst forth. "You son of a bitch!" I shouted at him. "How could you do this to me? How could you leave me here, alone, when we were at the top of the heap? Where do I go now? What do I *do* now, you son of a bitch, you son of a *bitch*!"

And it kept coming. The anger raged out of me. And the love. And the terrible, horrible regret and pain and loss. I hated him for leaving me alone and I loved him for being the brother I'd lost.

And in the deepest, most essential part of me, I knew that what had departed that day was irreplaceable. Never again would I have the kind of shared success that we, as young *wunderkinds,* had owned for a year and a half. Eighteen short months, and the memory of them would have to do me for a lifetime.

The funeral was massive, and very moving. Typical for Jerry, it was SRO—Standing Room Only. Everybody who knew and had been touched by him packed the Rodeph Sholom Temple at 83rd Street, between Columbus Avenue and Central Park West, to its outer walls, and spilled out onto the sidewalk. Roz Russell sat next to me and held my hand through the entire ceremony, which seemed to go on and on and on. Jerry's father flung himself on the coffin, screaming, "My son! My son!" until he was gently disengaged and led, weeping, to his seat. I swam in and out of that morning, sometimes concentrating, sometimes remembering, sometimes drifting in space.

And then, the rabbi paused, coming to the end of his eulogy. "In the words of Adler and Ross," he said, softly, " 'You Gotta Have Heart / All you really need is heart'. . ."

And the tears flowed, not only from me, but from everybody in that sanctuary who loved Jerry, and knew him, and knew what he stood for in this sometimes heartless world, which had been given a mere twenty-nine years of his matchless brilliance.

And now he was gone. And here I was. Alone, the way I'd been when I was young, and frightened. As frightened of the future as I was now, at this dark and terrible moment.

II
The
Long
Shadow

6.

M Y father, Clarence Adler, was a masterful musician, a peerless teacher, and a great man. He participated in a score of important, timeless, famous musical activities. But the one activity he never participated in was my boyhood.

And yet, he cast a shadow, as deep as my thwarted love for him and as long as the length of my life.

He grew up in Cincinnati, in the midst of a colony of immigrants who had come over from Frankfurt in the summer of 1856. My grandfather, Leopold Adler, was a streetcar conductor; my grandmother took in laundry and boarders. Between the two of them, they managed the food and the clothing for their seven children and themselves.

Clarence was the second boy in the family, and he learned at a very early age a lesson in basic survival that he never forgot, and never forgot to practice: You had to eat, and you didn't eat without working for it.

According to his recollections, every day, at 5:30 A.M., from the time he was seven years old until the time he was twelve, he rolled out of a warm bed and on to a cold paper route.

One balmy day in late spring, when he was eight, after he'd dropped off all of his papers, he decided that, instead of going to school, he would explore the city beyond his neighborhood.

The way he remembered it, he walked around for nearly an hour, and then strolled into a small side street. Music was soaring out of a second story window in a third rate apartment house in the middle of the block. He was drawn to the sounds as certainly as if he'd been destined for them.

The idea of danger didn't invade his mind. He climbed the apartment house stairs, and on the second floor, he homed in on the source of the music. In an apartment whose door was half open, someone was playing a piano.

My father pushed against the door, tentatively. It opened further, and he slipped in. At a concert grand, a dark, athletically built man sat, bringing a Beethoven sonata to a dramatic conclusion. As quietly as he could, my father attached himself to the wall behind the pianist.

He'd never heard anything like this in his life.

When the piece was over, the man turned around, slowly. My father remained riveted to the spot. He was in for it, he knew. A trespasser, not only in somebody else's apartment, but in territory outside the one assigned to him by the *Cincinnati Enquirer.*

But what occurred next both calmed and mystified him. With a voice that was like an arm around my father's shoulders, the man, without the least hesitation or surprise, asked, "Did you like the music?"

My father nodded. Vigorously. He'd more than liked it. It had been thrilling. Better than riding his bike. Better than ice cream.

"Come here."

The man held his hands out to my father, who came to him. He gathered up the young, dazzled boy, and put him on his shoulders. "Let's have a ride and talk," he said.

While the man, who introduced himself as Romeo Gorno, circled the room with my father around his neck, he asked all the questions that would unlock young Clarence Adler. What was his name? Where did he live? What was his father's name? Why wasn't he in school?

And then, he posed one final, fateful question. "Would you like to play the piano, too?"

My father didn't hesitate for the space of a grace note. Yes. Of course he would. Right away. And immediately, as soon as he could transfer him from his shoulders to the piano bench, Romeo Gorno gave Clarence Adler his second piano lesson. The first, my father often stated, was the greatest pedagogical experience in his life—the conversational ride around the room on Romeo Gorno's shoulders.

Of course, music hadn't exactly been absent from my father's life before that important afternoon. The day at his parents' boarding house might have begun in work, but it ended in music. There was a gramophone and a piano in the front parlor. Summer nights were long and light, and not at all silent.

So, maybe it was Providence that provided my father's musical education. Or maybe it was coincidence, aided and abetted by my grandparents' tastes. Whatever it was, it produced a child prodigy, and before he was out of short pants, my father was into Mozart and Beethoven.

And pretty soon, he was out of Cincinnati.

By the time he was eighteen, he'd become a striking figure, one who refused to fade into a crowd. He was short, slender and sensitive looking, with a huge shock of very black hair, a prominent nose, and long, tapered hands.

Women, both older and younger, were attracted to him, and the first of the former was Mutti Markbright, the wife of a prominent Cincinnati businessman. Taking him under her protective wing, she initiated him into the ways of the world and lovemaking. It was no one-night farewell to virginity. Mutti Markbright was more gentle and knowing than that. And probably more demanding. For four years, while Romeo Gorno continued to teach my father the nuances of the piano, Mutti Markbright schooled him in the nuances of the bedroom.

At the end of that time, he'd learned about as much as he could from each of them. And whether it was because her husband found out about her relationship with my father, or whether she was beginning to realize the lack of a future for them, Mutti, though deeply in love with the young musician, sent him off to Berlin to study with the great pianist, composer, teacher, intellectual, and world-renowned wit, Leopold Godowsky.

It was the spring of 1908. Berlin was a center of music in that last decade of innocence for Europe. Godowsky was a lodestone who attracted the finest minds on the continent. A scientist, a pianist who ranked with the great musician and statesman Ignace Jan Paderewski, a towering intellectual, he wasn't just a man who ground out concert pianists; he believed that wit and wisdom and understanding were what gave a performer's performance depth. And what made that performer an interesting person, besides.

In Godowsky's well-populated salon, my father studied more than music; he heard as much about poetry and politics as he did about instrumental technique. Einstein, who'd just published his first theory of relativity, dropped by to play passable violin and swap a few stories. Isadora Duncan floated in and out, unannounced (and later floated my father willingly into her bed). Paderewski, more revered by musicians than the Pope, listened in stony silence one morning, while my father played for him. And then nodded his head in approval.

But out of all of those five years in Berlin, it was one summer afternoon in 1913 that remained most vividly in my father's memory.

He was taking his midmorning walk in the park, when suddenly, several men, dressed like extras in the throne room scene from *The Student Prince*, thundered by him, on horseback.

One of them dropped a leather packet, and it landed alongside my father. "Wait!" he yelled after them, "you dropped something!"

Shocked silence from the other strollers in the park. My father didn't notice. "You dropped this!" He yelled again.

The horsemen reined up. One of them turned his mount around and rode over to my father. My father handed him the packet.

The man thanked my father and then asked what he did, why he was in Berlin, where he was from. The usual niceties. The mention of Godowsky's name raised his eyebrows.

Finally, he turned his horse, ready to ride on.

Then, he paused. "You must come and play for me. Give my adjutant your address, and he'll arrange the time, and notify you," the man said, smiling.

"Where will you—"

"At the Palace," concluded Kaiser Wilhelm, as he rode away.

At just about the same time, in Mobile, Alabama, a very pretty girl by the name of Elsa Adrienne Richard was growing up splendidly. No boarders in her home. No laundry. And only a civilized amount of music.

Her parents hadn't made the trip from Europe to Government Street in Mobile in steerage. They were Sephardic Jews, who traced their ancestry back to sixteenth-century Spain, where their name was Ricarda. When the Inquisition drove them to Holland, they made the trip on a ship whose passenger list included another Sephardic Jew named Spinoza.

In Holland, they became the Rickardts; when they wandered into Germany, they were still the Richardts. By the time my mother, Elsa Adrienne, was born, they were The Richards of Mobile.

Elsa Adrienne Richard was a woman of many contrasts. Delicate of features and soft of voice, she possessed an interior of tensilized steel. When she was fifteen years old, she leaped from a twenty-foot pier into the roiling waters of Mobile Bay and saved the life of the son of the governor of Alabama. He weighed 240 pounds; she weighed a mere 108, and yet she managed to calm him, gather him to her, and pull him ashore. For this, she won that state's highest medal of bravery, and a proposal of marriage from the governor's son. She accepted the first and declined the last, and went back to her quiet and dutiful maturing process as a protected Southern belle.

Her parents, despite Elsa's determination to manifest the stronger side of her nature, were dedicated to bringing her up genteelly. No hard edges of the world were going to bruise her, not if Mr. and Mrs. Richard had anything to do with it. They saw to it that she had her Southern upbringing whittled to a fine, delicate point by the best schools in Mobile, and when she was seventeen, she was shipped up North, like many young girls of well-to-do Southern families, to study music. Not too much music. But enough to get by in conversation and to play violin for family musicales.

At the same time, the musical son of a Cincinnati streetcar conductor had settled comfortably into New York. And he and Elsa Richard would meet under the kind of romantic circumstances that most seventeen-year-old girls of that age dreamed about, but hardly ever experienced.

It happened at one of those regal dinner parties wealthy patrons of the arts threw in New York City a few years before World War I.

Candlelight burned. Wine flowed. Conversation made acquaintances of strangers. Directly across from Elsa Richard sat a young, handsome, black-haired, and very successful pianist. Still in his twenties, he'd made his New York debut with the New York Philharmonic under Walter Damrosch. He'd been the pianist with the Kneisel Quartet. He'd succeeded Arthur Schnabel in Berlin as the pianist in the Hekking Trio, and now he was the pianist with the Letz Quartet. He was going places, and he wondered if she'd like to accompany him to some of them—to the piano, for instance, to turn pages?

How could she refuse such a lovely offer from such a cultured young man, particularly one whose eyes seemed to see not only what she looked like, but what she thought, too? Nobody spoke so quickly in Mobile. Or thought so quickly. Or moved so quickly.

Four years later, they were married, and living at 730 Riverside Drive. A year later, a daughter, Jane, was born. Three years later, Jane died of a mysterious stomach malady.

The loss practically destroyed my mother; it would be two years before she could even imagine having another child. My father was tender with her; he spent less time at the Bohemian's, a musician's gathering place, and more time at home; he began to cut piano rolls and to scale down his professional appearances.

In the midst of this, on August 3, 1921, I was born. I began my education at a nursery school whose name and look now escapes me. All I can remember of those years is one morning when nobody arrived at the school to escort me home. I walked the few blocks downtown myself, and arrived home to an empty apartment and a locked door. Scared and confused, I went to the superintendent of the building, who took me in and fed me lunch. Backwards. We began with dessert and ended with soup, and maybe the sheer inventiveness of that lunch emblazoned it in my memory. It's all that remains with me of my nursery school years.

My parents skipped me over the first grade, and I began my real education in the second grade at Columbia Grammar School, at 5 West 93rd Street—something I also remember very little about, until sometime in the middle of that same year.

Imagine a spring day, in 1929. It's May, and I have a crush on my second grade teacher, Miss Peterson. I'm not alone. Practically every other guy whose sap is rising is feeling the same way this day, because Miss Peterson is looking especially lovely.

It's three o'clock, and although I'm supposed to be studying arithmetic, what I'm *really* studying is Miss Peterson.

And then, without warning, my mother appears in the doorway of the schoolroom. I look at her. I look at Miss Peterson. And suddenly, I realize I'm the luckiest guy in that room. Oh sure, other guys have their mothers call for them. That's nothing special. Their old ladies come by with their matronly cloche hats and orthopedic shoes and bodies that look like vases.

But my mother, in a blue dress with white polka dots, standing in the classroom door, is pretty. No. She's more than pretty. She's beautiful. And in a different way from Miss Peterson. And I realize, with a rush of pride, that there are *two* beautiful women in my life, and I like the idea a lot. It's a fateful appreciation of beautiful women, full of premonitions for the future.

The spring of 1929 would be the last time I'd see Miss Peterson, and the last I'd see of Columbia Grammar for a while. That year, we moved to 336 Central Park West, a block away from Columbia Grammar. And in September 1930, for some reason, I was enrolled in Ethical Culture School, thirty blocks south. I'd spend the third and fourth grades there, and have my first taste of show business.

It happened in the spring. It was at some sort of seasonal pageant, a mulligatawny of a lot of disconnected acts. I'll never forget how

My mother, Elsa Richard Adler, around 1935, (ABOVE). My father, Clarence Adler.

Ninth grade at Columbia Grammar School, 1936. I am third from the left in the middle row, (LEFT, ABOVE).   The family home in Lake Placid, New York, we called Karinoke, from the Iroquois meaning "Place of the Beautiful Song," around 1930, (INSET, LEFT).   My first collaborator, Philip Springer, and I in 1948, (ABOVE, TOP).   Columbia Grammar School Dramatic Society, 1938, (ABOVE).

Jerry Ross and I, 1953. (ABOVE, LEFT). Hermione Gingold in *John Murray Anderson's Almanac*, 1953. Jerry and I wrote some of the music for this show, (BELOW, LEFT). My sons Christopher (left) and Andrew, ages 3 and 5, with a friend in 1957, (TOP). A self-portrait of my first wife, Marion Hart Adler.

Hi Chris
Your Pals

Howdy
Doody
&
Buffalo
Bob

From left, Janis Paige, John Raitt and Buzz Miller, in the confrontation scene in *The Pajama Game*, (TOP, LEFT). Carol Haney (center) with dancers in "Steam Heat," from *The Pajama Game*, 1954, (TOP, INSET). Dress rehearsal of the Finale of *The Pajama Game*, May, 1954, (INSET, BOTTOM). Gwen Verdon as Lola, (TOP, RIGHT). Bob Fosse, center, rehearsing the dancers in "Two Lost Souls," from *Damn Yankees*, 1955, (RIGHT, BOTTOM).

G wen and Eddie Phillips in "Who's Got the Pain?," (ABOVE, LEFT).   A publicity still of that devil, Ray Walston, and Gwen, from *Damn Yankees*, (BELOW, LEFT).   Sally Ann Howes, my second wife, at the time she was starring in *My Fair Lady*, 1960, (TOP).   Leonard Lyons, Bob Hope, myself, Margaret Truman and Horace Sutton at Sardi's, 1955, (CENTER).   Somerset Maugham, Sally Ann and myself at Villa Mauresque, 1960, (BELOW).

"Something Big," from *Kwamina*, 1961, (TOP, ABOVE). The company for the White House press and photographers gala honoring President Kennedy and Prime Minister Macmillan, 1962, (ABOVE). President Kennedy delivering what Variety called "the wittiest speech in history," at the gala honoring him and Prime Minister Macmillan, (RIGHT, TOP). In the Oval Office with the President, Danny Kaye and Judy Garland, 1962, (BELOW, RIGHT).

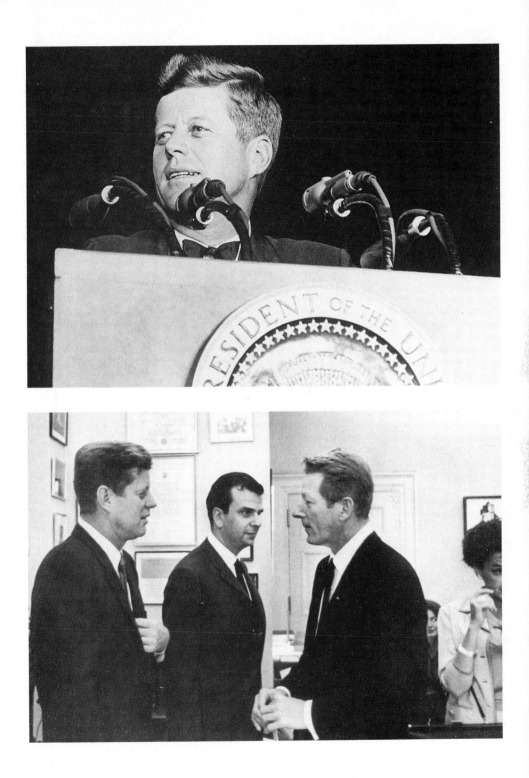

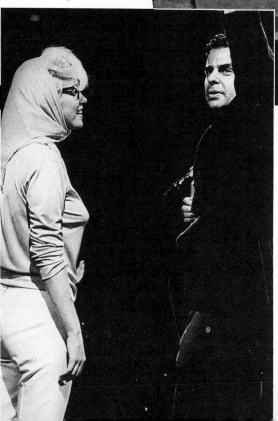

The roster for the Birthday Salute to President Kennedy, 1962, (TOP, LEFT). Harry Belafonte and Miriam Makeba in a duet, (ABOVE, INSET). Here I ask Marilyn Monroe to project when she sings "Happy Birthday" to the President, (BELOW, LEFT). Jack Benny demonstrating his impeccable timing, (ABOVE, RIGHT). At rehearsal, Maria Callas needs no advice from me on how to project....Nor does Jimmy Durante, (CENTER).

Kirk Douglas at rehearsal, (ABOVE, LEFT). Shirley MacLaine and Jimmy Durante. A view of the stage and environs, (RIGHT). Ella Fitzgerald in performance, (INSET, ABOVE). The President and Vice-President, with their ladies, (INSET, BELOW).

A birthday cake is presented to the President, (INSET). Marilyn's song is the hit of the evening, (RIGHT). The roster for the "Presidentical" honoring the anniversary of JFK's inauguration, at the National Guard Armory in Washington, D.C., 1962.

INAUGURAL ANNIVERSARY SALUTE · HAPPY ANNIVERSARY, MR. PRESIDENT! ☆ ☆ ☆

Produced and Staged by Richard Adler ☆ ☆ ☆ ☆ ☆ ☆ ☆ ☆ ☆ ☆ ☆ ☆ ☆

STAR SPANGLED BANNER · John Bourdon, Conductor · Orchestrated by Sid Ramin ☆ ☆ ☆ ☆ ☆ ☆ ☆

ANNIVERSARY OVERTURE · Hal Hastings, Conductor ☆ ☆ ☆ ☆ ☆ ☆ ☆ ☆ ☆ ☆ ☆ ☆

GENE KELLY ☆ ☆ ☆ ☆ ☆ ☆ ☆ ☆ ☆ ☆ ☆ ☆ ☆ ☆ ☆ ☆ ☆ ☆ ☆

YVES MONTAND · Robert Cantello, Conductor ☆ ☆ ☆ ☆ ☆ ☆ ☆ ☆ ☆ ☆ ☆ ☆

ANTONIO and his FLAMENCO BALLET ESPAÑOL ☆ ☆ ☆ ☆ ☆ ☆ ☆ ☆ ☆ ☆ ☆ ☆

with Carmen Rojas ☆ ☆ ☆ ☆ ☆ ☆ ☆ ☆ ☆ ☆ ☆ ☆ ☆ ☆ ☆ ☆ ☆ ☆ ☆

and Paco Ruiz · Luis Torrán · Paavera Ruiz ☆ ☆ ☆ ☆ ☆ ☆ ☆ ☆ ☆ ☆ ☆

SHIRLEY BASSEY · Raymond Long, Conductor ☆ ☆ ☆ ☆ ☆ ☆ ☆ ☆ ☆ ☆

GEORGE BURNS & CAROL CHANNING · Robert Hunter, Conductor ☆ ☆ ☆ ☆ ☆

PETER, PAUL & MARY ☆ ☆ ☆ ☆ ☆ ☆ ☆ ☆ ☆ ☆ ☆ ☆ ☆ ☆ ☆ ☆

KIRK DOUGLAS ☆

JOAN SUTHERLAND · Richard Bonynge, Conductor ☆ ☆ ☆ ☆ ☆ ☆ ☆ ☆ ☆ ☆ ☆ ☆ ☆

PRINCESS OF MOROVIA or (CAROL BURNETT) ☆ ☆ ☆ ☆ ☆ ☆ ☆ ☆ ☆ ☆ ☆ ☆ ☆ ☆

Assisted by Dick Aliman ☆

DIAHANN CARROLL · Peter Matz, Conductor ☆ ☆ ☆ ☆ ☆ ☆ ☆ ☆ ☆ ☆ ☆ ☆

NEW YORK CITY BALLET Excerpts from "Stars and Stripes" ☆ ☆ ☆ ☆ ☆ ☆ ☆ ☆ ☆

Choreography by George Balanchine · Costumes by Karinska · Robert Irving, Conductor ☆ ☆ ☆ ☆

Music by John Philip Sousa · Orchestration by Hershy Kay ☆ ☆ ☆ ☆ ☆ ☆ ☆ ☆ ☆ ☆

Featured Soloists: Allegra Kent · Arthur Mitchel · Edward Villella ☆ ☆ ☆ ☆ ☆ ☆ ☆ ☆

ANNIVERSARY FINALE ☆

LYNDON B. JOHNSON · Vice President of the United States ☆ ☆ ☆ ☆ ☆ ☆ ☆ ☆ ☆

JOHN F. KENNEDY · President of the United States ☆ ☆ ☆ ☆ ☆ ☆ ☆ ☆ ☆ ☆

BEDFORD S. WY

MRS. HALE BOG

JOHN M. O

MRS. MARGAR

MRS. DOROTHY VR

RICHARD M

VANCE H

MICHA

embarrassed I was at my getup as a horse. My turn had me pulling a chariot, while somebody played, on the piano, Beethoven's "Turkish March." Even then, I had enough taste to know that anybody pretending to be a horse would look like a jerk.

Of course, my mother thought I was terrific. She was always there, applauding me, taking me to the children's concerts at Carnegie Hall on Saturday mornings, and, when it was in town, to the circus at Madison Square Garden. She'd also take me to museums, and when I'd say why I liked a Picasso, for instance, she'd reply, "You as the viewer are on the same artistic level as the artist. I'm sure Mr. Picasso would be impressed by the way you saw that." And I'd feel very important, and flattered.

My mother—my lovely, talented unusual mother—wasn't only generous with her time. She had a certain generosity of spirit that flooded my childhood with sunlight. I knew she loved me. It was as simple and important as that. There was nothing of the dark complexity that marked my relationship with my father, none of the changing seasons of our moods. It was always fair weather around my mother, and I continued to be grateful for the bright bounty she gave me all the days of my youth.

But in spite of all of this, I was plagued by her one overriding limitation: She was a woman, and because she was a woman, she couldn't do what I wanted most—she couldn't take me to a Yankee game.

A father had to do that, and other boys' fathers did. They took their sons up to the Bronx, to Yankee Stadium. They clowned around with them. They spent Saturdays with them.

Mine had taken on piano students now, and he either taught, or cut piano rolls, or concertized. The Depression and hard times were upon us, and he probably was feeling the pressures all heads of families were feeling those days. It took up all of his time and most of his energy. Looking back, I suppose he had only so much to give. And whatever he had left at the end of each day, he gave to my mother. There didn't seem to be much left for me, even though I ached for it.

There was, for instance, the incident of my second grade composition. It was the first sustained writing I'd ever done. The teacher had assigned 100 words, and I'd written not 99 nor 101, but exactly 100 words. I was thrilled. My mother had read it, and she'd told me she thought it was wonderful. I couldn't wait for my father to sit down at the dinner table, read it, and praise me too.

My mother and I put the composition on his plate. He didn't seem to notice it. My mother told him what it was. He picked it up and read it. I held my breath.

He dropped it on the tablecloth. "You wrote this?" he asked.

I nodded, too excited to look at him.

"What's so special about it?" he asked, and turned back to his dinner.

I was crushed. I was devastated. The impact of this particular rejection left its mark on me for the rest of my life. But what's amazing to me, when I look back at it, is that, even then, as much as my father seemed to reject me, I never stopped striving for his approval. And I treasured the times, during my early boyhood, even though they were few and far apart, that my father spent with the entire family.

Some Sundays we'd go to a Chinese restaurant that was at the top of a flight of stairs at 86th Street and Broadway. My father would lead us up those stairs as if we were about to discover some obscure and precious treasure.

Later, when I could be trusted to use the right fork at the right time, he'd take us to the Lotos Club at 5 East 66th Street. That was a very, very big deal indeed—or at least it is in my memory. Once, my father'd been an officer of the club, and he was still a member during the Depression. So, we were seated in the best room, the downstairs bar. It was mostly mahogany, and relentlessly elegant. There was crystal glassware and linen tableclothes that were starched as stiffly as shirt fronts. Around the bar, for me to sneak looks at, there were paintings of gorgeous nudes done by James Montgomery Flagg, who was, more often than not, sitting at the bar when we came in. He was a very tall, very thin, highly distinguished looking man with a craggy face, a shock of blue-gray hair, and deep circles under his eyes. He'd often join us after dinner, and light up a cigar with my father.

Once, we took Fannie Hurst, another family friend—and, in my memory, one of the kindest, most loving people in the world—to dinner, and that was a *very* special occasion. She was at the height of her fame then, and whenever she signed autographs, she'd draw a lily beside her name. Pretty strange, I thought, and said so, at the time, to my mother.

"It's her symbol," she answered, mysteriously.

Years and years later, when I was married to Sally Ann Howes, and living in Saddle River, New Jersey, I invited Fannie Hurst to speak at the Saddle River Country Day School, where my children were being educated. I had two dogs then, and she admired one, a Yorkie named

Samantha. I gave Samantha to Fannie Hurst, and she immediately renamed her Lily.

"Why?" I asked.

"Everyone important to me is named Lily," she answered.

My closest friend in those days was E. Charles Straus. The E was for Edwin, a name he loathed. I called him Eddie, and later on, when we were roommates in college, he asked me to drop the Eddie and call him Charles. Charles and I shared just about everything in my boyhood but my collection of presidential buttons. They were very special to me, and we met over them during the Hoover-Smith election, in October 1929. We also got into an argument over them that same day, in front of 336 Central Park West, where Eddie lived, too, six floors above me. We went to his father, a lawyer, to settle the disagreement, and he settled it, amicably. And from that time forward, we were the fastest of friends.

So, I wasn't alone in my childhood in New York. If Eddie wasn't around, my father's students always were. In fact, there was, it seems to me, an endless parade of pianists that came through the front door at 336 Central Park West, and stayed. And drove me crazy with their playing.

Not all of them, of course. There was Paulina Ruvinska, who was much older than I, and very, very sweet. She used to take me out in my baby carriage when *she* was eight, and I used to dream romantic dreams about her when *I* was eight.

And there was Poldi Mildner, two years older than I, who was Austrian, and plump, and had blonde braids, and no command of the English language whatsoever. Later, when I was thirteen, my father gave me three dollars to take her out on a date, and I did, and fell absolutely and foolishly in love with her. The trouble was, I was too afraid of rejection to try to kiss her when we got home. After all, she *was* an older woman. Her importance in my life terrified me, and she mistook my fear for coldness, and that was that.

Which was a shame, because my libido, still carefully under wraps, had been treated to a healthy massage one Saturday night two years earlier, when my mother foolishly and wonderfully told our maid, Mary Snead, to bathe me.

Mary was a very pretty Polynesian looking Black woman—young, leggy, bosomy, and very flirtatious. I'd seen my father's friend Max Rosen, a well-known violinist, back Mary up against a wall, and, while she giggled, move his body back and forth against her. At the time, I didn't have the faintest idea what he was doing to her, but it looked like fun.

That Saturday night, very businesslike and brusque, she ran my bathwater, and told me to get undressed. After I'd settled into the warm water, she kneeled down beside me and began to soap me. Slowly. Her hands sent little tingles of pleasure through me. They got better and better the lower she soaped. Finally, she brought her hand between my legs and very gently rubbed my privates.

It was the most pleasurable tingle of all, and I asked her to keep doing it.

She pulled her hand away. "I only do that for money," she said, folding up the washcloth.

"How much?" I asked, breathlessly. I would have robbed the Morgan Guaranty Trust for another tingle.

"Fifteen cents," she answered.

Paradise was within my reach.

The next day, I gathered up three deposit bottles and took them to the delicatessen on Columbus Avenue.

And every Saturday bath night, from then on, the pockets of my discarded trousers weighed down with change, I would lie back in the warm, sudsy water of the bathtub while Mary Snead gently led me through a new and lovely wonderland.

The only problem was putting Mary's lessons to work with girls my own age. Somehow, it wasn't the same.

And the other, older women who joined the parade through our front door were hardly interested in me as a sex object. Besides, they were friends of my mother, and taboo.

Or they were like poor Mrs. Rafael Joseffy, who brought forth feelings of sadness and respect. She was a huge woman who had a thick German accent and dressed as if she were still in the nineteenth century. Her cloche hats, high-waisted button-down blouses, and endless skirts were always a little frayed. She had a huge mop of mousy gray hair that she wore in a bun on top of her head, and, try as I might, I can never remember her not weeping.

She had a lot to weep about. Her husband, who was dead, had been a world-class pianist, as great as—maybe greater than—Paderewski. He'd founded and been the first president of the Bohemian Society, that fraternity of fine musicians, and my father was the Society's first secretary.

All of the money Rafael Joseffy had left to his wife and son had been used up in his son's trial for fraud. The son had been convicted, and was in Sing Sing, and Mrs. Joseffy had devoted her life to him. And now she was very poor, and perhaps a little crazy, and my father always gave her money. He didn't have it to give, but he gave it anyway, and whenever Mrs. Joseffy left, she left behind her a trail of silence and despair—and admiration by my mother and me for my father.

So there it was. I was on a roller coaster built partly by me and partly by my father. Sometimes he took me out and showed me off. But those times were few and precious, which is probably why I remember them so well. Most of the time he ignored me, and so, through practically all of my early boyhood, my father and I lived in a kind of cloud of ambivalence. He was a gracious, kind, and demanding person to his students, his friends, and my mother. They probably got the best of him. I probably got the worst.

So, I resisted the musical knowledge he might have given to me.

Would I take piano lessons?

Not on your life!

Of course, my father could have made it easier. He could have offered to teach me himself, instead of shunting me off to one or more of his students. I wanted my father to teach me. But he wouldn't, or couldn't.

Oh, I tried learning to play the piano for a while. But the house was full of little people, barely able to climb onto a piano stool, who could rip off concertos at the drop of a conductor's hand. While I was struggling through "The Happy Farmer." It was a hopeless situation. I knew I'd never play like one of his prodigies, so why try? I gave it up for baseball. And I wasn't too good at that, either.

What I didn't realize was that, in spite of my obstinancy, music was unconsciously seeping into me.

Every night, while I was trying to read in my room, the thunder of my father's voice would roll through the wall. "No. NO! I told you SLOWER!" he'd roar, and the pianist would go back and work through the piece at the pace of a glacier melting.

Years and years later, when music and I had become inseparable, and I was training Broadway choruses, I'd use exactly the same technique. I would, in fact, imitate many of my father's teaching techniques—The Adler Method—that crept, in my early youth, through the wall of my bedroom and into my subconscious.

I'd use his gentle persuasion and insinuation of phrasing, without which music is as mechanical as the turning of a turbine. I'd echo his way of seeing and hearing and speaking and instructing ("More of this; less of that, put a little ritard here—more softly there. Energy. It needs energy here—") and it would become as much a part of me as my own thought processes. Decades down the road, both the singers in my shows and I would benefit mightily from that early, subliminal absorption of my father's brilliance during my rebellious youth.

Afterwards, late at night, the house would become as quiet as a mute singing. And I'd listen. And sure enough, I'd hear the creak of the knob on my father's "dumb" piano. It was an upright that had no keyboard and thus made no noise when you hit the keys. It just gave you a physical workout. And if the workout seemed too easy, there was a round knob at the left of the lowest note that could be adjusted to heighten keyboard resistance.

No wonder my father couldn't take me to a ball game. If he wasn't teaching, he was cutting piano rolls. If he wasn't cutting piano rolls, he was exercising at the dumb piano. If he wasn't doing that, he was practicing hand isometrics, or wearing a weird contraption that was supposed to stretch his hands.

Or else he was talking music with his musician friends who dropped in between lessons or on Sundays. Or playing poker with them every Saturday night.

But through all of this fancied neglect and real rebellion against my father's profession, in spite of the errors in judgment that we both made, he was teaching me, through the example of a man consumed by his art, a truth that time has proven to me, too: Music is a jealous mistress. Give it your absolute attention, and it'll treat you beautifully. Neglect it for a while, and it may walk out on you.

The parade of famous musicians that walked through the doors of our apartment was endless. But the three men I remember most are associated in my memory with a place a long way from Riverside Drive. The great French cellist Horace Britt, the eminent French flutist Georges Barrère, and the man I called "Uncle Pierre"—Pierre Monteux, the immortal conductor who, ten years before I was born, introduced Stravinsky's *Rite of Spring* to the world—are all associated in my memory with a musical gathering place miles north of New York.

In 1924, when I was three years old, my father was convinced by some of his friends that he should have a place in the country that was his own, a place where they could all make beautiful music together. He withdrew the last of his savings and threw in with three friends and some other visionaries to buy 110 acres of woodland and buildings in the hamlet of Averyville, about three and a half miles north of the Lake Placid railroad station and four miles from the center of the town of Lake Placid, New York.

He and my mother named it Karinoke. My mother was into numerology at the time and this was a favorable numerological change from the area's Indian title, Ka-ren-i-o-ke, which, in Iroquois, meant "place of the beautiful song."

Karinoke wasn't exactly that at first. But it became a place of beautiful song when my father turned it into a music colony.

Karinoke and I grew up together. After a couple of years at Ethical Culture, I went back to Columbia Grammar School, and graduated from there. I still have a great affection for Columbia Grammar. But I have a different kind of affection for Karinoke.

7.

K A R I N O K E was a paradise for a boy, and for a musician. But my first memories of it were as a boy who thought of himself as anything *but* a musician.

I can still see the sprawling, fieldstone and shingle house with its green metal roof, where we lived, and the rambling barn my father and his cohorts had turned into an auditorium (my father called it the "barnitorium"). Outfitted with church pews he'd bought from a church that had burned down, it became a rural Carnegie Hall and a summer retreat for much of the greatest musical talent of the age. Every June, from as early as I can remember, until I left for college, we packed up the family car and headed north from New York City to our own Tanglewood.

The concerts held in that barn where my mother decorated the beams with balsam bows and lit the candles on the wrought iron candelabra that framed the stage were magnificent. Every Sunday afternoon, sprinkled among the Buicks and the Chevies and the Fords, chauffeur-driven Dusenbergs, Rolls Royces, Pierce Arrows, Marmons, Reos, and Austins purred up a dirt driveway, kicked up clouds of dust, rocked across our lawn, and parked in the open lot against the endless hills.

Although I resisted playing music, I'd grown to love to listen to it, particularly on those sweet summer Sundays, when we'd roll open the barn doors, so that the overflow crowd that spilled up the hillock on the edge of the forest could see, as well as hear, the players.

To me, Sunday nights were the crown jewels of the week, when, after all but a large handful of musicians and audience members had left, we crowded into the candlelit dining room where my mother had set out, on our huge, heavy oak dining table, a buffet fit for royalty: ham, roast beef, turkey, baked beans, paradisekraut—which was a concoction of sauerkraut with tomato paste and honey and onions—and a dessert of ice cream and schnekken, those intensely rich, supremely sweet, and habit-forming buns that none of us, not even children my age, should have eaten, but did, eagerly.

After dinner, there would be chess games, and my father would sit down and play with me, and it would be a deadly serious match. He was very German, very strong, very stubborn. So was I. He never let me win, and I suppose that was a valuable lesson, too, although I resented it at the time. Still, I learned never to approach anything—a game, work, a relationship—without a desire to win, honestly. From an early age at Karinoke, I never expected to be treated any differently than as an equal.

Still, every once in a while, in some deep, adolescent part of me, I wanted my father to bend a little, just a little, and let me win; to show his love by softening up, if only for a moment. I saw how warm and affectionate he was with other people. No one ever said an unkind word about Clarence Adler, and no one had a reason to say an unkind word about him. Except me, in my boyhood, and in the confusion of my growing up.

And yet at times I saw how gentle and understanding he could be with me, when he wanted to be. One day, I'd opened the drawer of his bureau and found a sheaf of condoms. I ran to the kitchen, got a pair of scissors and chopped little holes in every one of them, hoping in my childhood fixation of the moment, that it would make me heir to a brother or sister. When he discovered the carnage I'd caused, he treated it with amusement and love.

If we'd been more open with each other, if we'd been able to bring our feelings to the surface more often, our relationship might have been happier and less ambivalent. But we were who we were, stubborn, self-contained, demanding.

And so, it seems from the vantage point of now that I spent much of my boyhood wishing for what could never be. If my father only had a little of my mother's softness, I thought. If he'd only be a little personal, if only *he'd* give me the piano lessons he asked one of his students to give to me.

On the surface at least, I was blasé about it all, overused to a surfeit of geniuses on the premises: Rosa Ponselle, the great soprano singing in the barnitorium, Mischa Elman, Toscha Seidel, Godowsky, my father's teacher, playing piano sonatas. And one of my father's more gifted students, Aaron Copland, composing and banging out his "Music for the Theatre" in The Clouds, a little shack pasted against the side of a hill on the property.

Forever afterward, I would call Copland "Dyata," because he shouted while he worked through some of his musical phrases. "Dyata, Dum dum DUM!" he'd scream from his perch on the side of the hill, while I held my hands over my ears. Little did I know that years and years later, I'd do exactly the same thing when I began to compose.

But then, I thought that most of the musicians, including Copland, were pretty stuffy in person, and better to listen to when they were playing than when they were talking. All, that is, except my "Uncle" Pierre Monteux. He was short, barrel-chested, smoked huge, heavy cigars, and always intervened for me when I wanted to do something my parents had forbidden.

Of course, this had its consequences as well as its advantages. One night, when I was six years old, I pleaded and cajoled my parents to let me go to the movies in Lake Placid to see *The Phantom of the Opera.*

No dice. It was too scary and I was too young.

But I had a French ace up my sleeve. Uncle Pierre was on the premises, and all I had to do was wait for him to walk through the door. I figured that after that, I was a sure bet to see the film.

And I was right. *"Mais certainment,"* he said, his black walrus moustache curling up to his cheekbones when he smiled. "A fine, French, classical story. The boy will be better for having seen it."

And he was wrong, dreadfully wrong. I had nightmares for weeks, and avoided chandeliers for months.

The part of my childhood I spent in Karinoke I spent alone, not, I think, because it had to be that way, but because I made it so. I prolonged my universal and abiding dislike of the parade of prodigies that my father now taught at Karinoke. I still wanted to play baseball, because it was the kind of thing "regular" kids did—the kind of regular kids who didn't devote their lives to music.

The kids at Karinoke *wouldn't* play baseball, because they didn't want to take a chance on breaking a finger, or injuring a wrist. Arnold Pomerantz, for instance, was a particular target of my disdain. He had a head that was too big for his body. He couldn't run fifty yards without puffing. But he could play the piano at the age of nine with such dazzling virtuosity that audiences would stand up and cheer.

So what? I thought. I didn't care about what he *could* do. I concentrated on what he *couldn't* do, and so I cut myself off from yet another companion my own age.

On the other hand, Jean Barrère, the son of my father's close friend, the great flutist Georges Barrère, and who was a little older than I, was that rare combination, a musician and a regular guy. Like Uncle Pierre. One July day, Jean and I whittled some wood and banged the pieces together to make two swords, which we used to duel with each other. We got into a frantic fight, up and down the hills, in and out of the barn, and I was determined to win, just as I was when I played chess with my father. I slashed and lunged and shouted—and all of a sudden, the end of my wooden sword started flinging blood around the barn, and Jean was grabbing at his neck.

I yelled. My mother came, on the run, took one look at Jean, and bundled him into the car. She took him into town to the doctor, to have the wound stitched, and Jean was brave and close lipped, and never blamed me for it. But I blamed myself, and I figured I'd lost the one friend I had at Karinoke. And when he left because he had to, I figured it was because of what I'd done.

Ironically enough, years and years later, Jean Barrere would reenter my life, when he became the stage manager of *The Pajama Game.*

At Karinoke, there were other incidents that deepened my feeling of isolation. As incredibly talented, as world-renowned as my father was, he made very little money. And I was ashamed of that, particularly when I had to perform the chores around Karinoke.

The two bitterest ones were making the Sunday ice cream and working the gasoline-powered water pump. In the early thirties, everyone had an ice house, and ours was near the back porch of the main building. Every winter, the Wescotts, who took care of the place during the off-season, hauled thirty-six-inch cubes of ice they'd cut out of Lake Placid up the hill to the ice house, filling it for the summer.

And every Sunday, I'd haul down the ice tongs from their hook on the back porch, open the ice house, dump three cubes of ice on the lawn, hose off the sawdust that covered them, pulverize the ice with a hand pick, pour the crushed ice into the freezer container that surrounded the cream and sugar and flavor, pour rock salt over that, and then settle down to a long session of cranking. When the crank would no longer move, the ice cream would be ready, and my reward would be to lick the paddle.

There was no reward whatsoever, on the other hand, for turning on the water pump, which was in the heart of a forest a mile from the house. Looking back on it, the place in which it stood seems idyllic. At the time, it was grim, and I couldn't see anything beautiful in that gorgeous spring that bubbled up in the nearby spring house. I'd pour the gasoline into the tank, crank the motor, and get it started. The pump would force the water uphill, for a mile and five-eighths, to a reservoir. From there, gravity would nudge it through a series of pipes downhill to the house.

My job was to haul the gasoline to the pumphouse, and start the pump—and that was the hateful part of it, because when it was cold, it would cough and spit and refuse to start, or else the crank would buck back at me and nearly break my arm. After tussling with this machinery, I'd hike back to the house; then, when it was time to shut off the pump, I'd hike out again, turn it off, and trudge back.

It was a long, boring tour, and after a couple of summers of this difficult dullness, I grew smart enough to put just enough gasoline into the tank so that it would run for two and a half hours—which was plenty of time to fill up the reservoir. I prided myself on shaving two miles of hiking from my daily chores.

But one day, dirt got into the unattended gas line, and my father gave me hell for being lazy.

He gave me hell a lot in those days, and in many ways. In some of his more thoughtless moments, he beat me at games of ego, and made me think even less of myself than I already did.

Take, for instance, the day he humiliated me in front of Frankie Freedman. Frankie was a pupil of my father's. She was nineteen when I was sixteen, pretty, a flirt, very shapely, and I had a wild crush on her, which was probably nine-tenths lust. But when you're sixteen, lust and love are interchangeable.

It was a hot, sunny, August morning in 1937. By then, I had a little car that I'd bought for sixty-five dollars, a 1931 Model A Ford Cabriolet. It was my prize possession, and I'd nicknamed it "Scrappy" because (a) it had a lot of pluck, and (b) it was one step away from the scrap heap. It was not only my pride and joy, it was the facilitator of my income. I'd charge twenty-five cents a ride from Karinoke to the village and twenty-five cents back, and that summer, I raked in three hundred and fifty dollars.

On this particular morning, I was shining her up, washing the road dust off her, polishing her maroon finish to a fine, blinding patina. I'd done the outside, and had climbed into the driver's seat to dust off the interior, when Frankie Freedman and my father strolled by.

My father wasn't immune to Frankie's charms, either. He was always wrapping his arm around her shoulders, and doing other little things that made me resentful.

Frankie looked especially alluring that morning, and she seemed particularly fascinated with what my father was saying to her.

They stopped alongside the car, and my father came over and said something to me. I don't remember what it was. I probably wasn't listening to him anyway. I was too interested in devouring Frankie Freedman with my eyes and my imagination.

I must have answered him impolitely, without thinking, because the next thing I knew, *he* was furious. He walked over to the hose I'd been using, picked it up, dragged it to the car, leaned it on the top of the open window, shoved it inside the car, and pointed it directly at me. The water was still running and a high pressure geyser roared through the car, soaking me, the upholstery, the dashboard, the steering wheel—and I guess a little of my father, too.

I was humiliated, mortified, furious, and most of all, vengeful. I'd get even, I thought. Just wait. I'd get even.

And that night, I tried, in one of the silliest ways possible. Out of a clear blue sky, at the dinner table, I said, "Fuck." Just "Fuck." No logical reason. No connection with the conversation. Just "Fuck," because I knew it would make my father as furious as I'd been this morning.

And it did. He ignited. He leaped up from the table and slapped me across the face, as hard as he could. It stung like hell, but I gulped back my real reaction and said, "I didn't feel anything."

This seemed to infuriate him even more, and he slapped me even harder. Nine times he struck me, before he finally stopped, and stormed from the room. My face felt as if it had been raked with a steel comb. My mother was in tears, the dinner had been devastated. The swollen imprint of my father's hand remained on my cheek for many hours. I'd learned, for the first but not the last time, the price of fighting back.

What waste we lay to relationships when we're young and careless. There was so much I didn't know in those days, and so much I misinterpreted. I didn't know that love from a parent—or from anyone else, for that matter—chooses its own way of expression. I see now that my father was expressing his love to me in the only way he knew, by being strong and trying to teach me to be the same. By giving me standards. By trying to teach me to be independent. That was his way.

But I saw none of the love behind the actions. Like most adolescents, I was more concerned about the effect he was having on me than what he was doing. My shame over our lack of money must have hurt him, terribly. But he didn't let on, and I kept on giving vent to my shame, not understanding that my father was wealthy in ways that a boy my age couldn't see. He had respect; he had distinction. He was a sensitive and great artist. My mother and all of the adults treated him that way, and he reacted warmly to it.

But in the thirties in Karinoke and New York, my mother would be the only one who seemed to take the time to listen to *my* adolescent problems, and to fill *my* enormous need for love and affection and praise.

So, I turned to her and others for support for my fragile, adolescent ego, and I was lucky. One of my friends in New York was Martin Poll. Today, Marty's a successful movie producer. But in those days, his chief connection with show business was through his Aunt Selma Tamber, who was the professional manager of Chappell Music Company, the biggest music publisher in the world.

One Saturday that fall, Marty called me up at our New York apartment. "Would you like to go to the theater today and see a musical?" he asked.

"What's a musical?" I countered. I honestly didn't know.

"It's a play with songs," he answered. "My aunt Selma has tickets."

I thought a minute. "How much?" I asked.

"Nothing. She'll give us the tickets."

"Great," I said, and we were off, downtown, to Radio City, where Chappell's and Marty's Aunt Selma were located. She was a gray-haired, businesslike woman, whose severe exterior disguised a vast interior of kindness and gentleness. She had eyes and attention for no one but Marty and me when we walked into her office that day.

"See that man over there?" she whispered, as she handed us two balcony tickets to *On Your Toes*. There was a small, stooped man, shorter than we were, with thin hair and a neutral expression on his face, leafing through some music sheets in the next office. "That's Lorenz Hart," she said, and Marty nodded appreciatively.

"Who's Lorenz Hart?" I asked my friend as we took the elevator down to the street.

"He's the lyricist of the show we're gonna see," he answered, as we hit the sidewalk and headed for Roth's Bar and Grill at 49th Street and 7th Avenue.

"What's a lyricist?" I asked him.

"A man who writes the words to the songs," Marty explained, as we walked into the bar and grill for a hot pastrami sandwich, a bowl of baked beans and a lot of free pickles, all for thirty-five cents.

So, I saw my first musical, at the Imperial Theatre, and it not only had lyrics by Lorenz Hart, but music by Richard Rodgers—with whom I'd eventually work—and book and direction by the man who would, eighteen years later, have a monumental amount to do with the launching of my theatrical career: George Abbott.

That day, I was hooked. From then on, almost every Saturday, Marty and I would take the subway downtown, for a nickle apiece, pick up two free balcony tickets, stop by Roth's Bar and Grill for a sandwich and free pickles, and see a show.

I don't remember all of them. I do remember being excited beyond belief by everything the Group Theatre did, including *Johnny Johnson,* with music by Kurt Weill and lyrics by Paul Green; and Clifford Odets' *Golden Boy,* with John Garfield, Elia Kazan, Luther Adler, and a gorgeous actress named Frances Farmer, with whom I of course fell immediately in love.

All of these people, with the exception of (alas) Frances Farmer and Kurt Weill, would play very large roles in my life, and when I look back on those last days of my adolescence, I marvel at how destiny interwove their lives with mine at the precise moment I needed a direction and an abiding purpose. Nothing at that moment attracted, or intrigued, or consumed me as much as the theatre.

—Except, perhaps, Karinoke, for it was in the hills of the Adirondacks surrounding that Place of the Beautiful Song that I finally experienced my only moments of boyhood closeness with my father. Not in the music colony itself, when he was absorbed in his music and his students. And not at Lake Placid High School, during the years my parents decided to stay until October. I attended classes there, and once, my father was invited to give a recital at an assembly. I was, true to form, embarrassed beyond belief, beyond good taste. I knew, I just knew my father would embarrass me by saying something, so I slunk down in my seat as far as I could, trying to make myself invisible.

And he did.

After his first selection, he stepped to the edge of the stage, pointed at me and said, "That's my son, Richard. He's embarrassed because I'm playing a concert here, and he doesn't like my being a musician, instead of a baseball player."

It charmed the audience and mortified me. I should have been touched. Instead, I thought I'd die.

But in one magical place, in the hills above Karinoke, it was different, for my father, and for me, and for us together. I spent my happiest, most exhilarating, most joyful moments on Mt. Marcy, and Whiteface. When I was eight, I'd climbed Whiteface, with my Uncle Ben and Al Miller, who was a handyman around the place. It had made me, for a long time, the youngest person ever to climb that mountain.

So, when the world and my relationship to my father began to weigh too heavily on my shoulders, I'd take off, and hike into the mountains, who were my closest, most loyal friends, the companions who never ignored me, or fought me, or talked back.

But—and I never questioned this ambivalence, nor realized it, until much later in my life—it was here, too, in the mountains, that I felt *closest* to my father. On early, very early mornings in the summer, we'd take walks together, on Averyville Road, above Karinoke. My father liked to take his constitutional in his pajamas and his bathrobe, the robe open and streaming like a silk flag behind him, a cigar clamped in his teeth and protruding forward belligerently, so that he reminded his musician friends of a pajama-clad Brahms. He was a short man, only about five feet six or seven, but he walked very fast, and, until I was fifteen or so, I had to run to keep up with him. It would take many years and scores of walks before I would finally be able to first equal and then pass his pace.

What was important in those last days of my adolescence was the time and the place we were sharing, both of which were particularly precious to me. There was the profound and lonely character of the mountains that I would return to, again and again, for the rest of my life. And most significant of all, there was the fact that I had a chance, in their quiet eloquence, to share them with a man I loved more than I would dare admit.

So, time and growing up passed—even though I figured they never would—and the moment came to leave one set of conflicts and fulfill-ments and meet another.

Some boys agonize for months over the right college. I made up my mind overnight, after a fateful trip to the library. The book I picked up was Thomas Wolfe's *Look Homeward, Angel.*

It seemed like a good story to me. Hefty, but good, and I threw myself on the bed in my bedroom one afternoon when I was sixteen to read it.

Dinnertime came, and my mother called me. I was so captured, so enraptured, so completely lost in the book, I mumbled, "I'm not eating."

My mother never questioned my motives, only my actions. "What are you, sick?" she asked.

"No," I answered. "There's just some reading I have to do."

And that was exactly what it was. I *had* to read that book, at that moment, in that state of mind. It was probably one of the pivotal experiences of my life. It was certainly one of the most far-reaching, for at six o'clock the next morning, when I finally finished the last of the 864 pages of *Look Homeward, Angel,* I knew that the only college I could attend would be Thomas Wolfe's alma mater, the University of North Carolina at Chapel Hill. I was Eugene Gant. I was Thomas Wolfe. I was obsessed.

But what a glorious obsession! I finally, over my mother and father's mild protestations, applied to and was accepted by the University of North Carolina (I'd also been accepted by Cornell, the University of Chicago, and the University of Pennsylvania, all of which I'd summarily turned down).

Once accepted, I dreamed almost nightly of being there, and one dream became so vivid, so tangible, I came to believe, in later years, that it really happened, and told it as if it had.

In the dream, I was a freshman at the University of North Carolina at Chapel Hill. One fall afternoon, shortly after I arrived, I decided that I had to visit Asheville, Thomas Wolfe's hometown and the setting of *Look Homeward, Angel.*

In the dream, I hitchhiked there. It took me thirteen hours, and it was early evening when I reached this lovely Southern city, high up in the Great Smoky Mountains. I wasn't hungry; I wasn't tired; I was determined to pursue a ghost. I went straight to the Old Kentucky Home—called Dixieland in *Look Homeward, Angel.* The door opened, and there stood Eliza Gant, Mrs. Wolfe, Thomas Wolfe's mother. I was eighteen, I was in paradise, and I was scared to death.

Moments that seemed like eternity passed, and then I finally stammered, "I've hitchhiked all the way from Chapel Hill, to talk to you about your son, who changed my life. I read *Look Homeward, Angel* a couple of years ago, and all I wanted to do was to come to the University of North Carolina and do everything he did. May I come in, Mrs. Wolfe?"

She looked levelly at me for a minute, and then she invited me in.

And there I was, in the middle of the reality of the fiction.

We had a cup of coffee, and we talked about her son and the profound effect he had had on me. And then, Tom's older sister came over, and we talked some more.

I was invited to stay overnight, and I slept in the bed in which Tom's brother Ben had died, behind the unfound door, beneath the leaf, near the forgotten faces. "O lost, and by the wind grieved ghost, come back again," I whispered to the darkness. And he did, gently and purposefully, sliding me into sleep. When I woke within the dream, I felt reassured, reborn. I was determined to go back to Chapel Hill, an eighteen-year-old freshman, and follow in Thomas Wolfe's footsteps. All the way to fame. But not, if I could help it, to an early death.

Chapel Hill in actuality was no disappointment; it was the college town of my imagination made tangible. There were two movie theatres, some clothing stores, a dry cleaners, some greasy spoons—among them The Greek's, where, for twenty-five cents, you could warm your interior on a winter's morning with a heaping order of eggs and Smithfield ham—and Harry's Coffee Shop, and Danziger's Vienna Coffee Shop, whose owners later became landlords for Eddie Straus and me.

South of Franklin Street, the main street of the town, lay the campus. A quadrangle, defined by enormous, flowing trees that were probably there before the country was founded, dominated and defined it. Its walks were unpaved Catawban clay paths that strung together the classrooms, dormitories, and administration buildings. Various, eclectically designed structures bordered this quadrangle immediately; among them, the student union, Graham Memorial, where I would occupy an office as editor of the literary magazine and where I would host a very important reception in my sophomore year; and Battle Vance and Pettigrew, the ancient dormitory in which I would spend my senior year.

In the midst of the quad stood the most venerable campus landmark of all, The Old Well, a small and stately gazebo that housed a fountain and a working well.

Cameron Street bisected the campus, and on one side of it was South Building, which was the Main Administration Building; south of that was Wilson Library; across Route 54, or Raleigh Road, was the source of many of my audible memories of campus life, the Bell Tower, a huge brick structure filled with bells that chimed out a plenitude of melody and information: joy after a football victory, liberation for vacation, and the hours for those of us dashing desperately for classes. Beyond that was Kenan Stadium, in the heart of a woodland, and to the left of it, in an orderly row, a track, a playing field, Woolen Gymnasium, a swimming pool complex, and "The Tin Can," a huge Quonset hut that served both as the women's gymnasium and the site of our fanciest dances, the ones in which the girls would become floating clouds of crinoline, and the males would spiff themselves up proudly in white tie and tails.

I plunged into the life of Chapel Hill as if I'd been directed there by some other force—which, I see now, I must have been. Why, for instance, would the manager of Everett dorm, my freshman living quarters, be Terry Sanford, the future governor of North Carolina, and for fourteen years, president of Duke University, and, after his retirement from Duke, the freshman United States Senator from North Carolina? Why would one of my very first freshman buddies be Lou Harris, the future pollster? And why would I meet Meg McKay at the beginning of my sophomore year?

Meg was a very soft, very lithe, very poetic looking lady, and she was older than I, which suited my Thomas Wolfe syndrome perfectly. She was worldly, a lissome twenty-two to my untutored and bony eighteen—and three and a half minutes after I met her, I was once again deeply and irretrievably in love. She was, after all, an older woman, and sensitive and well-read, and, like Wolfe's mistress, Aline Bernstein, of and in the theatre. Well, a person majoring in theatre was a person *in* the theatre to me, in those fervent, imaginative, and romantic years.

Meg McKay gave me love and understanding, which I probably needed more than her body, which she steadfastly refused to give me—"all the way," that is. It didn't matter. I was madly, adolescently, idealistically in love, enough so that I went with her, one afternoon, to her graduate playwrighting class.

The class was taught by the famous playwright Paul Green, who had won a Pulitzer Prize in 1927 for his play *In Abraham's Bosom,* and who had written *Johnny Johnson,* one of the Group Theatre's plays I'd seen on a Saturday matinee with Marty Poll. I'd remembered the feverish poetry of the lyrics to the Kurt Weill music, and I could barely contain myself as I took a seat at the back of his classroom.

He was a handsome, well-built man with a shock of curly black hair, salted with gray. His face was craggy. His eyes crinkled repeatedly into an omnipresent smile. A few afternoons in his class, and I became aware that he was a loving, benevolent, strong man, who never raised his voice or his opinions without a reason. And then, he did it as a homespun philosopher, a brilliant, articulate farmer, who was as at home in Eastern philosophy as he was hunting possum among the 'simmon trees behind his plantationlike home in Greenwood. A year later, he took me hunting one midnight, to flush the possums from the trees, to experience the dark wonder of the nature that spread in green waves around and beyond the campus.

His graduate classes discussed and demonstrated the dialectics of playwrighting. Scenes or acts of plays in progress written by the students were read and dissected, brilliantly.

I couldn't get enough of these classes. In the same way that I had been hooked in those theatre matinees with Marty Poll, I was captured by everything that happened in Paul Green's playwrighting classes.

I kept coming back, first, because of Meg McKay, and then, because of Paul Green. I was a sophomore, auditing a graduate class, and I had Meg to thank for that. But I would forever thank Paul Green for first inspiring me into thinking that I might write for the theatre.

In my junior year, fired up by this extraordinary man and his ideas of theatre, I took an undergraduate playwrighting class and wrote my first play, which I titled *The Black Damp*. It was a fierce, dark, sincere, and simpleminded melodrama about coalminers being ravaged by both their boss (an allegorical equivalent of Hitler, named Heller) and the black lung disease of the title.

It was an important work to me. It resonated with my ideas and my indignations. And unfortunately, it also proved that I could never be a serious playwright.

It didn't matter. I was still obsessed by the theatre. A year before, I'd joined the Playmakers, founded by Frederick H. "Proff" Koch, the man who invented folk theatre. My acting career was short and undistinguished, but it was one more block set in place at Chapel Hill in the foundation of theatre that I was building in my young life.

My sophomore year was full of major events. All during my freshman year, I'd read the *Daily Tarheel*, the campus newspaper, as religiously as any student. And my dissatisfaction with its coverage of the theatre—in fact, of the arts in general, was boundless. Here, I thought, we had people like Paul Green on campus, and the *Tarheel* was devoting most of its space to sports. Not that I had anything against sports, but the arts deserved more than the two lousy lines they got on the back page.

So, I devised a plan to rectify the problem. My idea was to form The

Carolina Workshop, designed to integrate the creative arts and promote and project them more adequately to the student body. I'd start by inviting a famous person in the arts to the campus, someone who would be both popular and prestigious enough to draw attention.

I presented my case to The Grail, a UNC honorary society. They liked it and gave me fifty dollars to establish it. I was bowled over. Fifty dollars in 1940 was enough for a college student to eat on for ten weeks.

I went back to my rooming house and composed a letter to the then greatest living American poet, the laureate Robert Frost. I asked him if he would recite his poems for the students of UNC. I offered him the fifty dollars The Grail had given me.

Three weeks later, I got an answer, in longhand, saying in essence, Yes, he would be happy to come to Chapel Hill on October 23 to recite his poems, but he couldn't accept the offer of the fifty dollar honorarium.

I dashed around, lining up his accommodations, reserving Hill Music Hall, which had an eight-hundred-seat auditorium, getting posters printed, putting stories in the local papers.

On the afternoon of October 23, 1940, Robert Frost arrived—this simple, portly, white-haired, gentle, and gigantic man. Paul Green knew him, and, with some of the other faculty members, I was eased through the first greetings.

But the introduction of Robert Frost to the student body, which had crammed Hill Music Hall to overflowing that night, was left to me. It was not one of my happier moments. Here I was, a stringy kid of nineteen, brash enough to plan something like this, but frightened out of my wits as I trudged tentatively up to the podium to introduce the great poet.

I opened my mouth. Nothing came out. I was frozen with fear. I couldn't see my notes and I couldn't extemporize. What would I do?

Moments seemed like centuries. I swallowed, and began again. And again. And again. And again: Air. On the fifth try, words finally came.

The rest of the evening was a gigantic success. For two hours, Frost held his audience captive. Simply, directly, movingly, with impeccable phrasing, he spun a web of words that snared everyone in that room. And at that moment, realizing the effect that his adroit phrasing had upon the reading of his poetry, I closed a link in my mind. New York came back to me, and my father's words through the wall of my bedroom. His relentless emphasis, his constant teaching of the phrasing of certain musical passages came back to me with a jolt. It was a direct parallel. It meant so much. Phrasing was all, in the reading of poetry, and the performance of music.

Later on, we had a reception, with punch and cookies, in the lounge of the student union in Graham Memorial. It was just as packed as the reading, just as overwhelming, just as stimulating. I hovered around the fringes of the masses of people who hovered around Robert Frost.

Sometime near midnight, when this triumphant evening finally ended, I handed Frost my copy of *This Generation,* a compendium of English and American Literature in the twentieth century. I opened the book to his lovely poem "To Earthward," with its words that, at that intense, romantic moment in my life, meant more to me than a promise of success:

> *. . . I craved strong sweets, but those*
> *Seemed strong when I was young;*
> *The petal of the rose*
> *It was that stung.*
>
> *Now no joy but lacks salt*
> *That is not dashed with pain*
> *And weariness and fault;*
> *I crave the stain*
>
> *Of tears, the aftermark*
> *Of almost too much love . . .*

I asked him to inscribe something to me above the poem. He did, and although the book was stolen during the war, I treasure the memory as much as the happening that magical night.

Decades later, a national magazine stated that The Carolina Workshop had been the first venture of its kind in the South.

At the end of that fateful year, my short but heady relationship with Meg McKay came to a sad and quiet close.

The previous winter, I'd brought her to New York for a weekend. My parents couldn't have been nicer; Meg and I went to see *Citizen Kane* and we loved it and talked about it with high and shared excitement.

But there was something wrong. Out of the context of Chapel Hill, beyond the bubble of that special, circumscribed place, things just weren't the same. There was an edge of uncomfortableness that I could neither cure nor deny.

Still, back at Chapel Hill, this diminished, and that spring, we decided to spend the summer between my sophomore and junior years together. At the end of June, we presented ourselves at the door of her parents' sumptuous home in Beverly, Massachusetts.

And now, our dreams froze under the unremitting, analytical gaze of Meg's father, who seemed to have all the warmth of an Alaskan tundra, and all the conversational graces of a statue. Well, come to think of it, why not? Here was his daughter, a lovely, promising twenty-three-year-old beauty. And her choice for a companion was a scrawny, unemployed, badly clothed, nineteen-year-old Jew from New York.

Three days later, frozen out of the McKay household, I moved into the Boston YMCA, which was near Symphony Hall, and searched the help wanted ads for a summer job. I found one, as a runner on the *Boston Globe*. But I was unhappy. And it wasn't long before my unhappiness deepened to misery. My pride had been more than damaged, it had been nearly demolished.

And besides, Meg in Boston was more like Meg in New York than Meg in Chapel Hill. The premonitions I'd had the previous winter became facts of life. Within a week, a very noticeable gap had begun to form between us. It soon widened to a chasm. It was obvious that what we had was over, and no amount of dreaming or wishing was going to restore it.

So, I packed up what few clothes I had, and hitchhiked to Lake Placid, and Karinoke, and my parents. I was happy to be home, happy to be warm again. My parents were surprised to see me; I'd told them I'd be gone for the entire summer. But they weren't surprised at the outcome of my romance with Meg McKay. It was something they accepted with the kind of relief that proved they'd seen it coming all along. They'd known that the relationship was only an interim booking.

I never saw Meg McKay again. Years and years later, when *The Pajama Game* was in Boston on its way to its New York opening, I got a phone call from her. She was married and had children and was living in Boston, and was happy. And so was I, for her.

Now, looking back on that summer and the one that followed, I realize something that neither my parents nor I surmised then: Probably, even if Meg's father hadn't been so protective and so uncivil to me, I wouldn't have lasted the summer in Boston. I wasn't nearly ready to live away from home. I really wasn't ready for anything more than another "go" at college.

The following summer, Howard Richardson and Bill Berney would offer me the opportunity to work in a summer stock theatre in Maine. Howard and Bill were to collaborate, in 1945, on the hugely successful and moving folk play, *Dark of the Moon*. Howard had directed me, in my freshman year, in a one-act play by Connie Smith called *Banked Fires*. Now, he wanted to give me a beautiful opportunity to increase my knowledge of and my experience in the theatre. But I would turn him down in favor of Karinoke, which was more than a beautiful place. It was my last barricade against growing up.

The winter of my junior year, spurred on by the success of the first venture of The Carolina Workshop, I put together a five-day Festival of the Arts. This time, there were plays written and directed and performed by students; a concert with music written and performed by them; a ballet; student painting, sculpture, and photography exhibits; and the festival's main event, a panel of honored guests from the arts. I had no money to offer anyone, so I decided to stay close to home. Paul Green agreed to appear on the panel, and so did James Boyd, a historical novelist who wrote *Drums* and who lived in Pinehurst, not very far from Chapel Hill. I talked Claire Leighton, a fabulous English woodcut artist who lived in Chapel Hill, into participating, and—laying my embarrassments over his profession finally to rest—I invited my father and his friend, stage designer Lee Simonson, who was one of the three founders of the Theatre Guild, to come to Chapel Hill and round out the panel.

The festival—and most certainly the highlight panel—was a major success. My father talked intelligently, persuasively, and probingly. I felt an unaccustomed flush of pride.

I'd picked the panel's topic: *The Artist in Wartime*. It was 1941, and the war was coming to our campus as certainly as it was to every other campus. It was something you talked about intensely and incessantly, late at night, in bull sessions—but only as an insinuation, something that was dangerous but distant.

And that was its location for a while. And then, late one December afternoon of that same junior year, the distance collapsed.

I'd spent the day with a married friend of mine, Barry Farnol. He was a real, functioning playwright, and that particular, crystalline afternoon, we took an inordinate amount of time talking and wandering through the tobacco fields of Chapel Hill. It was an intense point in both of our lives, when every thought was new and untried, and we loved turning these thoughts over in our minds like fine jewels, inspecting them for flaws—accepting them, rejecting them, testing them against other thoughts, but most importantly of all, experiencing them.

After a few hours of this, Barry asked me to come back to his place for a bite of lunch. His wife was in New York for the weekend, and we figured we'd settle in for an afternoon of shmoozing and music.

While he fixed lunch in the kitchen, I turned on the radio in the living room.

And in one split second, my world came apart. Comfort was gone, the clear vision of a foreseeable future was gone, the simple certainty of our youth was gone. Pearl Harbor had been bombed.

The next day, I did what thousands of kids my age did the Monday after. I skipped classes and took the train to New York to enlist.

I walked into the Navy recruiting office at 100 Centre Street, ready to fight for my country and, hopefully, to be able to finish my education. There was, I knew, the V-7 program, that allowed you to graduate, and then become an apprentice seaman for thirty days. If you passed that training, you became a midshipman for ninety days—a ninety-day wonder, who completed three years of education as an ensign in three months. That was for me.

But I apparently wasn't for the Navy. I was turned down. For a "marked malaclusion," which means, in dental lingo, an overbite.

I was furious. I turned to the recruiting officer, and snarled at him, "What do you expect me to have to do—*bite* the Japs?"

He wasn't amused, and I figured that Navy recruiters elsewhere might be better able to recognize a good man when they saw one.

But again, I was turned down; this time in Raleigh, and for the same reason.

It couldn't be possible, I thought. Maybe they were lying to me. Maybe their Jewish quota was filled. Maybe I just wasn't presenting myself the right way.

I got on a train to Richmond, Virginia, and marched into the recruiting office, impersonating a confident man.

To my amazement, I was examined and welcomed with open arms into the Navy's V-7 Program, without any crap about an overbite.

So, I went back to Chapel Hill, and, true to my plan to follow in Thomas Wolfe's footsteps, became editor of the literary magazine, *The Carolina Mag.*

I divided my first edition (which was to celebrate the magazine's centennial) into three sections: Pre–Civil War; Post–Civil War; World War I to the Present. In the last section, I printed a one-act play called *The Return of Buck Gavin.* It was undoubtedly the worst play I have ever read. It made no sense; it was clumsy; the language was awful; there was nothing that was good about it. But nevertheless, I printed verbatim, this play written by Thomas Wolfe when he was eighteen, at UNC.

Heading it, in a boldface box, I wrote the following emprecation: "Future writers of the world, read *this* and take heart!"

My junior year was a busy and happy one. I was tapped into the Golden Fleece, the highest honor in the University—an honor my son Christopher would also achieve, thirty-three years later.

And on June 2, 1943, my senior year came to an end. I graduated, while my parents looked on, my mother expressing everything, her eyes full of tears, and my father wrapped tightly in a quiet, enigmatic silence. When it was over, my mother embraced me and told me how proud she was, and how thin I looked and how now she was going to fatten me up as soon as I got home.

My father pressed my hand, strongly and briefly. Our eyes met and then darted away. I think both of us wanted to throw our arms around each other. But it wasn't time. Not yet.

I took one last look around the campus. But I knew I'd already left, the moment I'd walked out of Paul Green's study the night before graduation. He'd talked to me, in his quiet, understated way, for perhaps half an hour that night, and then, we'd both risen, and looked at each other for a long moment. He'd extended his hand, and gripped mine strongly. "Richard," he'd said, as he opened the door of his study for me for the last time, "don't ever let them kick the enthusiasm out of you."

After the ceremony, my parents and I packed up my belongings, four years of bits and pieces of my growing up. We took the train, the long, musical ride that Thomas Wolfe had described so lyrically in *Of Time and the River.* Emerging from my Wolfe's lair, I was leaving behind that romantic way of experiencing the world—not forever, mind you, but in that certain way and in that great abundance that only youth can survive.

We took a taxi from Penn Station to the apartment. It smelled like the past, like home. It was good to be back, among familiar furniture in familiar rooms.

I picked up the mail from the hall table. And there, sitting on top of the pile, like a harbinger, was a large manila envelope that said, in big, heavy letters: U.S. NAVY. I tore open the envelope and read my orders, commanding me to report for active duty in Chicago in seventeen days.

College was over. Thomas Wolfe had never written about, nor ever dreamed of becoming a midshipman.

ठ.

" A D L E R ! Stow your gear along the port bulkhead and bear a hand!"

I was in Abbott Hall, on the campus of Northwestern University, at 730 Lakeshore Drive in Chicago. That part of the university was all Navy now. And ten seconds after I'd arrived, so was I. Obeying the CPO's orders, I placed my suitcase along the lefthand wall, and went to work. Oh, did I go to work. We all did, in those days and nights at the height of World War II.

My dorm room in Abbott Hall housed three men, three beds, three bureaus, and three desks. And when we weren't in class, we were at these desks, studying as hard as we could, fighting to stay in the program. It was tough; it was grueling; every day, somebody we knew flunked out, which drove us on to study even harder.

"The smoking lamp is out!" a military voice would crow over the miniature loudspeakers in the hallways every night at 9:30. And the lights went out. But with me, the studying went on. I lined the closet with my sheets, so the light wouldn't show under the door.

Midshipman Adler was deadly serious. He wanted those ensign epaulets badly. A perfect score in a subject was a 4.0. If your average was 3.0, you didn't have to take final exams. I made *exactly* 3.0 in every one of my subjects. Not 3.1. Not 2.9. But exactly 3.0, on the nose—the way I'd written that composition of precisely 100 words when I was in the second grade.

This time, the reward was sweet and instantaneous: Those of us with 3.0 averages were liberated every night at 6:00 P.M. We'd dress up in our midshipman blues and head out on the town at 6:01. But not before we'd stop off to whistle at the poor bastards who hadn't made it, and were confined to the P Room. Navy Lingo is funny. The P Room is where you study and the Head is where you pee.

I played hard in those days. My philosophy was plain, live for today, and live completely, because who knew if tomorrow was even going to arrive? Of course, you have to be young to be able to abuse your body that way. And I was young, and resilient, and maniacal about having fun.

In the neighborhood, there were these two bars, one called Rickett's and the other Madame Galli. They catered chiefly to midshipmen. And what deals they gave us: During Happy Hour, from 5:30 to 7:00 every night, midshipmen could have all the beer they could drink, and all the shrimp they could eat—for nothing.

We had the run of the city. Midshipmen were automatic members of the exclusive Chicago Yacht Club, and could use the clubhouse at any time; we could ride free on any public conveyance. We were Navy and this was war, and everybody liked us for who we were and what we were doing.

As the day of our graduation neared, we ninety-day wonders had to roll up our sleeves. The course intensified. Our heads were stuffed full of Navy knowledge, and our bodies were tight and strong. I took to the physical regimen with vengeance and joy. I loved it, as I do to this day. Push-ups, sit-ups, running the obstacle course—I lapped it up. I did it all with ease.

But there was one goal I couldn't seem to reach, and for all my 3.0 average and my enthusiasm and my mastery of everything the cadre threw at us, I shuddered every time I was assigned to one corner of the Northwestern gym.

There, hanging from the ceiling, eighteen feet over our heads, was a series of ropes, positioned like an enormous bead curtain. At the sound of a whistle, squads of us would be ordered to climb the rope to the very top without using our feet, slap the ceiling, and come down.

Some of my buddies shimmied up like monkeys. A few others slogged skyward, puffing like steam turbines, but they made it.

I couldn't. I'd grab the rope, placing one hand over another, pulling myself toward the top. I'd get halfway up—and suddenly, my arms would give out. I'd push, pull, strain, and get to within three feet of the ceiling. And then, all my strength would leave me. I'd be totally helpless. I'd urge myself on, grit my teeth, curse at myself, but my arms just wouldn't respond, and I'd have to wrap my feet around the rope to keep my hands from getting burned, and slide back down.

"What's the matter, Adler, don't you like our rope?" the Battalion Commander would shout at me when I took myself, trembling, off the bottom of it. "You wanta be Navy—or not?"

Of course I did, more than anything in the world. But my arms just wouldn't obey my mind.

The time grew shorter, and my determination grew deeper. Every morning now, I'd psyche myself, tell myself that this was the day. And every day, three feet from the ceiling of the gym, my arms would turn to jelly.

Finally, a week before graduation, I decided it was now or never.

And so, that morning, determined not to fail and be left behind as an enlisted man, I didn't look right or left or up. I said a small prayer, closed my eyes, and grabbed the rope as if it were my worst enemy's neck. And then everything faded to black. I don't remember anything at all until, with a giant yelp of joy, I slapped the ceiling, and finished my training.

On the morning of October 28, 1943, a proud bunch of midshipmen marched from 730 Lakeshore Drive to Navy Pier on Lake Michigan. We marched in, platoon by platoon, as midshipmen. We walked out with that big gold stripe as ensigns.

Life seemed to be accelerating. We'd be in it, now, in no time. We were all given one week passes. I spent four days with my parents in New York, and then left, on the Silver Meteor, for my assignment in Norfolk, Virginia, the headquarters of the First Fleet. I planned to take this crack train to Raleigh, stop off at Chapel Hill, see my old buddies for a day, catch another train in Raleigh, and arrive in Norfolk in time to pick up my orders for my first duty assignment as a Naval officer.

Shortly before we were to leave from Penn Station, I settled into my eleven dollar reserved coach seat, wondering what new adventure waited for me. The adventure turned out to be petite and beautifully put together. She took the seat next to me, and we struck up an immediate conversation, which led to a couple of drinks in the club car. She was on her way to Columbia, South Carolina, she told me over the second whiskey sour, to spend some time with her husband, a colonel in the Army Air Corps who had just returned from heavy fighting in Africa. She hadn't seen him in fifteen months, and she missed him a lot. So she said.

I was on my way to Raleigh, I told her, so we'd be keeping each other company for a while. We struck it off well; we laughed a lot and made a few other friends in the club car, which was crowded and convivial, full of servicemen headed to embarkation ports, and young women, like my coach companion, on their way to spend some time with other servicemen before they left for overseas.

We went back to our seats. It was nearly midnight, and someplace near Baltimore, they turned out the lights in the car. We held hands, and then we began to kiss. It seemed as natural as saying hello, and by the time we got to Washington, we'd decided to get off the train and take an overnight detour to a hotel.

The next morning, we bid each other an affectionate farewell, two travelers with happy memories. She went on to her husband in Columbia, and I went on to Chapel Hill, where I dropped in on some old classmates and professors. I'd been away from UNC long enough to miss it and not long enough to feel the distance of time and events. Still, I was happy that it was only a two-day visit. As close as I felt to Chapel Hill and the people there, it was the past. And I was anxious to see what the Navy had in store for my present and my future.

My orders were waiting for me at Norfolk. I was to report to the USS *Fayette, APA46,* for transport to Cristobal, in Panama, on the Atlantic side of the Canal Zone. The ship was packed with five thousand marines, headed for the Pacific Theatre of War. We all had good, rowdy times aboard, punctuated by long, poker-playing nights. I'd learned to play poker from watching my father in his regular Saturday night games in the dining room of our apartment on Riverside Drive. He was a reckless, emotional poker player, who rarely won. Still, he'd sit down regularly with heavyweights like Sam "Roxy" Rothafel, the founder of both the Radio City Music Hall and its competition, the Roxy Theatre; Leon Leonidoff, the producer of the stage shows at the Music Hall; and Erno Rapee, the conductor of the Music Hall orchestra. And practically every time, he'd lose his shirt.

When Roxy died, I think his widow must have been thinking of all the money her departed husband had won from my father when she called him and said, "Listen. There are some very lovely things here that Roxy left, and I'm sure he'd want you to have them, to give away or keep, or whatever."

My father said, "Fine." The next day, the doorbell rang, and there stood Roxy's chauffeur, supervising the delivery of 250 tuxedos. For the next two weeks, my father feverishly gave away tuxedos to every delivery boy who came to the door, and every elevator man and doorman in the neighborhood.

Near midnight of the sixth night at sea, we were routed out of our bunks by a call to general quarters, and ordered to don lifejackets. We'd almost reached the Canal Zone, and we were completely blacked out, as was all shipping.

We were lined up on deck. It was immensely still, relentlessly dark. Suddenly, a brilliant orange flash burst like a grim surprise on the horizon. Before the roar of it reached us, another flash erupted, closer. Then a third, and a fourth. We were in the middle of a wolf pack of German U-boats, torpedoing ships on either side of us.

I don't remember being frightened, only awestruck. The war had abruptly become tangible and dangerous to me, and yet it seemed as if I were merely a spectator.

We docked safely, shortly after midnight, at Cristobal, and I said goodbye to my poker-playing buddies. Every single one of them would die, needlessly, in the landing at Tarawa two weeks later. The Navy would miscalculate tide information, and send their landing craft in at low, instead of high tide. The boats would run up on reefs and become sitting targets for Japanese machine guns. The news would hit me in my gut. I mourned for them. But like everyone in any war, I was also, secretly and guiltily relieved that it had happened to someone else, someplace else. Nothing tests your morality more often and more thoroughly than being in danger during a war.

At Cristobal, I presented my orders to the officer in charge and was sent on to Balboa, on the Pacific side of the Canal. The narrow gauge railroad ride was a constantly astonishing one. Tourists would pay a bundle for this, I thought, as I rattled my leisurely, scenic way to Balboa, where I would be stationed for a while as a duty officer, billeted at the Submarine Officers' Mess.

It was a cushy job, and I made friends fast. We were a close crew of officers—Commander Jake Tallman; Lieutenant Fred Berdan (who could be mean, and hound you if he didn't like you, and so was nicknamed "birddog"); and an older communications officer, Lieutenant Woodland, who was called "Troopship." They were all Naval Reserve officers, but they knew their way around. I was the youngest officer there, and I learned early to respect these men. We all got along well.

But my tour ashore was shortlived. Within a month, my orders for sea duty arrived. I was assigned to the *YP285*, an ancient hulk of a converted tuna boat that maintained a watch patrol along an imaginary line in the Pacific between Cape Mala and Pines Bay—which was affectionately labeled penis bay.

Our job was to challenge, with signals, all incoming vessels. It was important to safeguard the Canal at all costs; I'd already been made dramatically aware of the presence of the enemy.

The *YP285* was certainly no sleek siren of the seas. Every square inch of her was used for communications equipment and some armament. And that left no room for amenities. There wasn't even a head aboard. If you had to go, you hung your rear end off the fantail. If the weather was bad, and the sea was high, your bottom got a free bath.

And the sea *was* high, much of the time, which meant that I spent most of my off-duty hours below decks, in my bunk. My first week aboard the *YP285* proved to me that I could get seasick at the drop of a stern. Most of the time, I felt like dying. When I was at my worst, suffering from the dry heaves, my fellow officers would make my life a little bit worse by dangling greasy pork chops in front of my face. Some fun.

At the end of two three-week tours on the *YP285*, I managed to convince the medical officer that I'd be the most useless ensign in the Navy if I was sent to sea again. I was transferred back to shore duty, back to Balboa, but not to Commander Tallman and my old crew.

Tallman had been transferred, and replaced by a Commander Cruse, whose name should have been Queeg—the demented skipper of the USS *Caine* in Herman Wouk's stoic novel *The Caine Mutiny*. He was a ruddy faced, Jew-baiting psychotic, and he took an instant dislike to me. Within my first day under his command, he had assigned me to polishing brass fixtures and serving every night on the midwatch, from midnight till 8:00 A.M.

The happy family we'd been under Commander Tallman was no more, and so I removed myself as far as I could from base headquarters and my tormenter.

I found an apartment in a posh section of Panama City, as an escape. It cost me more than I could really afford, but I figured it was worth it. Even if I had to live on the base, I could spend my time off there, away from this madman.

For a while, I frequented the Blue Moon joints, the row upon row of bar/nightclubs that gave Panama City its honkytonk character. Sailors were frequently seduced and robbed in these dives by beautiful women from all over the world. But I had an advantage. I spoke Spanish. I'd visit a particular bar, and after the first night, after I'd been approached by one of the girls, I'd be left alone, unless I really wanted a companion.

The other sailors, not knowing the lingo, would meet a girl, sit with her, and watch, dazzled, as she'd order "un trago," every ten or fifteen minutes. It was a dollar shot of what looked like whiskey, but which was really tea or cola. The girl got fifty cents; the house got fifty cents; and the sailor got screwed, but it didn't even tickle.

Not that I was an eternal spectator. I got around a lot in Panama City. First, with an Argentinian woman I met in a Blue Moon joint, and then with some elegant and glamorous women I met through Mosa and Rita Havivi. The Havivis were an older couple, and Middle Eastern Jews. He was a cellist. We met at a party in my neighborhood one night, and he immediately locked in to my musical background, such as it was. From then on, the Havivis saw that I was well fed and introduced me to some of their friends in the American colony. Through them I met Amy Sartain. She was the society editor of the *Panama American,* an English language newspaper; she was beautiful, well educated, articulate, and worldly. She loved making love, but she wanted no emotional involvement, and that suited me fine. She was thirty-four; I was twenty-two; it was a Thomas Wolfe fantasy once again.

Years later, in the 1950s, I got an unexpected telephone call in New York. A lovely, achingly familiar voice flowed from the receiver. "Richard?" it said. "This is Amy Sartain. I'm in New York. I'm married to a sea captain now, but I'd love to see you."

I trembled. All of those magic times in Panama rushed back, and I said of course, and made a date to meet her for lunch at '21.'

I arrived early, full of memories. I waited. And waited. And waited. I searched the face of every beautiful woman who entered '21.' There was an endless parade of them. But no Amy Sartain.

Time passed, and I was about to leave, when I felt a gentle tap on my shoulder.

"Richard?" a familiar voice said, softly. I turned around, and faced a white-haired lady, a quite old, quite dignified, white-haired lady. It was another Thomas Wolfe fantasy come true, but this one had a title that Wolfe's editor had given it: *You Can't Go Home Again.*

I made other friends in Panama City, and ran into a few old ones. I met my former college roommate, Paul Kolton, on Amador Beach. He was in the Army, and stationed in Panama, and married, and we spent a lot of time reminiscing, planning our lives after the war, and just generally raising hell.

And I also became very close friends with Dolly Grey, who worked with the Admiral of the Panama Sea Frontier, Fifteenth District. The Admiral was called the "flag," in Navy parlance, and Dolly was nicknamed "the flag bag."

It was an affectionate title. Everyone who knew Dolly loved her. She was a warm, understanding friend, someone I could laugh with over my sexual adventures and with whom I could share my troubles. One of the troubles I shared with her was my lousy life under Commander Cruse, who seemed to delight in finding more and more brass for me to polish.

"He can't do that," said Dolly, when I told her about it.

"What do you mean?" I countered. "He's my commanding officer. He can do whatever he wants."

"No he can't," she insisted. "You're an officer. He can't order you to polish brass. It's against Navy regs."

And so, a way out of a lousy situation presented itself, without my even asking for it. I knew it was dangerous, going over the head of my commanding officer to the Admiral of the Panama Sea Frontier, but I'd been taking uninterrupted shit from Commander Cruse for six months. I figured he had a little coming back.

The Admiral was livid when he found out about Cruse's orders, and got me transferred immediately to Colombia. I was grateful, but a little sad to leave Panama. I'd made good and lasting friends there, and I'd had some happy times, and some memorable ones.

A week before I was to leave, Paul Kolton and I spent the night at a home owned by a friend of mine on the outskirts of the city. There was an all night party; I'd brought a lady; he hadn't, but it didn't prevent him from having a good time with the rest of the guests.

At six in the morning, he and I slipped away, to report to our duty posts. We opened the front door. And gunfire erupted all around us. Figures dashed across front and back yards.

"Son of a bitch. It's another revolution," said Paul, as he flung me to the ground. "Come on," he said. "We've got to get to work."

So, keeping very low profiles and staying under the paths of the bullets, we crawled on our bellies to his staff car, lifted ourselves into it, started it, and gunned it out of the neighborhood.

A few hours later, I was on a transport, flying to Colombia. My destination was Soledad, a small airfield twelve miles from Barranquilla. There was a Blimp Hedron (Navy for squadron) stationed there, which was charged with reconnaissance work, spotting Nazi U-boats. I was assigned to it, and I looked forward to the change from polishing brass in Panama.

We landed. The door of the plane opened, letting in a rush of stifling, tropical air. It was something I would learn to breathe and live with for a year and a half. Only the Persian Gulf has a hotter climate than Barranquilla. And, if my memory is at all trustworthy, Barranquilla beats the Persian Gulf handily for off-the-gauge, nonstop humidity.

I picked up my gear and started down the ladder to the tarmac. Suddenly, small rifle fire exploded from a tangle of trees bordering the tarmac. "Get down!" shouted the seaman who'd come out to help me.

"What the hell's going on?" I yelled back, as we hit the hot asphalt.

"Revolution," he explained, and we crawled on our bellies toward a nearby hangar. It was all very friendly. Like I'd never left Panama.

My CO was Lieutenant John Temple McGinnis. He was exactly forty years old, from Texas, and struck me at first as a ramrod straight, unforgiving Navy man. He wasn't. He was, on the contrary, a pussycat, who would constantly call me "The Ensign," and who would later became a good friend.

Life in Soledad became very much like it had been in Panama before Commander Cruse. The officers—there were six of us—were a great bunch of cutups, and I was accepted into the inner circle immediately. The Blimp Hedron was immense, and consumed most of the airfield at Soledad. The rest of the space was given over to a squadron of six PBY 5As.

We were billeted in Barranquilla, and my memories of that post are soaked in humidity, heat, and passion.

Temperatures of 130 degrees Fahrenheit weren't uncommon. When you took a shower, you'd start to sweat as soon as you began to towel off. We were issued salt pills, which we took three times a day, to steady the liquid balance in our bodies.

Our belongings were stowed in footlockers by our bunks, and, because of the humidity, each one of these lockers was outfitted with a small light bulb, encased in a metal cage. The light burned night and day. If it didn't, you ended up with a footlocker full of mildew moss.

We slept naked, under mosquito netting, and after a while, the temperature began to mean less and less to me. I slept soundly, with very few cares and hardly any interruptions in those days.

Until one night.

I'd gotten to bed late, after spending a tour of duty with the Shore

Patrol in Barranquilla. It seemed as though I'd just closed my eyes when I was jolted out of a deep sleep. I shot bolt upright in my bed, wide awake and surrounded by raging fire. Men were shouting; dark shadows dashed through the flames; the entire barracks was consumed by an immense cloud of black smoke.

"Fire!" I yelled at a couple of sleeping forms on either side of me, who popped up as if they were on springs.

"Get the hell out of there!" shouted a voice from outside of the Quonset hut. "Get out!"

I didn't need any further orders. I didn't even bother to undo my mosquito netting. I burst through it, and, stark naked, ran as fast as I could through the open door of the hut and out into the night.

Somebody's shirt had fallen onto the light bulb in his footlocker, and caught fire. By the time the fire had finally burnt out, every mosquito net, every blanket, every sheet, every mattress, and every stitch of clothing we owned had been reduced to black, acrid ashes.

It was a hell of a mess, and we shuffled around Soledad in castoff bits and pieces of uniforms for a couple of weeks, until we could reorder and receive our own.

Barranquilla possessed one large, rather luxurious establishment named the Hotel del Prado, and every Saturday night, we'd go there to dance the *porro,* a local variation of the rhumba. It was a civilized, satisfying, fun night out, something like a dance in a hotel courtyard in Fort Worth, Texas. The fact that I spoke the language once more provided me with a high speed highway into the fraternity of native Colombians there.

I enthusiastically gravitated toward the young women, and one night, a gloriously beautiful, eighteen-year-old girl attracted my immediate attention. And devotion. She was one part Caucasian, one part Indian, one part Black; her name was Adelita Losada, and I, as usual, was smitten.

I chased her for months, and she played it very cagey. She made it known to me that she had many boyfriends, and she wasn't about to tie herself to one man.

I turned on every charm I'd learned, and invented some new ones. I pleaded, I cajoled, I demanded, I promised. And finally, after several months of chasing, and false chastity, and frustration, she let me into her bed and her life. And all of a sudden, I had a woman who was absolutely, endlessly—and eventually, oppressively—devoted to me.

Her passion was bottomless, but so was her possessiveness. She cooked for me, waited on me, waited *for* me, and grew angry and tearful when I didn't report for duty in her bedroom. It got to be more of a job than a love affair, and I started to volunteer for more and more nighttime Shore Patrol duty.

The Shore Patrol had plenty to do in Barranquilla. There were a lot of whorehouses, a lot of whores, and a lot of venereal disease. Weekly short-arm inspection on the base always climaxed in a wholesale handing out of sulfa drugs.

I often wondered why it was worth it to so many seamen. The whorehouses weren't pretty places. They were designed for efficiency, and they got the job done. The first floor was usually a bar and a dance hall. Upstairs, there was a series of doorless cubicles, forty little hutches lined up, opposite each other, along a dimly lit hallway. Inside of each cubicle, there was a bed and a washstand and a whore, and from early evening till early the next morning, the girl hardly ever left her bed. When business slowed for a few minutes, and the snaking line of seamen broke, the whores would pack ice into their crotches, to cool down the machinery.

It was a total turnoff to me, and I wouldn't have been caught dead as a customer in one of these dives. I only went there as the duty officer with the SPs, to make sure the customers weren't rolled or murdered, and to break up the inevitable fights that exploded every payday.

But one night, in one of these miserable sex factories, I encountered a prostitute who attracted me. God knows why. Maybe it was the oppressiveness of Adelita Losada's devotion. Maybe it was self-destruction. Maybe it was adventure. But I was undeniably attracted to this skinny, unbeautiful, but mysteriously alluring prostitute.

Every time we patrolled her place of business, I'd arrange to talk to her, or buy her a drink, or dance with her. And before long, we'd made an arrangement to meet at her house for a voluntary "freebie" after she finished work.

She was, needless to say, a marvelous, unusual lover. She had techniques that hadn't been invented yet. And I was intrigued enough to come back for more.

And then, Adelita found out. One night, in bed, she turned to me and asked if I was seeing someone else.

"Yes," I said, "but—"

"And do you have sex with her?"

"Yes," I blundered on, "but it's nothing. It doesn't mean anything."

There are times when the truth is discretionary, and this was one of them. I was only twenty-two, and I had still to learn this; I figured that when Adelita rolled over, away from me, she was just showing her displeasure. I was wrong. She reached under the bed, swung around, and came at me with what seemed to be the largest, sharpest knife I'd ever seen.

I didn't wait, I didn't argue; I threw off the covers, and, naked again, leaped from the bed. It took me only a split second longer to leave Adelita's bedroom than it had taken me to flee my flaming barracks the night of the fire, but that was only because I stopped to scoop up my clothes. Fortunately, there weren't any early morning strollers out to see me hopping down the street, climbing into my uniform, in full retreat from one of the angriest women I would ever know.

I don't mean to paint a monochromatic picture. It wasn't all heat and humidity and passion and violence in Colombia during World War II. The country was much more than that. It was beautiful—a lush, color-splashed, surprising collection of landscapes that never ceased to astonish me.

And I made other, less volatile friends, among them Mrs. Myron Reed, an older American woman who drove me, one steamy afternoon, to Cartagena, the ancient, seacoast village whose seawall had been built in the sixteenth century as an ornate and useless safeguard against pirates.

This whole part of the world was a new and exciting discovery for me. One week, partway into my hitch, I accompanied General Brett, the commanding general of the Panama Sea Frontier Area, and Lieutenant McGinnis to Curacao, that spotlessly clean, clarified island in the Caribbean. We had lunch at the Piscadera Club, and I swam that afternoon in water that was almost invisible, it was so clear. And again, I felt that same fulfillment and peace that I'd experienced in the mountains surrounding Lake Placid and the fields beyond Chapel Hill.

Time passed; Normandy was invaded; the war turned in our favor. I'd put in a year and a half on the Panama Sea Frontier, and now I was eligible for a weekend in San José, Costa Rica. After the humid one hundred and twenty degree-plus heat of Colombia, San José, high in the mountains, would be a cool and lovely paradise.

Of course, we sailors didn't go there just for the climate.

Every Saturday evening, a unique parade took place in the Parque Central, the small, tree-lined square of San José. The young girls of the city, dressed in their weekend finery, would circle the square in a clockwise direction, and the young men of San José—and the U.S. Navy—would stroll in a counterclockwise direction. It was a slow mating dance, choreographed with impeccable control and unstinting dignity.

It was, in fact, all very civilized, all very proper, all very traditional. It was the custom to make one complete circuit of the park. And then, the next time around, if you were struck by a particular young girl, it was also the custom to meet her eyes. If she returned the look, you joined arms and the two of you left the park together. If she looked away, or at the pavement, you kept on circling, searching for another pair of friendlier eyes.

I don't recall how many circuits I made, but I do remember the beautiful girl I met, and with whom—according to tradition—I spent a glorious weekend.

What a tradition. No wonder San José was Shangri-la for every sailor on the Panama Sea Frontier.

In December 1944, just as the Battle of the Bulge began, I flew to New York, to begin a thirty-day leave. It was bitter cold in Manhattan that particular December, and the city was crackling with life, full of servicemen eager to have a good time.

I was happy to be home. My attitude toward my father's students had mysteriously changed. They didn't look odd, not at all. In fact, one of them, a seventeen-year-old piano student named Margery Abrams, appealed to me instantly. We struck up a conversation; I asked her out; and within two days we were dizzily in love.

We arranged to be together every day and every night. I spent less and less time at home. It was, I was sure, going to be the best thirty days of my life in New York.

And then, my father stepped into the middle of the love affair. One of his friends and sponsors, it seemed, was Siegfried S.H. Kahn, a wealthy manufacturer. S.H. had a daughter named Winifred, who was nearly my age, and not particularly popular. It was important, for my father's friendship and the continuance of the sponsorship, for me to take Winifred out.

He asked me, politely, to do it. I declined. I wouldn't dream of it. A night away from Margery was an eternity misspent. "I won't do it," I said, simply. But that approach was totally ineffectual.

I was going to take her out, and that was that. Once my father had made up his mind, Moses couldn't have changed it. I'd take her, he decreed, to see *Carmen Jones*, Oscar Hammerstein II's resetting of Bizet's opera in a present day parachute factory, with an all-Black cast; we'd go to the Russian Tea Room for a drink afterwards, and then I could do what I wanted. But this, my father said, in terms that broached no argument, would come first.

I was furious and upset. Here I was, twenty-three and part of a fighting military machine, and my father was still casting his long shadow, dulling the bright moments of my life. And I was powerless to counteract it, because I was under his roof and therefore his influence.

I explained my predicament to Margery, and told her I'd call her as soon as I got home. I guaranteed it would be early. She was moderately understanding, although I had a feeling she was crying.

So, I had the date with Winifred Kahn. I found her immensely unattractive, and she probably didn't think I was a terrific bargain, either. We had a conversational evening, saw the show, went to the Russian Tea Room, and then set out to find a taxicab.

It was bitterly, cruelly cold. I wasn't used to this kind of weather; my blood had undoubtedly thinned from my year and a half in the subtropics. And to complicate matters, it was wartime; there were few taxis and many customers, and it took us more than half an hour to finally hail down a cab. By this time, I was chilled to the marrow.

I dropped Winifred off at her apartment, kept the cab, and headed home. By the time I'd gotten inside the door of my parents' apartment, I was burning up with fever. Goddamn the cold, goddamn the date, goddamn my father for forcing me to go on it, I thought, as I crawled, shivering violently, into bed. I'd sweat the cold out tonight under piles of blankets, and then, no more of this. Margery and I were old enough to make our own decisions, and we'd make them, by God.

But the next morning, my fever had risen, and later that day, I developed pneumonia. I was too sick to be moved to a hospital, so I spent three weeks at home in bed. One night I almost died and Dr. Kaunitz, our family physician, spent the entire night at my bedside till the crisis had passed.

Because of the pneumonia, my thirty-day leave stretched to eight weeks, and Margery and I made the most of it. By the time I'd boarded a Naval Air Transport Service DC-3 for Miami, she'd become the girl at home, waiting for and writing to her man in the service. The plane developed engine trouble over northern Florida, and we made an emergency landing on the beach at Daytona. It didn't faze me; I had more important things on my mind. All I could think of was getting to a telephone booth and calling Margery. I missed her almost enough to desert.

We wrote for a while when I got back to Colombia, and kept up our correspondence after I was transferred back, to Panama Sea Frontier Headquarters, where I became an operations officer. And then, one day, the letter waiting for me at mail call was a "Dear John." And that was the end of yet another eternal love affair.

In a few months, the war ended, too. A few weeks later, on a boat packed with returning veterans, I sailed into New York harbor. I was given duty as the Leave and Liberty Officer at Lido Beach, Long Island, prior to being mustered out. My Navy days were drawing to an end, and practically in my own backyard.

9.

T W O years earlier, in the rocky days and nights of my sea duty on the gallant tub *YP285,* I'd passed my non-throwing up, off-duty hours reading a book that would inform and transform my entire, post-service life. The book was *The Fervent Years,* Harold Clurman's reportorial recollection of the history of The Group Theatre.

Nothing, I realize now, happens by accident. Reading that book became one more act in a series of forward movements that would ultimately deposit me in my happiest professional home, the theatre.

The central female character in the Clurman book was his wife, Stella Adler. He wrote about her like a man in love. And there, tossing around on the sea, throwing up whenever I tossed too much, I fell in love with both the theatre and Stella Adler.

I sublimated this for the duration. But now, in 1945, while I was spending my last days in the Navy at Lido Beach, that feeling came back. I was twenty-four; I had time on my hands; the Navy had taught me that brashness sometimes won you a prize. And so, one day, I telephoned the Clurmans.

Stella answered the phone and my heart raced. "My name is Adler, too," I said, rapidly, "and I'm a young naval officer, and I've read *The Fervent Years,* and I'm anxious to meet you, and I'm a student of the theatre and—"

Her voice was cold and austere. Later, she would tell me that I was so sincere and sweet and intense, she couldn't help but be intrigued. She invited me to come to their apartment, at 161 West 54th Street, the following Sunday, from three to four in the afternoon.

I could hardly contain myself. The next Sunday, I got to the Clurman neighborhood at least half an hour early, and wandered the streets until three o'clock. Stella Adler met me at the door. And instantly, the

157

feelings I'd had at sea while I was reading the book rushed back. I was blinded by this gorgeous, statuesque, fascinating, Helen of Troy who was about to sink the ship of my judgment, with one, consuming look. I was in love. Again.

I stayed from three to four that day, all right—from three in the afternoon till four in the morning. And those thirteen hours were a bounty beyond value.

They were there, the famous theatre people I'd read about. Clifford Odets, Franchot Tone, Mordecai "Max" Gorelik, C. Edward Bromberg, Elia Kazan, Sanford Meisner, all of them, talking, reminiscing, planning, planting the seed of informed fascination with the theatre in me so deeply that it would never, from that afternoon forward, cease to grow.

Stella seemed to be fascinated by me, or my youth, or something, and so I was invited back to the Sunday salons, where somebody new always appeared to eat her salads, drink her champagne, and to talk, intensely or brilliantly or wittily. One afternoon, it would be Charles and Oona Chaplin. Another, it would be Maxwell Anderson and Thornton Wilder, or Canada Lee, or another young theatre aspirant my age named Marlon Brando.

Gradually, I was drawn into the group. And then, Stella and I began to meet each other elsewhere. She'd take me to the theatre, where we'd sit in choice seats, and see Vivien Leigh and Laurence Olivier in *Antony and Cleopatra,* Olivier by himself in *Oedipus Rex,* and Maurice Evans in *Hamlet*—an experience in which our seats turned out to be *too* choice. Evans was both a fine actor and a master spitter, and those of us who sat in rows one through five received the full force of his shower.

It wasn't very far from an orchestra seat to a bed. Stella was, at times, bizarre and eccentric. One night, during a huge party at the Clurman apartment, I suddenly got deathly sick. I ran a high fever, and began throwing up. Stella put me to bed in one of the maid's rooms. I figured I'd die; but I didn't, and within a couple of hours, I was feeling better.

I was breathing easily, thinking about rejoining the party, when the door opened. It was Stella. I thought she'd simply come to check on me. Instead, she closed the door behind her and slipped into bed, next to me.

I was terrified. "Harold's right down the hall," I protested.

"Shh," she said.

"But—"

"He won't come in," she whispered. She was, as she would continue to be for many months, the mature woman taking care of everything for the young and frightened—but willing—man.

During all those years that Stella and I carried on our torrid and secret affair, Harold never seemed to know about it . . . or if he did, he didn't care.

I'd convinced my mother and father that it would be only right for me to invite some of my friends from the Clurman's salon to dinner at our home.

It was a memorable party. I was still in the Navy but I lived at home with my parents at 336 Central Park West. They had a large dining room with stuccoed walls that my mother had painted with a mixture of oranges and browns so that the entire room glowed in the candle-light, which illuminated the faces of the people I most admired. Sanford Meisner and his wife Betty; Clifford Odets and *his* wife Betty; Stella, with her long blonde hair pulled back primly, sitting next to Harold; and Irwin Shaw, the jokester of the group, funloving, vibrant, looking more like a football player or a butcher than a fine playwright and novelist. In college, I'd played the sixth corpse in his powerful anti-war one-act play *Bury the Dead*, and I could barely contain myself this evening, thinking that the man who had written *that* was sitting here, as *my* guest! His lovely wife Marion was next to Clifford, and I was next to her, and at either end of the table were my mother and father. My father, sensing the moment and its importance to me, stayed in the background.

I sat back and let their talk about The Theatre and the people who made it vibrate wash over me. My role that night was more river pilot than anything else. Whenever the conversation dipped, even a tiny amount—which it hardly ever did—I'd steer it back to talk about the Group. At the time, I think I did it because I was fascinated by the concept of it. Now, I'm sure I wanted to impress my father, too.

Some time, just before dessert, Irwin Shaw and Clifford Odets got into it. Irwin loved to bait Clifford, who was taciturn, introspective, brilliant, and relentlessly serious. Irwin, I think, got him started on the subject of some of his ideals, like the labor union movement, and after Clifford had been holding forth for a good five minutes, he finally had to pause for breath.

Irwin leaned across the table and, very quietly, punctured the argument. "Clifford," he said, "the trouble with you is you live in a Red Ivory Tower."

I think Harold sensed how much I loved hanging around the periphery of the theatre. He made me his unofficial assistant, and even listened to my young, uninformed, and sincere suggestions.

One night, when Maxwell Anderson's *Truckline Cafe* was being cast, I had dinner at Harold and Stella's. Harold was directing the play, and over dessert, he complained about how much trouble he was having casting the role of the murderer.

"What about Marlon?" I suggested.

At the time, Marlon was playing the young Nils' in *I Remember Mama*. He also happened to be the boyfriend of Ellen, Stella Adler's daughter. Ellen was a beautiful, black-eyed, black-haired, eighteen-year-old version of Jennifer Jones, and she and Marlon were having a big romance.

Harold paused a minute, and then said, matter of factly, "Good idea. Good idea."

The next day, Marlon got the part. And, because I was Harold's assistant, I had the good fortune to be backstage and watch Marlon work.

I remember how serious and concentrated he was. And I particularly remember how he created an unforgettable entrance before his one big scene. In the play, he'd escaped from prison, and he'd been hiding at sea from the police. Before he'd come on stage, he'd stand under a shower with his clothes on, and while he was soaking wet, do push-ups to make himself look tense and distraught.

And then, he'd walk on stage, and give a riveting performance, one which would ultimately earn him fantastic reviews. And out of that— because "Gadge" Kazan was one of the producers of *Truckline Cafe*— came the part of Stanley Kowalski in Tennessee Williams' *Streetcar Named Desire*, which made Marlon an overnight star.

So, I was continually in the presence of peerless performers and creators. One night, after a run-through of *Truckline Cafe*, Harold, Gadge Kazan, Wally Fried, Max Anderson, a young girl, and I went to a Viennese cafe called the Blue Grotto, on 45th Street, between 6th and 7th Avenues. The young girl had been at rehearsal, and I figured she was somebody's daughter.

Midway through dinner, Harold leaned over to me and whispered, "Talk to that girl. She's brilliant. She's *very* interesting."

"Maybe. But she's fourteen years old," I whispered back.

"She's nineteen," answered Harold. "Try it."

So I talked to her, and she *was* brilliant, and interesting and talented. Her name was Julie Harris.

She was just an insecure fledgling then, fresh out of Yale Drama School and living at Miss Hewett's, a kind of finishing school on the East Side. We got to be friends, and one night, after I'd finally been mustered out of the Navy and had rented a maid's room on Fifth Avenue, she came up to the room with me. She picked up a copy of George Bernard Shaw's plays that rested in my tiny bookcase. She sat down, that night, and read the entire *Saint Joan* to me, from beginning to end.

I was transfixed. She closed the book and smiled. There was a beat of appreciative silence, and then I said, "Julie, you *have* to become the First Lady of the American Theatre."

She blushed and smiled. "Oh come on, Richard," she said. "Stop that."

And then, finally, there was Mama Adler, into her eighties in 1946, fragile and needing care, and at the other end of a theatrical career from Julie. Once, when Harold was out of town with *Truckline Cafe* and Stella was also out of town, with Turgenev's *He Who Gets Slapped,* they asked me to look after Mama.

One night, I wandered into Harold's study. There was a closet with its door partly open. It was full of scrapbooks, piled ten feet high. I climbed onto a chair, and took down one of the books from the top of the pile. I began to leaf through it. It was part of a reportorial account of the Group Theatre, from its beginnings.

For the next two hours, I consumed the books, hungrily, one after the other, reliving those days of privation and glory, so absorbed in them that I didn't notice Mama Adler walk into the room.

She sat there for a moment, and then sighed. I came out of my trance. "I'm sorry," I said. "I was—"

"It means very much to you, doesn't it?" she said, softly.

"Very much," I answered.

"It does to me, too," she continued, and then she began to tell me about her long acting career in Moscow and Vienna, how she'd starred as the young girl in Tolstoy's *Resurrection.* And as she talked, she began to relive the part. Gradually, strangely, the years began to drop away, and her voice became stronger and more youthful, and she began to glide through the room like a dancer, a young dancer on a stage in Vienna, nearly three-quarters of a century ago. It was ghostly and wonderful, as were her words: "It means very much to you, doesn't it?"

One Sunday afternoon at Stella's, I overheard Canada Lee discussing a play he owned called *On Whitman Avenue*. Canada was the biggest Black star in the world at the time; while I was in Chapel Hill, he'd appeared as Bigger Thomas in *Native Son*—the dramatization, by Paul Green and Richard Wright, of Wright's shattering, best selling novel. I had been sent to New York to review it for the student newspaper The *Daily Tar Heel*.

Now, he was trying new waters, as a co-producer, with a fellow named Mark Marvin, of a play by Maxine Wood, about a Black family moving into a white suburb of Detroit. This, mind you, was 1946. And in ideas and subject matter, *On Whitman Avenue* was years ahead of its time.

It was a simple, straightforward, touching play, and it struck something deep and personal in me. When I'd been a student at Chapel Hill, I'd gone out with a girl named Ouida Campbell. She lived in a small town called Carrboro, adjacent to Chapel Hill, but eons away in time and thought.

One night, when I was visiting her, we heard a terrible commotion at the end of her street. We came out on her front porch, just as a police cruiser careened past, its lights flashing, its siren wailing. At the end of the street, near a huge tree, a carnival-happy, probably drunk gang of white men was about to hang a young Black man. The rope was around his neck, and he'd fainted from fright. But before the crowd could finish its grisly business, the police waded in and broke it up. The picture of that—the sounds, the faces of the crowd, and the terrified rag doll of a young man with a rope around his neck would stay with me.

Now, in 1946, lynchings were still a fact of life in the South, and neighborhoods in the North were still segregated strongholds. So the play was an enormously daring one, and Canada Lee was determined to produce it.

I decided that I wanted to be part of his venture. I'd saved twenty-five hundred dollars in the Navy. I gave it all to Canada, and came aboard the sinking ship of *On Whitman Avenue*.

It was as much a crusade as a production. We all believed in the play, fiercely. Margo Jones, who would later start one of the first regional theaters in America, the Dallas Repertory Company, was directing, and it was a work of love for her.

We opened at the Cort Theatre, to mixed notices. A day of hardly any ticket sales, and it was obvious to all of us that the box office wasn't going to be able to keep the play alive. So, I was dispatched to churches, labor unions, and synagogues to crusade about the qualities that made it worth seeing and worth saving. I spent long, heated evenings exhorting audiences to support this noble, and to me at that time, important play.

But nothing I or anybody else did could keep *On Whitman Avenue* open. We closed fourteen weeks later, another daring and worthwhile experiment dead of avoidance by the public.

I stayed in touch with Canada and Margo, and particularly with Mark Marvin, who was a man stalked by failure and tragedy all of his short life. He later married an actress named Blanche Zohar, a lovely, sweet, good person who became the director of a children's workshop. She and Mark had two children; one of them was born a deaf mute.

Neither Mark nor Blanche ever made much money; they always lived on the brink, and one desperate day, Mark took an overdose of sleeping pills, and died.

Blanche found him, and, refusing to believe that he was dead, with great difficulty picked him up and laboriously walked him around the room, pouring coffee into his inert mouth in a desperate and futile attempt to revive him.

I went to the funeral, in a hall somewhere in the West Seventies. It was packed. Mark and Blanche had many, many friends who'd been touched at one time or another by their kindness and their tragedy.

The eulogy was delivered by Mark's brother, Herbert Klein, the distinguished documentary filmmaker. At the end of it, Herb paused, and said, "And now, let us give Mark Marvin the tribute he so richly deserved but never got in the theatre or in life."

And he began to slowly applaud. And gradually, one by one, the congregation joined in, until there was a crescendo of tremendous applause, as if a hit show had just opened, and the curtain had come down, finally, on a great evening.

I was twenty-five now. It was time to make a living, time to be on my own. I was in a curious place. I wanted to, I *needed* to be my own person. And yet, being back in New York, in the surroundings of home, all of the old uncertainties and insecurities rushed back.

Sure, I'd taken steps to leave. But not enormous, lasting ones. The Navy had been a place of no responsibility. It hadn't done much for my growing up.

It was Stella who would nudge me into real adulthood. In her own way she introduced me to the world.

In the 1945–46 Broadway season, she appeared in the Tyrone Guthrie production of *He Who Gets Slapped,* an extraordinary production in which she was merely magnificent. By March 1946, the play had traveled to Washington, D.C. On March 10, she phoned, and commanded me to come to Washington, to be with her.

It was my father's birthday, and, except for the time I'd been away at college or in the Navy, it had always been a family celebration. But the birthday took a backseat to my desire to be with Stella. Without a pause or a second thought, I booked myself on a plane and flew to Washington.

That night, at dinnertime, I called my father to wish him a happy birthday. My mother answered the phone. She was her usual and constantly warm self, thanking me for calling, certain that my father would be delighted that I thought of him.

There was a long silence, while she called him. The phone was set down. I waited, apprehensively. Finally, the phone was picked up. It was my mother. "He won't come to the phone. He won't speak to you," she said, and guilt hit me like an artillery barrage.

I spent a bad weekend in Washington, torn in three simultaneous directions. First, there was my wish, my desire, my need to be with Stella; then, there was my guilt over not being with my father on his birthday; and finally, and most important of all, there was the realization, unearthed by the confrontation between the first two, that I was, dammit, an adult now, and should be able to live my life the way I wanted to live it.

The battle raged. One part of me argued like a trial lawyer for my rights as a twenty-five-year-old individual. The other wanted to sprint to the airport, hop a plane, and get home as fast as possible.

And the guilt over that weekend of turmoil and realization wouldn't end when I came back to New York the following Monday. It would, in fact, never entirely leave. When I had my own children, I would be compulsive about sharing their birthdays with them. One year, ten years into the future, I'd leave for London one evening, participate in a business meeting, leave it, and go directly to the airport so that I could be back in Connecticut for Parents' Weekend at Salisbury Academy, where my son Andrew was attending school. And ten years after that, I'd turn down a dinner invitation from a president of the United States to honor a dinner commitment with my children.

But now, in 1946, it was time to turn away from the Nembutal days of the Navy, Stella's salon, and the shelter of my parent's apartment. It was time to establish myself, by myself. I'd been living on the rim of greatness for over a year, basking in the reflected light of theatrical geniuses, but I'd done nothing for young Richard Adler.

When I finally made that decision, after several more weeks of agonizing, Stella and I began to drift apart. It was natural and appropriate. We'd both come along at the right moment in each other's lives, and now that moment was over.

My father eventually forgave me for not being home for his birthday; looking back on it, I see that he nearly always forgave me, in one way or another. In fact, one night at the dinner table, in a move that now seems almost like compensation for his rejection of my second grade composition, he brought up the subject of my writing. I'd written some poems after I'd left the service, and my mother had shown them to him.

"They're good," he said. "Maybe good enough to be set to music. Why don't you write some songs with Phil Springer?" Phil Springer was one of the few pupils of my father who wrote popular music. He was a student at Columbia University, five years my junior, and an aspiring composer and pianist.

My father introduced us, and after an initial parrying period, we began to write together. Of course, my father never thought of it as anything more than a diversion, something to make two young men happy in their leisure time. Making a living came first, and he went about helping me do that, too.

My parents had two old friends, the Rosetts, a sweet and gentle, white-haired couple who came for dinner now and then. Max Rosett was the production head and a vice-president of Conde Nast Publications, and one night, after some urging from my father, we talked earnestly about opportunities for young writers. The outlook was no brighter then than it is today. In fact, it was probably worse. There were tens of thousands of returning veterans in the marketplace that year, all eager, all determined, and some talented. And every one of them was looking for a job. It was a buyer's market.

Still, Max Rosett promised to help. And he tried, but he couldn't find me anything at Conde Nast. He did, however, introduce me to

Fred Norman, the publisher of the *New Yorker* magazine. Fred Norman didn't have anything at the *New Yorker* for me, either. But *he* introduced me to someone in the public relations department at Celanese Corporation of America. And here, the bell finally rang. Celanese was looking for someone to fill an entry level PR job.

But, in the same way as today, "entry level" meant somebody with some experience. And I had none.

It didn't slow me. The next day, I culled magazines and newspapers for enough unsigned articles to convince Celanese that I had the right kind of background to qualify as an entry level writer. I pasted them into a scrapbook, and passed them off as my own.

It got me the job, at sixty-five dollars a week, first as an apprentice, then as a writer of public relations releases about the charms of acetate yarns, the triumph of viscose over nylon, and the romance of textured plastics. I remember more about it than I want to, particularly the part where they learned that I could speak Spanish, and gave me the added task of translating their releases for the Central and South American market.

Still, it was a living, and it was only nine to five, and it gave me the means that I needed to move away from home.

And move away I finally did, shortly after the second paycheck. It was my true liberation, the first time in my life that I would depend upon myself, and only myself. Was I scared? Of course I was. But I was damned if I was going to show it.

The digs I picked weren't exactly grand. They were, in fact, crummy. But they were in possibly the best neighborhood of the city, 73rd and Fifth Avenue. In fact, I went to Tiffany and braggadociously ordered some raised letter stationery. Today, 923 Fifth Avenue is a beautiful structure. But then, it was the former Guggenheimer brownstone, once a grand residence, now a dilapidated dump, filled with a weird assortment of unmatched people. The maid's room at the extreme top of the building was empty, and the rent was thirty-two dollars a month.

It was a tiny, oddly shaped room, with a miniature terrace and a glorious view of Fifth Avenue. My parents furnished it with odds and ends from everywhere. The desk came from the New York apartment; so did a bureau and an armchair; the bed was an imitation colonial bunk from Lake Placid; a lamp and a bookcase—from which Julie Harris would one night pluck *Saint Joan*—were Karinoke contributions, too. Altogether, it was eclectic but cozy, and what was most to the point, it was mine.

There was no bathroom; nobody had a private bathroom on the top floor, and it was in these communal places that I met some of my bizarre housemates. There were drug peddlers. There was a Colombian journalist named Olvero Perez. There was a Polish refugee, an intellectual-turned-photographer named Szygmunt Lytinski. There were at least two call girls on a lower floor, and, a year later, after his door had been kicked in by the FBI and he'd been hauled off, we discovered we'd had a spy on the premises, too.

Celanese didn't exactly pay me the kind of money that would allow me a roaring social life. But I did what I could, and one of my happiest nights out was going to basketball games at Madison Square Garden, particularly those in which North Carolina was playing.

A bangup matchup of that particular winter was between North Carolina and NYU. Tickets were hard to come by, but I bought two, and made plans for a big evening out with my current girlfriend.

And, as luck would have it, three days before the game, she broke her leg.

"Go on to the game without me," she said.

I compared the two evenings: a chance to be with her or a chance to be at the Garden by myself and 30,000 screaming fans, none of whom I knew. "I'd rather be with you," I said. "I'll see you at 8:30."

That would give me enough time, I figured, to try to get a refund for the tickets. With what I was earning at Celanese, I couldn't afford to just give them away.

So, the night of the game, I joined the long line at the Garden box office. I wasn't sure they'd take the tickets back, so I clutched them in my hand, hoping that somebody might see and buy them.

As I was nearing the window, a tall man in a dark overcoat approached me. "Want to sell those tickets?" he asked.

"Yes!" I shouted, relieved to have my problem solved.

"How much do you want for them?" he asked.

"What I paid for them," I said. "Five dollars."

He smiled. "Okay. I'll buy them," he said. And I stepped out of line.

He reached into his pocket and brought out his wallet. But he didn't reach in it for money. He waved it in front of me. There was a police badge pinned to it. "You're coming with me," he said.

"What for?" I cried.

"Ticket speculation," he snapped, and read me a long regulation I had seemingly violated.

He grabbed me by the arm, whipped me around, and guided me

through the crowd to the Garden office, into which he unceremoniously shoved me. Some other young men were standing there, all of them evidently full-time scalpers. They didn't look any happier than I, but they were much calmer. They knew what was coming, and it happened swiftly. We were all herded into a paddy wagon and taken downtown, to the Tombs, the city's ancient and foul smelling lockup.

There, we were searched, mug shot, fingerprinted, and tossed into a huge bull pen.

I wasn't exactly in uniform for the place. Practically everybody else was dressed for survival on the streets. And practically everybody else also looked like they'd been there a lot, and knew the ropes. I was Mr. Innocence, hooked, netted, and floundering.

One other man was dressed, as I was, in a suit and an overcoat. I gravitated to him. We drifted into conversation, and he opened up immediately. He was a printer, he said, and his boss had been bullying him. So, he'd socked him.

"What are you charged with?" I asked.

"Assault and battery," he said, cheerfully. "I've been here for five days. My trial comes up tomorrow. Look. You've never been in a place like this before, have you?"

"No," I said.

"Okay. Now, they're supposed to give you one phone call, but they don't always do that, so you'd better give me your father's phone number. I'll be out tomorrow, and I'll give him a call."

"You mean I've got to stay here all *night*?" I asked him. "I didn't do anything. They can't—"

"Yes they can," said my new friend. "They can do anything they want."

There was a commotion on the other side of the bull pen. "Oh oh," said my friend. "Here we go again."

Two cops were shoving a beautiful, extravagantly gowned Black lady into the bull pen. She was the only woman among possibly fifty men.

"I thought this was the men's—" I began.

"Come on," said he, as we walked over to the crowd, now gathered around the two cops and the woman.

"Take off your clothes," ordered one of the cops.

She hissed at him.

"Take off your clothes," he repeated, moving closer to her.

And she did. Slowly. First the jacket. Then the gown. The stockings. The garter belt. The bra. Finally, she stepped out of her panties. And an enormous penis popped forward and settled down between her— his?—legs. The bull pen ignited into wild applause, and the nude transvestite bowed—a deep, practiced, nightclub bow.

I'd never seen anything like that before. I was learning. "Being in jail is like travel. It educates you, fast," said my friend. "Now are you going to give me your father's number?"

I wrote out my parents' phone number on the envelope that had, until a few hours ago, contained two tickets to a basketball game, and handed it to him.

An hour later, we were herded out of the bull pen, and up to the sixth floor, where we were shoved into cells. I got no sleep whatsoever. I felt filthy, and exhausted, and upset, as if I'd been on a week-long binge with no stopovers for ablutions.

At six in the morning, a trustee handed me a broom. "What're you in for?" he asked. It was the jailhouse greeting, replacing "How are you?" on the outside, and delivered with about as much sincerity.

I told him.

"You made a call yet?"

I realized I hadn't, nor had anyone on the right side of the law informed me that I could. I shook my head negatively.

"You got any money?"

I'd stashed a ten dollar bill in my shoe, on the advice of another jailhouse veteran I'd met before being sprung from the bull pen.

"Give it to me. I'll make a call for ya," said the trustee, and I handed over the ten and my parents' number. It and the trustee disappeared, never to be seen or heard from again.

The day dragged on. Every other hour, we were let out of our cells for exercise. I asked two guards if I could make a call, and they ignored me. Lunch, as much slop as breakfast, came and went. I began to feel more and more isolated and terrified. How long would I be here before somebody started to miss me? And how would they find me once they did? It was all very depressing.

Finally, at 5:30 that afternoon, a guard unlocked the door of my cell. "Adler?" he shouted, "Get your gear. You're leaving."

"What's happening?" I asked him.

"You've been bailed out. Hurry up," he said, expressionlessly.

My Uncle Ben, who worked on Wall Street, and who could be counted on in any and all emergencies, was waiting for me downstairs. The printer, had, indeed, called my father, and my father had called Uncle Ben, who doled out a hundred dollars, and set me free.

I hugged him in thanks. And, as I went home, showered, shaved, and changed into black tie to attend the wedding ceremony and party of Count Rodolfo Crespi, at the home of financier Robert Lehman, the president of the Metropolitan Museum, I became acutely aware of the contrasts life hands us, in the interest of education. I would never again be quite so naive as I had been, twenty four hours earlier, standing on line at Madison Square Garden, thinking that the return of two extra basketball tickets was a simple matter.

A few weeks later, I had to get a lawyer and had to go to court. I was exonerated and given an apology by the judge.

It was a good, eventful life. I hated the eight hours I spent chained to a desk at Celanese, but I loved the rest of the time. Most weeknights, I'd go over to Phil's place at seven or seven-thirty, and we'd write songs until early in the morning, till we were both so bleary eyed and worked out we no longer made sense.

I'd stumble home to my colonial bed, and the next night, we'd be back at it, working our asses off and savoring every minute of it.

It was then that my father arranged that derogatory lunch with Phil Spitalny, who read my lyrics and advised me to forget the music business and throw all of my energies into Celanese Corporation of America. But even that stuffy pronouncement from an imposing radio-television personality couldn't discourage me. I knew what I wanted, and I was learning my craft the best way possible—by doing it.

And eventually, Phil springer and I got published. When Connie Haines recorded our song "Teasin' ", we knew that the work we were doing, and that gave us such joy, could satisfy the public, too.

Phil wound up his studies at Columbia. And I subconsciously wound up my life at Celanese. I'd been with them—and I hadn't been with them—for four years now. My salary had climbed to ninety-five dollars a week, which wasn't bad in those days. But as my salary escalated at Celanese, my interest in copy writing declined. The late nights writing songs with Phil first nibbled at, then took huge bites out of my daytime concentration.

So, logically enough, one day in 1950, I was called into the office of the vice-president in charge of public relations, and fired.

It didn't bother me much. In fact, it made a decision for me that I was unable to make myself. I was free to do what I wanted, full time. Phil was delighted when I told him, and so were my other friends on Tin Pan Alley—Al Hoffman and John Jacob Loeb and Bob Merrill, who had just shared with me his technique of composing on a toy xylophone. Everyone was happy about it but my father.

And he was predictably furious. How could I jeopardize a secure job by doing something as unpredictable as lyric writing? he asked, shaking his head.

And then, sure enough, I began to feel guilty. His anger and despair tapped a barely hidden vein of insecurity in me. I had a certain amount of chutzpah in those days, but not enough to drown out a pounding heart when I put it to use. In the dining room of my parents' apartment, in the presence of my father's overwhelming distress, I began to think that maybe I'd been too cavalier with Celanese.

But this time, it didn't last. Once I was out of the apartment and back on the street, the thought and the guilt dimmed. All I had done, after all, was to try, by casting a little light myself, to dissipate that long shadow of my father's disapproval and censure.

And now, my trying would turn to success—in a dimension I hadn't yet imagined. In the clarifying summer sunlight of my twenty-ninth year, I headed toward the Brill Building, and the most important, fateful, fortuitous meeting of my life.

III

ANOTHER
WILDERNESS

10.

C O L E Porter's words rang like bells in my ears.

"Write by yourself. I do it. It's easy."

And the more they rang, the more impossible it seemed to even think of doing anything without Jerry. I couldn't visualize myself by myself. I was a collaborator, that was what I was, and so I was only half an equation. And no incomplete equation has ever been solved.

I called Judy, and told her about Cole Porter's suggestion. She thought for a minute. "He's a survivor," she said. "Jerry was a survivor. Maybe—"

And then she broke down, and we went through it all again, as we did practically every day. How cheerful Jerry had been about the operation. How good he'd felt when he decided to go ahead with it. "I feel so good I want to feel perfect," he'd told Judy that summer. And the doctors had told him that the operation was ninety-nine percent safe, and that he'd be able to swim again, and play golf, and really begin to enjoy the money he was making for the first time in his life.

And what the hell was it all now? What were promises? Dust thrown in your eyes so you couldn't see the truth.

Still, maybe, I thought, maybe Cole Porter had a point. If I eased myself into it, if I went at it at my own speed and in my own way, I might be able to pull it off.

Long ago, I'd traded my toy xylophone for a tape recorder. I'd sit down with it and dictate the melody, the inner line, the bass line, counterpoint, passing tones, the whole schmeer.

I tried. Every day for a week I faced the tape recorder, but not the music. Nothing, absolutely nothing came forth.

I called Judy. "Look," I said, embarrassed at having to put it into words, "would you mind coming over and just sitting in the room while I compose?"

She didn't mind at all. She was as anxious as I to walk those same paths that Jerry and I had together, and to rerun some of our routines. If videotape had existed in those days, we would have watched whatever we had of Jerry over and over. Anything to resurrect some part of him.

Judy sat in one corner of the studio, and I sat in another, and for a few days, she watched me compose. The first song I finished was about a guy who had to take three buses to meet his girl. It was a song, naturally, about Jerry and Judy and their courtship. He'd taken three buses to get from his parents' apartment on the lower East Side of Manhattan to the upper Bronx, where she lived.

It wasn't very good, and neither were some of the other attempts I made in the next couple of weeks. Cole Porter's advice wasn't going to take, and one afternoon, I looked across the room at Judy and shook my head in absolute bewilderment.

She began to smile. It was the first time I'd seen her face brighten since I'd come back from St. Louis. "Here we are," she said, "I'm a mess, and you're a basket case, and what does it all mean?"

One night, I was invited to a dinner party at Arlene Francis and Martin Gabel's apartment at the Ritz. Jule Styne, Harold Arlen, Alan Jay Lerner, and a group of very knowledgeable and intriguing people were there.

After dinner, Jule Styne, in his typical, loving-to-perform way, raced to the piano, and started to play and sing that exquisite, extraordinary medley of his. Everybody gathered around the piano, encouraging and applauding him vigorously.

When Jule'd finished, somebody said, "Now Harold, It's your turn." And Harold Arlen, very humbly, very quietly, sat down at the piano and played and sang his incredible songs incredibly well—"Stormy Weather," "The Man That Got Away," "Come Rain or Come Shine." Everyone was mesmerized by the simple eloquence of the man.

When Harold had finished, Arlene said, "Now Alan, though you're a lyricist, we know you play. So let's hear from you." And Alan Lerner was pushed to the piano, and since, as a boy, he'd studied with Clarence Adler, he played pretty good piano. He sang the songs from *Brigadoon, My Fair Lady,* and *Paint Your Wagon.*

When Alan finished, the guests turned to me. "All right, Richard," they said, "Now you."

"But I don't play," I said, as offhandedly as I could.

"Come on," said somebody. "Of course you play. How can you write music, if you don't play the piano?"

"I really don't play the piano," I repeated.

"That's impossible!" they insisted.

"I don't know how to play!" I said, getting a little impatient.

Jule Styne interceded. "It's true. He doesn't play the piano," he said, "but tell you what, Richard, I'll play for you. I know your songs."

Now I was really becoming uncomfortable. "Jule," I said, "we haven't rehearsed together. I can't do this."

But the gates had been opened, and the partygoers wouldn't take no for an answer. I didn't want to; my judgment told me not to. I knew the value of performing properly, with rehearsal. But I did it anyway.

And it was awful. Jule did the best he could, but he really didn't know the songs. He played wrong chords, and set the songs in keys that were out of range for me. I was shriveled with embarrassment.

That night, when I went home, I resolved that there would be no more of this. It was time I got over the ridiculous block I was carrying around because of my father's students. I was going to learn to play the piano.

I did some research, and discovered that Coleridge Perkinson, a jazz musician, would be the best teacher for me. I called him, made an appointment, and things began to happen. He taught me a little harmony, a little theory, and some keyboard technique.

By the end of a year, I'd become pretty good.

That same year, I got an assignment to go to Hollywood and write a film score. I accepted it with high intentions. I was anxious to put my new musical knowledge to the test.

I reported for work at Warner Brothers, sat down in my assigned cubicle with its obligatory piano, and with my lately acquired skills, got ready to write.

Nothing happened.

Absolutely nothing.

I went back, day after day, and the same horrible vacantness visited me. I tried, I sweated, I agonized. And it never got any better. So, on the verge of a nervous breakdown, I resigned and headed back to New York.

When I got back to my studio, I picked up the telephone and called Perkinson. "Perk," I said, "we're going to have to stop."

"That's crazy, man," he countered. "You're doing great!"

"Yeah. I'm doing so great I can't write anymore," I said, and bid goodbye to Perk and my aspirations for orthodox composition.

It took me almost a year, and some intense analysis from my psycho-analyst, Dr. Bak, before I could unlearn what I'd learned, and compose again.

"This time, it was the lessons that were blocking you," the doctor explained. "You had something before that worked. It should work again for you."

And eventually, it did. Playing the piano had been, as Dr. Bak had said, erecting a dam that prevented a flow of music that was originating somewhere beyond me. I wasn't sure, but it seemed as if I were not a composer but a conduit; as if I just had to open myself, as naturally as possible, to a flood of sounds, searching for an outlet. And that's what I did, from that point onward.

March arrived, the month for the Tony Awards. Even though the nominations weren't announced in those days, rumor had it that *Damn Yankees* was a shoe-in to sweep the musical prizes. Its opposition was stiff compared to today's standards: Cole Porter's *Silk Stockings* was in the running; so was Hague and Horwitt's *Plain and Fancy* and Rodgers and Hammerstein's *Pipe Dream.* And Gwen had a major opponent in Carol Channing, who'd starred well in a bad musical called *The Vamp.* But the word was out: *Damn Yankees* was in, and big.

So, elation and sorrow sparred to a draw inside of me, as I once again donned black tie, to get ready for yet another hotel ballroom, still another awards ceremony. Only this time, it was different. There'd be an aching vacancy that no amount of people or praise would be able to fill.

I'd prepared a speech, in case the rumors were true, and picked up Judy. It was only appropriate that we should go together, to fight the memories, if nothing else.

And the memories were there, all right, like Fellini ghosts. We had a huge table of twelve or fourteen people, and the whole gang was gathered—Mr. Abbott, Bob Fosse, Bobby Griffith, Hal Prince, and Hal Hastings, our musical director. This time, instead of Dick Bisell, there was Doug Wallopp; instead of Janis Paige, Gwen; instead of John Raitt, Ray Walston; instead of Eddie Foy, Jr., Russ Brown; instead of Carol Haney, Jean Stapleton.

And instead of Jerry, no one.

It was a happy, excited, and very closely knit group that went quietly crazy with anticipation that night. The same close camaraderie of theatre people encased in an enclosed situation was repeated. But it would probably be the last time this would happen. Television entered the picture that night. It was the first Tony Awards ceremony to be televised, though it wouldn't be the last. And television provided the most dramatic moment of the entire ceremony.

Until then, the proceedings had been fairly loose. What happened merely happened, in its own time. But television, with its strict time requirements, changed all of this. The dramatic awards ambled along at their usual casual pace, and nobody thought that they'd affect the musical part of the program. They never had. But by the time our time had come, television time was running out.

The rumors had been right, and maybe a little conservative. This time, we swept practically everything—best actor, best actress, best supporting actor, best score, best choreography, best book of a musical, best direction, best producing organization, best musical direction, best stage technician, and best musical. It was triumphant. It was overwhelming.

And, to the television producers, it was also a perfect solution to their time problem. One of the directors, sweat cascading from his chin, his eyes wild with tension, dashed over to our table and whispered, rapidly, "Please. I know this is a big occasion for you, and I know how much it means for all of you to be up there and be honored. But we're almost out of time. Would you please *all* go up there at *once?*"

We blanched. The director read the horror and anger on our faces, and plunged ahead, hysterically. "AND THEN," he went on, "after we go OFF THE AIR, we can go back and have the INDIVIDUAL speeches. But if we do that now, NONE OF YOU will get on. So PLEASE—"

What could we say? We all began to push back our chairs, ready to mount the dais *en masse.*

But Bobby Griffith stopped us. "Wait a minute," he said, and he took Judy by the arm. "I think Judy Ross should accept for all of us. Don't you?"

Judy protested. "I couldn't," she said, "I wouldn't know what to say. I'd come apart up there."

"You're the only one who should do it," Bobby repeated, gently leading her away from the table.

She looked at all of us. "Are you sure?" she asked.

We were sure, every last one of us, to the bottom of our beings.

And so, one last time, Jerry Ross got the credit he so richly and eternally deserved.

And I had another Tony Award to put in my bookcase. If Jerry and I had been together, it would have opened the door to a barrage of offers. The phone in our studio would have been ringing night and day. We, after all, were being talked about as the new Rodgers and Hart, the new Rodgers and Hammerstein.

Now, half of the act was missing. In a split second I had gone from an exclamation point to a questions mark. and I was an unknown quantity. And in show business, nobody wants to take a chance with an unknown quantity. Besides, rumors had circulated for the past year that Richard Adler was the brains and the business part of the team, and Jerry Ross was the talent. I was, the story went, the PR guy, the pusher, the fighter, the aggressive business element, the administrator, the salesman—in other words, the prick.

It wasn't true. We were equals, and we always, in our friendship, in our collaboration, in our business dealings, split it down the middle. We complemented each other, as clearly as a formula in physics. His musical abilities were more developed than mine; I was a natural lyricist. His ill health denied him the energy and the time to fight for four extra fiddles in the pit orchestra, or for the integrity of one of our songs, or for the justified billing. I became the spokesman for the duo, the arguer simply because Jerry had neither the physical strength nor the emotional makeup for it.

So the phone didn't ring. The offers didn't pour in. And the only way I was going to fight this misapprehension of my role in the collaboration was to follow Cole Porter's advice. But I was immobilized. Even the first efforts that I was able to urge forth in the weeks following Jerry's death seemed to have been nothing more than final spurts of leftover energy. Yet, I knew, undeniably, that the longer I stayed that way, the more credence the rumors would gather. It was a dark, distressful time, probably the darkest of my professional life so far. And it would take a transcontinental trip and some California sunshine to illuminate it.

Warner Brothers had bought the movie rights to *The Pajama Game.* It was scheduled to go before the cameras that summer. I'd stored that news in the back of my mind, and there it remained until one morning, when a first-class round-trip air ticket to Los Angeles arrived in the mail from Warners.

My first impulse was to chuck it into a wastebasket, and tell them to get another musical advisor. I couldn't go through all that again, working with Mr. Abbott and Bob Fosse and John Raitt and Eddie

Foy, Jr. The memories would pile too high. I'd be buried under the avalanche.

And then I thought, wait a minute. Maybe this is something that's being handed to me by a benevolent fate. Maybe, in the presence of people I know and like, doing something familiar, doing something I could do in my sleep—

"Do it," said Judy Ross, when I phoned her about it. "I'll be out there myself in a month or so. We'll prop each other up if we have to."

"Do it," said Bob Merrill, when I talked to him about it over lunch. "I have to be out there in a couple of weeks myself. We'll take in the sights."

And slowly, it began to come together. Bob and I had known each other long enough and were close enough to be able to spend time in each other's company with respect and care. "Look," I said, getting a brainstorm over dessert, "have you ever been to Las Vegas?"

"No."

"Neither have I. Suppose I cash in the first-class ticket for a couple of economy tickets, with a stopover in Las Vegas? Would you come with me?"

He looked at me for a minute. He knew damned well that I was scared to death about breaking out of the grim comfort of my depression. "Okay," he finally said. "We'll have a ball and make a bundle."

So, I traded in the ticket and picked up two economy seats on a plane that would get us into Las Vegas at 2:30 in the morning. We were young, and Las Vegas was open twenty-four hours; I figured we could gamble all night, get a couple hours of sleep and take another plane to Los Angeles. I'd be there just in time for my appointments the next morning.

Bob showed up at Idlewild Airport with his luggage and a small white envelope. "Listen," he said, while we were on the check-in line, "We want to be fresh to gamble, right? So, what we do is take a couple of sleeping pills when we get to the airport. We'll have a good night's sleep and then knock 'em dead at the blackjack table."

It seemed like a first-class idea. In those days, propeller-driven planes took seven hours to get from New York to Las Vegas, and sleeping was the best way I could imagine to spend seven hours in the air. So, just as they were calling our plane's departure, we took the pills.

We climbed aboard, asked for a couple of pillows, and settled into our seats for a blissfully ignorant flight. In a few minutes, the pills took effect, and we drifted sweetly off to sleep.

I was dreaming, I guess, when the stewardess nudged me awake.

"God, what a smooth ride," I said, fighting to wake up.

"We haven't left New York," she said.

That chased the dream. "What do you mean?" I shouted.

"We have engine trouble," said the stewardess, smiling brightly and trying, unsuccessfully, to awaken Bob. Everybody has to deplane."

"Deplane?" Her airplane jargon was making no impression on my stupor. I began to drift off again.

"Get off!" she shouted, poking me awake.

"Why?"

She repeated the whole procedure to me again, and both of us went to work on Bob. It was turning into a long, long night.

The stewardess finally deplaned us, and we and the other passengers settled down to spend four fitful hours in the waiting room, while the airline brought in another carrier. Bob and I were as groggy as a couple of amateur drunks, too doped up to stay awake and too nervous about missing our plane to fall asleep.

Two and a half hours later, we were reloaded. By this time, the effect of the pills had worn off. We spent a sleepless six hours in the air. By 5:30 in the morning, when we finally touched down in Las Vegas, we were a couple of certified zombies.

But we were game zombies. We staggered into the casino in our hotel and tried to concentrate on gambling. We went from one table to the next, and lost most of what we'd set aside to begin our winnings.

"What the hell," I finally said to Bob, after both of us had tried unsuccessfully to concentrate on our blackjack hands. "Let's get some sleep." And that's what we did.

I was actually trembling as I approached the Warner Brothers lot on the first full morning of work. But once I was there, time seemed to collapse. It was home; it was natural; it was almost easy. The film was already deeply into preproduction; Mr. Abbott was working with Stanley Donen, who would be co-directing the film; Bob Fosse was recreating the dances; the film was adhering very closely to the original.

My task was to train the ensemble and Doris Day, who was playing the Janis Paige role. A mass of freckles and beauty and good spirits, she was a genuinely sweet person, and a joy to work with. She had an agile mind, and a sure musical sense, and teaching the songs to her was a breeze.

It was so natural that a couple of days into rehearsal, I thought why not give her a new song, one I'd write myself? It would help her, help me, and possibly help my future. So, I sat down with my tape recorder, and then with a musical secretary, and wrote a ballad for her called "The Man Who Invented Love."

She loved it. It laid in her range, it had nice lyrics, and what was most important, it was right for both her and the character. I played it for Mr. Abbott and Stanley Donen, and they liked it, too. It was a sure bet for the film, a breakthrough for me. My career was slowly re-engaging its gears.

What I didn't know at the time, nor did anyone else, was the ultimate fate of the song. It would never be heard. It would end up on the proverbial cutting room floor.

But, in retrospect, that was the least important role the song played in my life. What was most important was that I'd written it. I was functioning by myself. I relaxed and enjoyed California, and moved into a small but lively residential hotel.

Among my fellow residents were Bob Merrill, Bob Loggia and his wife Marjorie, and Tony Randall. Tony got a particular kick out of me, the Easterner encountering movie moguls for the first time on a day-to-day basis. I'd come home, frustrated and exasperated, and sigh, "They just don't understand!"—because they didn't.

I must have repeated the same routine every day without knowing it because, from the first week onward, Tony would appear at the pool or in the lobby, stop me, and say, in a despairing voice, "They just don't understand!" And to this day, every time he and I meet, he fixes me with a baleful stare, shakes his head, and intones, mournfully, "They just don't understand!"

Nelson Riddle, who was the musical director on the film, invited me to sit in on a Frank Sinatra recording session. It was awesome. Sinatra, I learned, rarely needed more than two takes. In an hour and a half, he recorded four songs, and they couldn't have been improved upon. It was phenomenal, and I told him that when I met him.

He brushed it aside. "So you're Adler," he said, with a half smile as we left the studio. "I'm Sinatra, the schmuck that turned down 'Hey There.' "

So, I mended in the California sun. The music was recorded; the film went into production; my job was finished.

I was in no rush to get back to New York. Life was easy in California, and memory-free. Hollywood was an active, busy place in 1956. Television was just a passing fad. The big stars were still the mainstay of the film industry. That it would all change in a few years might have been predictable, and was probably very much on the minds of some of the decision makers. But in 1956, the performers all thought of themselves as movie stars first, foremost, and always.

Groucho Marx hadn't become a game show host yet; he was a star who had only just begun to dim. He was a boyhood idol of mine, and it was a great thrill to meet him.

I'd run into his wife Enid on the Warner lot, and she in turn introduced me to a young girl named Joy—who was just that—and invited the two of us to dinner at the Marx home.

Joy and I arrived at the appointed hour and were met at the door by Enid. The house was bright and tastefully decorated, and the walls of the entryway were filled with an array of gorgeous paintings.

"These are wonderful," I said to her. "Who did them?"

"I did," she answered, simply.

I was astonished. "I didn't know you were—you really painted these?"

She laughed. "Yes."

I wandered around the room, truly excited over the paintings. "This one," I said, gesticulating at a landscape, "and that," and I pointed to a portrait, "are *particularly* fine."

"You like them."

"Yes."

"Good," she concluded. "I'd like to give them to you."

"Oh, I couldn't do that," I remonstrated. I was embarrassed, not because I'd overpraised them, but because of her impulsive generosity, which I thought she'd regret later.

"No," she insisted, linking her arm in mine and escorting me to the living room, "I've really decided to give them to you."

And sure enough, the next day, a package arrived at my hotel. It was the two paintings, carefully wrapped. I called her and asked her again if she hadn't been too impulsive, and she repeated her words of the night before. I relaxed. I was pleased, and honored, and put them where they could be seen.

A couple of days later, the phone rang. It was Groucho. He dispensed with the preliminaries and got right down to the subject of the paintings. "Now Richard," he said, "about those pictures. You know, you really can't do that. It's not right. Those frames alone cost me five hundred bucks apiece."

I knew frames, and if they were worth five hundred dollars, I was Picasso. "Well, what do you want me to do?" I asked him. "Do you want me to give them back to you? I don't want to offend Enid."

"No no no no no," he added, quickly, "not that. But something's got to be done."

I got the drift. "Would you allow me to pay for the frames?" I asked.

"Well," he said, as if he hadn't been driving at it all along, "All right."

So, I sent him a thousand dollars, and thought to myself, I don't really have a lot of luck getting paintings for nothing. First, there was Maugham and the Lautrec. Now, there's Groucho and the Enid.

I stopped.

The Lautrec. Maugham. The Villa Mauresque. When I'd been there, one of the conversations we'd had was about turning *Of Human Bondage* into a musical. He'd been intrigued by the idea, and had mentioned it again when he'd come to London for *Pajama Game*'s opening.

Well, why not? I thought. I'd proved I could write a song. The next test would be to see if I could write an entire score. I began to pack my bags. Hollywood had served its purpose—in spades.

As soon as I got back to New York, I wrote a letter to Maugham, outlining my plan for the musicalization of *Of Human Bondage*. If I could get a preliminary okay from him, I said, I could begin to cast it, look for a Mildred, get some preliminary backing, and then, with that money, begin to write.

The reply came back within two weeks. He was intrigued. He'd like to meet with me and discuss it further. He still thought it was workable, and I had his blessing to begin.

I read the novel again. Twice. I took notes. I started an outline. And then, as the shape of the show began to form in front of me, I began to realize that I had taken on an enormous project, perhaps too much for a first outing, particularly for someone who was used to working with a collaborator.

I talked it over with Bob Merrill. He was interested. He took the book, read it, and became more interested. And I became more excited. But the ducks had to be in a row before we could begin. My confidence wasn't that solidified, nor was his.

So, in midwinter of 1957, I went to London, to get a cast on paper that could be used to gain both backers and Maugham's signature on a contract.

I had another, personal motive in auditioning in London rather than in New York. The separation agreement with Marion had originally stated that she could only live in New York State. Shortly after that, she'd asked me for a modification. She was a British subject; her home as a child had been in London; she wanted to go home.

It was a tough decision, but one I had to make in her favor. How could I honorably stipulate where another human being could live? It would be a long way to go to see my sons, but I could understand her anguish and her wishes, and so I'd agreed to the modification. Shortly after that, she and Andrew and Christopher had gone to London and settled in to a house in Mayfair. Now, I was looking forward to more quality time with my boys, the treasure of my first marriage.

The Pajama Game was still playing at the Coliseum, so I set up a series of general auditions there, and canvassed some of my friends for suggestions for a female star.

Kenneth Tynan knew the ideal woman. Her name was Sally Ann Howes. "You've just got to see her, Richard," he enthused. "She's the most beautiful woman in the world. *And* she sings better than anyone alive. *And* she's a brilliant actress. *And* a marvelous comedienne. A true English rose. Well, you simply *must* meet her."

I knew that Kenneth was given to hyperbole; still, I'd be a fool to ignore such an enthusiastic endorsement. My assistant called her agent, Harry Foster. He suggested that I see her in *A Hatful of Rain,* in which she was then starring with Sam Wanamaker. I sent back a reply: I wanted to hear her sing, too, and she certainly wouldn't be singing in *A Hatful of Rain.*

Days passed and no further word came from Harry Foster. I had one more day of auditions to conduct, and then I was booked on the *Liberté,* back to New York. On the last day, Harry Foster came into the theatre. I still hadn't found my Mildred, and the lineup that morning didn't bode any better than those before it.

He introduced himself and said, "Miss Howes is coming here today."

"Good," I answered, turning my attention back to the stage.

"But she's not going to sing for you," he added.

"What do you mean?" My attention flicked back to him.

He settled in his seat. "She's much too big a star to sing for anybody."

I was furious. "Anybody?" I said, forgetting about the stage entirely. "Am I anybody? Is Somerset Maugham anybody? To hell with her. Tell her not to bother. I wouldn't talk to her anyway."

He seemed genuinely distressed. "She just won't do it; I know that."

"Then forget it," I said. I already had.

The next auditionee entered from the wings and handed her music to the pianist. I jotted a few notes. And then, the staccato tapping of high heels clicked down the aisle toward me. Harry Foster turned around in his seat, then whispered to me, "Here comes Miss Howes now."

Good, I thought. I'll tell her who I think she is. I wheeled around, the first words already formed: Who the hell do you think you are, I said, in my mind, Who in hell are *you* to say you won't audition—

But the words died, unsaid. Kenneth Tynan was right. She was the most beautiful woman in the world. More delicately formed, more blonde, more exquisite than anyone I could remember ever seeing.

I rose to meet her. "Miss Howes," I said, "I hear you won't sing for me, but would you like to have lunch?"

She paused for a fraction of a moment, her blue-green eyes evaluating me. And then she said, as musically as if she'd been singing for me, "That would be very nice."

After lunch, we went to my rented flat on Charles Street, and spent the afternoon increasing our fascination with each other. By four o'clock, I was besotted, and I broke a date for that evening to take her to supper after the performance.

It was a whirlwind, a major reordering of the atmosphere. I convinced her that she should pick me up at my flat at 9:30 the next morning. The two of us would meet my children at South Street. My mind and my plans were in fast forward.

She loved Andrew and Christopher and they responded immediately to her. Marion was out of town, and it was just as well, as later developments would prove. In less than twenty-four hours, Sally and I had coveredsixmonthsofpreliminaries.

And it wasn't over. In the taxi to Victoria Station, where I was to catch the boat train to Southampton, I pleaded with her to come with me, just as far as Southampton. There was another train returning to London that would get her back before makeup and curtain time that night.

"Absolutely not," she said, smiling, her exquisite features too perfect for any man to bear, much less leave.

I pleaded my case like a barrister before the bar, and she relented, with a tiny laugh. "I don't know what we're beginning, Richard," she said, "I haven't had time to think."

I wasn't about to let her think long enough to have doubts. As soon as I was aboard the *Liberté,* I sent her a cable; at sea, I radiophoned her; in New York, I phoned and wrote and phoned and wrote again. Aly Khan couldn't have pursued Bettina with any more singlemindedness than I as I went after Sally Ann Howes.

And there was good reason, beyond the instant physical attraction I had for her. Everything that had turned the marriage between Marion and me sour was reversed with Sally Ann. Marion was insecure about her talents, unrealized professionally, and resentful of my successes. Sally Ann was secure about her talents, had long ago realized her professional ambitions, and was now building upon them. She'd grown up in the theatre; her grandfather was the London producer J.A.E. Malone, and her father was the great British comedian Bobby Howes, with whom she'd appeared, to tremendous critical acclaim, four years previously, in the London production of *Paint Your Wagon.* It had been her touching portrayal of the daughter, both on and offstage, of Bobby Howes, that had prompted Alan Jay Lerner to cast her as Julie Andrews' replacement in *My Fair Lady.* In early 1958, the New York leads would be coming to London, and Sally Ann would be going to New York to recreate Eliza Doolittle there.

So, we were equals, I felt. One person's success wouldn't tread on the other's confidence. But most of all, I loved her, enough so that I wanted to spend every moment with her. I wrote impassioned letters, beseeching her to spend a month with Bob Merrill and me, in the house we'd rented in Westhampton, Long Island. She finally agreed, and arrived on July 13, the week before her birthday. And she stayed, not for a month, but for the entire summer. By the end of August, she'd agreed not only to star in *Of Human Bondage,* but in my life.

Now that we had our leading lady, Bob and I got down to work on the musicalization of *Of Human Bondage* with a vengeance. By the middle of September, we'd dented the first act pretty thoroughly.

Sally Ann was slated for two television appearances in England, and so had to leave, but I talked her into coming back immediately and staying with me until she went into *My Fair Lady,* in February.

By this time, we'd decided to be married as soon as my divorce from Marion became final. And so, we moved in together in my apartment at 130 East 67th Street.

And the trouble began.

Somehow, Marion found out about Sally Ann and me. And the news apparently drove her crazy. She bombarded me with insane telephone calls that could only have originated in the head of a woman who felt herself scorned. "I'm going to expose you to the newspapers!" she said, in one particularly vitriolic exchange. "I'll expose you, and bury your career, and I'll ruin hers! She'll never open in *My Fair Lady* when I get through with both of you!"

I bluffed, I cajoled, I tried to joke her out of it. But secretly, I was worried. My career wasn't exactly in the public eye, but Sally Ann's was. I didn't have the right to jeopardize the great chance she was getting with *My Fair Lady*.

I finally decided to lay it out to those who would be making the major decisions in our lives for the next few months. I went to Herman Levin, *My Fair Lady*'s producer, and told him the story. He chuckled. "Don't worry," he said, "it'll be good publicity."

That was encouraging, all right. At least Sally Ann's job was safe. Now it was time to look out for my interests. I visited my lawyer, Sidney Cohn, and outlined the mess for him.

And he laughed, too. "Don't worry about it," he said. "What kind of damage can it do you? Be happy. You know what Shakespeare said. All the world loves a lover."

Yeah, I thought, as I hung up the telephone. But Shakespeare doesn't know what *Marion* said. Still, I could relax now, think about the future, and get back to writing.

For some reason, Sidney Cohn's words stayed with me for the next few days. And before long, the quote from Shakespeare began to transform itself in my mind and melt into a rhythm, and a rhyme scheme. "Everybody Loves a Lover . . ." it began, and wouldn't let up until I set it to paper.

A few days later, I had a dummy lyric, and I liked it, and said so one lunchtime to Bob Allen, a composer I'd known from the old Tin Pan Alley days. We went to his studio, and before long, we had a song, and a good one, one that felt like a hit.

Bob and I both owned publishing companies. Mine was Andrew Music, and his was Korwin. We flipped a coin to see who would publish the song. Bob won. He took it with him to the Coast and showed it to Doris Day, who had told me just a month previously that she was looking for a novelty song. She liked it enough to record it, and "Everybody Loves a Lover" became a smash, instantly. In three weeks, it became number one on the Hit Parade. And after that, it became number one all over the world.

Marion didn't follow through with her threats, and we reached a kind of a détente; Sidney Cohn called and told me that the final divorce decree would probably be granted by the first of the year.

Sally Ann and I decided to get married as soon as the divorce became final, but this meant taking our honeymoon before we got married. She had to go into rehearsals for *My Fair Lady* on January 4, so there'd be no time after the marriage. We went to Key West, ran into David Susskind and his family, played a lot of poker, and had a sunny week as a make-believe man and wife.

We didn't have long to wait to make it authentic. On January 3, 1958, the day my divorce became final, we were married in Arlington, Virginia. It was such a romantic, passionate courtship, full of conflict and resolution and danger and fulfillment. How could either of us have known that this would be the character of our marriage, too?

I got down to work on an idea I'd discussed with David Susskind in Key West. There, under a blazing sun, with the blue Atlantic lapping at our feet, we'd talked about two TV musicals, one for autumn, one for Christmas. The October musical would be an adaptation of *Little Women*; the Christmas musical would be a treatment of O. Henry's short story *The Gift of the Magi*, and it would star Sally Ann. David and I would co-produce, and I would write the music and lyrics.

At the time, I'd had deep doubts about my ability to follow through on the project, but now, with my life falling into place, I plunged into it energetically.

Little Women had an all-star cast—Jeannie Carson, Florence Henderson, Joel Grey, Margaret O'Brien, and Risë Stevens. It appeared on October 16, as an hour special on the CBS network. The reviews were good, though, as *Variety* correctly pointed out, ". . . trimmed as it was for the hour's length, and garnished besides with eight songs from Richard Adler's fruitful cupboard (not to count the reprises) Louisa May Alcott's eye-watering evergreen for youngsters emerged on the picture tube as a fluffy petit four for dainty palates with not much to sink the choppers into."

On December 9, we followed up with *The Gift of the Magi*, with Sally Ann and Gordon MacRae starring. Though the national reviews were good, the New York reviews were bad. But they made no difference to the public, apparently. The ratings were excellent, the sponsor was delighted, and both shows would be replayed the following year.

It was an important exercise for me. Cole Porter was right. I could write both words and music alone.

It was also an affirmation of a hope for Sally Ann and me. We proved that we not only weren't professional threats to each other; we could work together, and beautifully.

It was 11:30 Saturday night, during the run of *My Fair Lady.* I picked up Sally Ann backstage at the Mark Hellinger Theatre. She was in her dressing room; her stage makeup was off and her face still glistened from the cold cream that had removed it. She was putting on some lipstick. Her lips were pursed to make sure the lipstick was correct. She rose, wriggled into a tight-fitting chiffon silk dress, slipped into a pair of pumps, grabbed my arm, and we were off to 760 Park Avenue where our friend Tyrone Power had rented the penthouse for the winter of 1958.

The cab let us off at the northwest corner of 72nd Street and Park. We rang the doorbell, and in a few seconds, Ty greeted us, wearing an apron over his trousers. He ushered us into the study, an intimate, well-appointed room with African and pre-Columbian artifacts casually placed in easy-to-notice, well-lit corners.

Peter Ustinov and Laurence Olivier were seated across from each other and laughing over some quip about the British stage. We all exchanged greetings as Ty prepared drinks for us and excused himself to return to the kitchen to a shepherd's pie he was preparing for our midnight repast.

He came back shortly with some beluga caviar and uncorked a bottle of Dom Perignon champagne. Our host, as gracious as he was handsome, asked me about my work and wondered if he could come over to hear it sometime.

The phone rang and Ty picked it up. "Hello," he said with customary resonance. His face quickly turned serious. "I'm going to take this in the other room, Lana." He excused himself, saying he would be right back.

Nobody paid much attention, and Larry got up and did his soft shoe routine that he was preparing for the film, *The Entertainer.* We all cheered the brilliant interpretation of the second-rate vaudevillian and laughed generously at the cockney accent he emoted. Olivier's genius was particularly pleasing to Sally Ann, whose cockney was also perfect for *My Fair Lady.*

Suddenly, we noticed that quite a good deal of time had elapsed since Ty had left the room. He'd been absent over half an hour. We began to discuss the mysterious call that kept our host away for so long and hoped the shepherd's pie hadn't burnt to a crisp. Ten minutes later, Ty re-entered, looking drawn and pale. "Listen," he said, "I'm terribly sorry but something has come up and I'm going to have to call off supper."

He seemed extremely agitated. The room was filled with an atmosphere of anticipated gloom, and in response to our concern, Ty turned to each of us slowly and said, "We're good friends." He hesitated. "I guess I'd better tell you."

His voice faltered slightly. "Sit down. That was Lana Turner calling from California." (Lana and Ty had been lovers many years before and had remained very close friends.) Ty explained that "poor Lana" had been living with a gangster, a handsome young thug named Johnny Stompanato. That was fairly common knowledge as the gossip columns had worked over the relationship pretty thoroughly.

Lana and Johnny had just had a terrible argument in Lana's apartment. During the course of the fracas, Johnny, who had been drinking heavily, started beating up Lana, Ty was explaining, his voice just a level above a whisper.

Suddenly, Lana's thirteen-year-old daughter Cheryl Crane rushed into Lana's bedroom, and tried to stop Johnny from hitting her mother. Johnny shoved the child away. Cheryl ran out of the room and came back with a butcher knife.

Ty's voice became almost inaudible. She saw Stompanato on top of her mother with his hands around her throat. She plunged the knife into Johnny's back. Stompanato was dead!

Lana was hysterical, and had called Ty for advice. She hadn't spoken to anyone and didn't know what to do.

We sat there stupefied, and then we all asked Ty what he had said.

"Call the police, and call your lawyer, and tell them the truth," Ty replied.

We left. As I went out into the street, I asked Sally Ann, "What do you think *really* happened?"

I felt a sadness for Ty having been saddled with the tragic responsibility of guiding his great friend through her hideous problem. What could Ty do to help Lana and Cheryl? And how would the papers treat the happening? At that moment, only five of us knew this horrible secret. The next morning the whole world would be talking about it. A year later, in a California courtroom, Cheryl Crane would be acquitted.

Ty never lived to see the outcome of this drama. He died of a heart attack on November 15, while filming in Spain.

Sally Ann stayed with *My Fair Lady* for a year. When her run as Eliza Doolittle ended, the time came for us to take our *real* honeymoon. Sally Ann and I decided to sail to Italy on the *Cristoforo Colombo,* drive from Naples to Rome, then fly to Nice and see Maugham at the Villa Mauresque. Bob and I had finished a draft of the script and score for *Of Human Bondage;* we liked what we'd written, and I was anxious to close the deal.

During the run of *My Fair Lady,* we grew close to Judy Ross and her new husband, businessman Elliott Coulter. Elliott and I both loved to play cards, and Judy and Sally Ann got along famously. We invited Judy and Elliott to come along on our deferred honeymoon. Sally Ann and I thought it would be great fun, and we wound up having a marvelous time together, despite a few glitches. Our stateroom turned into a wading pool with six inches of water in it when I left the porthole open one night during a storm; Sally Ann got deathly ill from taking vaccination shots; I got even more deathly ill from eating tainted chicken in Rome: and Judy threatened to kill Elliott and me in cold blood, if we didn't stop playing gin rummy.

At the end of two bounteous weeks, we bid goodbye to Judy and Elliott in Rome, and flew to Nice. On the way, three of the airplane's four engines conked out, and for a while I wondered if the trip was really going to be worth it. But one look at the setting sun on the Mediterranean as we circled the Nice airport and drifted slowly and smoothly in for a landing, and my spirits soared. I couldn't wait to show Sally Ann the Villa Mauresque.

We descended the staircase from the plane in high, but shaky spirits. It was a warm, bright day, and there was a long walk from the plane to the terminal. As we began the trek, I noticed a crowd of people standing near the entrance gates. As we drew nearer, it seemed as if they were carrying mirrors. The reflection of the setting sun was sending off little detonations of white and yellow light from the group.

I strained to spot Alan Searle. I figured that if there were any congestion at all, he'd be well away from it. But he was nowhere to be seen.

We were closer to the crowd now, and I could see that they were journalists. The sun had been reflecting off their camera lenses. Who was famous enough on our flight to draw that big a gathering? I wondered.

And then, as we approached the gate, I saw the venerable, bent frame of W. Somerset Maugham. I was thrilled and touched that this great, eighty-five-year-old man would personally make the forty-minute trip from Cap Ferrat to greet Sally Ann and me.

The photographers surrounded us. They posed Sally Ann on one side of Maugham and me on the other, and shouted and flashed away like a bombardment. I tried to concentrate on smiling, but in the middle of the melee of shooting, I felt a sharp elbow, digging me repeatedly in the ribs.

I turned, and Maugham was chuckling. "B-B-But R-R-R-Richard," he said, "I d-d-d-didn't know y-y-you were s-s-so f-f-f-f-famous."

And so began a week of high hilarity and ribald jokes, many of them at my expense. Sally Ann was, as I knew she would be, enchanted with the villa and with Maugham, who did everything he could to make our stay memorable. He was the perfect host. Our every wish was met, before we wished it. Our bathroom was stocked with stores of different varieties of soap, shaving creams, after-shave lotion, cologne, and bath salts; we were wined and dined, at the villa, and one unique evening in an Arab restaurant in old Nice, where the order and the check were written in Arabic on the tablecloth.

By the end of one week, Maugham had put his signature to the contract that would legally allow Bob and me to turn *Of Human Bondage* into a musical. "R-R-Rodgers and Hammerstein asked me. T-t-t-turned them down," he said, warmly. "B-b-b-but I like you, Richard. I think you're the m-m-m-man to d-d-do it."

And oh how I wish he'd been right. Now that the contract had been signed and sealed, Bob and I invited David Merrick to my studio at 130 East 67th Street to listen to the completed book, music, and lyrics of *Of Human Bondage*.

We made him comfortable, and launched into the show. As the first act unfolded, David Merrick seemed to grow older and sicker. He looked like a man who'd eaten something that had violently disagreed with him. He looked disconsolate. He seemed distracted.

At the end of the first act, I drew Bob into the other room. "Look, Bob," I said, "I can't go on with this. I just can't go on. He hates it. He despises it. What's the use of wasting his time and ours?"

Bob shook his head slowly. "No," he said, "I think we should do the rest of the show."

"But he won't *buy* this show! You can *tell*!" I insisted,

"Just calm down, Richard," Bob soothed me. "We have him here now. Let's do the show."

So we did, and I fully expected David Merrick to get up and leave, at any moment.

Instead, to my absolute astonishment, he stayed to the last note, rose, shook himself free of his apparent sickness, and said, "I like it. It has a marvelous score. There are nice things in it. But—"

Oh oh, I thought. Here's where the words match the look on his face.

"But," he went on, "I won't produce it with that book. The book has to be rewritten."

We exhaled, in relief, and asked him for advice about librettists.

He suggested Bella and Sam Spewak, who had, ten years before, written the enormously clever and successful *Kiss Me Kate* with Cole Porter. We met with them, and they agreed to take on the job of reworking the book.

A couple of months passed, and they delivered the new libretto. It was dreadful.

We sent it on to David Merrick, but we knew before we put it in an envelope what his reply would be. And what the replies would be from the other producers to whom we'd send it after he turned it down.

Once more, my career had ground to a halt. Sally Ann's, on the other hand, was soaring. She'd been a huge success in *My Fair Lady,* and was reading new scripts daily. She'd appeared on TV on the "Bell Telephone Hour," the "Perry Como Show," the "Ed Sullivan Show," and the "U.S. Steel Hour."

But her most prestigious dramatic role on TV was in a CBS production of Hemingway's *The Fifth Column.* Richard Burton and Maximilian Schell were her co-stars. It was a major production, and the rehearsals were intense and long. My time was my own now, so I picked her up after rehearsals, and we'd spend quiet dinners together on the West Side of Manhattan, near the studio.

One night, Richard Burton came along, just for a drink, he said. Within half an hour, he'd dominated our dinner, bragging about his sexual prowess and naming names, which I thought was in inexcusable taste. It didn't take long for a mutual antipathy to develop between the two of us.

"Not a very nice man," I said to Sally Ann on the way back to our apartment.

"He's rather charming, actually," said Sally Ann. "Has some really wonderful qualities."

"They weren't very visible tonight," I said, and I would never, it turned out, be treated to them, for it was Richard Burton who would be responsible for creating the first real trouble in my marriage to Sally Ann.

It was he, it turned out, who would encourage Maximilian Schell to direct his charms toward Sally Ann. My suspicions were slightly raised, when, as rehearsals continued, she devoted more and more of our dinner conversation to Schell, to his sensitivity as an actor and a man, to how much he admired me, and to how anxious he was to meet me—all of which struck me as excessive.

One night, after *The Fifth Column* had been produced, live, to very good reviews, Sally Ann and I went to a party at which Schell and Burton and most of the cast of the show had also been invited. Schell, as I supposed, didn't seem all that interested in meeting me and talking about my shows.

When 2:00 A.M. arrived, I said to Sally Ann, "Let's go home."

"I don't want to go home," she replied.

"It's late," I insisted. "There's work tomorrow."

"You go home and I'll come later," she said, levelly.

And I did, but I had a sick feeling in my stomach. For the next few days, Sally Ann was distant and out of reach. I wasn't quite sure what was going on in her mind, but I knew I had to do something about the situation.

Schell was staying at the Algonquin Hotel, and the next morning, I called him there.

"Hello, Max," I said, when he answered the phone, and before I'd had a chance to go into my prepared speech, he began to talk about the fantastic woman he had in his life. "I want to marry her," he continued, "but she's already married to some songwriter."

On and on he went, obviously thinking I was somebody else. I muttered a few monosyllables, and hung up.

I was sick. I knew that no matter what happened from this point onward, the relationship between Sally Ann and me would never be the same. When trust dies, there's hardly any hope for a marriage. But in the midst of the proof of this, I didn't want to believe it. I wanted it all to be a huge mistake.

When Sally Ann got up, I was prepared to confront her with what I knew and what I hoped. But before I'd had a chance to begin, she dropped a bombshell. "Look," she said, obviously uncomfortable, and concerned for my feelings. "I might be in love with Max. I don't know. I want to spend two days with him, to find out."

I didn't know what to say. It was an honest admission, an understandable confusion. It was lousy for my ego, but it was straightforward. She wasn't trying to delude me, so it wasn't really cheating. And I also remembered the two days that Marion had spent, years ago, to sort out her doubts about marrying me. And that had ended happily.

"Okay," I said.

In a day and a half, Sally Ann was back, and the business with Maximilian Schell had ended. She swore to me that she never went to bed with him, and though it was difficult, I chose to believe her.

We resumed our marriage, trying to pretend that nothing had happened, that life together was just fine. But it would never be as it had been. It would, from that time forward, be tinged with distrust.

I tried to ignore the fallout. We spent more time in each other's company, and I cast about for ideas so that we could work together again. Maybe that would erase this, I thought. Maybe it would bring us close enough so that our mutual need to wander and explore—which we'd been able to control until now—could be bested.

I was searching for ideas and collaborators. One day, I had lunch at the Colony restaurant with super producer Leland Hayward. Talk came around to a project we'd discussed earlier, the musicalization of the Audrey Hepburn—Gregory Peck film, *Roman Holiday.* He'd put me in touch with Carolyn Leigh, a brilliant lyricist. We'd tried to collaborate. It didn't work.

"I think I'd like to try *Roman Holiday* alone," I said to Leland that day.

"Fine," he said, and I got to work.

Leland liked what I did, and brought in Robert (*Tea and Sympathy*) Anderson to write the book. It was good. I performed the score for the complete NBC brass. They liked it, and the financing was in place.

We cast Elliot Gould as the photographer, and Liza Minelli, then only eighteen, was set for the Audrey Hepburn role of the princess. She was enthusiastic about the score. She would take songs home with her, and would come back beaming. "Mama loved this song; Mama loved that song," she would say. Having Judy Garland like my stuff made me feel terrific.

And then, the bottom dropped out. Leland became ill—very ill. Everything went on hold. One by one, our stars drifted away. And the property ultimately reverted to its original owner, Paramount Pictures.

A few months before the Maximilian Schell episode, I'd picked up the *New York Times.* Buried on a back page, there was an article about the son of an African tribal chief who'd attended Oxford on a scholarship. A brilliant man, he'd spent seven years there, and had earned his M.D.

Then, his father died, and he was called back to Africa to assume the leadership of his village. He went, but by now, he was no longer a mindless practitioner of the ancient ways of his tribe. He'd absorbed not only the knowledge but the values of another culture. He brought modern medicine with him—and, by implication, a totally alien way of life. The *Times* article chronicled his fight to wrest the will of his people away from their witch doctor.

It was a fascinating tale, and something had clicked in me when I read it. The story had conflict—the basic ingredient of drama—on a multitude of levels. But more than that. It dealt with a contemporary problem. It had an exotic setting. It offered an opportunity for an entire smorgasbord of musical thoughts. If a love story were added, it could complicate the conflict and humanize it. And if the love interest were a *white* woman, that woman could be Sally Ann.

It was certainly unorthodox material for a musical, but then again *Of Human Bondage* wasn't exactly a backstage story, either. This story had all of the elements of riveting drama, and all the potential of being an exciting, different sort of show. I wasn't sure *how,* but I knew it had potential. And so, I'd put it on file.

Now, as if fate were taking a hand and determining my destiny once more, Sally Ann and I were invited to a cocktail party. One of my idols, Adlai Stevenson, was there. I knew what Stevenson stood for, and I was thrilled to see him again. When I was first introduced to him, by my dear friend, the equally humanistic Mary Lasker, he'd just been defeated for the presidency, and had come back from the Belgian Congo, where he'd spent time observing tribal life. We'd discussed this at length.

Now, three years later, at Mary Lasker's, that first conversation came back to me, and I reminded him of it.

"Yes. The Belgian Congo," he said, "The most exciting area in the world, and full of contrasts. You can be in a modern city like Stanleyville one minute, and then, a few miles away, you can be in the most primitive village, where human sacrifice is still practiced."

I talked with Stevenson for a long time that night, and the next day, I began to sketch an outline of a musical that combined my story with some of his perceptions. I knew I needed a librettist. But I also knew that it was a show whose music and lyrics I would write alone.

And so, *Kwamina,* my first theatre piece without Jerry, was born.

M Y search for a librettist ended at another party. This one took place at the home of Robert Alan Aurthur, the playwright and television writer whose play *A Very Special Baby* hadn't won him any prizes, but whose television dramas *Man on a Mountaintop* and *A Man Is Ten Feet Tall* had garnered him two Sylvania Awards. Sally Ann and I were there through the good offices of Mel Brooks, who, with his cohort Carl Reiner, performed, that evening, for the first time ever, their classic, excruciatingly funny routine, "The Two Thousand-Year-Old Man."

When we'd dried our eyes from laughing, Robert Alan Aurthur and I got into a conversation about plots. I tried the African one on him, and he nodded his head enthusiastically. "I had a classmate in Graduate School at the University of Pennsylvania in 1946," he said. "Kwame Nkrumah."

"You mean the president of—" I said.

"Yes," he nodded. "He's the president of Ghana now, but then he was just a graduate student. And he had these glowing ideals. 'Change everything now!' he used to tell me. Then he became president, and he found he had to deal with the fetish men, the witch doctors." Aurthur sighed. "Now his philosophy is 'I won't bother you if you won't bother me.' They're powerful. The witch doctors. Supernaturally powerful."

It was a beginning, a tentative joining of interests, and, in light of what happened afterwards, it probably should have ended right there.

But I was naive. I loved *A Man Is Ten Feet Tall*, particularly in its expanded, movie version, starring Sidney Poitier. I felt that in it, Bob had shown that he had a thoroughgoing knowledge of the vision, sensibilities, and mental processes of Blacks. What I overlooked was that there was a world of difference between the thinking of Black

Africans and Black Americans. And although Bob had a great depth of understanding of the American experience of Blacks, he would never wholly comprehend the *persona* of the Black African. And that would constitute a fatal flaw in our show.

Years before, Oscar Hammerstein had said to me, "Nothing can ever work, no matter how great the songs are, if the story isn't right, and the people don't ring true." He was talking about *Very Warm for May*, the flop he'd written with Jerome Kern. Oscar had been uttering a universal theatrical truth.

Of course, I didn't know that it would eventually apply to our show in that spring of 1960. Bob and I began to meet, every day, on the same bench in Central Park, near the Metropolitan Museum of Art. More dimensions began to be added to the project, as he recalled a young Navajo Indian he'd met in New Mexico a few years ago. The man had gone to the University of Chicago to study medicine, and came back with a non-Indian from Chicago as his bride. The oldsters in the tribe refused to accept either his bride or his new ideas. Everyone greeted him with hostility—except the children. "But the old people are dying off," he'd told Bob. "I just have to work with the children, and wait."

And so we had our theme. And each day, Bob would come up with new ideas. One time, he arrived excitedly, after having read Richard Wright's book *Black Power*, which talked about Wright's trip to a small village in Ghana, on the eve of that country's independence. He'd encountered fear and silence and revelation, as the village waited for the fetish men to pick ten human sacrifices to accompany their dead chief to paradise.

Our show would take place on the eve of an African nation's independence, too. And its main character—and its title—would be *Kwamina*, which was not only a variation on Kwame Nkrumah, the man who had brought the strands of the story together for us, but an African word that meant "Born on Sunday."

It was a new beginning, then, in a host of ways. And it felt right, from the start. Sally Ann had been excited by the idea as soon as I'd told her about it. She, as much as I, felt that working together would bring us closer together.

And, as I plunged into the writing of the score, I found that it came easily. Astonishingly so. In many cases, the music and the words came together simultaneously.

I was enjoying myself, too. I was working, really working again. Ideas exploded. I determined to write two scores—one with an African feeling for the Africans; one with a Western feeling for Sally Ann and the other European character, called Blair. The music that emerged was like nothing I'd ever written before. It refused to follow set patterns of popular music, but, like the theatrical songs Jerry and I had written, it flowed smoothly, acquiring its shape from the shape of the scene in which it fit.

Other pieces began to fall into place, as if they'd been meant to all along. Some time after the book and most of the score had been written, I discussed the show with Johnny Schlesinger, a friend of mine and the head of one of the two wealthiest and most powerful families in South Africa. He questioned me carefully about the subject, about the production, about the music. The more questions he asked, the more excited he seemed to get.

"You've got to play me some of the music," he finally said.

I agreed, and invited him to come to my studio at 130 East 67th Street, where my pianist and musical secretary, Herbert Shutz, played the songs I'd written and I sang them.

Johnny seemed to be in heaven. "Do you want to be involved?" I asked him.

"Yes," he answered.

"How much of it do you want?"

"All of it."

I shook my head. "No, really, Johnny, how much?"

"All or nothing," he said.

He was a friend of mine. "It's a risk," I said, in spite of my belief in what I was doing. "It isn't a commercial type show. It's a message show. It has miscegenation in it. It's not going to be a money show. It's just something I want to do."

And there it was. While I was talking to him, a number of uncomfortable truths I'd buried came to the surface. This show *was* a personal crusade. It probably wouldn't be a big commercial success. And we were going to have to scratch around to get the $400,000 at which it would capitalize.

Johnny stood his ground. "I don't care what you say, I want this show. All the way. All or nothing," he said. "I think it's great."

And so, he committed for $400,000, and we were completely and instantly financed.

Now, with these pieces in place, finding a producer was no problem. His toughest task—raising the money—had already been accomplished for him. Still, we wanted the best, and we got him in the person of

Alfred de Liagre, who had produced *The Voice of the Turtle*, *The Madwoman of Chaillot*, *The Golden Apple*, and *J.B.*, among a host of other adventurous and magnificent ventures.

Agnes de Mille, who, since *Oklahoma!* had become one of the most prestigious choreographers on Broadway, was hired to stage the dances. Tony Richardson, who had brilliantly staged *Look Back in Anger* and *The Entertainer* in London and New York, was our first choice for director, and he was eager to do the show, and gave us a verbal assurance that he would. But film studios in London and Hollywood were already aware of his cinematic skills, and he had to beg off after a very juicy offer to direct the film version of *Look Back in Anger* turned up.

So, we hired Robert Lewis, who had done fine, sensitive work with *Brigadoon* and had staged an exciting Harold Arlen–E.Y. Harburg–Fred Saidy show called *Jamaica* the previous season.

Our musical director would be Colin Romoff, an extraordinarily gifted musician.

Will Steven Armstrong, who had designed a brilliant, suggestive set for *Carnival*, did the same for *Kwamina*. His thirty-two-foot round-table that, in various revolves, showed an African village and a clinic from several distances and perspectives, was hugely inventive. But it created its own set of problems. It made a hideous, grinding noise, always dissonant to what was being performed. In the early performances it was terribly distracting; later on, the grinding was softened, but it never reached the *pianissimo* that would satisfied me. And I turned against revolving sets forever.

As we went into rehearsal in the summer of 1961, it felt like coming home, when home is a place of accomplishment and fulfillment. The score was met with enormous enthusiasm by the cast. I'd largely achieved what I'd set out to do. My African music sounded African, though it really wasn't, any more than "Bali Ha'i" is a South Seas song. A little exploration of true African music had convinced me that even half an evening of it would have been very difficult for theatre audiences. So, although I used a five-tone scale for the welcoming chant and a Bantuesque approach for "Nothing More to Look Forward To," a plaintive duet, the music was designed merely to work in each given situation. That the situations were more numerous and varied than most musicals till that date was a challenge. But the solutions, I felt, were good ones. Or, at least, most of them were. Some didn't work.

And, from the time he first began to set his ideas to paper, Bob Aurthur had trouble with the book. Then, to add to that, there was the fact that he'd never written a musical before. He was dealing with a medium whose demands he really hadn't mastered. But he was a responsible, dedicated man. Looking back, I think that perhaps the very magnitude of the task crippled him. He wanted to make it human, to deal with the larger issues, to balance them, and—and here is where we probably all went wrong: to attempt to make it acceptable to American audiences of 1961, three years before the Civil Rights Act.

Miscegenation in a musical had always been a tricky subject. How far could we go with it? We had cosmic things to say. How many of them could we put onstage without the show becoming ponderous and pedantic? We were dealing with an exotic locale. How exotic could we let it become before it became inaccessible?

We were asking for trouble, but it was exciting trouble, and we entered the thickets of rehearsal with our eyes open. We had a marvelous cast of fifty Blacks and two whites. Johnny Sekka, a native African, had originally been cast as Kwamina. But the demands of the role had exceeded his skills, and we'd replaced him with Terry Carter.

I wanted Brock Peters to play Kwamina. He was a magnificent actor and a beautiful singer with a deep, rich, baritone voice. To me, he was interesting looking, and not at all the conventional leading man type. And unfortunately for that reason, nobody else liked him.

So, Brock Peters played the witch doctor, and Rex Ingram the tribal chief, and their power was palpable, from the very first readings. And Sally Ann was miraculous. She was beautiful, she read brilliantly and sang like a musically advanced angel. She was simply the best musical performer I had ever written for, and she loved my music. The show was working on a multitude of levels, for all of us.

And then, the trouble began.

From the first rehearsal, there was unrest and tension among the players, a simmering resentment that the vast majority of the cast was Black, and the production staff was white, with the sole exception of Albert Opoku, a Ghanian choreographer and dancer who was serving as technical consultant to Agnes de Mille, and James Wall, our general stage manager.

The dances were brilliant but the book still didn't work, and, as we dug into rehearsals, Bob couldn't seem to resolve its problems. Songs had to be moved, rewritten, written anew.

As we advanced further into rehearsals, I began to experience differences with Bobby Lewis. My training had been under George Abbott, and I was probably applying much of that perspective to the show. But

I could clearly see that Bobby wasn't bringing the spectacle and the personal story into balance. The spectacle was swallowing up the story.

And, some of the songs I'd written just weren't working.

Well, that was what out of town was for, and so, at the end of August, we headed for Toronto and the O'Keefe Center. It was a terrific theatre. And Toronto was a very long way from New York— long enough away for us to work on the show in comparative privacy.

We were all nervous when we arrived there. We knew we had something—but it wasn't really a show yet. It was a bunch of separate parts, some of them brilliant. But a cohesive work it wasn't. We had four weeks in Toronto—a week of rehearsals and three weeks of performances—and then another three weeks in Boston to fix it. I'd been part of a team that had done just that with *Damn Yankees,* and I felt we could do it now.

So, we opened on September 3, 1961. It wasn't a good opening. The first act was too long. The applause was sometimes thunderous, particularly for Agnes's superb dances, and for some of the songs. But more often than not, it was merely polite; a danger signal.

The next day, the reviews were split in our favor: Two were favorable, one was negative. Hugh Thompson, of the *Globe and Mail* bolstered Bob Aurthur and me by stating that "[*Kwamina*] has an overwhelming sincerity which carries impact . . . Authors Richard Adler and Robert Alan Aurthur have taken a dramatic safari into Africa and returned with a worthy trophy."

But our own sense of the show and the audience reaction was much closer to Nathan Cohen's opinion in the *Toronto Star,* that the show was "listing from bad basic construction and injudicious ornament. It needs a crisis repair job in the worst possible way."

I in fact had lunch with Cohen two days later, and found him to be an articulate, intelligent, and savvy man. He had good suggestions, some of which we utilized. He followed the show to Boston, and became one of our staunchest supporters.

But back in Toronto, it was crisis time. I rolled up my sleeves and went to work. One of the first songs I jettisoned was one of my favorites, "Barbarians." It was sung by the witch doctor, and was a twist on the accepted use of the word. In the lyrics, white Western civilization emerged as barbaric.

It was met with stony silence from the audience, and it was apparent that the hostility it engendered could damage the show from that point forward. The audience resented the comparison. By the time Bobby

Lewis brought it up at the following morning's meeting, I'd already determined to cut it.

The mood was intense, as it generally is on the road, but there was also a slowly rising edge of hysteria that was beginning to insinuate itself about *Kwamina*. As days went by, changes were made . . . but were they for the better? This would have been the time that Mr. Abbott would have taken an iron hand to the proceedings. But Bobby Lewis had no iron hand. In fact, the further into trouble we got with the show, the further he seemed to move away from the center of it. And without that strong anchor of direction, the show began to founder.

Some of us began to assume directorial chores, and this was a mistake.

But a few of our ideas worked and the second week in Toronto, *Kwamina* began to improve. I had business to take care of in New York, so I felt comfortable enough with the situation to fly east for a couple of days —and I needed a little time away from the tension. I'd written seven songs in Toronto, to try to shore up the book.

Before I left, I'd personally set the opening number, "The Cocoa Bean Song," a choral piece written in five-part counterpoint. It was tough musically, but the chorus was singing it beautifully. Each of the five groups was cohesive and expressive, and when they were brought together, as the song built and built, it was thrilling, musically and dramatically, and got the show off to a rousing start. The audiences loved it, and so did I.

I got back from New York in time to catch the evening performance. It was horrifying. "The Cocoa Bean Song" was a shambles. The mounting excitement that had been in it when I left for New York was gone. And the reason was apparent to me from the first few notes. The number had been completely restaged. The vocal groups had been broken up and redistributed around the stage, and the entire musical impact, the rising crescendo of sound was dissipated and garbled because of it.

I was furious. I dashed backstage and demanded to know who had restaged the number. Agnes said she had. And she had done it with the best intentions, and within a system of "everyone for themselves" that had established itself in Toronto. I pointed out the damage the restaging had caused, and the next afternoon, we spent an hour putting everything back the way it was. It was wasted energy, and had consumed valuable time that should have been spent elsewhere, but it was typical of the compounding troubles of the show. What else could go wrong? I asked myself, as yet another partially happy, partially dissatisfied audience filed out of the O'Keefe Center.

Plenty, I was to discover, that very night.

We were all working under intense pressure, now. The Toronto run was ending, and we were still doing major rewrites, every night. Nerves were frayed; tempers were as raw as a January wind.

I was particularly tired, and when Sally Ann and I finally dragged ourselves up to our suite, I told her I was going to bed immediately. We'd agreed to sleep in separate bedrooms; she needed her rest to face the daily rehearsal and performance schedule; I worked best in the early morning. I didn't want to disturb her. We kissed each other good night and I crawled into my bed and fell asleep immediately.

About 5:00 A.M., I got up to go to the john. As I came out, I noticed that Sally Ann's bedroom door was open, just a crack. It was usually closed tight, to protect her from my work habits. I wondered if she was all right. I pushed the door open and entered her bedroom, and stopped dead in my tracks. The bed was empty. The front door was slightly ajar.

I sat in a chair facing the door, waiting.

Three-quarters of an hour later, she came in. She let out a little cry when she saw me, and then admitted, as rapidly and as straightforwardly as she had about Maximilian Schell, that she'd been with Terry Carter. It was something that was fairly common in the theatre, leading men and leading ladies getting together, but in our case it was more than that. It was, unconsciously, a monumentally destructive act. She'd practically carved a trail for herself. She could have shut the bedroom door before she left. She could have said to me that she'd gone out for a walk. But in some perverse way—again, I am certain, unconsciously— it seemed as if she actually wanted to be caught.

I was hurt, minimized, betrayed, cuckolded. I exploded. The problem was not only one of marital infidelity.

It was far more crippling than that. What about rehearsals now? A show in trouble brings the people in it closer together. I'd have to face both of them every single day and night now, for the rest of the Toronto run and the entire Boston run. She wasn't only hurting me; she was hurting herself, and Terry Carter, and the show.

I was a wreck. I needed some advice about this, my latest crisis.

I phoned Dr. Bak, my analyst. He listened patiently, and then said, "It's one of the most destructive, and self-destructive acts I can imagine. You needed help. I think she does, too."

Sally Ann and I finished Toronto in polite silence. Each of us was a professional; each of us buried, as much as we could, the knowledge and the hurt, but it must have spilled over into the show.

On the flight to Boston, I turned to Sally Ann. "Look," I said, "I know this sounds crazy, but I still care about you. There's something I want you to do."

"What's that?" she asked.

"I want you to go into psychoanalysis," I replied.

She nodded. "All right," she said. And she did.

In retrospect, I can see that a large part of the blame for these acts should have rested on my own unprepared shoulders. Even though I was in my late thirties, I wasn't yet sufficiently emotionally mature to cope with the enormous demands of a husband-wife relationship, especially when both are theatre professionals. More than probably, my own insecurities and anxieties got in the way of the relationship. Instead of having a "we'll fix it" attitude, I clung desperately and defensively to my bruises.

Sally Ann completed her analysis in five years. And I know it helped her enormously.

But by then, we would both know that the marriage had really been over for years. It had been wounded in New York and it died in Toronto.

I will, however, always be grateful to Sally Ann Howes for the kind, tender, and adoring way she treated my two sons. She remained a mother to them for always, and when, later, Christopher became terribly ill, Sally Ann took leave of her devoted husband and came to live in New York City to be the supportive person she is intuitively.

We postponed the Boston opening for a night, claiming mechanical troubles. But the troubles were deeper and more enduring than that, and the critics and audiences there were split, as they had been in Toronto. Two reviews were favorable, two were on the fence and two were unfavorable. Elinor Hughes in the *Herald* called it "Big, colorful, and courageous," and it was that. But Eliot Norton, of the *Post*, turned thumbs down on us.

We toiled hard in Boston. I was strung out. Bobby Lewis seemed to be sleepwalking through his paces, and I was willing to give him the benefit of fatigue, until one odd and disquieting evening.

I was in my hotel room, and I decided to phone Delly, as we called our producer Alfred de Liagre, in New York. For some reason, the phone lines crossed, and I came in on a conversation already in progress. Bobby Lewis was talking, and he was slaughtering me, running me into and below the ground to Delly.

Delly was defending me, and the more he defended me, the more Bobby Lewis bitched, and I mean exactly that.

On and on it went, while I listened, silently. They hung up, and I hung up.

The next day, I walked into rehearsal. Bobby was standing in the right wing, and I walked over to him. "Bobby," I said, "you don't like me, do you?"

His eyebrows elevated. "Oh no, Richard," he answered, "that's not true. I adore you."

And then I let him know that I'd heard his diatribe, heard his ten to fifteen minutes of verbal massacre. I never once raised my voice; it was all delivered in bittersweet tones with a dash of carbolic acid.

But when it was over, it was over, and there would be no love exchanged or lost between Bobby Lewis and me from that point onward.

And so, we'd all reached a new nadir. By October, when we were to open in New York, Bob Aurthur and I were fighting. Elinor Hughes had said, in the *Boston Herald,* "If *Kwamina* were as good as its best portions—namely, the Agnes de Mille dances and Richard Adler's songs—it would be a sure Broadway hit. Unfortunately, there's serious book trouble."

There had been book trouble from the very first day, and although it had improved since Toronto, the book was still weighing the show down. Looking back, I don't suppose Bob was given the kind of help he needed from the rest of us. Each of us on the production team was more knowledgeable about theatre than Bob. We could have helped him more.

But even if we had, we ourselves hadn't solved still another problem, and that was a major dilemma that had grown from our own emotional attachment to the material. We were dealing with something we believed in, and yet we also fervently wanted a hit in New York. And so, we didn't really resolve the issues at the end of the show. We copped out. Perhaps if we'd been grittier and more realistic, the thematic force of the show would have been great enough to carry it through. But we sent the two lovers—and the audience—off with the dream that, in another time, another place, it might have been different.

I didn't know when I wrote the following lyric that I'd be describing not only the relationship between the lovers, but also that between Sally Ann and me:

> *Another time, another place;*
> *Somewhere behind the moon*
> *Way out in outer space . . .*
> *Another world will have to do.*
> *Another world is where there is room for me and you.*
> *And we might find it*
> *If we could be*
> *On top of Everest or miles beneath the sea.*
> *And you could hold me forever in your embrace*
> *Another time, another place.*
> *And I could love as much as you would allow*
> *But this is here, and this is now.*

And so we opened in New York, at the 54th Street Theatre—now the George Abbott—on October 23, 1961. And flopped. Badly. We lasted for thirty-two performances, and closed on a very sad Sunday night.

It had been an embittering experience. Much has been said and written about flop sweat—the feelings you get before you fail. But not enough will ever be said about the feelings *after*. They're sometimes too terrible to record, and excavating the memories of that time almost amounts to masochism.

When it was over, I had more than the postpartam blues. I was blackly, deeply despondent. I knew I'd written the best score of my life. And that was reinforced the week after the show opened, first by a laudatory article by *New York Times* music critic Irving Kolodin, then by a phone call from Harold Arlen, who said it was one of the finest scores he'd ever heard; and finally and most touchingly by my father, who, after the opening night performance came up to me, and said, "I haven't understood what you've been doing up till now. But I understand this. And I like it. You're a fine composer, a fine musician."

I put my arms around him, and hugged him, and all of those contentions of the past disappeared like mist when the sun starts to shine. It was as if, with one accomplishment, I was no longer the young boy tagging along after my father as he strode, like Brahms, through the

Mr. Hitchcock and I wait for rehearsal to begin. Al Hirschfeld's drawing of the "Presidentical," 1962, (MIDDLE). Rehearsing with Bobby Darin, (BELOW).

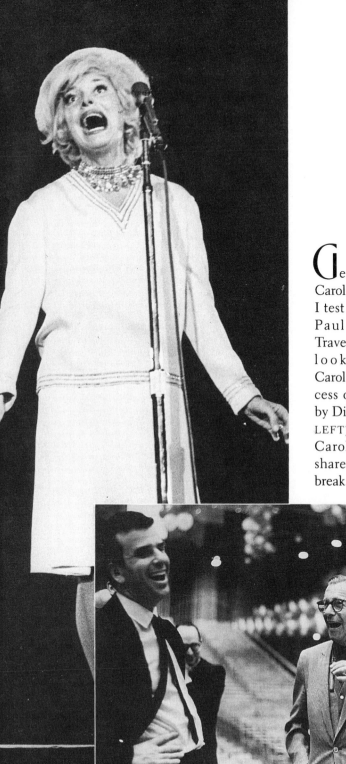

George Burns and Carol Channing in a duet. I test the microphone for Paul Stookey as Mary Travers and Peter Yarrow look on, (TOP, LEFT). Carol Burnett as the Princess of Morovia, assisted by Dick Altman, (BOTTOM, LEFT). George Burns, Carol Channing and I share a laugh during the break.

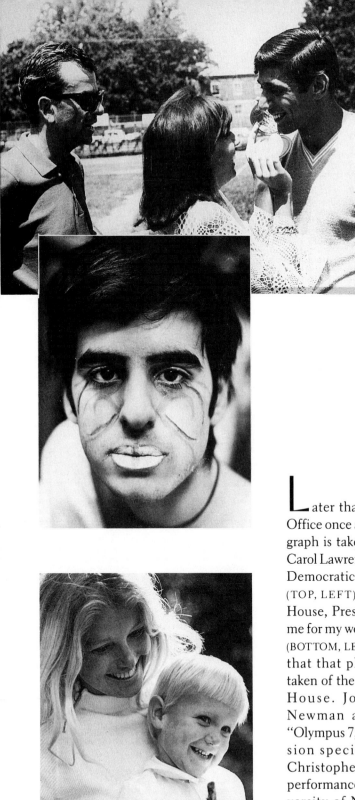

ater that year, I visit the Oval Office once again, where this photograph is taken of me, Lena Horne, Carol Lawrence and members of the Democratic National Committee, (TOP, LEFT). From the White House, President Kennedy thanks me for my work on the Presidentical, (BOTTOM, LEFT). I discover later that that photo was the last one taken of the President in the White House. Joe Namath, Phyllis Newman and I on the set of "Olympus 7," one of the ABC television specials, (CENTER, RIGHT). Christopher in make-up before a performance in college at the University of North Carolina, 1972. Ritchey and Robbie (Age 3) (LEFT).

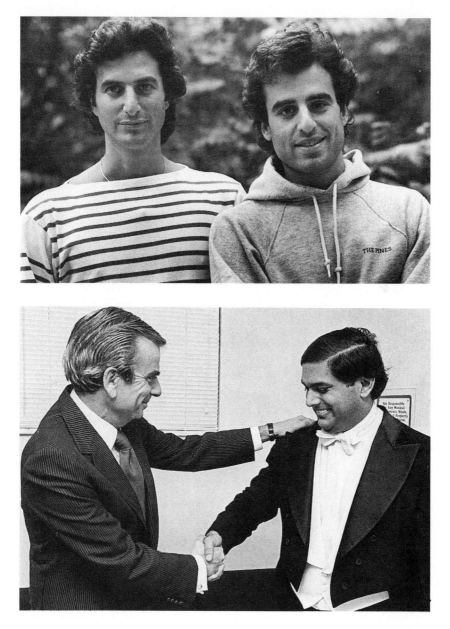

Richard Rodgers at the piano, surrounded by Benny Goodman, Al Simon, Celeste Holm, myself, Sheldon Harnick and Dorothy Rodgers, at Lincoln Center in 1975, (TOP, LEFT). A publicity still for the revival of *The Pajama Game* in 1973. From left, George Abbott, Hal Linden, Cab Calloway, Barbara McNair and me at the piano, (CENTER). Mr. Abbott, Patricia Birch and I at rehearsal of *Music Is*, 1976. (BOTTOM, LEFT). Andrew (left) and Christopher, 1980, (TOP, RIGHT). I congratulate conductor Rohan Joseph at the world premiere of "Yellowstone Overture" at Carnegie Hall, November, 1980.

With Charles Ketchem, conductor of the Utah Symphony, rehearsing "Wilderness Suite," February, 1983, (TOP, LEFT). Chancellor Christopher Fordham after presenting me with the Distinguished Alumni Award from the University of North Carolina, (CENTER, LEFT). With the National Park Service Rangers at the Chattanouga Chickamagua National Cemetery, 1981. I'm the one without the hat, (BOTTOM, LEFT). In London with Mary Adler, my fourth wife, and David Susskind, when the recording of "Wilderness Suite" was released, 1984, (TOP, RIGHT). At a luncheon at the State Department in London at the European premiere of "Wilderness Suite." Pictured with me are my son Andrew, his then-wife Michele, and the Countess of Dudley, (ABOVE).

Sam Goody's window promotion of "The Lady Remembers," (TOP, LEFT). In Southampton in 1985 with Laura, my mother, and Mary, (CENTER, LEFT). With Susan Ivory and my stepdaughter Ritchey, (BOTTOM, LEFT). Ritchey at the Grand Palace in Bangkok, 1986, (ABOVE, TOP). In Paris, March, 1987, with Susan and Andrew and daughter-in-law Bea.

In London, 1987, with Susan, Harold Pinter and Lady Antonia Fraser, (TOP, LEFT). With Buddhist monks in Thailand, 1987, (CENTER, LEFT). With my good friend, U.S. Senator Terry Sanford of North Carolina, (BOTTOM). Susan and I with Mitch Miller and his wife, Joan Peyser, in Lake Placid, (ABOVE, TOP). With Gershon Kingsley recording the score of my ballet, *Chicago*, on the synthesizer, 1987.

The marquee for *Chicago*, in Chicago, (ABOVE, LEFT). Mayor Harold Washington receiving the title page from the score of *Chicago*, and in exchange giving me the key to the city, (BELOW, LEFT). My mother on her 93rd birthday, November 15, 1988, (TOP, RIGHT). My radiologist, Dr. Lewis B. Harrison, his wife Ilene and daughter Barbara, with myself and collaborator Lee Davis, in Southampton, 1988. Here I am with beard on my Colorado river trip, 1987.

With Dr. Eugene Callender, president of the SYDA Foundation, in Lake Placid, 1989, (TOP). Home in Chapel Hill, (CENTER). In the spirit of true collaboration, with Bill C. Davis during a grueling session on "Off-Key."

countryside of Karinoke. I'd caught up—in my mind and in his—and what a profound achievement that was.

And yet, all of this was being dulled by the failure of the show. I was angry at Bobby Lewis, at Bob Aurthur, at myself for not taking a still-stronger hand when I knew it was coming to pieces. I was angry at Sally Ann, angry at my naivete and bad judgment in placing the burden of the salvation of our marriage on the show.

And I was angry at the public, which reacted much more hostilely than the critics at our audacity in portraying the love of a white woman for a Black man onstage. The hate mail roared in even before we opened in New York, and spit forth from the mailbox long after we closed. It was vituperative and vile, and Sally Ann had to bear the brunt of most of it. The very bottom was reached one day during the first week of the New York run, when she received a piece of used toilet paper in an envelope.

It was particularly devastating, because I had no idea that the out-pouring would be so violent and negative. Now, looking back on those times, I suppose it was sadly predictable, particularly in the light of what happened a mere thirty days after we closed. A month after we shuttered, in exactly the same theatre, Richard Rodgers opened *No Strings*. The parallels were eerie and ironic. It was the first show that Dick had written after the death of his collaborator, Oscar Hammerstein II. It was a show for which he had undertaken to write both music and lyrics. And, it was a show that dealt with miscegenation.

But. In *No Strings*, the story was about a *white* man in love with a *Black* girl. In 1961, that made all the difference in the world. Before the civil rights movement, there was a Janus-headed, Southern heritage that informed American tradition: It had, in nineteenth century America, been perfectly acceptable for white plantation bosses to have their way with Black female slaves. But let a Black man touch a white woman, and a lynch mob would have him before sunrise. We'd dared to place the Black man–white woman equation on a musical stage, and so, while Dick's story remained unresolved, as ours did, the public accepted its relationship, while angrily rejecting ours.

And yet, who knows? Maybe if our book problems had been resolved, we would at least have had a chance. Oscar Hammerstein's words, "Nothing can ever work, no matter how great the songs are, if the story isn't right, and if the people don't ring true," should have rung in my ears during rehearsals. Walter Kerr voiced what was our most abiding and damaging problem. "[*Kwamina*] is in general . . . a thing of

enormous good will and as much bad writing . . . [It] makes one wonder
. . . whether the show has its eye on the United Nations or United
Artists," was exactly on the money. I was flattered and warmed by his
and others' praise for the score, but a score is only a part of a show,
and if the show is buried, so is the score.

This is why I thought it was pointless to record *Kwamina*. But
Capitol Records was adamant, and set a recording date for the Monday
after the show closed. It was probably a first: No other show up to that
time had made an original cast recording *after* the show closed, and I
pleaded with Joe Csida, the A&R chief of Capitol, not to do it. "Do
a Peggy Lee album of my songs, or something like that," I begged.
"Don't put us through a cast recording."

But he was adamant, and we recorded it in one four-hour session.
One shot Charley, as they say, and it sounded like it to me.

And again, I was wrong. The album, released three months later to
avoid bucking Christmas, became a best-seller. And today, it's a collec-
tors' item.

The world in 1961 was a puzzling place to me, and it became more
so when I received a call from a man named Bud Gruber, the Chairman
of the Board of the P. Lorillard Tobacco Company. He invited me to
have lunch with him in the company dining room. He had something
important, he said, to discuss with me.

I accepted, and partway through lunch, he mentioned that he'd liked
"Everybody Loves a Lover," enormously, and wondered if I'd be interested in writing a jingle to advertise Newport.

Newport? I wondered aloud. What's that? The cut of beef? The
society playground in Rhode Island? The Jazz Festival?

He laughed. Newport was a new line of mentholated cigarettes that
Lorillard was planning to introduce the following fall.

I shook my head. "I can't do *that*," I said.

"Why not?" he asked.

"I'm a production writer."

And then he mentioned the money he'd pay me to write the jingle,
and I thought, yes. I *can* do *that*. But I still held him off, telling him
I'd have to get back to him in a few days.

Jingles were an art form to which I'd paid little attention. As far as
I was concerned, they could have been written on the moon, by aliens.

But now, motivated, I went home and listened. Avidly.

I was impressed. Some weren't bad at all. Some were straightforward melodies that said what they had to say honestly and rapidly. The lyrics accomplished their task. And many were well performed.

I called Gene Puerling, who headed the HiLos, the best and most individual vocal group of the late fifties and sixties, and asked him to bring the HiLos to my studio to sing for me. The group showed up the next day, sang, and knocked me out. They did songs with harmonies in sevenths, nineths—and elevenths, which was astonishing, but I quipped, "Have you ever heard of thirds? Or—God forbid—*unison?*"

They laughed. "That's the most effective harmony there is," said Gene Puerling, and I knew I'd found a vocal group that could do absolutely everything.

So, I called Bud Gruber, and accepted his offer. He put me in touch with the head of Young and Rubicam, the advertising agency they were using. We reached an agreement on a contract that allowed me to control the entire creative process, from writing through recording.

I wrote the Newport jingle; they liked it; we recorded it. And it would run for *eleven years*, and be popular enough to end up in countless juke boxes throughout the nation. Dance arrangements were requested for college proms. And it would win the National Association of Advertisers Award as best jingle of the year.

I followed Newport with jingles for Kent, York Imperial, and Hertz (which would run for nine years). *Newsweek* magazine headlined me The King of the Jingles in a two-page article.

I didn't write jingles with my left hand. I worked with as much dedication and exactitude as if I were writing a score for a musical. And I followed through on the recording sessions, with the same attention to detail. In those days, there was no laying down of tracks, no patching of tape. You did a take, and if it wasn't right, you did it again. One recording session ran to 104 takes before we got it right. At the end of it, the HiLos could hardly speak.

The best part of that year was the fun of it: I was having a good time, and making an enormous amount of money. I didn't feel self-conscious one bit—not even one night on the John Crosby television show. I'd been asked to appear with Abe Burrows and Alan Jay Lerner. When Abe was introduced, the band played "The Girl with the Three Blue Eyes." When Alan Jay Lerner was introduced, they played "I Could Have Danced All Night." When I was introduced, I expected "Hey There," or "Whatever Lola Wants," or "You Gotta Have Heart."

Instead, the orchestra launched into the Newport Filter Cigarette Jingle.

Alan leaned over to me and asked, in a hushed voice, "Did you write *that*?" To this day, I haven't figured out the implication behind his question.

IV
CAMELOT

12.

" O N E   moment please," the operator said. "The White House is calling."

I thought for a moment. Did I have any dry cleaning at the White House Cleaners around the corner? I didn't think so.

A woman's voice, soft-spoken, obviously educated, came on. "Mr. Adler?" she asked.

"Yes," I answered.

"This is Mrs. Lincoln."

(Though history wasn't one of my strong subjects, even I knew that Mrs. Lincoln was dead.)

"President Kennedy's secretary," she continued. "Mr. Adler, will you please hold the phone? The President wishes to speak with you."

I chuckled. Sammy Davis, Jr., did a Kennedy impression that was terrific, and he wasn't above getting an actress in to help him play an elaborate hoax on his friends. I waited for Sammy to come on the line.

It was the female voice again. "Mr. Adler," she said, softly, "here is the president now."

Sure, I said to myself. The president of the synagogue.

But then, that unmistakable, often imitated Boston accent emerged from the phone. "Hello Dick," said the voice. "How are you?"

"Good afternoon, Mr. President," I said, controlling myself. God, I thought, Sammy's really improved. This is fabulous.

And then, the voice at the other end of the line began to reminisce about the time we'd met backstage in Boston, during the tryout tour of *John Murray Anderson's Almanac,* and went on to resurrect our conversation previously at the dinner party in the home of Mrs. Julian Rogers in Brookline, Massachusetts.

I began to perspire. I hadn't told Sammy anything about these events. This was no joke. This *was* the President of the United States!

"Like to speak to you, Dick, about something I want you to do. Can you come down to Washington, say, next Tuesday at three o'clock?" he asked.

Could I? I would have made it through the Hellespont without a boat, if it were the White House at the other end.

But why me? I thought, as I hung up. And what did he have in mind?

My suspicions returned. Possibly, just possibly, I might get thrown out on my ass.

I appeared, as instructed, at the entrance to the West Wing of the White House at 2:45 the following Tuesday. On the shuttle flight down from New York, my imagination had run wild. What was it the president wanted me to do that he couldn't discuss over the telephone?

My name was on the visitors' list, and I was escorted into the Fish Room, where I sat alone for a quarter of an hour until Mrs. Evelyn Lincoln came to lead me to her desk, a few feet away from the portals to the Oval Office.

So this is real! I thought to myself, exultantly. Here I *am*, actually about to be taken into the office of the President of the United States!

What could he want of me? I puzzled. Could he want me to be a spy? Could he want me to be an undercover agent who'll be parachuted into the Kremlin, a—

And then the doors opened. And there he was, the President of the United States, John Fitzgerald Kennedy, in the taut and well-tanned flesh, smiling, as handsome as a Hollywood star, and a hundred times more imposing. He was standing easily and with great authority, framed in those famous, oval, double doors.

"Hello, Dick," he said, and extended his hand.

I walked into the inner chamber of the central nervous system of the Free World. The President seated himself in the famous rocking chair, gestured for me to sit down, and said, "Lou Harris has told me a lot about you."

I relaxed. So that was it. My old college buddy from Chapel Hill, and now one of the leading pollsters in the country. Fate was working overtime again.

We talked about various mutual acquaintances, and about having met before. He reached over and picked up a coconut shell that had been laminated in plastic. "Do you know what this is?" he asked, handing it to me.

I turned it over in my hands. I recognized it. It was the very coconut shell into which he'd stuffed a message, a cry of help after the sinking of the *PT109*. I knew the story well, of how he'd swum from Japanese held island to Japanese held island to Japanese held island, alone and in terrible danger, and how he'd almost drowned, but had never given up hope. If that message had been picked up by the Japanese, he would have been found and killed. But fate had treated him kindly, as he knew it would. The Americans had discovered it, and it had all ended in a miraculous rescue, an affirmation to the President that he was leading a charmed life.

"Dick," he said, leaning over and returning the coconut shell to its appointed place, "I guess you're wondering why I asked you to come here."

"Yes, Mr. President," I answered.

He'd gotten the idea, he went on, through Lou Harris, that I would be the best man in the country to do a big combination gala and forty-fifth birthday celebration for him at Madison Square Garden, in New York, to help raise money to cover the deficit from the Presidential campaign.

Would I do it?

I'd never staged anything in my life, but if I could teach myself to write jingles, why couldn't I teach myself to stage a show that would be worthy of a charismatic president? It wouldn't be a variety show; it wouldn't be a musical. It would be—and I coined the word on the spot—a "Presidentical." With this kind of concept, I could approach the top performers of the world to do a show for President John Fitzgerald Kennedy, for nothing.

I of course answered yes.

"Good," he said, rising and extending his hand. "Welcome aboard."

I left the White House, floating on air. Working in Washington, and for a president for whom I had the same affection that just about everybody in the arts shared in 1962! I was eager to proceed, especially for this man who had also invited Robert Frost to speak at a very important occasion.

I broke the news to Sally Ann, who was preparing for a starring role as Fiona McClaren in a City Center revival of *Brigadoon.* She was excited, delighted, and offered all the encouragement and help she could. And I knew I'd need it when I found out from Lou Harris that, because of his adamant endorsement, I'd beaten out both Leland Hayward and David Merrick for the job of producing the Presidential Birthday Gala.

As it turned out, I was given an opportunity for a tryout before the main event. I'd scarcely assembled a staff when a call came from Merriman Smith, the senior member of the White House Press Corps. He'd heard that I was the new showman on the premises, and he wondered if I'd stage a one hour entertainment for a party that was to be held at the Shoreham Hotel, for "President Kennedy and Friend"— the friend being British Prime Minister Harold MacMillan.

I seized the opportunity. I figured that hiring topnotch entertainment was a priority. I put Sally Ann and Gwen Verdon together in top hat, ties, and tramp outfits, to sing Cole Porter's "A Couple of Swells." I invited Benny Goodman and his quintet, Peter Sellers to deliver a monologue, and I put a chorus of singers together to do a salute to the American musical theatre.

And as a special feature, I hired Eliott Reed, who did a priceless impression of Kennedy at a press conference. I was taking a chance, but I figured that if it worked, the President would get a big boot out of it. If it didn't, *I'd* get the boot.

We rehearsed at the Shoreham the day of the party. Once through the Reed routine, and I knew that he was going to stop the show. I went over to Peter Sellers, and told him I thought we should revise the running order. "Peter," I said, "you'd better go on ahead of this, because it's going to—"

He held up an imperious hand. "I'm the star of the show, and I'm going on next to closing."

Okay, I thought, it's your red wagon, and I turned my attention back to the business of getting the show routined.

The evening began with a small reception and cocktail party for forty or forty-five people. We assembled, waiting for the president and Mr. MacMillan to arrive. And for the rest of my days, I will carry with me that indelible picture of their entrance into the Shoreham that night.

MacMillan was a distinguished looking man with a flowing white moustache, the perfect picture of a proper British statesman. But the President was absolutely unique, uncommon, extraordinary. He'd just come back from Palm Beach, and his suntan had deepened to a glowing shade of ochre; he had a blue cornflower in his lapel, his eyes sparkled as if he'd just been told an enormously funny story; he held himself proudly erect, in spite of his painfully crippled back. He was the tallest, the most brilliant, the most overpowering man in that room—and in my life.

That very afternoon, in the middle of rehearsal, presidential assistant Kenny O'Donnell had drawn me aside, and confided to me that the President thought it would be discreet if I would stop writing jingles during the time I was working with the White House. Just so there could be no hint of impropriety and improper influence from the business sector, as he put it.

Simple, innocent days. Simple solutions, when you think of the convoluted Washington scandals to come. I of course agreed.

Over three thousand press people were in the ballroom at the Shoreham that night, and I arranged myself at a table next to the president's, so that I could watch his reactions.

The show moved right along, and received wild applause. The President seemed to be enjoying himself. And then, Eliott Reed came on, and absolutely brought down the house. His bit was timed to run seven minutes. With laughter and applause, it stretched to ten.

I kept glancing nervously at the president, who was laughing as hard as anybody. But he was also feverishly making notes, as fast as he could.

Eliott Reed exited; Peter Sellers entered, and, as I feared, with an absolutely hilarious routine, laid an *egg*.

The finale worked beautifully, and then the President got up to speak, and with better timing, better material, and a better delivery than any professional comedian you can name, wowed everybody. It was one of the funniest speeches I've ever heard—and the following Wednesday, *Variety* headlined it "Wittiest Speech in History." *Time* and *Newsweek* devoted a couple of three full pages to this prime example of Kennedy wit and wisdom, drawn from some hastily scribbled notes, and set down while a satire of himself was crackling around him.

Afterwards, I had a small party in my suite at the Shoreham. I invited Pamela Turnure, Jackie's press secretary, Hal Prince, Sally Ann, Gwen Vernon, Bob Fosse, and Peter Sellers. Everybody was buzzing about the hilarity of the evening. Everybody, that is, except Peter Sellers, who sat in not so splendid isolation in a corner chair, brooding darkly.

I'd taken care of the curtain raiser. Now it was time to begin work on the main event, the Birthday Party fundraiser, which was to be held at Madison Square Garden, on May 19. I went to performers I knew and some I didn't, and they all accepted eagerly: Judy Garland, Danny Kaye, Jack Benny, Jimmy Durante, Maria Callas, Shirley MacLaine, Ella Fitzgerald, Peggy Lee, Nichols and May, Harry Belafonte, and

Henry Fonda and Gregory Peck as *compères,* to emcee the proceedings.

It was certainly a different way of casting a show. No lawyers, no agents haggling over contracts. Just a short telegram, signed "John F. Kennedy and Richard Adler," inviting the performer to appear. And the greatest stars in the world practically stumbled over each other to accept.

There was only one spot left to fill, and that was the moment that a huge cake would be wheeled into the Garden and "Happy Birthday" would be sung to the President. The logical way to do it would be to bring back Maria Callas and have her launch forth with the song. But I wanted it to be unique, and unexpected. Who, I asked myself, could be expected to do the unexpected?.

The name came to me lined in marquee lights:

Marilyn Monroe.

I'd met her a year earlier, at the Actors' Studio, where I'd audited some classes.

I knew she was slated soon to leave for California to film George Cukor's *Something's Got to Give,* and I was aware of her mercurial habits and temperament. But I thought it was worth a try.

I went to the Actors Studio, and pulled Marilyn out of class.

She looked at me with those frightened, haunted, and helpless eyes. After all of her successes, she still seemed as unsure as an ingenue auditioning for her first part.

"Marilyn," I said, "I'm staging a big show for the Democratic Party at Madison Square Garden on May 19—President Kennedy's birthday. And I want you to sing 'Happy Birthday' to him."

Her face relaxed, and she smiled, as if she'd been given a diamond bracelet. "I'd love to do it," she said, and then added, "And I *will* do it."

I knew her reputation for unreliability and tardiness, and she seemed to know I knew it. "I not only want you not to be late," I said, "I want you to actually be there."

She nodded. "You won't have to worry about that."

"Fine." Now, *I* could relax. "And I want you to sing it a certain way," I went on. "I'll write some special material to give it a little more body. I want you to sing it straight, not in a breathy voice. You know. Straight."

She nodded again, vigorously.

"One more thing. What'll you wear?"

"A black, high neck, flowing dress," she said, putting a reassuring hand on my arm.

And so, I released the information to the press.

A firestorm erupted.

Hundreds of telegrams arrived at the White House, protesting Marilyn Monroe's appearance. Catholic groups objected. Congressmen objected. Three senators even called me personally, objecting. Finally, the chairman of the Democratic National Committee phoned, demanding that I remove her from the program.

I was, by this time, of two conflicting minds. The show biz side of me was as stubborn as a mule just before lunch. It wanted to go forward with Marilyn. I'd made a responsible, knowledgeable, entertainment decision.

The other side of me was wracked by aggravated insecurity. Maybe I'd really made a senseless mistake. Maybe I'd be responsible for getting the second impeachment of a president of the United States, I mused to myself.

There was only one way to resolve it. I put in a call to the White House. I told the President about the opposition to Marilyn, and exactly from whom it came, and—what did he think?

"I think it's a great idea, Dick," he said. "Goodbye, and keep up the good work." And he hung up.

As soon as word got around that the President liked it, everybody liked it. The Catholics like it. The congressmen liked it. The senators liked it.

Everybody but me liked it. Some small burr of doubt had attached itself to my conscience, and the itch wouldn't go away. I wanted to be sure that nothing was left to chance about Marilyn's appearance. I wrote a set of special lyrics to lead into the birthday song. The words referred to Kennedy's public blast at Roger Blau, the president of U.S. Steel, for the irresponsibility of the steel industry's pricing policies. Set to the melody of "Thanks for the Memory," it went:

> *Thanks, Mr. President*
> *For all the things you've done,*
> *The battles that you've won,*
> *The way you deal*
> *With U.S. Steel . . .*

I made a record of it and sent it off to California, reminding Marilyn, right on the record, that she was to sing it as I did—full out, no baby-voiced breathiness. *Please.*

The middle of May arrived, and Marilyn came back to town. I made an appointment to hear her. She set a bizarre hour for the meeting: eleven o'clock at night at her apartment. Hank Jones, the great jazz pianist, would be there to accompany her.

I arrived on time, and Marilyn came to the door in a pair of tight-fitting black slacks and a loose-fitting Pucci silk shirt.

"God, you look great, Marilyn," I said. "You've lost so much weight."

"I know," she said. "Look." And she lifted up the shirt, to show me her waistline—all the way to her neck. And it was true. Just like on the famous calendar photo.

I carefully gave her a wide berth, sitting opposite her. She began to pout, and drink wine, very fast. She was obviously overreacting to my lack of response to her charms.

I knew I had to do something, so I got up and put my arm around her shoulder, reassuringly. "What difference does it make?" I said to her, but she kept on pouting, until Hank arrived.

I quickly said, "It's getting late, so let's hear the song." Hank began to play, and she began to sing. And her delivery was the very opposite of what I wanted and had clearly requested. It was pure, baby-voiced breathiness. I left her apartment in a major funk. Tomorrow would be an enormously busy day for me. I had to conduct a full technical rehearsal. There were hundreds of things to do with a large cast of stars, choruses, and ballets, and the temperaments of the stars with which to contend. I needed to be fresh, but I got little sleep that night. The burr of doubt about Marilyn had turned into a field of cactus. I was almost certain that her spot would be an embarrassing disaster.

That morning, the tech, with full cast and a sixty-piece orchestra, lurched through its frenetic paces. There were many problems, of course, but Peggy Lee proved to have the only irritating temperament. By and large, it went well. Marilyn appeared, and couldn't have been nicer. But she declined to sing.

My nerves were shot. After the rehearsal, I walked over to the Hotel Pierre, where Jack Benny was staying, and went up to his suite. He was my friend, and I wanted some stroking.

He was in a pair of black pajamas, propped up in bed, resting. His manager, his press agent, and a group of friends were in the living room of the suite. I poured out my worries to him. He looked at me searchingly for a moment, with those big, beautiful, spaniel eyes, and then he said, "Schmuck. What kind of an idiot are you, anyway—using Marilyn Monroe to sing 'Happy Birthday' to the President. Get somebody else."

"But the show's tomorrow," I protested.

"Get somebody else," he repeated.

I was relieved. Jack had solved my problem for me. I called Shirley MacLaine, who was staying at the same hotel and told her I wanted to talk to her. When I got to her suite, I poured out my problem.

She smiled. "Don't worry," she said. "It'll be all right."

"No it won't," I insisted. "I want you to do it."

She bit her lip. "You can't fire Marilyn Monroe," she said. "I'll do anything you want me to do, but you really should think about the repercussions."

Think about it. That's what I'd been doing for days. There was obviously only one person who could resolve this mess, and he was staying at the New York White House, the Hotel Carlyle. I knew he had a few more important things on his mind, things like running the country, but he'd told me to call him anytime there was a problem. Anyway, I knew that JFK liked to talk show business. So, I plunged ahead, and dialed the number.

It took him a good fifteen minutes to come to the phone, and there was an edge to his voice. He sounded irritated. "What is it, Dick?" he asked. "What's wrong?"

"It's Marilyn," I told him.

"Now look, Dick," he said, impatiently. "You called me on this before. I told you I thought it was a perfectly fine idea. I assured you. What can be wrong?"

"Listen, Mr. President," I said. I took an exceedingly deep breath, and I emoted, in slow, very breathy tones, with long, long pauses, "H-h-h-h-a-a-a-a-p-p-p-p-y B-b-b-b-i-i-i-r-r-r-th-th-th-th-d-d-d-a-a-a-a-y, t'you."

The president laughed, heartily. "It'll be all right," he said.

"But what about the press, Mr. President? I don't want you to be embarrassed."

"They'll be gone by that time. It's the end of the evening. It'll be all right, Dick." And he hung up.

I breathed a sigh of relief. I was off the hook no matter what happened. I got a good night's sleep.

The show went magnificently. Everyone was great, because they *were* the greatest of the theatrical greats. That sort of a show could never have been produced except under those extraordinary circumstances. Everything went without a hitch, although I worked like a madman, conducting the pace of the show over an intercom from a box high up in the Garden, behind the presidential box.

I had two phones, one to the pit, one to backstage. I was constantly on one or the other, refining tempos, goosing up the audio, warning, encouraging, nudging, tightening. But I was also nervous about something else. One look at the secret service swarming over the premises that afternoon, and a horrible thought instantly swept through me: This was a public arena, and public arenas were where nuts with guns try to kill heads of state. And there were blackouts between the acts . . . the blackouts that night were lightning fast, I assure you.

Finally, the moment for the entrance of the cake—and Marilyn—arrived. The snare drums started a terse roll.

Peter Lawford stepped up to the microphone and announced, "And now, ladies and gentlemen, Miss Marilyn Monroe." He gestured to the wing, the spotlight swept to it, and there was no Marilyn.

He did it again. "And now ladies and gentlemen . . . " Still no Marilyn.

It was part of the act. On the third try, Marilyn entered—but not, as she assured me she would, in a conservative black dress. The outfit she wore looked, in Adlai Stevenson's words, "like flesh with sequins sewn on." It was so tight, she had to walk like a thirteenth century Japanese geisha.

I held my breath as she wiggled to the microphone. The orchestra began, and so did she.

And it was simple, and wonderful. She sang it absolutely straight, and brought the audience to its feet, joining in with her in a full-throated birthday wish of happiness to the President.

The show ended as it had begun; filled with incredible, thrilling dimensions. The crowd cheered for several minutes, while Marilyn stood in the spotlight, tears in her eyes. She'd been kidding all along, and I'd fallen for it.

We created history that night, and, sadly enough, the possibility exists that through a set of interlocking circumstances, I became involved, as did many others, inadvertantly and unconsciously in the dark and downward spiral of Marilyn's final, self-destructive months.

After the show, I found out that she'd walked off the set of *Something's Got to Give*, to appear at the gala, and that she'd been fired from the picture because of it.

Arthur Krim threw a party for the President, the cast, and me at his townhouse at 45 East 69th Street. It was a heady experience to be part of this very different world, and I felt like the new but privileged kid on the block as Sally Ann and I stepped out of my limousine in front of Arthur's house, which was cordoned off.

The sidewalk was full of police, secret service men, and reporters. In the middle of them was Merriman Smith.

"Merriman," I shouted, "what are you doing, standing here like this? Why don't you come in with us?"

"Are you sure?" he asked.

"Of course," I assured him, and led him past the secret service men standing at the entrance.

It was very bad judgment on my part. You just don't do that when you're invited to a private party for the president, particularly this president. And I soon discovered why.

Partway through the evening, Marilyn Monroe arrived, escorted by Arthur Miller's father, a softspoken man with an enormous shock of snow white hair. She seemed radiant and relaxed.

Bobby Kennedy came over to me immediately, and asked me to introduce him to her. I did, and from that point onward, he and Marilyn spent the rest of the evening together, dancing and drinking wine. It wasn't a very comfortable sight, particularly since Ethel was there.

The next day, Merriman called me. "Guess who paid a visit to me this morning at 2:00 A.M.?" he asked.

I couldn't imagine.

"The secret service," he said. "They weren't very happy that I was there at all last night. And they wanted to be extra sure that I didn't write about Marilyn and Bobby."

"Are you going to?" I asked.

"Of course not," he answered. "I'm not a gossip columnist." I felt terrible, not only because he'd been intimidated, and I'd invited him to the party, but also because the secret service was involved in that kind of censorship.

I would never have dreamt that that would be the last time I would ever see Marilyn. Three months later, she would be dead from an overdose of barbiturates.

A wire service story then would name me as one of the six people responsible for her death. It would be a horrible, tasteless, groundless accusation, based upon my having asked her to do the birthday gala.

And yet, I suppose there was a grain of truth in it. I'd also introduced her to the President and to Bobby Kennedy, and who, to this day, knows the real story of what that led to? Everyone who had been at all close to Marilyn in those last months of her life was a part of a calamitous playing out of a distressing story. We were all characters in a heartrending tragedy.

What happened to that gifted and tragic waif is as much a mystery to me as it is to almost everyone, and I felt the horror and the waste of it deeply when it happened. I'd also introduced her to Ralph Roberts, a University of North Carolina acquaintance of mine who had become her masseur and confidante, and the last person to see her alive. Ralph called me the day after it happened. He was devastated, destroyed. And he swore that Marilyn Monroe did not commit suicide.

The summer turned into autumn, and I settled into the job of staging another Presidentical.

The President was insatiably fascinated with show business and the people who worked in it. He read *Variety* every week. He summoned me for walks in the rose garden, during which he'd pump me for stories about the performers I knew. I think these walks and exchanges of gossip were part of his relaxation from the pressures of State. I treasure to this day the memory of those quiet and sometimes revealing moments.

He was a complex man, of many moods and facets, wise and thoughtful, and unsparing with himself, as I discovered at the time of the second Presidentical.

This one was staged at the National Guard Armory in Washington before an audience of just under twenty thousand, and it featured Peter, Paul, and Mary, Joan Sutherland, Yves Montand, Carol Burnett, George Balanchine and his New York City Ballet, and Kirk Douglas and Gene Kelly as twin emcees.

I had my problems with the politicians on this one, too. I planned to end the program with the pas de deux and the last movement of Balanchine's *Stars and Stripes*. It would be a stirring and appropriate finale, and I was elated that Balanchine was going to bring Arthur

Mitchell and Allegra Kent in from New York to dance the pas de deux.

But, when press reports began to circulate about it, the Democratic National Committee got timid. A Black man and a white woman had never danced publicly before Washington audiences, and the Committee thought it imprudent.

They met with me and told me to eliminate Kent and Mitchell.

I was outraged. Without a thought, I rose from my seat, snapped my briefcase shut, and said, "You'd better get yourself another boy." And I walked out. I was the showman; they were the politicians. I didn't try to tell them how to run an election.

And sure enough, the president got wind of the meeting, and within a day, I received a call from the Democratic National Committee, apologizing, and telling me to use my judgment in staging the show. And so, for the first time in history, a Black man and a white woman danced onstage in Washington, D.C.

When it ended, the cast and I piled into limousines and were whisked across town to the vice-president's house for a midnight dinner. The President preceded us, and was already relaxing in the living room of Lyndon Johnson's home when we arrived, sirens screaming.

President Kennedy was in show business heaven, gossiping and joking with the entertainers, and halfway through the dinner, he leaned back in his chair and asked me, "Dick, when are you going to do the second show?"

I didn't have to think twice. "Right after dinner, Mr. President," I said, and I immediately began to circulate among the tables, collaring the performers. "You're going to be on again," I whispered to each of them, and when they looked up at me with a startled expression, I added, quickly, "The President of the United States is commanding you."

And so, at 1:30 A.M., the entire cast assembled in the hallway and on the staircase of the Johnson house. I stood on the sixth step, presenting, and the President sat no more than ten feet away.

Partway through Peter, Paul, and Mary's number, Paul Stookey broke a string on his guitar. He kept on playing, and at the end of the number, which was punctuated by wild applause, I said, "You see, Mr. President, what happens when greatness meets greatness? You bust your gut."

The evening got brighter and brighter. Yves Montand sang; Carol Channing sang; Joan Sutherland sang; Gene Kelly and Kirk Douglas fooled around; and then Gene went over to the president, took his arm, and pulled him up in front of the audience. "Come on, Mr. President," he said, "it's time for a couple of Irishmen to sing a song."

The pianist struck up "The Wearing of the Green," and they sang. It wasn't exactly a performance that would have gathered a bouquet of rave notices. The President had a poor voice, and couldn't carry a tune. And he knew it. He smiled, and stood tall, but he was blushing like a little boy. It was a picture I'll remember, but one that John Kennedy apparently wanted to forget quickly. After the applause, he suddenly announced, "Well, I've got to go now," and he and Jackie and her sister Lee Radziwill left.

My White House assignment proceeded apace. Sally Ann and I bought a house in Upper Saddle River, New Jersey; she continued to do television shows and a second revival of *Brigadoon* at City Center.

And then, at 3:50 A.M., on Sunday, April 20, 1963, the phone rang in our bedroom. Still drugged from sleep, I picked up the receiver and said, "Yes?"

The connection was bad. There was static. It was a cable call or a radio phone. "This is the United Kingdom calling Richard Adler," an operator said.

"This is Richard Adler," I replied.

A woman with a slight German accent came on. "Richard?" she said, "I have sad news. Marion died this morning."

Suddenly, sleep left me and I sat up straight, like a shot. "Oh my God," I said, "I'm so sorry. I'm so terribly sorry."

"Can you get over here right away?" the voice continued. "The funeral is to be tomorrow—and the children—"

My God, the children, I thought. "Yes. Yes, I'll come right over."

Poor, dear Marion. She'd had an anneurism a year and a half ago, and it had paralyzed her left side. I'd gone to England then, and helped her find a clinic in Switzerland. And miraculously, she'd recovered the use of her left side. What the hell could have happened?

"Who was that at this hour?" asked Sally Ann.

I told her it was Evi, Marion's sister. I told her Marion had just died. I told her I had to get on a plane right away and get over there.

We got out of bed and went down to the kitchen. I put the kettle on the stove, picked up the phone, and called Pan Am. I booked myself on the 10:00 A.M. flight to London.

Suddenly, I realized it was Sunday and that my passport was in the safe deposit box of a bank of 57th Street and Madison Avenue, in the city. I panicked. What could I do? I looked at my watch. It was 4:14 A.M.

I started to think. I could never get anyone to open the bank so that I could get into my safe deposit box to collect the only document that would allow me, under any circumstances, entry into the U.K. That was too complicated. I didn't know the names or whereabouts of any of the bank officers.

"What am I going to do?" I asked Sally Ann.

She looked vacant. "Could you wait until Monday, and take the night flight?" she suggested.

I shook my head. It just didn't wash. To miss the funeral would be wrong. The children, I knew, were away on spring break with friends in Bournemouth. They'd have to be collected and told—and then brought back with their belongings to Saddle River. All of this had to be dealt with, with delicate candor and at once—and by me.

Suddenly, I got an idea. Senator Javits—Jacob K. Javits, the great and powerful U.S. senator from New York. Jack Javits was a cherished friend. We were close. Close enough even for me to do the unspeakable to a man who worked terribly hard for God, Country, and the State, and who needed all the rest he could get.

So, at 4:30 A.M. on that dark Sunday morning, I picked up the phone and dialed Jack at his apartment in Washington. He answered and sweetly assured apologetic me it was okay. I explained the circumstances. He simply replied, "Richard, go to your plane. Everything will be taken care of. I'm sorry that you have to take this trip."

I hung up the phone, knowing here was a *real* friend. Two and a half hours later, while I was packing, I received a call from one of Jack's aides. He told me all arrangements had been taken care of. I would be met at Idlewild Airport and escorted through immigration, and would receive the same courtesy at London's Heathrow Airport. And then, anytime after that, I could pick up a temporary passport at the American Embassy. I said one hundred silent "thank you's" to the wonderful friend who had arranged the near impossible for me.

I checked into the London Hilton. My English friend, Nymon Libson, whom I had met through Danny Kaye in the South of France eight years before, came over and took me downstairs to the coffee shop for a snack and a chat. We talked about Marion, what a beautiful mother she'd been to our children—always so generous with her love.

The next morning, I got up early, shaved, showered, dressed, and then cabbed to 2 Templewood Avenue in Hampstead. Here, Omi ("grandmother" in German) lived in stately splendor in her large, Tudor-like brick manor and her formal garden, which was now abundant with blooming spring bulbs.

Here, at 2 Templewood, Marion had lived as a younger woman before we'd met. Here, I'd come to meet her family when Andrew was on the way, after Marion and I had known each other only three months. Here, we all had decided the best thing to do was for Marion to get a divorce from her first husband and for the two of us to marry. Here, with our youth and good looks and spontaneous enthusiasm, and our "pregnant" situation, our presence had unwittingly shifted the attention from sister Evi and her fiancé, Walter Simpson, whose formal marriage plans were temporarily, at least, pushed into the background. Here was I, once again, because of tragic circumstances, reunited with a family I had not sorrowfully broken with through the mechanism of divorce, years before.

Omi descended the stairs slowly, aided by daughter Evi and son-in-law Walter, and followed by her husband Biba. Her eyes were red from long hours of crying. She saw me and burst into fresh tears. The scene called for embracing.

Then, wiping away her tears, she said, "Ja, Richard, you must be hungry. Come, let us go into the dining room and have some *gut* breakfast."

No one ate too much. The sumptuous buffet of cereals and eggs and delicious English bangers, bagels and cream cheese and Scotch salmon, was barely touched. Full table—empty appetites: Omi, Evi, Walter, Biba, and Betty Retter—the children's godmother and Marion's best friend, who had flown from New York earlier to be with her during the last stage of her terrible illness. And finally, at the end of the table, sat David Wakeling, the young Englishman with whom Marion had lived for several years.

It was an inharmonious group, brought together by a cruel and sad circumstance, all trying to mute the dissonances of this unwanted gathering. All were truly sorrowing for a young and vital person who had left the scene too soon. The formalities of society forcing the gathering of this motley cast filled me with distaste, and yet, I knew it had to be. Later on, I would discover how appropriate had been my feelings of discomfort.

The burial at a Golders Green Cemetery, without benefit of religious service, was especially gloomy. Clouds hid the sun. A light English drizzle added a filtered, grain-like texture to the background. The simple, unadorned pine box was lowered into the eight-foot deep, rectangular grave, the digging of which had barely been finished as our little group arrived. When the coffin struck bottom, I heard a macabre rattling from within—Marion's final protest to her untimely departure from earth to earth.

The following morning, David Wakeling picked me up in his sporty Jaguar convertible. He'd offered to chauffeur me, since the children were staying with his sister in Bournemouth. We spoke very little. A few miles beyond Southampton, we motored through a lovely woodland called the New Forest. I saw small herds of wild, beautifully marked ponies in various shades of brown and gray. I decided immediately that this peaceful forest would be a far better setting for the children to hear the sad news of their mother's death than the hotel rooms I'd booked in Southampton.

The children, now nine and eleven, were dressed in identical blue serge short pants suits, with white shirts and bowties. They looked wonderful. We exchanged hugs and kisses enthusiastically, and I mused at how tall and grown-up they were.

From the back of David's car they squealed with delight at the prospect of seeing their mother again. It had been almost four weeks. Continually, as we sped along the highway, they would ask me how she was. "How's Mommy feeling?" they queried.

"Fine, fine, very well indeed," I would reply. "I'm looking for a good place where we can get out and see the wild ponies and then I'll tell you all about it."

Suddenly, I saw an idyllic little glen where a group of ponies was peacefully grazing. "Please stop here, David," I said.

He pulled the car off the road and the three of us got out. David had been instructed by me to stay in the car.

The trip to the glen was a very wet one. By the time we reached it, our shoes were caked with rich, English mud. We headed toward a fallen tree. This was beginning to feel like the most difficult moment of my life.

"Sit on that log, boys," I whispered. I sat down on a large rock. I faced the two little boys as they seated themselves. They looked so small to be on the verge of hearing such calamitous news.

I took a deep breath and began. "You know how you've been asking me over and over how Mommy is—and I've been telling you she's fine. Now you know how much pain and suffering she's had these past two years. Well, Mommy is fine *now,* for where she has gone there is no more pain, no more suffering. You see, boys, Mommy has died.''

There was silence for a few seconds. And then, Christopher began to cry hysterically. Andrew didn't move a muscle. His jaw tightened a bit and his face drained of color. He turned to stone.

With Andrew a statue, and Christopher now screaming as he sobbed, I felt desperate. I didn't know what to do.

I looked around and saw a nearby brook. In the brook was a bottle. I shouted, ''Boys, pick up stones and smash that bottle in the stream!''

Mechanically, they obeyed, and in seconds, the bottle had been smashed. That gesture helped, but it wasn't enough to break this spell.

In those days, I smoked. I quickly took out the package of Players I'd brought with me and said, ''Now look, boys. I think this occasion deserves one cigarette for each of us. I want you to puff a cigarette down to the filter and then I want you to promise me you'll never smoke another.'' I handed a Players to each boy, took one myself, struck a match and lighted the three cigarettes.

The sun was peeking through a cloud as it was beginning to set. The three of us just stood there, without saying a word. Two little boys and a grown man puffing cigarettes in a wooded glen with wild ponies nearby.

Christopher had stopped crying. His face twitched a bit. His mouth was taut. He coughed once or twice. Andrew looked hollow-eyed, but the color slowly returned to his cheeks. Nobody said a word. We walked back, through the mud, to David and the Jaguar.

It was important to occupy every moment of the boys' time. We checked into the hotel, went immediately to a restaurant and had dinner, and from there, took in Frank Sinatra's *Pal Joey* in a nearby movie theatre. The next morning, we embarked on a whirlwind of activity—the antique car museum, the boat yard, lunch, the park—and finally the *S.S. France,* which we boarded that afternoon. By evening, we were well on our way back to America, to an unprepossessing house in Upper Saddle River, New Jersey. Except for a couple of summer visits to Omi, it would be years before Andrew and Christopher would really return to London, and then they would go there separately, as two individuals leading lives so disparate that they might be inhabiting separate solar systems.

From the moment at which each of them had been assaulted by the juggernaut of the news of their mother's death, they would proceed upon their own distinct, opposite ways. And I would play an integral role in this, because they would live with me until they were grown.

Sally Ann was magnificent. From the moment we turned into the driveway in Upper Saddle River, she gathered my boys in, loving them without question and caring for them without restraint. Later, I would let her adopt them legally, although I kept custodial control. When our marriage had finally run its course, she would remain constantly in touch with them. No mother could have been closer to her own children than Sally Ann became with Andrew and Christopher.

But, unhappily, Andrew, as he entered the protective shelter of Sally Ann's giving arms, drew away from mine. His transformation into a mute statue in the wooded glen in Bournemouth was no temporary withdrawal. Perhaps it was his method of self-preservation; perhaps it was an expression of some repressed and hidden anger that he harbored against me, as he perceived, through the eyes of a child who rightfully expected the presence of both parents, that I had forsaken him, as well as his mother; perhaps it was an affirmation of some hidden suspicion that he was unworthy of being loved, and had therefore been deprived, by an avenging fate, of the love and the persons of first his father, and then his mother, and both far too soon. Perhaps it was a combination of these and a hundred other reactions to a thousand other injustices that he had experienced. But for whatever reason, Andrew stepped away from me that day in Bournemouth, and has yet to fully return. Even so, as adults, now living on different continents, we seem to love each other a lot, and get along eminently well.

The four of us moved into a larger house, at 101 Chestnut Ridge Road in Saddle River, New Jersey, to give us all more room. But as the months unfolded, I found that room wasn't the problem. In an almost medieval acting out of their grief, the boys fought—endlessly, furiously, remorselessly.

Christopher was my clone, so much like me in fact, that I thought I was seeing a home movie of my life. He was bombastic, tempestuous, brilliant, flamboyant. Andrew was just the opposite—quietly brilliant, but laid-back, reserved, and introverted. He was, in some respects, easy to discipline. He didn't revolt overtly. And he seemed only to draw close to Christopher and Sally Ann.

He was two years older than his brother and much stronger. He taunted Christopher because he knew he'd get a rise out of him. Anyone could get a rise out of Christopher. And to my everlasting regret, I'd join in with Andrew, and play this game. It was fun.

It would just be words when I was there. But when I wasn't in the same room, the teasing and taunting would invariably erupt into blows. Andrew would say something tormenting, and Christopher would become enraged, and then the fight would start.

Finally, it became apparent that the only way to stop the battles was to separate the combatants. And so, sadly but inevitably, I enrolled them in different boarding schools, Christopher in Millbrook, in upstate New York, and Andrew in Salisbury, in Connecticut.

Two years later, Andrew would begin to paint, and I would encourage him mightily. And he would become a fine artist. Out of the darkness and the silence and the inwardness, something beautiful and unique would emerge. It had, of course, been there all along, waiting for the sunlight.

Plans for the third anniversary of President Kennedy's Inaugural began and during one of our Rose Garden walks, the President confided to me that he'd decided not to ask Lyndon Johnson to run on the ticket with him for his second term. His choice for vice-president this time would be none other than my old friend from the University of North Carolina at Chapel Hill, the now Senator Terry Sanford, then Governor of North Carolina.

"Knew he was a friend of yours. Thought you'd be interested," the president said, in characteristic understatement.

I could barely contain my joy, and told him so.

And then, shortly after that, President Kennedy asked me to be a trustee of the new performing arts center that was being constructed along the Potomac. I accepted with great happiness and humility.

So, it was with a light heart and total commitment that I began preparations for the Third Anniversary of the Kennedy Inaugural. It would be fine and entertaining, but it would probably pale next to the presidential to end all presidenticals, which would be held the following year, when John F. Kennedy would begin his second four years in office. None of us, for a flicker of an instant, believed that he would lose that election.

On the morning of November 20th, 1963, I appeared at the White House to pose for publicity pictures with Lena Horne, Carol Lawrence and the President. After the session, he drew me aside. "Dick," he said, "How would you like to go with me to Bobby's birthday party tonight?"

It was another command, but this time, I couldn't obey it. It had only been a few months since their mother had died, and I'd promised Andrew and Christopher that I'd have dinner with them that night.

I declined, politely. "I'd love that, Mr. President," I said, "but I can't, because I promised my two sons I'd have dinner with them."

A slight frown drifted across his features. He wasn't accustomed to negative answers to his invitations. I plunged on. "And besides," I continued, "I have to go to San Francisco the next day."

President Kennedy went on, enthusiastically. "Then why don't you come with me to Dallas," he said, "and continue from there to San Francisco? It'll be cheaper, Dick."

And again I had to decline, because my meeting couldn't be postponed, and I wouldn't be able to make it if I took a detour to Dallas with Jackie and the President. He accepted my turndown with a smile and patted me on the shoulder. "Well, maybe next time," he said, and walked out of the Oval Office.

The board room of Young and Rubicam in San Francisco was oak-panelled and opulent. We all sat around a huge table, drinking coffee, eating sandwiches, batting ideas about. I was growing restless. I wanted to get to a quiet place, by myself, so that I could shut out the endless repetition of slogans. I wanted to write the damned jingle I was flown out there to write.

Suddenly, a man burst into the board room. "The President's been shot!" he yelled.

I wheeled around. "You dirty Republican son of a bitch," I seethed, even though I didn't know him. "That's not humor. That's sick." I was enraged. I wanted to choke the bastard.

The man looked at me, stricken. "No no no," he said, softly. "It's true. He's really been shot."

I raced out of the room. In the center of office cubicles, a crowd had gathered around a TV set. Grim-faced announcers were reading bulletins. Every one of them confirmed the horrible news: The man, who, only forty hours ago had invited me to come with him to Dallas, was dying.

I grabbed a phone and called Governor Sanford. "What are we going to do?" I asked him, and by this time I was crying, as was half the nation. "I don't know, Richard," said Terry.

I hung up and dialed Lou Harris. I had almost the same brief and pathetic conversation with him. And then, like a somnambulist, I wandered mechanically back to my hotel. I went up to my suite, turned on the television set and stretched out on the sofa. The news was cataclysmic. The President was dead.

The sheer awfulness, the magnitude and horror of it overwhelmed me, and pummelled me into sleep. When I woke, the familiar tones, the music of the man and his Boston accent, filled the room. He was on television, making a speech.

I sat up. Joy flashed through me. It was all a dream! I'd been sleeping. I'd dreamed that the president had been assassinated, and now I could wake up.

And then, I tuned into the words. They were familiar ones, from a speech I'd heard, months before. It was no dream.

I sat back disconsolately and remembered the coconut shell he'd shown me the first day I'd met him, the first time he'd displayed all of those artifacts and mementos of *PT 109,* all of the reminders that, to him, reaffirmed his charmed life, his invulnerability in times of mortal danger. He'd been casual about security during his thousand days in office, too. The secret service men assigned to him were always on the run, always aware that he might be a target. I'd taken great pains to the blackouts at the end of the acts in the presidenticals. I wanted covering darkness for as little time as possible when the president was on the premises. I knew that the rest of us had to be particularly cautious, because the president was uncomfortably casual about his own safety.

And I was sure that it was that same feeling of faith in his own invulnerability that he'd expressed to me in the Oval Office only a few months before that had prompted him to leave off the bulletproof bubble on his open car in Dallas.

I packed, numbly, and caught the next plane East. Like most of us that day, and for the next few days, I had to be with people I loved.

I called the White House. I knew I wouldn't be needed there. And I also knew that, as my boys had needed me in times of tragedy, I needed them now. I wrote a long letter of consolation to Jackie. And I remained in the circle of my family during that endless November weekend.

There's a touching footnote to all of this. A year later, almost to the day, Jackie invited me to have lunch with her at her apartment in New York, at 1040 Fifth Avenue. I hadn't really gotten to know her at the White House. She'd been a distant, beautiful presence, but that was all.

Now, we had a quiet lunch, just the two of us, talking of the Camelot days in Washington. Somehow the conversation traveled to and rested upon President Kennedy's invitation to me to accompany them to Dallas.

Jackie looked up at me in astonishment, and grabbed my arm. "Dick," she said, urgently, "if only you'd come. Maybe you would have lost a suitcase or something. And we would have all had to wait until it was found."

Tears welled up in my eyes. It was such a desperate outcry, and so heartfelt; it was the most compassionate statement I'd ever heard her make, privately or publicly; and it summed up, eloquently and concisely, the feelings of all of us who had been touched by that immense and impressive presence:

"If only—"

But the reality was that the man was dead, and much of the dream would be shattered into a thousand warring segments. Camelot wouldn't be over for me, but it would be forever and irrevocably changed.

I N   December of 1963, I received my second call from the White House, inviting me to begin my second stint in Washington, D.C. President Johnson wanted me to serve in the same capacity with him that I had during in the Kennedy Administration.

And so I returned to a changed national capital. It would all continue—the policies, the dream, the Democratic administration that cared more for the people than for the privileged few. But it would be changed, as different as a hoedown is from a ballet.

Lyndon Johnson was a farmer, a rancher, a man of the soil. As glamorous as John F. Kennedy was, Johnson was homespun; as crisp and witty as Kennedy was, Johnson was earthy and even vulgar; as young and vigorous as Kennedy was, Johnson was driven and avuncular, a father figure in the energetic mode of Roosevelt and Eisenhower.

And this is in no way meant to seem pejorative. There was something enormously appealing about Lyndon Johnson. He had very large ears that stuck out a little bit, a big head, a huge frame, and huge hands. He was a big, rawboned man, but there was something very paternal and comforting about that. Merriman Smith called him the king, and recalled his giving an interview once from the vantage point of the toilet, which he was using at the time.

Some of the old faces remained at the White House, but by the time I arrived, in the middle of December, President Johnson had surrounded himself with new advisors with whom he felt comfortable— Bill Moyers, Walter Jenkins, Liz Carpenter, Jack Valenti, and a staff that had served him in Congress and as vice-president.

There would be no more walks in the Rose Garden for me; they would be replaced by some private dinners upstairs in the executive mansion, and a privileged entree into some of the most dramatic and important events of the 1960s. To me, President Lyndon Johnson was a warm, genial man, unfailingly kind. He never once raised his voice to me, although I saw his temper unleashed against others, and it was an awesome thing to see.

Shortly after I arrived in Washington, Mrs. Johnson announced that she wanted me to take on the staging of the thirty or forty minute short entertainments at the state dinners, too. The first, and therefore the most important of these, was scheduled for January, to honor President Segni of Italy.

I met with Mrs. Johnson and her social secretary Bess Abel. Mrs. Johnson asked me what I proposed for entertainment.

I'd given it some thought, with the idea in mind of balancing taste and diplomacy. "How about Robert Merrill singing Italian opera arias and the New Christy Minstrels singing American folk songs?" I suggested.

She nodded her accord.

"And," I continued, "Do you want me to get somebody like Lenny Bernstein as master of ceremonies?"

"Absolutely not," she said, unequivocally.

"Do you have somebody in mind?" I asked.

"Yes."

"Who?"

"You."

"Me?" I choked. This was going to be the first Johnson Administration state dinner. A very special guest list that included justices of the Supreme Court was being put together. It was one hell of a responsibility, and I accepted it, not without a small amount of trepidation— which escalated mightily when I discovered that President Segni didn't speak English.

And I didn't speak Italian, so I asked a friend of mine in Rome to translate the opening remarks I'd written into Italian and then write them out phonetically for me.

For years, my son Christopher remembered me wandering around the house in Saddle River, repeating, over and over, my two minutes of phonetic Italian.

It all went beautifully. My Italian must have been at least convincing, because at the end of the program, when President Johnson introduced me to the Italian President, who started rattling off something to me at a furious clip: in Italian. I just stared at him wide-eyed. I didn't know what the hell he was saying, but he evidently thought I did, and that I guess, in affairs of state, is what really counts.

President Johnson was reelected for a second term, beating Barry Goldwater by one of the largest margins in history. I settled into my own second season as the Sol Hurok of the White House, and planned the Inaugural Gala. For this one, I decided to invite Carol Channing, who was a friend of the Johnsons and an enormous smash in *Hello Dolly*, to sing the title song from her show, but as "Hello Lyndon":

> *Hello Lyndon.*
> *Well, hello Lyndon;*
> *It's so nice to have you here where you belong.*

I went to Carol and her manager/husband Charles Lowe, and suggested it. Both of them thought it was a great idea. But we also knew that we'd have to deal with David Merrick, who wouldn't exactly be thrilled about closing down a sold-out, hit show for a night and returning a houseful of tickets, while his star went off to sing for somebody else. No matter who that somebody else was, we knew that David Merrick would hit the roof.

"Don't worry," said Charles. "I'll take care of it."

I breathed a sigh of relief, and went back to Washington.

A week or so later, I released the cast list of the Inaugural Gala to the press, and two days later, the phone rang at home. It was a hysterical David Merrick. He launched into a gargantuan diatribe. It was heroic; it was Shakespearian; it eventually became hilarious, and I motioned to Sally Ann to pick up the extension and listen in. She never would have believed me if I'd tried to describe what was coming out of the receiver.

Finally, in a flourish worthy of Edmund Kean, David Merrick intoned, "Over my dead body will you get Carol Channing! You will never get Carol Channing! I don't care if she's been commanded to appear before God, and you're certainly not God! You will never get Carol Channing!"

But we *did* get her, and she was of course terrific, as was the entire gala.

Life in Saddle River was bright and relaxed, and just the right contrast to the gothic goings-on in Washington. Barbra Streisand and her husband Elliott Gould were good friends; we spent high-spirited times together tobogganing on Sundays with the kids on the hills around Saddle River.

The boys and I celebrated New Years' Eve of 1965 in Barbra's dressing room when she was starring in *Funny Girl,* and one of the sweetest and most memorable times I had with Barbra came about at a surprise farewell party for her before she left for England to star in the film version of *Hello Dolly.*

The guests were close friends, and each of us was to bring a silly gift.

Barbra had recently been given a small, white dog whose name I can't remember, and he was the recipient of her joy and attention. It gave me an idea. I rummaged through my bureau and found an old passport. I removed my picture and eradicated my signature. Then, while Barbra was napping one afternoon, Elliott and I propped the dog up in a chair, and I took a Polaroid snapshot of him. I had the picture reduced to passport size, and inserted it where my picture had been. I drew a paw print in the signature space, wrapped the passport, and headed for the party.

There was a plenitude of imaginative and funny gifts for Barbra that night. She opened them at the table. When she came to mine, she unwrapped it gingerly, opened the passport, and gasped. Tears came to her eyes, and she let out a whoop of laughter.

"That was so dear, so special," she said, as she hugged me in appreciation.

In 1965, I started taking out Lee Strasberg's daughter Susan. She was starring in her first big role then, as Anne Frank in *The Diary of Anne Frank.* She was lovely and petite, with wide eyes, a thirst for life that was infectious and a joyous, bubbling excitement that made her adorable, and I was smitten. We saw each other quite regularly throughout most of the play's run. But she was only seventeen, and I respected her youth. We didn't make love.

Right after she left *The Diary of Anne Frank,* Susan appeared in *Time Remembered,* with Richard Burton. His scruples were different. He and Susan had a prolonged and well-known affair. And I kicked myself for months for being such a gentleman, and such a chump.

Although the Cuban Missile Crisis and the Bay of Pigs Invasion happened while I was "doing my thing" with the Kennedy White House, the turmoil surrounding them took place behind closed doors and out of the sight and hearing of most of us in non-sensitive positions. In the Johnson White House, the many crises, large and small, that Mr. Johnson faced, and which eventually caused him to decide not to run for a second term, seemed to affect all of us, and I wasn't immune to some of the suspicions and troubles that plagued that administration.

The first of these occurred sometime during my second year of staging the galas and the East Room state dinner entertainments.

Out of nowhere, it seemed, the rumor began to spread in the White House that I was taking kickbacks from the artists I invited to perform in these shows. The story had it that prominent entertainers were slipping me money for the privilege of appearing at the White House.

At first, I shrugged it off as absurd. Who could believe such a ridiculous, illogical story?

But then, I noticed a subtle, yet relentless change in the atmosphere around me. I was getting the cold shoulder from just about everybody, including the President—which meant that he'd been fed the rumor too. Now, my own suspicions gave way to anger. Who could be so rotten? Who would want to circulate such a story? Nothing could have been further from the truth, but how did I go about countering it? I couldn't just march in to the President and say, "It's a damned lie and don't you believe it!" I wasn't exactly dealing with the production staff of a show; this was the government of the United States.

So, I did some asking around, and finally discovered that the rumor had reached Liz Carpenter, Ladybird Johnson's press secretary, and she'd been the one who had gotten to the President's ear. But what to do with this knowledge now that I had it? I was confounded. I didn't know how to proceed.

So, I turned to the woman I respected more than just about anyone I knew, Mary Lasker. She'd personally known every president who had served during her adult life, and she'd be able to tell me the protocol to follow.

Her advice was simple and direct. "Call up Liz Carpenter, make an appointment with her, go to see her, and tell her that it isn't so."

It was the obvious solution, one that fright and anger had obscured from me.

I followed Mary's advice, and found out a great deal about the politics that exist within the inner circle of government. I was straightforward and thorough. "Liz," I said, "I understand you've been told that I'm taking kickbacks from people to whom I give the privilege of performing in these shows. And I want you to know that I've never in my life accepted an unethical nickel from anybody. I'm outraged," I went on, "not only at the rumor, but that it seems to be believed—by everybody, without even questioning it—without coming to *me* about it. And I'm also unhappy that you apparently told the president about it, at his birthday party in the executive mansion."

She looked at me levelly and calmly, and said, "Yes. I told him."

"I don't know who told *you*, but if you're willing to tell *me*—" I went on.

"I can't," she said, shaking her head.

"I want you to know it's an out and out lie," I repeated.

She paused, and then smiled. It was a smile of finality. "I believe you," she said. And I knew she would follow through and tell the President, which she did. And also, that I would never know who had originated the rumor, or why. In a few days, the story evaporated, and life at the White House continued for me as it had before.

Shortly after this episode, the Walter Jenkins homosexuality scandal exploded. It was a malicious charade, and it, too, had all the earmarks of a palace intrigue. Walter was a good, honest man, and above reproach. I knew him and would stop to chat with him many times in his office, which adjoined the Oval Office. He was inexhaustibly dedicated to serving his president, who wasn't easy on Walter.

So, when he attended that fateful *Newsweek* party, I'm sure his fatigue contributed to his advanced state of inebriation. And I'm sure that it was then easy to set him up with a homosexual in a men's room, so that the scam could be played out.

It was a nasty scheme, and its repercussions went far beyond the White House—as they were meant to. I was at home in Saddle River the night it happened, but a day or so later, after the news broke in the national press, I received a phone call from a former girlfriend. It seems that she'd been visited by the FBI, and they'd asked her a lot of questions about me.

"And do you know what they said?" she laughed. "They said, 'We've had a lot of trouble finding you.' 'Why didn't you look me up in the phone book?' I asked them." They'd been particularly interested, she went on, in knowing if I'd ever mentioned Walter Jenkins to her.

I hung up, mystified and angry, and a little paranoid. The FBI? Questions about my relationship with Walter Jenkins? Who the hell were the people in the White House who had it in for me?

The telephone rang again. It was Hal Prince. He'd had a visit in his office from the FBI too. "They asked me a lot of questions about you," he said, "and especially about your connection to Walter Jenkins."

"Son of a bitch!" I exploded.

"Oh, and Richard," Hal continued, "they also asked me how and where you and I met."

"What did you tell them?"

"I told them," he answered, slyly. "I told them we'd met in the men's room at the Y."

Despite Hal's *reductio ad absurdum,* I was disgusted with being dragged into the dark subbasement of Washington politics. Still, when I got an inevitable call from the president's super aide, Jack Valenti, asking me to come to Washington, I was considerably less emotional about the whole matter.

I entered Jack's office. He was sitting at his desk. On it was a fairly thick manila folder. It was the FBI dossier on me. He explained the investigation and apologized for the FBI seige on some of my friends. I played dumb.

Jack shook his head. "You were friendly with Walter Jenkins, Dick, and the president ordered everybody who was close to him to be looked at this way."

"What did you find?" I asked him.

He ran a hand over the folder. "We found that you certainly don't fancy fellows. Quite the opposite." And Jack smiled.

President Johnson honored his predecessor's wish, and declared me a trustee of what's now called the Kennedy Center for the Performing Arts, and I remained a trustee for thirteen years.

National and international events proliferated rapidly for Lyndon Johnson. The background work for the passage of the Civil Rights Act had been set in place during the Kennedy Administration, but it was on President Johnson's watch that it finally cleared Congress and landed in the streets of New York City, Philadelphia, Mississippi, and Selma, Alabama.

I was fortunate enough to be alone with President Johnson in the Oval Office that day in 1965 when Martin Luther King led his historic march on Selma, the ultimate confrontation between the forces of bigotry and the forces of change, which would mark the positive turning point for the civil rights movement in the United States.

I remember musing to myself that afternoon about overlooked moments of importance in our lives. Years ago, Lou Harris had introduced Eleanor Roosevelt to me at a Roosevelt Day Dinner. We'd exchanged pleasantries, and then she'd motioned to a young Black man. "I want you to meet someone who's going to be an important person some day." And I remember the burning intensity in this young man, the brightness in his eyes, the strength in his handshake, and the shining articulateness of his thoughts. "This is Martin Luther King," she'd said.

And now, here he was, leading a movement that would change the face of America forever.

That day in the Oval Office I was fascinated by the Johnson style. He was like an orchestra maestro, conducting the entire proceedings— first on the phone to Judge Johnson (the brass), then to Martin Luther King (the strings), then to Governor Wallace (the percussion). I'm sure these men weren't altogether cooperative players, but it was clear that the President was in charge, and aware of every nuance as well as the bigger picture of the events of that day.

Partway through it, he turned to me and said, with a voice full of foreboding, "Dick, wouldn't it be terrible if Martin Luther King were shot? It would set the civil rights movement back a hundred years."

How could we have known then that his concern would be prophecy? We were entering an age of violence that would deepen horrendously as the years rolled on. And although President Johnson would be responsible for initiating the extraordinary and beautiful humanitarian advances of his Great Society, he would have one tragic blind spot that would, contrarily, contribute to the escalating violence in America and the world: He truly, deeply believed in the Vietnam War, and he simply couldn't understand those who opposed it.

I recall a hot August night, one of those heavily humid Washington nights when the mere act of breathing is a major undertaking. I'd been invited to have dinner with the president, his wife, and Jack and Mary Margaret Valenti. The air conditioning upstairs in the executive mansion was broken, and the heat hung in thick, sultry curtains around us. The president had his jacket and tie off, and there were spreading lakes of perspiration radiating out from under his suspenders.

Talk turned to the war that night, and in the middle of it, the phone rang. It was Mayor Richard Daley of Chicago, who would, in two years, be responsible for the police riots that would brutalize thousands of anti-war demonstrators in the streets of Chicago. The president took the call at the table. The conversation with Daley went on for a good twenty minutes, and when it was over, he was smiling. He turned to me. "That Dick Daley. He's a great man," he said, "the best there is. He's a great American."

Later, during coffee, I screwed up my courage and said, "Mr. President, I know it seems out of place for a man in my position to be making this suggestion, but can't you find it in your heart to end this war?''

He turned to me and, in very quiet, modulated tones, began to enumerate his reasons for believing in the validity of the war. They would be reasons he'd be repeating for the rest of his time in office, to a rapidly increasing coterie of critics.

And so, my White House days were drawing to a close. In 1966, I once again wrote a one hour television musical. This one was aired as part of the *Stage 67* series on ABC. The series concept was that of a repertory of mini-musicals, created by well-known composers and writers from the musical theatre. Steve Sondheim's *Evening Primrose* was one of these; my contribution was *Olympus 7-0000,* for which I wrote music, lyrics, and book—and produced it.

The story from which the show sprang bore a more than passing resemblance to *Damn Yankees.* This time, Mercury, instead of the Devil, came to earth to help a losing football team. Mercury was played by Donald O'Connor, and Larry Blyden, Phyllis Newman, and my old friend from *Pajama Game,* Eddie Foy, Jr., filled the principal roles. It was a success, garnering some of the best ratings and highest critical praise of the series.

So, as the Johnson years were winding down, I figured it would be natural and possible to return to Broadway and the musical theatre.

But Broadway in 1966 wasn't the Broadway of ten years before. The golden age of musicals had passed. The number of theatres had shrunk. Television, which had changed the entertainment habits of a nation and had gutted Hollywood, had begun to make inroads on Broadway, too. Production costs had skyrocketed, and real estate interests had begun to make it impossible to bring shows in for the manageable budgets we'd once known. As the available number of theatres shrank on Broadway, Off-Broadway was born.

But the milieu of Off-Broadway was alien to me, as was the popular music of the time. I wrote some songs. But my frame of reference and the music I wrote was, to the entertainment industry of the sixties, interesting but not ''today.''

Broadway hadn't begun to reverberate with rock. Not yet. There was a paucity of shows and theatres, an alarming shrinkage from the times I knew. *On a Clear Day You Can See Forever* was a classic musical, but it wasn't a great success, despite its lovely music and agile lyrics; *Mame* was, but it was mainly a series of wonderful star turns by Angela

Lansbury and a string of fine, working melodies; *Cabaret* was in the offing, but it would only reach its peak of popularity when Bob Fosse's film version deepened and widened it. Otherwise, Broadway was in turmoil and in trouble.

And so was I. The marriage with Sally Ann had run its course and sputtered out. She'd faithfully and seriously carried through with five years of therapy, but two years before, during the run of the musical version of *What Makes Sammy Run,* in which she'd played the role of Kit Sargent opposite Steve Lawrence's Sammy Glick, I'd suspected that she'd lapsed back into her leading man syndrome.

And yet, I couldn't blame Sally Ann. Our marriage was by then a marriage in name only. We still respected each other and still loved each other, as friends. But the deep and abiding and fulfilling commitment that two people have who are in love with each other was no longer there.

And so, in 1966, we decided to divorce. It was realistic, and it wouldn't change our warm feelings toward each other, nor would it diminish Sally Ann's contact with my sons, who were growing up at a furious rate.

We got the divorce and Sally Ann returned to England. I sold the house in Saddle River and moved into an apartment at the Dakota in New York City. Long before I'd even moved in most of the basics, I decided to throw a dinner party, to lift my spirits.

I got a caterer, and invited a group of interesting people—among them, Ann Ford, Mary Lasker, Jan and Chandler "Mike" Cowles, and Gina Lollobrigida. It was a beautiful meal, beautifully served, despite the lack of furniture in the rest of the apartment.

But halfway through dinner, gorgeous Gina Lollobrigida, began to look terrible. She leaned over to me and whispered, "Richard, I don't feel well. I have to lie down."

She could hardly raise herself from the table. I got her to my room, and put her onto the bed.

An hour later, she'd worsened, and I called an ambulance. The dinner party struggled on half-heartedly.

The ambulance arrived, and as the attendants were taking her out on a stretcher, Gina took off a ring that sported an enormous rock and handed it to me. "Hold on to this," she whispered.

One more piece of costume jewelry from a not-too-loaded admirer, I thought. I tossed it onto my bureau, and forgot about it.

A week later, she called me and asked me if I'd bring the ring to her.

"I have to go out," I said, "but I'll leave it with the doorman."

"Leave it with the doorman!" she squealed. "That ring is worth $750,000!"

"You mean you just handed me a $750,000 ring without telling me what it was worth?" I yelled. "Christ! I'm no gemologist. How would I know if it's real or not? If I'd lost it, you would have sued the ass off of me!" And I hung up the phone.

In 1967, I read a deliciously comic novel by Bruce Jay Friedman called *A Mother's Kisses*. It told a hilarious and sometimes touching story of a young Jewish boy whose wildly eccentric mother not only totally directs but absolutely consumes his life. And yet, there's something terribly sad and immensely lovable about her singlemindedness and her blindness to the consequences of it. It was full of wonderfully funny dialogue and situations; it dealt with growing up and growing away, and, although the ending of the book was inconclusive, I was sure that, being the major and marvelous writer he was, Bruce Jay Friedman could strengthen it and I approached him about turning the novel into a musical.

He was enthusiastic; so were Gene Saks and his wife Bea Arthur. A deal was made. Gene took on the direction of the show and Bea was cast in the lead. And ironically, she would be the only one to really profit from the project. Her role would become the basis for the character of *Maude*, her big hit TV show.

In 1968, however, the role of the strident, deadpan mother came and went, in and out of focus, as Gene Saks proceeded to over-collaborate with Bruce Jay Friedman. Bruce was and still is a miraculous writer. But Gene wouldn't let him be himself; with perfectly noble intentions, he hovered too close, supervising every line, and so draining every drop of spontaneity from the writing and the show.

It was in trouble from the start, but then again, other shows with which I'd been associated had been in trouble in the beginning, and some of them—well, one of them—had climbed out of it. I took the summer of 1968 off and rented a house in Watermill, Long Island, possibly to escape the inevitable.

My first few days there were isolated ones. I knew hardly anyone. One night, Maggie Newhouse phoned and asked me to escort her to a dinner party. Her husband Clyde, an art dealer, was in Europe, and this was a big party, and she didn't want to go alone. I accepted.

Partway through the evening, I was introduced to Ritchey Banker, a pretty, articulate, and vivacious blonde. I later found that she was in the process of getting a divorce. She had three children; she was bright, very social, and from one of the oldest families in the country. And she only seemed to have a couple of minutes to talk to me.

Maybe it was my feeling of being adrift, maybe my insecurities were working overtime, maybe I needed a change of association. Maybe Ritchey Banker was just the right person for me in the summer of 1968. Whatever it was, I thought she was dynamite. The next day, I ran into Pat Patterson, one of the handful of people I knew in Southampton. She asked me if anything interesting was happening in my life, I readily answered, "I met this terrific girl."

Pat knew Ritchey, and concluded on the spot that we were perfect for each other. Ritchey, she said, was dying to meet somebody interesting and she was just what I needed.

So, Pat arranged another meeting, and, during the course of that sweet summer, Ritchey and I got to know each other. She was involved with somebody else on weekends, and could only see me on Tuesdays, Thursdays, and Sundays, and that was fine, as far as I was concerned. A summer romance was about my speed in 1968.

But when fall arrived, and it was time to go into rehearsal with *A Mother's Kisses*, it dawned on me that we had a rapport that was enormously appealing. We had good, uncomplicated times together. Her life was an easy, circumscribed, uncomplicated one. It revolved entirely around New York City and Southampton, on tennis courts and in bridge games. It was a whole different ballgame from the life of a Jewish kid from the West Side of Manhattan, but it was a ballgame that intrigued me. I appreciated the simplicity of Southampton, the freedom from show business pizzazz, the seeming neutrality and re-moval from intellectual pursuits of the summer crowd. Almost every-body was either a banker or a stockbroker.

I loved the fresh air, the ocean, the greenness. And I was growing to love Ritchey; her honesty and sweetness and kindness grew on me, and I adored her three children: little Ritchey, Moby, and Robbie. Two were still in diapers. I'd forgotten what it was like to be with small children, and I found it engaging.

So, I bought a large house in Southampton, called The Gables, and asked Ritchey first, to give up her weekend boyfriend, and second, to move up the timetable of her divorce. I wanted to marry her. And she, it turned out, wanted to marry me.

"You're liable to be kicked out of the clubs and the social register," I warned her.

"It doesn't matter," she said.

"Are you sure?" I asked, "Remember grandma."

She did, and laughed. When I'd first started to court Ritchey, she'd asked me to go with her, one afternoon, to La Grenouille restaurant to meet her grandmother, for whom she had a lot of affection.

I'd of course said yes, and, in this elegant and understated eatery, on a warm spring afternoon, I'd met her grandmother, a quiet, erect, very elderly lady with bluish silver hair. She was just finishing her lunch, and we joined her for coffee.

She'd wasted no time with idle chitchat. Fixing me with a straightforward stare, she'd leaned forward, and said, enthusiastically, "Mr. Adler, I want you to know I *like* Jews!"

So, we'd had a genteel forecast of things to come. And come they did. We got married, and, because every marriage of everyone in the present social register appears in the following month's issue of the register, ours was duly noted.

A few weeks later, according to protocol, an application form arrived for me. I opened it, roared with laughter, took it into my study, uncapped my pen, and went to work. I was determined to fill out the application absolutely accurately.

Down went the details of my life and my lineage, all the way back to father's parents.

Paternal Grandmother's Occupation, it requested.

I giggled to myself and wrote, in a bold hand: *Laundress and Rooming House Keeper.*

Paternal Grandfather's Occupation, it demanded.

With a flourish, I penned in: *Streetcar Conductor.*

And then, wiping the tears of laughter off the application page, I folded it, put it in an envelope, and mailed it.

Needless to say, that was the last I ever heard from the scions of the Social Register. Or them from me.

It mattered not at all to either Ritchey or me. We were having the time of our life, and needed no help.

Meanwhile, on the road, *A Mother's Kisses* was coming apart. We were scheduled to open in New Haven, but I had my doubts. The book was mired down in rewrites; the show was, to put it mildly, a shambles. It was in far worse shape than *Kwamina* had been at this time, and alarm bells were sounding in me regularly.

By opening night in New Haven, Gene Saks had been working so hard on individual scenes with Bea, that the opening performance was actually our first complete run-through.

One look at what went on onstage that night, and I knew that the show had practically no chance of surviving. And yet, that's not the way you start a tryout tour, so I dug in and wrote some new songs, and we all worked hard. But the show didn't improve appreciably.

At the end of the New Haven run, I argued forcefully against going to Baltimore. We just weren't ready.

But my pleas weren't heeded, and we brought the show in. I held my breath. Ritchey came to Baltimore and held my hand through the agony of that opening night. And agony it was. The show played no better in front of a Baltimore audience than it had in New Haven.

It had its moments; every show does. The opening number, "Look at Those Faces," was a big success, launching the show formidably. Another tune, "When You Gonna Learn?" would later be recorded by Edie Gorme, and thus would enjoy greater longevity than the show. In fact, several of the numbers worked surprisingly well, and I've always felt that this was one of the best scores I'd written.

But it would be buried, very soon, along with the rest of the show. One look at the faces on an extraordinarily quiet audience exiting the theatre that night, and I knew it was time to cut our losses and run. And since I was co-producer as well as composer and lyricist, I had the right to propose this, which I did, at a very subdued production meeting the next morning.

Gene Saks disagreed, and balked at the idea of closing.

It was time for me to inject a large dose of reality into the proceedings. "Okay," I said, "I herewith withdraw from the project. If you want to get yourself another composer/lyricist, fine. If you want to throw out all my songs, fine. If you want to throw out half of them, fine. Whatever you want to do, do, but deal me out."

And I left the show that morning. Every instinct I had said that it was destined to flop, and flop badly. I'd done as much as I could, so I left, and went back to Southampton and the only part of my life that seemed to be making sense at the time.

The show closed in Baltimore. Gene and Bea salvaged the Maude character, and Bruce Jay Friedman and I salvaged a lasting friendship. But, except for that, A Mother's Kisses repaid nothing—not to its backers, and not to its creators.

Christmas vacation of 1969 arrived, and so did my sons.

Quietly, one night, with very little introduction and no fanfare whatsoever, Andrew showed me his portfolio. I was more than moderately impressed, and I told him so. What I didn't convey to him was that I loved his work for more than its skill and its revelation of his abundant talent. I was equally proud of his ability to deal with whatever mysterious depths resided in him, to put them in order and make them visual. Much of what he hadn't expressed to me or to those close to him had been finding its way to the pages of his sketch pads and the first canvases he'd attempted. And now it was manifesting itself in his own, distinctive, fascinating style.

I was also more than a little delighted that he'd decided to go to the University of North Carolina at Chapel Hill the next year. He was a good student. He could have gone elsewhere. But he chose Chapel Hill, and though Carolina is a top ranked university, I took his decision as an act of love toward me.

The three of us—Andrew, Christopher, and I—spent a quiet Christmas Eve together, having dinner and then going to the movies to see *Bonnie and Clyde.* We were home and in bed early.

At exactly five minutes before Christmas of 1969, the telephone rang. It was my mother. She was crying. "Daddy's dead," she said. That was all. Two words, and the man who had cast the longest shadow on my life, who had influenced me so profoundly, so thoroughly, almost every moment of my childhood and my adult life, was gone.

I hung up the phone numbly, threw on my clothes, and taxied to the apartment on Central Park West. My mother met me at the door, and we fell into each other's arms. Five minutes later, the undertakers arrived with a stretcher. I showed them into the bedroom.

My father did not look peaceful. His mouth was open, as if he were crying out, in protest or in pain. Or perhaps in surprise.

It was his time, I supposed, the end of yet another act. My mother was already trying to gather herself together. She would try to meet this as she'd met every crisis in her life, large or small, feeling it as deeply as it could be felt, and then, tucking it inside, adding it to the storehouse of experiences that had formed the structure of her life. I'll always remember my mother as a gentle monument; sensitive, sensible, and strong.

And yet, my father's death would tear her apart. They'd been married for more than fifty years, and it had been a romance of infinite depths and colors. She would come apart after the first, anesthetizing shock, and we would all gather around her, and, with a lot of love and care, help her to put the pieces of herself back together again.

Christopher would be particularly gentle and attentive, staying with her in the apartment for several weeks, taking care of her, talking with her, cajoling her slowly back to herself. My Uncle Ben, he of the generosity that, in my impoverished youth, got me to England and my first marriage, would take her on a trip to Japan, and later, when I would be on the Keedick Lecture Circuit, delivering a talk and a performance titled "From 1600 Broadway to 1600 Pennsylvania Avenue," I would take my mother with me, showing her the sights and the shops of California. And that would constitute her final mending from the shock of my father's death.

I stayed with her as long as I could at the apartment at Central Park West that sad night, talking quietly. But then, I had to return to my sons. I promised her that I'd be back the next morning.

I mused, as I walked to the end of the street to get a taxi, that my father had always hated Christmas. For as long as I could remember, he'd avoided it as much as he could. Could tonight, I wondered, as I slid into the warmth of the cab, be his final rebuke, his ultimate avoidance?

My eyes began to mist over. One more parting of the ways had arrived, one more loss, one more moment of letting go.

14.

T H E new decade of the seventies dawned darkly for me. I was in deep distress. The boys were growing up. The bills were coming in, right, left, and center; but the money to pay them was slowing to a trickle.

I don't mean to complain too tearfully, although I did then, plenty. I mean, I was far from poor; *The Pajama Game* and *Damn Yankees* would be my twin insurance policies for the rest of my life.

But the problem was, I wasn't adding to these policies.

Late in 1969, George Abbott had come to me with an idea for a revival of *The Pajama Game,* with an interracial twist. I'd liked the idea, but then, Mr. Abbott, who had at last asked me to call him George, had become involved in a minor disaster called *The Fig Leaves Are Falling,* and the project had gone on hold.

Ritchey spent the first summer of our marriage at The Gables, my multi-bedroom, multi-gabled, multi-mortgaged home on South Main Street in Southampton. It was right for the area: large, with a rolling lawn, a swimming pool, and a fine patio for fine summer evenings.

I felt a certain fascination in all that Southampton wealth. I liked the Meadow Club, with its Kelly green, grass tennis courts, enjoyed the wall to wall cocktail parties held every summer weekend, savored the dinner parties in the expansive Southampton mansions called by old world Southamptonians, "cottages." I loved the quaintness of the town with its many chic shops and little bistros.

Ritchey seemed to be the tonic I needed. Her sunny disposition matched the summer season; her sweetness and kindness formed a cushion against the real but bruising reality of the paralysis in my working life. And the children were immensely lovable. Who could want anything more?

We both shared a love of the outdoors, I'd thought, looking forward eagerly to camping trips, and mountain climbing, and exploring new wilderness areas. But Ritchey's idea of the outdoors at that time was Southampton, and a tennis court.

We went to London, and I was eager to show her the sights, and then to go out into the country, to experience the wild cliffs of Cornwall and the majesty of the sea at Devon. Her reaction was a thoughtful and tender release for me to go and have a wonderful time, while she went to the Curzon Club and played bridge.

She loved the theatre, and that was a bond that didn't wear out. But otherwise, our interests and the world in which we moved were worlds apart.

Before too many years elapsed, it was apparent to me that we'd made a mistake. We'd married before we'd really gotten to know each other, and once we discovered the mistake, instead of working at it, we stepped back and let the negativities take over.

My restlessness and ennui took a predictable turn. Kenneth Bilby, then the executive vice-president of RCA, and an old friend I'd known since 1948, called me one day. "Why don't you have lunch with me tomorrow?" he asked. "I'm bringing a very attractive lady along, and I think you'd like to meet her."

I accepted the invitation.

Ken's description of the lady was completely inadequate. She was a brown-eyed, auburn haired beauty, sophisticated, sexy, and worldly. She was Belgian, and spoke with a gentle accent, and the way that she looked at the world, herself, and me was direct and piercing. She in fact had an understated self-assurance about her that was enormously appealing and highly refreshing.

An electric current seemed to leap across the space between us the instant we looked at each other. I was positive enough of it to phone her the next day at the real estate firm for which she worked, and ask her to have lunch with me.

"I'm terribly sorry," she said, in a throaty voice that warmed me, even over the phone, "I'm a married woman. You're a married man. Forget it."

I was amused, but disappointed. How could I have misread things so thoroughly? I parried, in embarrassment. I was asking her to lunch, not to bed.

Or was I?

Meanwhile, on Broadway, revival fever was in the air. The only truly successful musical of the 1973-74 season was Steve Sondheim's *A Little Night Music*. It seemed to be the right time for *Pajama Game* again. George Abbott and I went to work on script revisions to accommodate the interracial motif.

I assembled the production team. Bert Wood, who had worked for Mr. Abbott as a stage manager became co-producer, and put together the stage crew. Nelson Peltz, a brilliant young business entrepreneur, raised a good deal of the money, and became associate producer. I'd always disliked the scene in which the reprise of "Hey There" was sung in the second act, so I wrote a song called "Watch Your Heart" to replace it. George liked it. Later, in 1985, I would rewrite "Watch Your Heart" into "If You Win You Lose," for the Leicester Haymarket Theatre's very successful production of *The Pajama Game,* and the song worked very well indeed.

We signed Hal Linden for the John Raitt role, Barbara MacNair for the Janis Paige part, and Cab Calloway to play Eddie Foy Jr's role.

We went into rehearsal, and George was his usual, peppery self, driving the show as if he were forty years old instead of eighty-five.

But.

It's probably doubtful that even Mr. Abbott at any age could have harnessed Cab Calloway.

Casting Cab seemed like a good idea at the time. He was a star with a following; he'd played Sportin' Life in *Porgy and Bess* with respectable success. We entered rehearsals with high expectations.

But partway into them, we knew we'd made a mistake. Cab Calloway may have been an effective entertainer. But his attitude was unforgivably unprofessional. Over and over, he would disrupt rehearsals, refusing to take direction, disputing with and snarling at Mr. Abbott and me.

And when we opened in Washington, at the Kennedy Center Opera House, he still didn't know his lines. His ineptitude threw everybody else's timing off, too, and slowed the overall pace of the show to a stumble when he was onstage.

Variety reported that "Cab Calloway . . . doesn't seem comfortable in the role"; and David Richards, in the *Washington Star News,* caught it all when he wrote that Cab Calloway's timing was off enough on opening night ". . . to set pajama production back six months."

When we moved into the Lunt-Fontanne Theatre in New York City on December 9, 1973, the reviews were all over the lot. There were seven favorable ones, five mixed, and five negative. Douglas Watt, in the *Daily News,* was ebullient, cheering that, *"The Pajama Game* arrived on Broadway bursting with vitality and sunny songs . . . and it was fun all over again"; Richard Watts in the *Post,* pronounced it "brilliant." And Brendan Gill said, in his *New Yorker* review, "Richard Adler and Jerry Ross . . . wrote their songs together—that is, each contributed to both the lyrics and the music, and this rare form of collaboration is perhaps the reason that their lovely handiwork gives the impression of having always existed and therefore of having been all simply and effortlessly come upon, rather than composed."

But somehow, even with a twelve-dollar top for tickets, the public stayed away, convinced by the particularly vicious attack on us by Clive Barnes in the *New York Times. "The Pajama Game, "* he wrote, "would not be on my list of the greatest American musicals—would it be on yours?—. . . Yet, the music still stands—especially in elevators."

We limped along for sixty-five performances, and then folded.

Shortly after *The Pajama Game* closed, I got another call from Ken Bilby. "Remember that lady we had lunch with a while back?" he asked.

"Yes," I said, without enthusiasm.

"Well, she just called me, and she asked me to take her to lunch. Today."

"Look, Ken," I said, "I've got a million things to do, and—"

"Wait a minute," he interrupted. "She asked me to ask you to come along. She said to tell you she'd made a mistake."

That very afternoon, we made another lunch date, this time for just the two of us. Our relationship began.

A year later, she rented a house in Marbella, Spain. She called me often, asking me to come and be with her. I was vegetating in New York. I wanted and needed her electric presence.

Ritchey had always been fair with me. Now it was up to me to be fair with her. I told her about Gisèle, without mentioning her name. I said I would try to work "the other woman" out of my system—that I wanted to stay with her.

Her reaction was calm. It didn't seem to surprise her, nor did it seem to displease her very much. She told me to go to Spain.

I caught the next plane to Malaga, where Gisèle met me. We drove down the Costa del Sol to Marbella, which was just beginning to transform its character from sleepy fishing village to playground of the international rich.

She and her two children were living in a small villa on a golf course high above the sea. The Mediterranean, as blue as a field of topaz, lazed benignly below us.

By the last night of my week's stay, I was beginning to feel a disquieting turbulence. Gisèle cried a lot that last night, because of my impending departure, and I tried to comfort her, but I had a sinking feeling that it was all becoming too complex. I was being swept into something I would regret, simply because I was restless.

Guilt plagued me. Ritchey had agreed that I should go to Spain, but she probably regarded it as simply a fling. I was concerned about Gisèle and her state of mind. And I felt guilty about being away from my work. I was a mess.

I was relieved to climb aboard the plane for New York.

But the minute I got to my seat, I began to think about Gisèle, and before an hour had passed, the feelings I'd been fighting against won out. I yearned to be back with her.

I was in trouble. I was in two wildly contrasting places, and neither one of them was the right place. There was the feverish joy of my relationship with Gisèle, and there was the rest of my life, a dark hole whose sides obliterated any daylight of hope. Nothing, absolutely nothing seemed to be working the way it should.

Time had passed rapidly. Andrew was about to graduate from the University of North Carolina at Chapel Hill. He'd had a respectable four years of college, almost interrupted once when he'd determined to drop out and, as he put it, "travel through the veins of America." I'd been able to talk him out of that and back to school, and now, a mature and individual young man, he was about to meet the world on his own terms.

Both the university and his life had prepared him well. He came to New York, and continued painting. Before long, a friend of mine, Solange Herter, saw and fell in love with Andrew's paintings. She in turn arranged for him to have his first major exhibition, at the Harkness Gallery on 75th Street, between Madison and Fifth avenues in New York City. The exhibition was a success, and Andrew sold many of his paintings through the gallery.

One day, he came to me and announced that he was going to move to Paris for a couple of years.

"You know, son, I'm going to miss you," I said, "and Paris is an expensive city. If you go there, you're on your own. Don't call me unless you're on your way to a hospital or a jail." I smiled. "And try to stay out of both."

He nodded quietly. We said our goodbyes. I loved and respected him enormously, and still do. And, standing in my living room that night. I admired his courage, too. He didn't speak a word of French, and he wasn't particularly interested in looking up my friends there. He wanted to realize his own talent in his own way, in his own place. And he would.

Within two years, he would return with a lovely girl, Michele Joan. She was French, and he would meet her in Paris, and he would marry her in my apartment at United Nations Plaza, where I would move after Ritchey and I divorced.

And very much later, when he and Michele had parted and he'd married Bea Wickrath in Munich, he would give me the most precious gift any son can give a father: a grandchild.

Andrew would continue to go his own way. His path in life would be a considered, steadily fulfilling one, in stark and dramatic contrast to the volatile, jagged, nearly spastic circles of my life and that of his mercurial brother Christopher.

V

CHRISTOPHER

15.

I F   it were possible to wear your heart on your sleeve, or anyplace else the world could easily reach, that's where my younger son Christopher would have worn his. If there'd been trumpets handy, they would have announced Christopher's decision to go to the University of North Carolina at Chapel Hill. If there'd been drums, they would have rolled. It seemed that he never did anything with less than full out, articulately expressed enthusiasm. He was a brilliant student; he could have had his pick of any Ivy League or other league college. But he chose UNC. "I want to go where you went, Daddy," he said one day, hugging me. And not only that, he did much of what I did, and more besides. By the time he left Chapel Hill, in 1975, he'd directed seventeen plays, been tapped for the university's highest all around honor, the Golden Fleece Award for Meritorious Service Academically and Extracurricularly, and had decided that he wanted to make the theatre his life.

Five years later, he would come to me with pages of lyrics, and ask me what I thought of them, and how he could improve upon them. And I would eagerly plunge into the task of tutoring him.

I taught him what I could. I remembered how, early on, I'd learned, from a pile of failures, that youth and enthusiasm and amateurism tell you to write too much into a song.

"It isn't what you write into a song, but what you write out of it that makes the difference," I told Christopher, because it was probably the most valuable rule any songwriter can learn.

I knew that the form of the popular song was changing, that the old thirty-two bar structure was being blown apart. But I also knew that no matter what the form, certain processes had to take place within the song. Frank Loesser taught it to me when he told me that the popular song is built upon cliches, but that each song should have a special corner that's utterly original.

This of course doesn't apply when you're writing show tunes. Generally speaking, a show song should be germaine to the mood of and the moment when it occurs in the show. Recently, Hal Prince told me that the quality he most remembered about the music and lyrics that Jerry and I wrote was their rightness for the show. They always, always helped the show move forward or inward, he said.

Christopher would listen carefully to my advice. Sometimes he would follow it—and sometimes he wouldn't. He would bark his shins on the world over and over because of his nature. He was my clone, my double, my mirror image, my despair, and my joy.

One morning, during the winter of 1975, Eddie Colton, who'd been my attorney on and off since before *The Pajama Game,* called me.

"Dick," he said, "I want to have lunch with you. I have something important I want to discuss with you."

We had lunch, and partway through, Eddie leaned forward and lowered his voice. "Dick, I'm going to let you in on a little secret," he said. "I think it might be helpful to you, and somebody else as well." He paused. Eddie was given to dramatic pauses. "That somebody is Richard Rodgers. He hasn't anything to do, and he's itching for a project. Do you think you might have something for him?"

Richard Rodgers! He was seventy-two now, and in frail health, but he was one of the remaining giants of the theatre. It was a golden opportunity.

I didn't have to think twice. "I'll have something tomorrow," I told Eddie.

Actually, an idea I'd already begun to research had been in the back of my mind for some time, as a possible project for myself. King Henry VIII was one of the most colorful figures of English history. Alexander Korda had made a wonderful film, *The Private Life of Henry VIII:* Charles Laughton had had an enormous amount of fun with this multifaceted character, who was, I found from my reading, tender, emotional, insanely jealous, ruthless, and gifted. It was he who had supposedly written the song "Greensleeves," and it was he who had definitely written some of the most beautiful love letters ever set to paper.

He was also a son of a bitch and a murderer, and no musical had yet been written with a son of a bitch and a murderer as its central character. But that important piece of knowledge somehow slipped past not only me but all of the people with whom I would become involved, in yet another doomed musical venture.

I was confident in 1974 that I could pull this one off, if I didn't overextend myself. Producing and writing the music and the lyrics had been a backbreaking and perhaps fatal overload in *A Mother's Kisses.*

So I decided to just produce this show, which would also leave me free to begin work on the music and lyrics for another musical that Mr. Abbott proposed to me at the same time, *Music Is,* based upon Shakespeare's *Twelfth Night.*

The next day, I phoned Eddie Colton, and asked him to set up a luncheon meeting with Richard Rodgers, whom I had already met a few times. We discussed the project, and he agreed to write the music, and a lovely friendship began.

For his collaborator, I suggested Sheldon Harnick—the lyricist of *Fiorello!, She Loves Me, Fiddler on the Roof,* and *The Apple Tree.* Sheldon had also contributed to my first Broadway venture, *John Murray Anderson's Almanac* those many years ago. And he was, besides being brilliant, a really likable man. He still is.

For librettists, I picked Jerome Lawrence and Robert E. Lee, who, with *Inherit the Wind,* had proved that they were marvels at bringing history to life onstage. But that would be a non-productive choice. They were fine in the context of straight plays, but at sea in a musical. Sherman Yellen, who'd worked with Sheldon on the unsuccessful but well conceived historical musical *The Rothschilds,* replaced them.

That fall I'd met Roger Berlind, an investment banker who'd been ripped to pieces by a shattering personal tragedy from which he was trying to recover. He'd gone to LaGuardia Airport to meet his wife and two daughters, who were flying in from a vacation. As the plane approached the runway, it was hit by wind shear, and went down, exploding on impact. Everyone aboard was killed instantly.

Roger had told me that, as an undergraduate at Princeton, he'd been involved in the Triangle Club productions. So, I proposed, as therapy, that he come in as co-producer, with financial wizard Ed Downe. He accepted the offer, and he's been producing successes on Broadway ever since.

Next, I went to the Shuberts, to ask them to invest in *Rex,* as the show was now called. We'd already received $100,000 from RCA, who would record the cast album. The Shuberts were willing to invest $150,000 and bring it into a Shubert theatre, *if* I could get Michael Bennett to direct it.

I tried. But his price was far too steep. I tried Hal Prince, but he was committed to Steve Sondheim's *Pacific Overtures,* and Jerry Robbins, who'd retired from Broadway and gone back to ballet. I made the rounds of other directors with solid experience in staging musicals, and they were all unavailable. So, I finally hired Ed Sherin, who had little musical experience, but who'd staged *The Great White Hope,* which had the same kaleidoscopic qualities we saw for *Rex.*

The decision cost me $150,000 of backing and a Shubert theatre, and, I think, the good will of the Shuberts. It was a considered decision that had to be made, and it turned out to be a costly one. In retrospect, I now see that I made a big mistake in not hiring Michael Bennett—at *any* price.

For a star, I had only one actor in mind: Nicol Williamson. I was told that he sang very well, and I'd seen him do several roles, including a smashing *Uncle Vanya,* under Mike Nichols' direction that year. For my money, he was one of the greatest actors in the world, and I was determined to cast him in the show.

I discovered that he was presently living near Stratford, right next to a castle that had once been occupied by none other than Henry VIII. Perhaps serendipity was on my side, I thought as I flew to London, rented a car, and drove out to Stratford, to keep a luncheon invitation offered to me by Williamson and his wife.

The home was a comfortable, British country retreat. I was let in by a butler and shown to the study, which had a full view of a sumptuous staircase. Five minutes passed, and there was a stirring at the top of the stairs. I looked up, and there, descending the staircase, was Henry VIII—redheaded, virile, reining in regal energy and fire. It was as if the character I'd envisioned had suddenly, precisely come to life.

We had a convivial, relaxed lunch. Nicol and his wife couldn't have been more charming. And to make it all perfect, as dessert neared, they both launched into melody, singing the songs from *Kwamina.*

Before I left, he'd agreed to do the part.

He was magnificent as Henry; few could have done it better.

But, unfortunately for us, and unknown to me at the time, he was a load of trouble—incredible antics fueled by copious amounts of wine mixed with brandy. It made for tumultuous times, in rehearsal, on the road, and in New York.

Rex's problems, however, didn't all originate or center upon Nicol Williamson's sometimes bizarre behavior. It was a show with a load of trouble, right from the start. If I'd had the same clear vision I'd had with *A Mother's Kisses,* I might have closed it in Wilmington, where we opened. But I reasoned that the show was in the hands of true professionals, with a freight train load of experience among them. I hoped we could pull it out.

Ned Sherin's direction was solid; Dania Krupska's dances were appealing, and the genius of Dick Rodgers, while not at its peak, was still in plentiful evidence. He wrote incessantly and easily. If a song didn't work, he wrote another one, without complaint. If that didn't work, he wrote another.

But unfortunately, collaboration with a legend had a negative effect upon Sheldon Harnick. Sheldon is a genius in his own right, but he was intimidated by Richard Rodgers. "It's a little like collaborating with God," he confessed to me one night, and when Marilyn Stasio caught up with us in Boston, and interviewed him for a lengthy article in *Cue,* he told her, "I'm consciously trying to avoid flashiness, the cleverness of the intricate rhyme. I'm trying to get more direct, more emotionally naked; to find fresh images to communicate genuine feeling. That's why I respond to Mr. Rodgers' music. It has such feeling."

Sheldon's evaluation was wrong, and Martin Gottlieb picked it up in his review in the *Post* when we opened in New York, when he said, that "Sheldon Harnick's lyrics . . . don't sound like Harnick. They sound like Hammerstein."

Still, that in itself wasn't enough to produce a bad show. Back in Wilmington, despite good reviews, it was apparent that we had major book problems. Henry VIII was just too nasty to exist as the central character in a musical. So, he was toned down, and by the time we'd gotten to the Opera House at the Kennedy Center in Washington, he was almost Mister Nice Guy.

Queen Katherine underwent a sea change, too. In fact, the only character that seemed to weather it all was Elizabeth, played beautifully by Penny Fuller. I know now, in hindsight, that Elizabeth was *the* fascinating person about whom the musical should have been written in the first place.

After we opened in Washington, I sent an SOS to Hal Prince in New York. I asked him to come down and see the show. And Hal came, and, as agreed, went back to New York without commenting.

Christopher had graduated from the University of North Carolina the previous spring. He wanted to go into the professional theatre, and I thought, what better way to know a show from the inside out than to break in as an assistant stage manager on *Rex?*

He got his taste of theatre, all right. He learned the ropes, literally, and saw it all, plus. One night, in Washington, some of the cast and crew went out for a few drinks in a neighborhood bar, and Williamson suddenly turned on Christopher. With bloodlust in his eyes and mayhem on his mind, he chased him out of the bar and up the street. Christopher nimbly got away.

In Boston, Williamson was often out of control. Sometimes he would show up for a rehearsal; sometimes he wouldn't. Sometimes he'd know his lines; sometimes he wouldn't. Caryl Rivers, in from New York to do a piece on us for the *New York Times,* had a chance to see our star in action, and it all found its way into his article. At one point, one cast member told Rivers, "You don't know if Nicol Williamson is going to be nice to you or punch you in the mouth," and one Saturday morning, after Williamson had missed a rehearsal of a new number that was to go into that afternoon's matinee performance, Rivers turned to me and asked, "Is he going to wing it?"

"You're learning," I said, furiously, and stalked out of the theatre to call Hal Prince. We needed a doctor, fast.

The Boston reviews, in Marilyn Stasio's apt words, ranged from "mixed to malicious." Hal arrived the next morning. Ed Sherin wasn't altogether delighted that he was there, but, as a solid professional, he knew we needed the kind of help Hal could provide.

And Hal did his best to assist, suggesting major and minor changes, moving numbers around, trimming and adding.

We postponed the New York opening for a few days, but it was a terminal case that even Doctor Prince couldn't save. We played forty-one performances, and then quietly closed.

I learned, then and there, that no matter how interesting or exciting a historical figure is, it's dangerous to use that figure in a show, because you can't change history without rebuke. You're stuck with what you have.

Fortunately, the George Abbott project needed my full attention, and so I plunged right into completing the score of *Music Is,* with Will Holt writing the lyrics. It would be a Shakespearian musical, with any luck much like Mr. Abbott's huge success of forty years before, *The Boys from Syracuse.*

We had the immense good luck to get Patricia Birch to stage the musical numbers and do the choreography. She'd worked with Hal

Prince on *A Little Night Music, Candide,* and *Pacific Overtures,* and she'd created a sensation with her dances for *Grease, The Me Nobody Knows,* and *Over Here.* Pat was very hot at the time, and we were all excited about *Music Is.*

We assembled a good, solid cast that included Christopher Hewett and Sherry Mathis. We capitalized at $600,000, and worked out an arrangement with the Seattle Repertory Company to launch the show in Seattle.

And so, in September of 1976, we headed west, with Mr. Abbott's 117th Broadway show, and my sixth. But who was counting? Every show is the first one when you're in rehearsal. And this show had a good, first time feeling about it.

I wrote my heart out. I poured forth a load of ballads, some quartets, a ribald comedy number for Christopher Hewett, a clutch of dances for Pat Birch, and an Elizabethan opening.

The book used more of Shakespeare than *The Boys from Syracuse* had; and there weren't a great many laughs in it when we got to Seattle in October. But the zest and spirit of the show was pure George Abbott, and Mr. Abbott was a great believer in on the road, out of town carpentry.

We opened to a highly appreciative audience on October 13, and the next day's reviews were good for the music, lukewarm for the book, and positive for the show.

Maggie Hawthorne, in the *Post Intelligencer,* summed up most of the Seattle opinion, when she wrote that "Abbott has . . . constructed a flimsy framework on which to hang songs. And that, perhaps, turns out to be the meaning of the show's title, for *Music Is* what this show finally has going for it."

Variety was there, liked it, and predicted a hit. So we rolled up our sleeves and began to work on the show, paring it, building the book, repositioning numbers, writing new ones.

As a co-producer, I felt that my biggest headache, and the largest problem for the show, was the scenery. It didn't work. Not at all. And so, we had to go back and build from scratch.

By the time we reached Washington, we had entirely new scenery and absolutely no money. But we also had a better show than we had in Seattle, and the Washington critics agreed with that estimate. They gave us across the board raves. Audiences went wild, stamping their feet and cheering. We had a hit. We were sure of it.

Preston Jones' *A Texas Trilogy,* a group of three full length plays about Jones' native state, went into New York just ahead of us, trumpeting its ecstatic out of town reviews. And the New York critics blasted it into oblivion.

We were all shaken by that. We took a lesson from it, and rewrote the ads for New York, cutting out any quotes whatsoever from our out of town, rave reviews.

Somebody suggested that we keep *Music Is* out of town indefinitely. "They love us in the boondocks," they said. "Why risk it in New York?"

And that was probably advice we should have heeded, instead of sneaking into town with no advance and no money.

At least we had fourteen days of hearty, pre-Christmas cheer. The preview audiences ate the show up. They cheered as lustily as they had in Seattle and Washington, D.C. The curtain came down on our last preview to a standing ovation.

And then, the New York press arrived. And that was the end of *Music Is.*

A few good notices couldn't stand up to the *New York Times'* unmitigated thrashing. Edwin Wilson, in the *Wall Street Journal,* seemed to sense what many of his fellow critics were about to do, when he wrote, "If [*Music Is*] does not succeed, it will be the audience's loss because it is the most exuberant, joyous, and carefree new musical on Broadway."

His words amounted to a whistle in the wilderness. We opened on Monday. The reviews appeared on Tuesday. I walked into the rear of the sixteen hundred-seat St. James Theatre during the Wednesday matinee performance, and counted heads. There were 113 people in the audience.

So, the closing notice went up, and we were out of the theatre by the weekend, after giving eight performances. The financial loss was staggering.

Mr. Abbott was as gracious in defeat as he would have been with a hit. He told me he loved the music. He told me that it hadn't been my fault, that there were two fatal flaws in the show: "The book wasn't good enough," he said, "and I should have made you write more Elizabethan music, like the opening number." And that was it for him. He'd closed the ledger on this show, and, characteristically, was ready to begin number 118.

But in spite of George's generous words, I was disgusted, I was mad,

I'd had it with Broadway and the musical theatre. The only compensation I received out of the experience of *Music Is* was once again working with the great George Abbott, watching this tireless man perform his theatre magic. Even though he said to me that his book wasn't good enough—and perhaps it wasn't—the aura of George Abbott will always remain special and beautiful to me, and the time I spent on this and other productions with him will be times I'll forever cherish. They form a bouquet that I've saved, pressing it carefully between the pages of my life.

That was the best of it. The worst was the realization that the theatre was in the grip of not so tender mercies. And if it had all come down to this, if a very, very small group of people could shape the present and the future of not only a hundred professionals, but of the entire Broadway theatre scene, modeling it to their tastes and their preferences and their prejudices, then Broadway was no longer a place I wanted to inhabit.

Whoever said that we should have kept the show out of New York was absolutely right. If we'd made that rash decision, the show might still be running.

But we hadn't. I'd hit bottom and I was mad as hell. What was going on? I asked myself. Was I going to stay on the flats of life forever? Was this all there was, my friend?

I needed a change of pace, but this time in my work, not my private life.

Shortly after *Music Is* flicked through Broadway, Twyla Tharp called me. She'd been impressed by the dance music I'd written for Pat Birch's dances, and she wondered if I'd be interested in writing a piece for her and her company.

"Ballet?" I said. "I've never written a ballet."

"You probably have, and you didn't know it," she laughed. "Why not give it a try?"

So, I called Dick Hayman, who'd done over two thousand orchestrations for Arthur Fiedler and the Boston Pops. I asked him to help me orchestrate the piece when it was completed. He agreed.

I began work on a tone poem which I called *Memory of a Childhood.* I sketched it out for six movements. It would be an average day in the life of a child . . . as I remembered it. Being a production writer, and being accustomed to developing a character, a scene—extending the mood of the scene beyond what the dialogue can do—was my customary modus operandi. So I reached back into the memory of my childhood. This was my script without a script. I started with "The Awakening" . . . how difficult it had been for me to roll out of bed, brush my teeth, eat, and tear off to school. I followed with "Playing Hookey." The motif was sly, mischievous. The third movement was "The Piano Lesson," which began with a scale and developed, fantasy-like, into a piano concerto. Number four I called "Going to the Movies." The first phrase expressed what we needed in those days when we were unaccompanied by an adult. With money in hand, we begged, "Mister, will you take me in, please?" Then I followed with runs and turns suggesting the flicks we saw starring Tom Mix, the Marx Brothers, Harold Lloyd and Charlie Chaplin. Then came "The Dancing Lesson." How well I remembered going to Miss O'Neill's dancing classes at the age of thirteen. We wore blue serge knickerbocker suits and white gloves so we wouldn't soil the little girls' pretty dresses. One, two, three, one, two, three. I mused as a slightly dissonant and purposely clumsy waltz theme became the basis for a lush ballet. The piece ended with "Evening Prayers" including a brief vocal with all the added "God blesses" a small child uses to manipulate the parent away from bidding him farewell for the night.

Dick and I sweated, and I learned about instrumental textures and strengths and impossibilities. From the time I was a child, I'd been exposed to the stylistic devices of the Great Masters, of Tchaikovsky and Brahms and Mozart and Beethoven and Shubert and Bach and Chopin. At the age of four, I could distinguish between them, and this gave me a solid background that helped our coaching sessions immensely. It was tough, but rewarding. And the piece was—okay. From the perspective of now, I can see that it was a hybrid, a suspension, partway between pop and serious. But both Dick Hayman and I were happy with it, and I sent it off to Twyla Tharp with a light heart and a handful of hope.

And she rejected it.

I was stunned. I'd laid myself on the line, going off in a new and strange direction, and rejection hadn't been part of my scenario.

I got on the phone to Dick Hayman. "Dick," I said, "do you think the piece is good?"

"Of course it is," he said. "I told you that."

"You're a conductor, right?"

"Right."

"And you know other conductors?"

"Right. And we're going to get the piece played," he said, with a tone of determination that matched my own.

And that's just what he did. He went directly to the Detroit Symphony. At first, they weren't interested. I was from another world. The fact that I'd had some success in the theatre meant nothing to them. But Dick persisted, and finally, they agreed to perform *Memory of a Childhood.*

The notices were great, and on the basis of that, Dick went to the St. Louis Symphony, which also accepted it and played it, and then, to the Chicago Symphony and the Boston Symphony, which performed it five times in its Youth Concerts.

It was exhilarating, like opening a window in a dark room. I'd taken a risk and the risk had paid off. Of course, it was a little lonely out there. There was nobody else to take the blame if you bombed. But if you hit, as I seemed to be doing, there was nobody else to diminish your joy, either.

Well, almost nobody. George Abbott heard the piece, and I asked him what he thought. He nodded his head, and gave me his succinct and straightforward assessment, as always. "It's good," he said, "but you're wasting your time, Dick. Get back to Broadway. That's where you belong."

And one sheltered corner of me echoed those sentiments precisely. I knew that George Abbott was theatre, and theatre was George Abbott. It would only be logical for him to say what he said. But some part of me also agreed, deeply, that I belonged on Broadway. As badly as my experience had been, there was something undeniably calling me back, a siren song that wouldn't quit.

And there was another bond that pulled me toward the theatre that I knew. Christopher had gone directly from *Music Is* into his first professional directing job. He'd directed a production of Harold Pinter's *Old Times,* at a little theatre on 62nd Street and Lexington Avenue, and it had been good. He had a feel for what would work on a stage, and I was happy that he'd found a niche.

Christopher had also come to me that week with some news that set me back on my heels.

"Daddy," he said, sitting down on the couch in my living room at United Nations Plaza. "I have something I want to talk to you about."

"What is it?" I asked.

"I know you're not going to like this," he said, staring out of the window onto First Avenue, "but I'm gay."

I was dumfounded. I'd had no hint, not at home, not on the road with *Rex,* not in his demeanor. I simply couldn't speak.

He looked up at me. "Are you angry?" he asked.

"No, of course not," I said, and I truly wasn't. But I was beset by conflicting emotions, none of which I could exactly identify. "Naturally," I said, "I would prefer that it were otherwise, for many, many reasons. It would be easier for you. It would be easier for a family relationship—" and I suppose I was thinking about grandchildren when I said this. They passed through my thoughts, and then disappeared.

I walked over to him. "Whatever makes you happy," I said. "That's what's important. If you're happy, then I'm happy."

And I could see in his expression that a great weight had been lifted.

The following Tuesday, Dick Hayman called me. The Metropolitan Brass Quintet, a fine, New York based brass ensemble, was looking for a short, original piece to play in a concert they were giving in the fall at the Music Barge in Brooklyn. I could get a commission to do it. What did I say?

I didn't know *what* to say. I'd done it once, but was it a fluke? Maybe not. Maybe that was the way to go. I accepted, but I wasn't comfortable with it. I'd had to hunt around for a subject for the first piece, and then I'd had to stretch to write it. I had to face it. I was much more comfortable entering into a theatre project than I was beginning an instrumental piece.

So, I called Bob Aurthur. We hadn't spoken since *Kwamina.* In the intervening years, I'd received over twenty requests to do *Kwamina* again, in several countries. And I'd turned down every one of them. But now, I thought, might be the time to make up and think about a complete rewrite of the show, and another try. The world had changed; attitudes toward race had been transformed; now might be the time to bring *Kwamina* back to Broadway.

Bob was in the hospital. I went to see him. We talked for a long time, and he was enthusiastic about rewriting the book of *Kwamina.* As soon as he got out of the hospital, we'd get together, we said, as we shook hands.

And then, several weeks later, I got the news. Bob Aurthur was dead.

Maybe, I thought, fate was trying to tell me something. Maybe it was trying to point me in a different direction.

16.

" L E T ' S get away," I asked Eva Malmstrom, a friend of mine in that summer of 1978.

"Where?" she asked.

"West," I said. I wanted to distance myself from the city for a while, leave my work and the setting for it behind and find a little perspective. I'd been told about a dude ranch in Wyoming, near Yellowstone National Park, where you could rent horses and be away from anything that even remotely reminded you of life in the city.

That was for me. And for Eva, too, who met me at Kennedy Airport that Saturday. We arrived at the Dude Ranch on a Tuesday morning, and plunged into the life of it immediately. The scenery was certainly wonderful, and the people, and the atmosphere. But I was an exercise freak, and it seemed to me that the horses were getting all of the exercise on this ranch. I needed a place to explore, on foot.

So, when Sunday arrived, and there were no scheduled activities, I suggested to Eva that we rent a car and go to Yellowstone. It wasn't necessarily number one on my list of places to visit, but I figured since it was so close, I'd be a good citizen and see it. Maybe it would have some walking trails. Eva agreed, eagerly. She hadn't seen the park either, and it was only 150 miles away. It would fill a Sunday nicely.

So, we rented the car and took a leisurely drive to Yellowstone National Park. It was a bright, sunswept day, with only a breath of a breeze. Innocuous, peaceful, ordinary. Gloriously deceiving, when I remember it in the context of what happened that day.

We drove into the park, like any tourists out for the scenery. And stopped. Stopped driving, stopped breathing. Even time seemed suspended.

There, spread like a primeval banquet before us, was a sight that must have been exactly the same as that seen by primitive beings, millions of years ago. A rhythmically contoured glacier lake, reflecting sky and trees and shoreline and us, stretched from one periphery of our vision to the other. Surrounding it, eerie emissions rose from some subterranean source: fumaroles of winding, ascending steam. Between and beyond them were more assertive geysers, their water fusing with the fumaroles' mists, and turning the shoreline into a billowing curtain of steam and spray.

There was nothing else, nothing to challenge the majestic motion, the seething serenity of that scene. It was this strange world and us, and that was all—except for an enormous woodframe building, fronting the lake, but miraculously not intruding upon it. It was almost as if it had been built as a piece of the countryside.

The building turned out to be the Yellowstone Lake Hotel, and I parked the car and immediately entered the lobby, strode up to the desk, and asked if they had a room. My hopes weren't extraordinary. A hotel like this, with scenery like this, would have to be booked months in advance. But this was the year of the gas shortage and the thirty-five percent drop in tourism, and, that Sunday, there was a room for us.

We dropped off what few things we had, and set out to walk through the surrounding landscape. It was a constantly thrilling, constantly unfolding panoply of colors and smells and textures. Pine needles soothed our senses for a mile. In the next, sulfuric steam stung our nostrils. We came upon a mud volcano, breathing and pumping and belching mud with its own secret rhythm. We stumbled upon more unmasked fumaroles, lightly hissing conduits from the epicenter of energy at the core of the earth.

And then, and then. We wandered up to the Grand Canyon of the Yellowstone, from its spectacular upper rim. The colors—the browns, siennas, yellows, reds, and hundreds of combinations of these, strung like layers in a rock-ribbed pastry that extended into infinity—were laid before us. We could see the upper and lower falls that fed the Yellowstone River that snaked through the bottom of the canyon, and that, along with other geologic forces, had carved and caused this fantastic layering of colors and textures over billions of years and millenia of storms and floods and calms.

And as I stood there, slowly and insinuatingly, I began to hear the colors. Actually hear them. They became music. Every hue had a tone; physical texture turned to musical texture; the shape and the form of the canyon became the shape and the form of a musical line.

My mind rushed back to a day in East Hampton, Long Island. I'd been sitting then with the great artist, Willem de Kooning, in his studio. We'd been lounging in a couple of rocking chairs in the midst of a roaring riot of bright colors, splashed on the floor, the walls, the furniture, and de Kooning himself, talking about the almost supernatural way that music came to me, how it was almost like pressing a button and unlocking the sounds.

"Yes, but *how* do you compose?" he'd asked me.

"Away from the piano," I'd answered.

"Aha," he'd said. "I draw with my eyes closed."

And so, another connection was made. de Kooning saw his colors in his head. And from that monumental moment in Yellowstone, when I first began to hear colors in *my* head, my whole way of writing and hearing and composing and experiencing life itself would be forever transformed.

We had to stay. That much we knew. I went back to the registration desk at the Yellowstone Lake Hotel and asked if they had a room for a few more days. They did.

Eva and I drove exultantly back to the dude ranch, where I cooked up an excuse about a dying uncle, and then, guilty over the shocked concern on the faces of the owners, left a week's rent behind anyway.

We had far greater riches to explore, and we wasted no time immersing ourselves in them. For nine days, we got up at five o'clock, every morning, just as the mist was rising like smoke from the lake, and birdsong blanketed the brush and the undergrowth like a thousand flutes playing.

After breakfast, we'd hike, endlessly, going more deeply into the park each day, coming upon herds of bison, elk, deer, and moose, foraging near the river, and in the lake. And as we plunged more deeply into the wilderness, it was as if we became part of it, and it became part of us.

I was insatiable. We flew back to New York, and immediately caught a plane for England. I wanted to go to Cornwall, to walk the cliffs of the Cornish coast. And we did. On windswept, rainswept mornings, we trod the treeless cliffs, and witnessed Ireland rising, wraithlike out of the sea, on the lip of the horizon. As rich as Yellowstone had been, that was how bleak the coast of Cornwall was, but it was all connected. It was all part of the same entity.

And it became obvious and essential to me in those weeks of one of the most monumental discoveries of my life: This planet of ours, I realized, was no inert mass, but a living, breathing entity, which cried out when you damaged it, and gave forth as much eloquence as a choir of angels. I was in touch with some greater energy here, some sense of connection to a power that I shared in common with nature. It was, I realized, the same feeling I'd had as a boy at Karinoke, and as a man, trapped in a train, marooned in Montana. It was a feeling that gave meaning not only to my existence, but to the existence of all of us. Grandiose, it was also simple. Intimidating, it was also as manageable as clay. I'd never given much thought to God before, but if God existed, I supposed, he was here, in this nature, and in me.

I went back to work like a man looking through a freshly polished window. I had my subject matter for the piece for the Metropolitan Brass Quartet. I called it *Yellowstone,* and I tried to set to paper and to note the colors I'd heard that memorable Sunday on the rim of the canyon.

But I still had a lot to learn about orchestration. I tried to run before I could walk, and I stumbled. Not in the public eye. The public and the reviewers loved the piece. But I knew that the sounds were not the sounds I'd seen and heard. The main theme, which I called "The Grand Canyon of the Yellowstone," was a sweeping, monumental one, written to capture the actuality.

But what I'd heard in my head was not what I heard at the Music Barge in Brooklyn. The quartet was first rate. And the lone trombonist was playing the subterranean pedal tones for all he was worth. "Give me more," I kept telling him in rehearsal. "More, more more! Super fortissimo! Triple f!"

And the poor guy gave all he could. But he only had one set of lungs and one trombone, and I'd been hearing a trombone *section,* augmented by a bass clarinet, a tuba, and eight basses.

Still, one trombone, one major brass quartet performing my work got me a commission, to write an overture for the American Philharmonic, an orchestra that, alas, no longer exists. They were good, and adventurous, and I plunged immediately into turning *Yellowstone* into *Yellowstone Overture,* in which a full trombone section and eight basses gave me all the grandeur I needed.

And this was an even bigger success, performed at Carnegie Hall. Now I heard the sounds purely as I'd imagined them. The colors translated and were reborn, and the reviewers were again happy with the results.

And so were two important and influential men.

One was the president of New York's premiere classical music radio station, WQXR. The day after the piece premiered, he called and asked me if it had been recorded. I knew that a tape that had been made at Carnegie Hall. I presumed it had been well-recorded, of broadcast quality, and I told him I'd try to get permission from the board of the orchestra and the musicians union to have it played over WQXR.

I got the permissions. The piece was played, and it became popular. Listeners phoned in, asking where they could get the record. And, of course, they couldn't, but at least *Yellowstone Overture* was gathering an audience.

And in that audience was the second influential and important man in my life at this time. Charles Z. Wick, whom I had met recently, had been in the audience at the premiere. A close personal friend of President Reagan, he was excited enough about it to arrange a meeting between James Watt, the controversial Secretary of the Interior, and me. The result was a governmental commission to write a major symphonic work celebrating the wilderness parklands of the National Park Service.

So here I was, thirty years after I'd started writing songs—beginning a new career. I was off the flats for good, and glad of it. Let Broadway be taken over by the cacophony of rock, I thought. Let electronic enhancement destroy the human contact that was the reason for theatre in the first place. I was on my way somewhere else.

In these high good spirits, I wanted to celebrate. And I wanted to celebrate with the people who meant most to me—my family.

I invited my mother, Andrew, his wife Michele, and Christopher to come with me to St. John's, in the U.S. Virgin Islands. I rented a house. We all met in Chicago at the opening of one of Andrew's exhibitions, and then flew together to the Caribbean.

It was a joyous reunion. For once in our lives, there were no clouds hanging over us, no crises, no ragged ends of problems to tie together. We relaxed in the sun and enjoyed each other and the fact that we were all well and in each other's company.

One afternoon, I wandered down to the beach alone. Suddenly, a soft, musical, female voice said, "Richard Adler."

I turned, and a pretty, blonde, green-eyed, aristocratic woman in beige slacks, with a gorgeous three-year-old child at her side was smiling at me. "Are you here with that pretty blonde?" she asked.

"Blonde?" I was trying to put the situation together.

"Eva," she said. "Don't you remember? We met at Nadja Stone's dinner party?"

"Yes!" I said, "You're—"

"Mary St. George."

"Mary St. George," I repeated, and added, "I'm not here with Eva." And so, my future wife Mary joined our party.

It was an abundant vacation, one that brought all of us a notch closer together. And that would mean that Christopher and I would draw closest of all. We horsed around, laughed together, argued, made up.

Earlier that same year, Chris and I had attempted to work together. The project had grown from an idea that Shirley MacLaine and I had tossed around when we'd met a few months before. It was an autobiographical musical about her. She was a very big star at that point, and we'd known each other for thirty years, ever since the afternoon I'd suggested she be the understudy for Carol Haney in *The Pajama Game.*

Shirley had been talking to me seriously about her spiritual practices; both Andrew and Christopher had started into meditating when they were in college. Shirley professed she was interested in exploring her journey through the universe.

"My life is strictly from marzipan," she'd joked, and I'd come up with the title *Strictly from Vanilla.*

Christopher's eyes had sparkled when I proposed that we collaborate. "Yes," he'd said. "Let's do that."

And so we tried. But we didn't succeed. Within a month the three of us locked horns.

I have to get out of this, I whispered to myself. If it's like this when we begin writing, what will it be like when we start *rehearsing*? So, I bailed out.

And Christopher had been furious. He'd railed at me, he'd cursed, he'd slammed out of my studio. It was obviously not the right time for us to fuse our energies—our talents.

Maybe later on, I thought, as we cooled off and love once again took over. Maybe one day.

Now, on the plane back to New York from St. John's, we sat together. I'd brought a pile of magazines to pass the time. Shortly after takeoff, Christopher reached into an envelope and drew out what looked like a script. "When you're finished with those magazines, I want you to look at this and tell me what you think," he said, handing it to me.

"Did you write it?" I asked him.

He nodded his head, rapidly.

I stashed the magazines into the seat pocket and opened the script. It was the first act of a musical libretto, entirely in lyrics. The title was *Jean Seberg*.

"About the actress," said Chris, nervously.

"I know," I said. Aside from Marilyn Monroe, there wasn't a more tragic figure in contemporary show business than Jean Seberg. The two shared the same self-destructive destiny. But a subject for a musical? I settled back, and dug.

And as I read, I grew steadily more exhilarated. Christopher's technique, his skill, his inventiveness, his sheer originality had improved tremendously. This was no amateur attempt. It was the work of a young, untempered, and inspired professional. I was bowled over.

I closed the script. "This is absolutely marvelous," I said, softly. "How did you do it?"

Christopher shifted in his seat. "Do you really think so?" he asked, excitedly. "Do you really like it, Daddy?"

"Yes," I said, and I put a hand over his.

He turned to me, his eyes bright now, nearly burning. "Would you like to write it with me?"

I felt a rush of blood to my head. A hundred thoughts flashed through my mind. Mr. Abbott. Jerry. Shirley MacLaine and *Strictly from Vanilla*. My resolution to stay away from Broadway. My love for my son.

"Yes," I said, almost instantaneously. "But I have to go on a couple of research trips for the Wilderness Project. And then I have to block out the piece. But I want to work with you. I'm sincere. I really want to do this, and with you."

I hugged my son, happy for both of us.

I went to Washington, shortly after we landed in New York, to meet Russell Dickenson, the director of the National Park Service. He was an extraordinary man who had risen from the ranger ranks to the top of the service, as director, and had still maintained his integrity and humane qualities.

He mapped out two trips into the parks, and Mary and I flew to Chapel Hill, where I received the 1981 Distinguished Alumnus Award at the University of North Carolina. From there we went to Gatlinburg, Tennessee, and Great Smokies National Park, and the beginning of an odyssey that would take us over thousands of miles and billions of years, for any trip into nature is a trip through time.

Wherever I went on this trip it was different, but it was the same. Wherever I went, the beauty was beyond description's reach. But there was a pleading for words and sounds to evoke the emotions that had been awakened. Wherever I went, the feelings were different, but they were the same—deeply stirred feelings, but with different colors and different sounds. Great Smokies, gracefully meandering through North Carolina and Tennessee possessed gentle rolling hills that were gorged with every imaginable color in every imaginable shade, reflecting the sunlight filtered through cloud wisps. The dust-flecked beams of light bounced off multi-trillion leaves, which made up this glorious, abstract kaleidoscope, this autumnal magic palette, this super-theatrical backdrop.

On we went, to Moab, Utah, where we met our guide, Thea Nordling, who would take us through Canyonlands National Park. And again it was different, and yet the same. Thea was tireless and articulate and possessed of libraries of knowledge, about the land, about its history, about its character. And about the common sense way to survive in it. She drove us in a jeep along Salt Creek, past precariously perched boulders, past mercurial quicksand pits, head-on in stomach-lurching inclines. It was a murderous trip. Our bellies felt as if they were jumping up to our brains.

The drama staged by nature displayed the unimaginable power of the canyon network: grotesque sizes and shapes, obelisks, arches, bridges that spanned far beyond even what wild imagination could conjure, rehearsed in the longest rehearsal—over a billion years of continual shaping. This drama, again irrepressible beauty, is always the same in that it creates a total feeling of being overawed by the total mystery of geologic creation. Only the settings, the varying formations of limestone, sandstone, and lava rock, and their wind and time and rain-fashioned sculptures, their Egyptian-seeming sphinxes, Nefertiti busts and pyramids were different.

Abandoning the jeep, we climbed iron ladders, to the tops of mesas, and dug into caves in the sides of sheer cliffs, into shelters that had been last inhabited before recorded history.

One of these caves contained pictographs that had been discovered a mere week before by a ranger. We were only the second group of people to gaze upon four figures, three of them copper-colored, one white, drawn on a cave wall. What story was the artist trying to tell, I wondered, what signature was he leaving behind for future millenia?

The Anisazis—the "Ancient Ones" in Iroquois—had once lived here, Thea told us, not only in this barren but beautiful rock, but throughout the Southwest. Migrating here in the second century A.D., they walked for thousands and thousands of miles across a land mass that once clogged the Bering Strait before finding their home in these red rock canyons. They'd planted every available acre of land with grain to feed themselves, and burrowed into what was left, setting up a civilization that lasted for a thousand years. And then, in the wink of an eye, because of some reason that history has buried, some cataclysm, an invasion or perhaps a crushing drought—they disappeared, in a fifty-year period, leaving everything just as it was the instant they vanished—graineries full of grain, tables set, weapons leaning against stone walls, utensils stacked serenely in abandoned kitchens.

What happens, I thought, one brightly polished day, in The Arches National Park, bordering Canyonlands in Utah, in the Chiso Mountains, on the edge of the flower-heavy Chihauahaua Desert of Big Bend National Park in Texas, what happens to us, who think we're so great and deathless?

A long life is a wink of an eye in the vast unfolding of the universe, I thought, as I clung to the sides of mountains that had been whittled by winds for eons, which had stood for billions of years. How do you, as a man, conceive of billions of years, how do you, as my boyhood idol Thomas Wolfe put it, "seek the great forgotten language, the lost lane-end into heaven, a stone, a leaf, an unfound door . . ."?

One way is to listen to the colors, and that was the reason for the trip, that was what it was all for and that was how it would all turn out. On we went, to the Petrified Forest, Canyon de Chelly, Mesa Verde, Chaco Canyon, and finally to Hawaii, where before dawn we walked the eleven-thousand-foot-high rim of the ancient, now dormant volcano Haleakala, where we were buffeted by winds that circulated, so that no matter where you turned—east, north, west, or south, you were hit in the face by the wind. Nowhere else were the forces of nature more capricious or more pervasive or more merciless.

And here again, I felt the same and yet it was different. That same deep stirring rose as I stared at the sunrise shooting rays into the crater of Haleakala. Everything was brown and black—red and black against a panel of iridescent blue. And far below, a sea of whipped cream clouds hid the rest of the world from view and one was alone with God, the mountain, the volcano, the crater, and the ancient Hawaiian Gods, Maui and Pele.

When I got back to New York, enough sounds had collected in my head and enough sights had been seared into my memory for me to begin work on *Wilderness Suite,* a six-movement symphonic piece, designed to capture time and space in the language called music.

I was happy to be back, happy to begin work, happy to be near Christopher. He was twenty-seven now, and we were closer than we'd been since he was a child. One day, he came to my studio on 83rd Street, obviously excited.

"What's on?" I asked him.

"I just made an appointment, for five weeks from now, with Marvin Hamlisch."

I'd suggested that Christopher find a composer with whom he could collaborate, full time. I knew Marvin and had introduced him to Christopher. He'd worked for me as a pianist, years before, and I liked his work very much. "Great," I said. "That's terrific. Show him everything you've got. Just don't show him *Jean.* It wouldn't be a good idea to show him something he won't be able to do."

Christopher agreed. "Daddy, I'm so looking forward to working with you. I'm excited about it," he said, and hugged me.

Five weeks went by. The evening of the appointment, Christopher again rang the bell.

"How did it go?" I asked him, as he slipped out of his jacket.

"It went great," he said, enthusiastically.

"What did you show him?"

There was silence.

"Tell me," I said, with rising disquietude, "What did you show him?"

Christopher turned away.

I walked over to him. My voice was level, but my insides were like lava. "You didn't show him *Jean Seberg,* did you?"

"I had to. It's by far the best thing I have," he said.

"You promised me you wouldn't," I continued, in mounting fury. "You promised me, because that's something for us to do! Something *you* said you so very much wanted to do with *me,* your father!"

Christopher's anger rose to meet mine. "Well," he said, bloodlessly, "he wants to do it."

And I erupted. And so did he. We screamed at each other, we stormed around the studio like a couple of maniacs. Finally, I threw him out, and it would be weeks before I would speak to him again. I was crushed. I was bewildered. I was hurt, probably more than I had ever been in my life.

Of course he had the right to collaborate with Marvin, or with anybody, for that matter. But what he had done to me was, in my eyes, so thoroughly thoughtless, so totally selfish, I could hardly believe that this was my own flesh and blood, treating me this way.

He'd come to me. He'd put together this dream, this possibility. And I'd opened myself to it. I'd done something I'd thought was beautiful, setting up an opportunity for Christopher, whose talent I admired and respected deeply. To write his first show with his father would, I thought, be a joyous experience, and I was really excited about the project's potential.

And so, it wasn't so much his decision to go elsewhere with the idea that hurt me; it was the thoughtless, self-centered way that he went about it.

If he'd come to me and said, "I want to do this with you, but look at the opportunity I have to do my first project *outside* of the family, on my own, with somebody important. Wouldn't you want me to have that chance?" I would have been disappointed, but I would have understood.

For I realized that Marvin, in Chris's eyes, represented success on Broadway. *A Chorus Line* and *They're Playing Our Song* had made Marvin a very hot property. And, for all of my success in writing "seriouser" music, I was as cold as yesterday's potatoes in the theatre. And *Jean* was a theatre piece.

We all recover from reasonable disappointments. It's the unreasonable ones that are difficult to take. It's being summarily rejected, steamrollered and humiliated that fills us with the kind of profound and lasting hurt that remains in the bones and the heart for a long, long time.

And that's what happened. I suppose, it *had* to happen between two such volatile people as Christopher and his father. For months, there would be an emptiness, a void that separated us, as we went our separate ways, until love and time healed the disruption.

I went back to work on *Wilderness Suite,* and concentrated on the parts of my life that were working well. And that included practically everything else.

Negatively, I'd received some disquieting news from Pamela Austin, the astrologer. Reading my chart, she'd remarked, "Somebody's going to die who's close to you, in exactly two years." I immediately thought of my mother. "No," she said, "It's not your mother. Somebody else close."

But I was certain that she meant my mother, and I grew more solicitous of her. She'd had a series of profound troubles in the past five years. Her second husband John had died, after a lingering illness. And then, shortly after we'd returned from the Virgin Islands, she'd fallen while boarding a bus and broken her hip. It had required a replacement, and I'd found an apartment for her a few blocks from me, so that I could keep in touch easily. She was nearing ninety, but her mind and perceptions were those of a much younger woman, and she made very few allowances for her physical age.

One day, as we were driving out to Southampton, to my summer home up the street from The Gables, I said to her, "I have something to tell you."

"Wait," she said. "Let me tell you. You're going to marry Mary."

"How did you know?" I asked her.

"I just know you're going to marry Mary," she said, with a light, knowing laugh. And that's exactly what I did. I was, and always would be, as transparent as rice paper to my mother.

Wilderness Suite unfolded easily, in one sustained burst of energy. It felt right, like the atmosphere that shoots through a late rehearsal of a show you know is going to be a hit.

But now, what I didn't realize was that the commission only guaranteed me a fee for composing the piece and getting it orchestrated. The commissioning body had no responsibility for having it performed. That was up to me, and for me this was indeed virgin territory.

I felt that having a recording contract couldn't hurt, and so I had a piano version performed for my friend and the president of RCA, Bob Summer. He seemed to like it, but made no firm committment to record it.

Still, there was interest, and it gave me confidence as I left for Houston, to meet with the board and the orchestra manager of the Houston Symphony. It seemed appropriate, I reasoned, to try a regional orchestra from a part of the country that was included in the piece.

I met with Gideon Toeplitz, the orchestra manager. We had lunch, and I left a copy of the conductor's score and a piano tape of the piece with him. He said he'd let me know. And when I left Houston, I had the unmistakable feeling that this would be the last word I'd hear from him.

Back in New York, I contacted Ed Block, whom I'd met at a dinner party given by Lou Harris. Ed was at one time the president of the American Foundation of the Arts, and the man responsible for AT&T's cultural programs.

He'd heard the tape of *Yellowstone Overture* and he was impressed. "You did the right thing by going to a regional orchestra," he said, "but I'd pick the Utah Symphony, if I were you. First of all, it's a very good orchestra, and second of all, Utah is probably the most important of the four corners states in terms of quantity of national parks."

Within a week, Ed had made an appointment with me with both the powers that were of the Utah Symphony, and its associate conductor, Charles Ketchum. I flew to Salt Lake City, met with them, left a conductor's score and a tape, and figured, this time, maybe.

A few weeks later, both Charlie Ketcham and Ed Block phoned and announced that the Utah Symphony was going to premiere *Wilderness Suite* on February 25, 1983. It would be performed, and later recorded by RCA at Salt Lake City's Symphony Hall, a magnificent auditorium that seated three thousand people. AT&T would sponsor both the world premiere performance and the recording.

This was heady news for a songwriter. I went to Salt Lake City two weeks ahead of time. The advance sale was not the stuff of fanfares. Only ten percent of the house had been sold, and it was obvious to me that some personal promotion was in order. I hit every television and radio station in the area, and by concert night, not even standing room was left.

Charlie Ketcham and I established a beautiful rapport from the first moment I arrived. He's an enormously talented conductor who's also finely tuned to the needs and concerns of the composer. To me, our method of working is the way it should always be between a living composer and a conductor.

At every rehearsal, I would sit with a small cassette recorder, and after each rehearsal, I would meet with Charlie, and we would go over the piece bar by bar. I would tell him what I thought was missing—in dynamics, in tempi, in phrasing, in section, in solo parts. The piece that was performed to a standing ovation on opening night was exactly the piece I had intended it to be.

That standing ovation, which went on for a very long time, didn't seem to impress the Salt Lake City critics. They panned the piece mercilessly, and it hurt. I'd again put my head on the block, trying something new, taking a chance, and the critics had crucified me.

But the hurt fled quickly, swallowed up in the excitement of the recording session, which took place the following day at Symphony Hall. Jack Pfeiffer, RCA's foremost classical record producer, who'd recorded all of Horowitz's RCA work, presided over a four-hour session that resulted in a beautiful, true capturing of the piece.

Shortly after that, *Wilderness Suite* began to be played by regional symphonies all over the country and in Europe. And, as it turned out, the two pans from Salt Lake City would be the only negative critical reactions the piece would ever get. In fact, the critic of the prestigious *Manchester Guardian* would, a year later, when *Wilderness Suite* premiered in London, give me one of the best reviews a composer could receive.

"When a highly successful Broadway and television composer decides to go up-market and write a concert work," the *Guardian* critic, Edward Greenfield, wrote, "there is a serious danger of his trying to over-reach himself in his efforts to emulate Beethoven. Happily Richard Adler, composer of such hits as *The Pajama Game* and *Damn Yankees*, has a very shrewd idea of his best assets as a composer, and *The Wilderness Suite* [sic] composed after an extended tour of American wilderness parklands, does exactly what that title suggests, gives a colourful and atmospheric picture in music of clearly defined subjects.

"It ends with the happiest volcano you could imagine. The last of the six movements was inspired by the volcanoes of Hawaii, and builds up slowly through cunningly scored passages suggesting subterranean rumbling up to the final eruption. What this and the other five movements shows very clearly is that though Mr. Adler may have won his spurs in the popular field, he is a very skilled orchestrator using a far bigger orchestra than can be contained in a theatre pit."

I was already off and running on two more commissions. The Chicago City Ballet now asked me to write a ballet based on my songs. I chose eight of them, five well known and three unknown, and called the ballet *Eight by Adler*. It would star Suzanne Farrell, prima ballerina of the New York City Ballet. Mary, my wife, didn't like the title when I recited it to her, asking for her opinion of it. "What's the matter?

Do you think it's bad grammar? Do you think it should be 'Eaten by Adler'?" I quipped.

The second comission had come from the Statue of Liberty–Ellis Island Foundation, to write a commemorative symphonic work for the Statue of Liberty Centennial. I'd name this *The Lady Remembers,* a title Mary suggested, and it would be the most difficult piece of music I would ever write, for many reasons.

Meanwhile, my relationship with Christopher emerged from the tent of silence we'd erected between us.

One day, he appeared at my studio, obviously in great distress. One look at the rivulets of care etching his normally unmarked face, and I knew something was wrong.

"It's George," he finally said. "I really can't take him anymore, Daddy."

He was talking about his roommate, George Barlow. He and Christopher had had a relationship for years, and it was marked by much tumult.

It was natural for him to ask me if he could move into my studio. There were two bedrooms attached to it; I'd long since turned the studio into a place of work and moved into Mary's apartment on the East River.

I agreed, on the following two conditions: No parties, and no rough-housing.

"Thanks, Daddy," he said. And yet another difficult time began for us. He moved in, and almost immediately violated the fragile trust we'd constructed. He abused his privileges; he threw parties; he invited hoardes of his friends in; and within two months, he'd clearly left the evidence of the drug habit he and his friends shared.

There was a terrible fight, a vituperative confrontation that climaxed in bitter, overstated accusations, flung like heavy artillery from both of us. We were like a couple of punchdrunk lovers—fighting and making up, fighting and making up, hating with the same furious passion with which we loved each other.

Once more I threw him out; once more we found ourselves on the far side of our thunderous relationship.

And still simmering at the center of it, like some interior theme, was his writing relationship with Marvin Hamlisch. I knew that Marvin had taken a strong hand with *Jean Seberg,* and thrown out a lot of Christopher's work—just how much I had yet to learn. It made me uneasy, and yet I knew that this was the way a show was written. The rewriting was most of it, but there was always the chance that the rewriting would become more than most, that it would take over entirely, and worsen rather than improve the original.

Still, Marvin was a pro, and, despite my residual hurt and outrage over Christopher's decision to work with him, I realized the value of the collaboration. Besides, after our last blowup, Christopher was having little or nothing to do with either me or my advice.

So, I returned to writing *Eight by Adler,* and blocking out *The Lady Remembers.* At least there, I reasoned, I was in control. Being around Christopher was a little like doing healthful exercise. You loved it, for all sorts of positive reasons, but it still hurt like hell.

We never remained apart for long. As certainly as the arrival of a season, I'd think of something I wanted to say to him, and as if nothing had happened to fling us apart, I'd pick up the phone and call him. Or, my telephone would ring at 7:00 A.M., and it would be Christopher, with a new idea, a problem, or a desire to just talk for a while.

One morning, in the spring of 1983, he called and casually mentioned that the lymph nodes in his neck were bothering him.

"What lymph nodes?" I asked him. This was the first I'd heard of it.

"They've been protruding for six months," he said, again conversationally. And again, I exploded. There was no safety valve, it seemed, when I was faced with a surprise from Christopher. "What?" I shouted. "You tell me this now?"

"Forget it, Daddy," he said, exasperated.

"No, wait a minute," I added, cooling down, as always, as fast as I'd heated up. "This could be serious. This isn't just a stomach ache."

I sent him over to Dr. Isadore Rosenfeld, a cardiologist and friend. He called me immediately. "Richard," he said, "how could you let this go this long?"

"I didn't know about it till yesterday," I replied. "I called you immediately."

"Well," Dr. Rosenfeld said, with a sigh, "We'd better do a biopsy on one of these things. There's no telling what it could be."

It scared both of us, and Chris agreed to the biopsy. And the news was good. It was benign.

But Dr. Rosenfeld wasn't satisfied. He called me again. "I want to go a lot further with this," he said. "I want a total blood workup. I'm not certain what's going on. I'm glad it's benign, but it could still be very serious."

I told Christopher, and he refused, adamantly. His doctor, Peter Seitzman, who took care of a large part of the gay community in the arts in New York City, minimized the whole procedure, said the tests wouldn't be valid anyway, and advised Christopher to forget it. "I don't like Rosenfeld," Christopher stormed. "I don't like his attitude; I don't like the way he reports to you instead of me. I don't like anything about him. I'm okay. Forget it!"

Finally, the time came to place *Jean Seberg* in front of an audience. The British National Theatre had agreed to produce it in London.

Christopher left New York in the summer. Mary and I followed, several months later, for the final rehearsals and the premiere and for the promotion of the British release of the *Wilderness Suite* recording.

Progress on *Eight by Adler* had moved forward splendidly. By now, I worked exclusively with Don Smith. He was more than a musical secretary to me. He knew me; he'd begun with me as the rehearsal pianist for the revival of *The Pajama Game,* and now he had become not only a close friend, but an echo chamber and a sharer of private, creative thoughts. Instinctively, he knew what I wanted and how I wanted it musically. And that instinct would never diminish, not for a measure.

Don and I still work together, practically every day. As the years go by, we've become endlessly and mysteriously attuned. It's as if we're one person . . . conjuring the same musical thought, with all of its subtext and subterranean voicings intact. We are each other's best help, and we represent, to me, the ideal, the rarely achieved possibility in personal, creative and interpretive relationships.

It was so different with Christopher, and yet the sheer fervor, the eternal battle in which we seemed to be forever locked, lent it a particular, passionate excitement that was very much like young love.

Two people who look alike, who think alike, who act alike—who have the same emotional flareups caused by the same kind of impulses, are bound to be in conflict. I know this now. It's when one emotion dovetails into the mood of another, when one person is the receiver and one is the sender that you don't have conflict.

That rarely happened with us, because we were both senders. And when I went to London in the fall of 1983, and sat in on an early preview of *Jean Seberg,* it became apparent to me that I had to send some help to Christopher—I was attending a potential theatrical disaster.

I could also see that it wasn't hopeless. There was hardly anything left of Christopher's original idea and text. Marvin had thrown out *everything* that Christopher had shown me on the airplane, and made him start over, from the beginning. And none of what he'd done since was nearly as good or as original as the original. But there were still three weeks until the official opening, and three weeks is a lot of time for rewrites.

I returned the next day with a pad and took notes. All of the anger and outrage I'd harbored since Christopher's defection to Marvin was subsumed in a mixture of theatrical savvy and love for a proud and talented son, who was about to place his talent and his pride on the altar of impersonal public opinion. I could help him—I *knew* I could—so I took copious notes, and then went backstage to convey them to Christopher.

He was distraught. He obviously knew, as did everyone connected with the show, that they were in trouble.

I suggested that we have a cup of tea someplace and talk.

He looked at the sheaf of notes in my hand. "What's that?" he asked, a rising note of distress tinting his words.

"Some notes," I said. "Let's go someplace and talk."

His face tightened. "Come here," he said, opening the door of an empty dressing room.

He closed the door behind him. "Daddy," he said, softly, but with the force of a shout. "I don't want your notes. I don't want your advice. I don't want you meddling in my show. You're not a member of this production team."

"What difference does that make?" I asked, my voice rising now, the anger winding itself up like a striking snake inside me. "I know the business. And you're in trouble!"

"You're right!" he shouted. "And I don't need your two cents!"

He slammed out of the room, and I went back to the hotel. "Let's get out of here," I said to a startled Mary. "He doesn't want anything to do with me. To hell with him. Let him face his own slaughter alone."

So we went back to New York and my fears proved conservative. The London press brutalized the show, Marvin, and Christopher. I'd never seen worse reviews, ever.

It was a considerably chastened Christopher who flew back to New York. He'd been brought down very, very low by the emptiness that had come after he'd poured his guts and his soul into a show, and then had it cruelly panned and consigned to the garbage heap by the critics.

I waited for the telephone call or the knock on my door when

Christopher would reach the other end of the pendulum swing and come to me.

And he did. And I was there for him, as I always would be.

Christopher was twenty-nine and resilient at the end of 1983, and he had faith in his talent. Within a few months of the *Jean Seberg* fiasco, he was back at work, again with Shirley MacLaine, on a one-woman show titled *Shirley MacLaine on Broadway.*

Christopher had flown out to California after he'd returned to America, to spend some time with Shirley at her home in Pacific Palisades. They went for long walks on the beach, sat on the deck of her home facing the sea, and evolved, together, a one-woman musical. It was Shirley's show, but Chris had helped in the concept. He wrote some of the lyrics and Marvin Hamlisch supplied some of the music.

It became a tremendous hit, a mega-success, and Christopher was flying high and free. He'd turned a defeat into the reason to triumph, and I was enormously proud of him. As we embraced after the opening, he poured out his gratitude. "Thanks, Daddy," he said, the intensity in him like a generating station. "Did you really like it? Were you proud of me?"

He was so open, so vulnerable at these times. I could hardly contain my love for him—and didn't.

Shortly after the show opened, Shirley reached her fiftieth birthday and Christopher created and engineered a spectacular celebration for her at the exclusive Limelight Disco, which was a converted church. He planned every detail, from an intimate party for thirty close friends to the extravaganza that staggered over a thousand people—and me.

I offered the opening toast at the small party, another production detail set in place by my son. It was a warm, affectionate time for so many of us who had grown up and grown older in the business together, and we were there that night to celebrate with Shirley.

After dinner, we joined the huge audience downstairs at the Limelight. Police surrounded the disco; barricades held back thousands of celebrity hunters. It was like a replay of the times of the Kennedy and Johnson presidenticals, except that now it was my son who was the impresario. And his instinct and his talent and—I hoped and believed—the example he himself had witnessed, once, at the White House, merged that night into one helluva show.

It climaxed with the wheeling in of a gigantic birthday cake. The lights dimmed. A spotlight probed through the cavernous darkness and focused on the cake. There was a fanfare, and suddenly, out of the cake, in white, spangled tails and top hat, sprang Christopher. Then, in an extraordinarily musical, clear, and sweet voice, he sang a brilliant and touching tribute to Shirley he had penned for her, using as music one of the numbers he and Marvin had written for *Shirley MacLaine on Broadway!*

It brought the crowd to its feet, cheering. I smacked my palms together till they all but bled. Tears ran down my face. It was one of the proudest single moments of my life—prouder to me than *The Pajama Game*'s opening night, more impressive than that first afternoon in the Oval Office with President Kennedy, more moving than the moment when Jerry and I first knew we could write together. My son had the world at his feet this summit-like evening, and I knew that I would treasure this time for as long as my memory and my life would last.

Exactly one month later, in June of 1984, the telephone rang. It was Christopher. His voice was small and shaky. He was crying.

"Daddy," the faint voice said, and then stopped.

A silence that seemed endless followed.

I tried to fill it. "Christopher. Is there anything wrong?" I asked.

Finally, he sobbed, "I've been to the doctor," he said, "and he says I've got abnormal blood."

"Abnormal blood? What does that mean?"

"Do you remember the lymph nodes? Daddy, I don't want to go to Fire Island this summer. I want to come out to Southampton with you," he said, and it was his way of saying that he'd made a terrible mistake, and now he was paying for it, and he was scared, and he didn't want to fight anymore.

"Of course," I said. "I'll pick you up on Friday."

My eyes were full of tears. I could hardly see to return the receiver to its cradle. The possibilities announced themselves like arriving trains. Lymphoma. Cancer. AIDS.

I was suddenly ungovernably angry. Christopher was only thirty! This was the forenoon of his life, a time of endless energy, of constant, enviable good health. It was unjust. It was unfair. And it all had such a familiar ring to it. I'd been here before and had heard these words, experienced these feelings with a partner I'd loved. And lost.

And almost instantaneously, Pamela Austin's words came back to me with an awful, imposing clarity. Someone close to me was going to die in two years.

And it was a year and a half.

I brushed it aside. It was too early to think that way. Way too early. Besides, we weren't slaves to fate. We used fate. We were accomplishers. And we'd lick this. Now was the time to bury the bad times, erase the negativity, and work together to beat the cruelty of a destiny that could, if you didn't fight it, tyrannize you.

In late spring, Christopher began to develop consuming sweats. He would perspire enormously, and this would bring on ungovernable trembling. It frightened him and concerned me.

"Come on," I said to him one day at the end of May. "We're going to the emergency room at Lenox Hill. You need tests your doctor isn't giving you. We're going to find out what's wrong, so we can have it treated. This is crazy."

He agreed, and we waited eleven hours before I finally buttonholed the supervisor, and said, "Look. You can't treat this boy this way. He obviously has a high fever. He must be given medical attention. You must have a private room."

And they did. They were obviously afraid of AIDS, an unknown quantity at the time. Given Christopher's life style, it was nearly axiomatic, and I, too, was afraid of it. Still, we were in the early days of diagnosis, and anything was possible.

Finally, they examined him and assigned him to a private room. His tests showed an enlarged spleen the size of a small football, and a devouring of red cells by white cells. More transfusions were suggested.

They went on for three weeks, and still, Christopher ran a continually high fever. He was suffering quite a lot.

Maybe, I thought, it was the blood transfusions. Mary and I went to see Dr. Marvin Cooper, his hemotologist.

"What's wrong with my boy?" I asked the doctor.

"I don't know," he said, shaking his head slowly.

"Does he have a form of cancer?" I asked, remembering the lymphomic fears.

"One thing I can tell you," Dr. Cooper said. "He doesn't have cancer."

But Christopher did have cancer, and the long, fierce, unfair battle was just beginning.

17.

O N the Friday of Father's Day weekend, 1983, I picked up Christopher at Lenox Hill. He'd undergone another round of transfusions, and his condition hadn't seemed to improve. But, in the fresh June air in Southampton, his spirits seemed to edge upward. As ill as he was, as weak as he was, he went to the pool the next morning and swam eighteen laps. I watched him with wonder. Rising like a young god out of the sunlit pool, he gasped, "I did it, Daddy." I toweled him off, praising him to the skies. He had guts; he was tough; the fear had been shoved aside now, and his indomitable spirit had taken over. We were both warmed by optimism at the end of the weekend.

But within a few days, I got a terrified call from him from a doctor's office on East 60th Street. He'd been in the middle of a lower barium series and had collapsed.

With the help of two interns, I bundled him into my car. He was delirious. At the suggestion of my friend, Dr. Matilda Krim, I rushed him to Sloan Kettering Memorial Cancer Center.

After a quick examination by Dr. Gold, an internist, and Dr. Sandy Kempen, who would become his new hemotologist, he was admitted for surgery, to be performed by Dr. Andrew Turnbull, a tall, imposing, and charismatic surgeon of extraordinary skill, who immediately took a personal interest in my son's case.

The atmosphere among the doctors wasn't a very positive one. It was as predictable as a forecast. I went to see Christopher two or three times a day, every day, and in between, I tried to get back to *The Lady Remembers. Eight by Adler* had been finished and was being readied for rehearsal in Chicago.

The exploratory took several hours and during it, Christopher's highly-enlarged, tumorous spleen was removed. Multiple cancerous lymph nodes in the abdominal tract were also excised. Dr. Turnbull had done a sectioning of the lower bowel, where there was a tumor about the size of a plum.

Christopher, then, was riddled with cancer and there was no denying the grim implications of it. Mary and I were there when they wheeled him in with drainage tubes sprouting, it seemed, from every orifice. Things looked very bad.

But within a few days, he was up again, shoving an I.V. tree around the halls, counting the once-around-the-floor laps, boasting proudly to me, through fever-bright eyes, "I did five laps last time, Daddy. Six tomorrow."

He would eventually do twenty laps, and I would encourage him every step of the way.

But one day, while he was sleeping, I wandered into a small vestibule outside of his room. Dr. Turnbull had left his chart behind. I opened the folder and scanned it, and what I saw numbed me. Scrawled unmistakably in Dr. Turnbull's handwriting was a description of the operation. The last sentence was, "The prognosis is terrible."

"I think I should get Andrew and Michele to come over, don't you?" I asked Mary, after I'd told her what I'd seen.

"Of course you should," she agreed, "and what about Sally Ann? She should know, too."

Mary was absolutely selfless, as was Sally Ann, who flew from London immediately, and spent untold hours, weeks, months with Christopher, comforting him, talking to him, making him laugh.

He kept extending his laps, and his sheer courage and determination transformed the entire floor. Patients and nurses alike would wave him on, and once I heard Dr. Turnbull, who was emerging from another patient's room. say, "Keep it up. You're doing great."

And he was. As his body shrank, his spirit seemed to grow. Maybe, I thought to myself, out of grit, in spite of what I'd read, maybe it would turn out well. Maybe he'd get better, after all.

Eight days after the operation, I received a phone call in Southampton. It was Sally Ann. She was calling from the hospital room. "You've got to get the doctor," she said. "Chris is in terrible pain, and nobody here seems to know what to do about it."

I called Dr. Turnbull's emergency number every twenty minutes, and the hospital every half hour. Christopher's temperature was steadily climbing. By evening, it had hit 105.

Finally, I found the doctor, told him of the problem, and hopped into my car. I must have hit speeds up to 100 mph on the Long Island Expressway, and when I got to the hospital, they'd already prepared Christopher for surgery. Peritonitis had set in, and they had to do another resection in the lower bowel. This would include an iliostomy.

The iliostomy was a particular nightmare for Christopher. Almost from the time he came out of the anesthetic, he lobbied to have it reversed. But before that could happen, he had to undergo chemotherapy, another ordeal that would claim most of his hair and more of his energy.

Thin as a rail, wearing a cap, he nevertheless was able to smile and lift our spirits. He'd become involved in yoga and meditation, and now with Andrew here, he practiced this regularly. I didn't wholly understand it, but if it gave him comfort, I was for it.

Our relationship entered a newer, sweeter, and deeper place. Christopher would, in those endless spaces when visiting hours had concluded, compose letters to me, each of which I would carefully preserve. "All along," he wrote to me once, "you have helped me deal with this incredibly painful and difficult test, which is by no means over yet. I love and admire you for all of it."

One night in early September, I stood in the doorway of his hospital room, and, in a flood of tactless sincerity, blurted out, "Christopher, I'd rather have you a shit and healthy than adorable and sick." And I meant it desperately. If there had been some power that could have reversed the last year, I would take him on any terms, at any time.

"Daddy," he replied, "how could you say such a terrible thing to me?" and smiled. He knew what I meant.

The chemotherapy treatments went on for two months. Christopher went from his hospital room to Marvin Hamlisch's apartment and back again. Marvin was wonderfully kind and caring about Christopher during those terrible months, turning the apartment he'd grown up in and which he'd kept for sentimental reasons over to him, seeing that he had everything he needed.

During that time, Christopher began to write a musical titled *Gideon Starr,* about a twentieth century Messiah. He showed me pieces of it as he wrote, and it was breathtaking. The lyrics fairly sang themselves off the page. It was beautiful and terrible. As his illness deepened, so, it seemed, did his talent.

At the end of three months, Christopher prevailed upon Dr. Turnbull to reverse the iliostomy. In retrospect, it was probably a wrong decision; and yet, in such a situation, wrong and right become merely different aspects of one long process of deterioration.

Christopher emerged weaker and sicker than he had entered the operation. He developed thrush, a yeast infection that started in his mouth and throat, and ultimately spread through his entire system.

His devoted Phillipine nurse, Nympha, rarely left his side. They were touchingly, totally dedicated to each other, and it was lovely to watch.

He was not getting better. This was obvious to everybody. He was in constant pain, and under heavy sedation. Sometime during that week, he wrote the last letter he would write to me. "Dearest Daddy," it said, "it's always so busy in here, so much activity and I get tired and the morphine makes me cranky, so I don't always get to express to you my deep love, my heady feelings, like being in love, that I feel for you, that I will always feel for you, that will grow and grow, if they can get bigger—There's nothing I like more than holding my daddy's hand and knowing that we are inseparably joined. Daddy, we have each other and that is a miracle."

The fifteenth of November was my mother's ninetieth birthday, and, off and on, for the past two years, Christopher and I had been planning a celebration of it. I'd made arrangements to hold the party at the Lotos Club, where my father had taken my mother and me on special occasions fifty years ago. I'd invited forty people, and it had been my secret wish that Christopher would feel strong enough to join in his grandmother's birthday celebration.

There had always been a special bond between them. After my father had died, Christopher had given my mother a little ring, and had said, as a child might say, "There, grandma. Now you and I are engaged." This, he thought, would keep her from being lonely.

But the morning of the party, Christopher called and said, "Daddy, I'm too sick. I can't come."

"Don't worry," I said, "you'll be missed, but you have to do what's best for you now. That's what's most important."

The party was beautiful. We filled the room with flowers. I'd gone to my old friend, Arthur "Punch" Sulzberger, the publisher of the *New York Times*, and bought multiple copies of the first page of the issue of November 15, 1894. It was the day my mother was born. They were at everyone's place setting.

At eight, we sat down to dinner; entertainment followed, and by nine-thirty we were onto cake and champagne.

And then, the door to the library opened. And there was Christopher, hauntingly thin and pale, leaning heavily on Nympha, and smiling that infectious, generous, loving smile. He blew a kiss to my mother, and entered the room.

I rushed over to him and embraced him, arranging him in a chair next to my mother. His face reflected the pain he was feeling, but the sweetness and love in his eyes warmed the entire room. He turned to me and said, very quietly, "I want to sing a song."

Marvin went to the piano. "What song?" he asked.

" 'Secrets,' " said Christopher, and Marvin began a lovely, simple ballad they'd written for *Jean*.

Christopher's voice rose, bell-like, in the room, pure and true and clear. But this night, it had another dimension I had never heard before, that no one who was there will ever forget. It was an angel singing.

Two weeks later, I was scheduled to leave for Chicago for the world premiere of *Eight by Adler*. Christopher had gone straight back to the hospital after my mother's birthday party.

"Should I go?" I asked Dr. Kempen.

"Go," he said, softly. "Nothing's going to happen while you're away."

So, I caught a plane for Chicago, and arrived at seven o'clock, and immediately phoned the hospital. Nympha answered. "He's not doing all that great," she said, "but there's nothing to worry about."

An hour later, I called the hospital again. This time, Nympha's voice had less assurance. "His blood pressure has dropped to sixty," she said. "They're taking him into intensive care. You'd better come back."

But there were no planes that night. I spent a sleepless seven hours until I could catch the 6:00 A.M. flight.

I arrived at the hospital at 10:30 that morning. Christopher was sitting up in a chair in the intensive care unit. A respirator was by his side, and two technicians were fiddling with it. Nympha was holding his hand. I looked at Christopher and tried to smile. There was terror in his eyes. I said something, I don't remember what. He didn't, or couldn't, answer. That was the last time I saw him conscious.

I put my arm around him. I held my lips very close to his ear. "Everything's going to be all right, Chris," I said. "I'm here now. You're going to be fine."

I stepped back, and they attached him to the respirator. And as I stood there, the ache of impending loss, which was now tangible and near, ascended like a choking wave in my throat, and I thought to myself, what can be worse than to lose a child that you've known since he was twenty minutes old, who's going to be thirty-one years old next month—your own flesh and blood? How can you measure the sadness, and the grief, the not-so-secret knowledge that you'll never, never see each other again, never be able to make over your mistakes, never be able to finish what you've only begun? Nobody can measure that. Nobody ever will.

Andrew and Michele and Sally Ann arrived, and we spent those last two days closely together, talking, embracing, supporting each other, while Christopher slipped slowly away.

That night, Andrew and Michele and I went into the room together. He was very white, very still. His eyes were closed and his breath was coming very rapidly. We gathered around the respirator. I leaned close to him, and, with infinite love and gratitude and faith, said, "Chris. Let go. It's going to be okay. You're going to be fine. Don't fight it. Go with it."

And that was the last I ever spoke to my son, or saw him. Wordless now in our grief, we clung to each other like blinded travelers in a storm, and slowly left the room. At 2:01 A.M., on November 30, 1984, Christopher died, just one month short of his thirty-first birthday.

18.

T H E R E were ugly, bureaucratic details to oversee. The death certificate. The choosing of a coffin. The making of funeral arrangements. Early that morning, Andrew and I took care of these details. At eleven o'clock, I called Shirley MacLaine, in California.

"Chris is dead," I told her. It was all I could manage.

"I know," she answered, calmly.

"What do you mean you know?" I asked.

"He died at two o'clock."

"Yes," I said, aghast. "How did you know that?"

"Because a blinding white light came into the room," she said, "and I sat all night with that light. And that light was Christopher."

Years later, she would name one of her books *Dancing in the Light,* and dedicate it to Christopher, and by then I would understand much more of what she went on to tell me that morning about his soul entering a vast field of energy, going back to its original form and transcending this plane to move on to its next station.

I'd known Shirley for thirty years, and during the five years before Chris's death, we'd become extraordinarily close. I talked for a long time with her that morning, and later on, I questioned Andrew about what seemed to me like complex metaphysical Eastern beliefs. I knew that out of respect for Andrew's adherence to Tibetan yogic custom, we would wait four days for the funeral, so that the soul could make its preparation both to leave the body and to embark on its journey to another astral plane. Andrew very patiently and lovingly explained all of this to me, and it made a kind of quiet sense, even though I didn't understand all of it.

Christopher had died of septic shock syndrome. He did not, as some newspapers erroneously reported, die of AIDS. Perhaps it all would have developed into that, if his poor, ravaged body had been able to sustain itself longer. But it didn't, and the medical report states unequivocally that he did not, at the time of his death, have AIDS.

He was cremated, as he wished, and on a gray, bleak, beginning of winter day, we took his ashes to the family plot in Hastings-on-Hudson. Marvin Hamlisch's cousin, a young and intellectual rabbi, presided over the services. They were mercifully brief and focused; we buried the finely sculpted urn containing all that was mortally left of Christopher next to my father, and silently drove back to my studio, where Mary and Sally Ann had prepared a small reception for the family and close friends.

It was tastefully and quietly done, as was everything that week. There was champagne, and little finger sandwiches and petit fours. And I moved through it all in a haze, a cloud of numbness, a suspension of contact with what was happening.

Then, as now, I thought that the gathering was a good custom, a good tradition. But I also felt vaguely uncomfortable, marginally dissatisfied. Ultimately in times of deepest grief, it seemed to me that social traditions were useless. What you should do when you're most distressed is what you feel most profoundly that you can do. That afternoon, I didn't want to make small talk and drink champagne. If talking were what should have taken place, then I would have preferred that it were a peaceful, metaphysical, philosophical discussion with Andrew and a couple of close friends, about death and about Christopher, and about what his life had been and might have been, and meant.

A week later, a memorial service was held at the Shubert Theatre. It was SRO—standing room only—packed to every available corner with Christopher's and my theatrical friends, paying their final respects to this brilliant, creative, and charismatic young man. The outpouring of devotion and love and respect was overpowering, and, as on so many occasions in my life when I was most profoundly touched or moved or affected—opening nights, closing nights, the death of Jerry—I drifted numbly through this, wholly there and yet simultaneously somewhere else that also encompassed this, and so made it nearly bearable.

The stage was sparingly, stunningly lit. There was a single podium, a piano, a row of chairs, and, upstage center, a more than lifesize photograph of Christopher, looking buoyant and boyish, his lick-the-world grin and young, godlike looks intact and untouched.

A long succession of tributes was delivered, each of them more touching and heartfelt than the next. Producer Michael Frazier, Christopher's friend, set the tone when he determined that "We are not here to mourn, but to *celebrate* Christopher Adler."

Hal Prince recalled Christopher's love of families, "He insinuated himself into them in a wondrous way," Hal recalled. "My wife Judy thought he looked like a Persian prince, and called him Mustafah. And Mustafah he was to us," he went on, remembering the time Chris went to Majorca to be with Judy and Hal. "He was determined to climb a very high, very rugged mountain," Hal said. "Nobody had climbed it before and nobody has since, as far as I know, but Christopher cut a branch from a tree and set out with some sandwiches, and he climbed to the top, and there he placed our standard. He claimed it for the Princes, with a torn T-shirt and a small American flag. It's still there." And then Hal paused. "We'll miss him very much," he concluded, softly.

Memories poured forth and piled high. Steve Sheppard recalled Christopher's mercurial changes of mood, his dictatorial giving of orders, his complexity. "He had so much to say, and so little time to say it," Steve remembered. And Liz Smith built upon this, when she said, eloquently, "He felt his life was incomplete; he couldn't live it fast enough." She turned to Andrew and to me, and she added, "I'll bet his family doesn't know how much he cared. He craved his father's approval and respect and love and he adored his brother. And he constantly marveled at how he had two real mothers. In the world of 'nay sayers,' he was a 'yea sayer.' Maybe he was some sort of angel. Oh well, later on." And she paused, tearfully. "But there now will be no later. Anybody can give you their talent. You can't keep them from giving it. Christopher gave us his everything."

North Carolina was represented by Peter Anlyan, his best friend at Chapel Hill, and by my close and treasured friend Terry Sanford, who reached out a hand of comfort that, in its profound caring, spanned the time since he and I had trod those same paths on the campus at UNC. "I hope that Richard finds the strength of God and his own strength to achieve the consolation that passeth understanding," Terry concluded, eloquently.

Members of the hospital staff who had worked in wonder around Christopher poured out their gratitude for his brief presence among them. Nympha recalled how much love there had been from the family, how I was there morning, noon, and night to hold Christopher's hand, how my mother cooked his favorite soup for him and how Mary brought him flowers and tea, how Sally Ann did his meditations with him, how Andrew helped him to understand his inner self. "Christopher did everything in his power to stay alive," added Dr. Richard Dolins, my psychiatrist and friend, and a constant, strong, and loving comfort to me and to Christopher in his last days. "I've never seen such love as he got from his family," added Dr. Dolins. "He didn't deserve to die, but he did deserve the love."

Dr. Dolins recalled that miraculous birthday party for my mother, and Christopher's angelic voice drifting on the air, singing of dreamers. It all came back, in a quiet rush, as Marvin Hamlisch went to the piano, quipping, lovingly, that "Christopher had the whole thing. He vibrated. If he could have played the piano, I might never have met Christopher Adler." And then, those clear and precise and revealing words were there, again, as they had been such a short time ago, telling as much about Christopher himself as about all of us:

> Certain dreamers have shooting stars they chase;
> There are others, with nightmares they must face;
> Sometimes dreamers are forced to leave the dreams far away,
> Sometimes they need to take the time
> To find treasures, and mountains we can climb.
> Maybe we dream to change the way we feel,
> 'Cause to dreamers, the real world can be unreal . . .

I was then, and still am in awe of the exquisite and sensitive expression revealed in these lyrics. In my estimation, Christopher would have become (and nearly was there already) a world-class lyricist—sensitive, profound, witty and powerful.

Ultimately, it was Shirley MacLaine who placed her hand on the pulse of the afternoon, who locked into the deepest part of my heart, and of Christopher's. Somehow, in that quiet conversation that she and I had had at eleven o'clock in the morning the day after Christopher's passing, I heard a door opening, and a new comprehension began to slowly enter. Not fully. Not so it was altogether noticed. I was too torn by tragedy to hear more than the cries of my own grief. But interlacing them, and warming me, were her words and the words of my son. And they were almost inseparable.

Shirley recalled how she'd first met Christopher when he was a few weeks old, and I'd brought him to the theater during rehearsals of *The*

Pajama Game, when she was in the chorus. She went on to recount the conversations she and Christopher had had about the spiritual Self. "We often remarked on how karmically bound we seemed to be," she said. "Not only Christopher and I, but I and the whole family. It was Richard who found me."

And for a brief flash, on the stage of the Shubert Theatre, it started to make more sense, what Shirley and Christopher and Andrew had been discussing so peacefully and naturally, during those last days. "Even though he fought so bravely to stay, he somehow understood and sensed that he would be pursuing another level of understanding," Shirley continued. "He approached [it] as a learning experience, because he knew that his real self would never really die. It would simply go on to another dimension . . . He never had any doubt that he was eternal, and that what was happening to him was part of a grander lesson which he himself had chosen to experience . . . Observing his graceful enlightenment was an extraordinary lesson for me."

Graceful enlightenment. It was what I had felt when Shirley had described the light of Christopher coming to her in her room in California. She recounted the story again, and the silence in the Shubert Theatre became complete and absolute, as if that light were, at that very instant, touching everyone there, too. "Chris adored the light," Shirley said. "The light of the stage. The light of attention. The light of his own soul. He very often spoke of love and light being the essence of all of us. Last week, when I spoke to him for the last time, he knew he was facing his final moments. He knew he would be leaving those final moments as he had lived his life. Completely, and in the [here and] Now. He would experience the transition from one dimension to the other with full learning and expanded awareness. He told me that."

She paused, controlling the emotion that was one large emotion, shared by every one of us at that moment. "This light [that came to me] was with me for several days," she said, quietly. "This light was Chris. It gave me energy. It gave me happinesss. I found myself living my own life more completely in the Now. Like his song for our show that exemplified his philosophy of life and his going on to a higher level of understanding."

And then, as Marvin played very quietly in the background, Shirley sang Christopher's revealing and lovely and profound words:

Now . . .
is what I was created for.

Now
I'm gonna let you know what I'm feeling.
Now
I must be emphatical,
I'm feeling plain ecstatical—Wow!
I might just float right up to the ceiling.
The joy inside me,
The smile you see,
Is for one reason alone.
The time and place
Where I want to be
Is—Holy Hot Damn—like where I am!
Now
The past is too historical
Now
The future needs an oracle,
Now
Is when you feel euphorical.
Trust me,
Your crowning achievement,
Your greatest prize
Will come on the day
That you realize
The moment you're living for—Wow!—
Is now.

And so, it was my turn. I remember that I was crying, as I had been all through the service. The morning swam in and out of focus, and I was thankful that it was all being recorded. I knew that otherwise, I would never, in the future, be able to recall a syllable or a sound.

I walked to the podium and grasped each side of it, the way a man who is being rescued grips the sides of a rope ladder.

"I'm going to try to get through this," I said, and paused. "My name is Richard, and I'm Christopher's father."

Andrew stood up, and came over to me. "—And I'm Christopher's brother Andrew," he said, softly, with great intensity. He stayed by my side.

"I've never had trouble, since I was a sophomore at Chapel Hill," I went on, fighting desperately to steady my voice, "when I introduced Robert Frost, in addressing an audience, but this is going to be tough." I paused again. I was determined to get through it.

"The floodgate of memory," I went on, "has been opened up. However, I'm not going to speak about the many wonderful experiences that I had. If I did, we might be here for hours. This is a memorial to Christopher that I wanted him to have . . . I wanted to share this moment with all of you, knowing how many friends he had, and we had. And I'm deeply moved to see the floor of the Shubert sold out. Standing room only in the back, which is lovely for Chris.

"My personal memorial to Christopher started several months ago, when I began a commission to write a long symphonic work celebrating the centennial of the Statue of Liberty. I told Christopher then that I was dedicating it to him. And he mistakenly thought that such dedications were for dead people. And I said, 'Not necessarily at all,' and I quoted a few instances. And the president of the record company and the publisher have promised me that they will have his name on every album, every piece of music that goes out. That's my memorial, that I've been working on through his illness. And I'm not finished yet.

"A lyric I wrote just before Christopher was born keeps coming back to me, and I'd like to recite it, if I can remember it. It's called 'Acorn in the Meadow,' and Harry Belafonte introduced it in 1954."

And I reached back, thirty years, to that first try at Broadway, that mystic moment when Harry had sung the song, and the words had come true once, and once only. Today was the second time:

> *Acorn in the meadow,*
> *Meadow filled with sun,*
> *Sun a' shinin' warm on the meadow,*
> *Tree begun.*
> *Baby in the cradle,*
> *Cradle filled with love,*
> *Mama smilin',*
> *Warm on the cradle from above.*
> *Some day my baby be a working man,*
> *Tree be mighty big and strong,*
> *Me, I'll sit in the shade of it,*
> *Just sit and relax all day long,*
> *Lord, I pray you help me*
> *Help me make him good.*
> *Help me make him gentle when he be grown.*
> *I can see it—*
> *Me in the shade of the acorn tree,*

He and his woman sittin' 'side 'a me
And maybe my baby with an acorn of his own.

And then Andrew, with a quiet, compelling dignity, stepped to the lectern. "Everybody's spoken so beautifully this afternoon, and I haven't prepared anything," he said. "But one thought that I had was that all that one can see is transient. And what you *cannot* see is eternal. And we've talked about memory, and the memories of Christopher. But I think that he's more present than ever.

"I'd like everyone who's here in Christopher's memory, and his present being, to join hands, while my father and I read two stanzas from his last project, *Gideon Starr.*

"I think that our existence here is to find peace in our selves, our souls. And Christopher has definitely found that, and he came to accomplish what he has accomplished for himself, and we must learn from this. And the fact that we're all here, and we can start with ourselves in this theatre, maybe it'll spread out."

Everyone in that crowded theatre joined hands then, and Andrew and I let Christopher's words fall like flowers on all of us, with our hands linked to each other and to him:

> *Through the clouds of our reflections,*
> *I drift to open air*
> *As I reach a deep blue clearing,*
> *Deep inside I know I'm nearing*
> *Some Universal Secrets we all share.*
>
> *As I float into tomorrow,*
> *I must leave behind today,*
> *There is so much I can learn here,*
> *And who knows when I'll return here?*
> *I'll just spread my wings and fly, far away.*

I felt a light within me, and it was growing, and it was Christopher.

This time, I had no rabbi to preach to me, and no Cole Porter to remind me. I had something infinitely more precious. There was the comfort and the nourishment of my son's spirit, his light, reminding me wordlessly and eternally, that, above all, and beneath all, You Gotta Have Heart.

VI

"You Gotta Have Heart"

19.

W O R K was my tonic; work was my cloak; work was my salvation. As long as I worked, my life had meaning. And so I plunged as deeply as I could into getting *The Lady Remembers* completed and performed. It had grown far beyond anything I'd done thus far. It was a much more internalized work, something dealing not only with the grandeur of the statue itself, but its more fundamental meaning: the immigrant experience, which denoted hope, illusion, and disillusion to me.

I researched the history of the statue exhaustively, and captured this in the opening movements, fusing *The Star Spangled Banner* and *The Marseillaise,* I chronicled the voyage of the *Isere,* with its pieces of the statue, section after section, fusing themes and stone, and then, turning to the cross-hatching of immigrant hopes and realities. Finally, I created an apotheosis of themes, bringing them together in an internal and external recreation of the statue in both spirit and substance.

It was in seven movements. Each of them was far more complex and ambitious than those of the previous work, *Wilderness Suite.* It involved, for the immigrant section, some soaring vocal interweavings, and for these, I'd engaged the Greek and Puerto Rican soprano Julia Migenes Johnson.

By the first week in December, I'd delivered a piano score to Bob Summer, the president of RCA records. Under the sponsorship of the Chrysler Corporation, which was also involved through its chairman Lee Iacocca in the Statue of Liberty Celebration, RCA was again going to record the work.

The year 1984 had been a year of mountains and abysses. I'd reached an age when honors started to come in. Prestigious honors. That year, I was elected to the Songwriters Hall of Fame, and made an honorary

Park Ranger by the National Park Service. My *Wilderness Suite* and *Yellowstone Overture* had been embraced by a number of environmental groups and used to give a voice to their values. I was being recognized on a multiplicity of fronts, and it felt good, particularly because President Kennedy had been the first person to receive it, posthumously.

I knew now, too, that the difficulties I'd had finding an orchestra for *Wilderness Suite* wouldn't carry over into my search for the orchestra and recording company of *The Lady Remembers.* This was a commemorative piece, and the commemorative celebration was imminent. Deadlines begat action. And sure enough, three major orchestras became interested. The St. Louis Symphony was my first choice, but before we could proceed to serious negotiations, a conflict in their schedule made it obviously impossible.

The National Symphony in Washington, D.C., was very interested in the piece, and, symbolically, it would have been appropriate for them to premiere it. But I had my reservations. I had certain fears about Maestro Rostropovich's understanding of what, despite its ethnic potpourri, was essentially a very American work.

And so, when the Detroit Symphony went eagerly to RCA with a proposal, I agreed to have them premiere and record *The Lady Remembers,* to be conducted by Maestro Gunther Herbig, a former student of Herbert Von Karajan. He had headed major orchestras all over Europe for years, had made many successful recordings in Europe, and had recently left his post in East Germany as the conductor of the Berliner Sinfonie-Orchester to assume the leadership of the Detroit Symphony.

I looked forward to another smooth sail into the premiere, similar to the one I'd had with Charlie Ketcham and the Utah Symphony. But from the very beginning, this project turned into a rocky, frustrating voyage. I asked Oleg Lovanov, the president of the orchestra and its manager, for ten hours of rehearsal time. He offered me four and a half.

"That's impossible," I argued. This is a complicated new piece, and it's a world premiere. It's an event. You have to give me more time than that."

I eventually got eight hours: two rehearsals in Detroit, one in New York, and two in Washington, where the piece would be premiered.

The first two rehearsals went well, with the exception of the fifth part of the sixth movement, in which the very Austrian Herr Herbig had difficulty with its more jazzy elements. I ran up to the podium and whispered into his ear, "Tell them to think of hot, sizzling Duke Ellington."

Mr. Herbig repeated, dutifully, in a heavy German accent, "Mr. Adler says for you to think of hot, sizzling Duke Ellington." They laughed, but they got it.

So, I was in a state of high anticipation and spirits when I walked into the first of the two rehearsals at the Kennedy Center. But the moment after I opened the door to the Opera House, I crashed into confusion. The orchestra wasn't rehearsing *The Lady Remembers* at all. They were deeply into Dvořák's *New World Symphony*, a substantial workhorse that most classical musicians can play blindfolded and unrehearsed. It was also on the program, and I figured, as I settled into a seat, that Mr. Herbig had decided to run it to get it out of the way.

At the end of the second hour, as my concern mounted, he put *New World* away, and turned to *The Lady Remembers*. There were still enormous areas of difficulties to be worked on and overcome. By the end of the rehearsal, the orchestra had only gotten through a little more than half of the number.

I went backstage, to the conductor's dressing room, with my notes, trying to hold back my temper and not display my anxiety. "Sorry you couldn't get through more of it," I said, delivering the notes, "But there's time to cover what we missed tomorrow."

Gunther Herbig splayed the pages on his dressing table and then, casually but firmly announced, "But Mr. Adler, your piece is not being rehearsed tomorrow."

"Oh yes it is," I said, a tiny hairline of anger starting to work its way into my words, "I have it in my memorandum."

"What memorandum?"

"Part of the arrangements I made with Lovanov."

"I am the conductor of this orchestra and Lovanov isn't," said Herbig, evenly and distinctly, "and I decide what is to be done and when it's to be done. I'm very secure with your piece and I have more work to do on the *New World Symphony.*"

The hairline of anger sprouted, but one look at Herbig's henchmen, his coterie of yes men, lounging about the dressing room, and I knew fighting for my rights would be useless. At least on that playing field.

I went directly to the airport, and before I caught the shuttle back to New York, I called Lovanov in Detroit. I poured out my concerns and my frustrations. "Not only did I not have a full rehearsal today, but he said I'm not getting a rehearsal tomorrow," I complained, "And if you consult *your* memorandum to *me,* you'll quickly see what's owed to me."

Lovanov agreed, and said he'd straighten it out with Herbig and call me tomorrow. I went to bed partially comforted.

"How did it go?" I asked him when the phone rang at my studio the next morning.

"You're not going to be very happy with what he said," answered Lovanov, in a subdued voice.

"What is it?"

"He told me this. He told me to 'tell Adler I'm *not* going to do the performance and I'm *not* going to record the piece. Tell him to get another conductor.' "

I slammed my fist onto the desk. What a childish, churlish, unprofessional thing to do! It was nine days from the world premiere performance, the black-tie, white-tie, invitation-only, whole-world-is-watching event that Chrysler was planning, and this "temperamental artist" was about to blow it to bits.

And then, as swiftly as my anger had exploded, a clarifying idea swept through me. It cooled the atmosphere. "Okay," I said, calmly, "he wants another conductor. I'll get another conductor. I'll get back to you."

Several months before, Nicholas Dodd, the young, imaginative British maestro, had agreed to perform *The Lady Remembers* in London as part of an all Adler concert. The London premiere was less than a month away, and we'd been discussing the piece by telephone at regular intervals.

I called Bob Summer at RCA, told him of my predicament, and about Nicholas Dodd, and he gave me the okay to go after the British conductor. Bob knew Nick's work, too, and endorsed him as enthusiastically as I.

Next, it was necessary to clear the change with the Chrysler Corporation. Jim Tolley, Iacocca's vice-president in charge of public affairs, and a friend of mine, was also cooperative. "Go after him," he said.

I crossed my fingers as I gave Nicholas Dodd's number to the international operator. Please let him be home, I prayed. Please.

He answered the phone. "How would you like to conduct the world premiere performance of *The Lady Remembers* with the Detroit Symphony at the Kennedy Center in Washington?" I asked.

There was a stony silence at the other end. Finally, Nick's gentle voice came on. "Why are you telling me this?" he said. "Is this a joke?"

"It's no joke," I answered, and explained the entire mess to him. "Can you do it?" I finally asked.

"Yes, but—"

"Okay," I said, "Call British Airways and see if you can get a seat on tomorrow's Concorde. I'll pick up the tab. Rehearsals start in New York at noon."

An hour later, he called back. He was booked on the Concorde. I phoned Lovanov in Detroit, and told him I had my other conductor.

"Who?" asked Lovanov.

"Nicholas Dodd. The Chelsea Symphony Orchestra. He knows the piece better than Gunther Herbig will ever know it."

"Fine," agreed Lovanov. Under the circumstances, the Detroit Symphony will pick up the expenses. I'll tell this to Herbig, and I'll call you in the morning."

At 7:00 A.M. the next morning, the phone rang in my studio. It was Lovanov. His voice was not untroubled. "I related to the maestro what you told me," he said. There was a pause. "The maestro has decided to do the piece after all."

"This is an outrage," I said, levelly. "A full-fledged outrage. What do I do about Dodd? He's already in the air."

Lovanov sighed. "Just explain it to him. Bring him over to the rehearsal. Tell him to stay as long as he wants, and have a good time. We'll pay the expenses."

Two hours later, the phone rang again. It was an excited and joyful Nicholas Dodd. "I'm here!" he shouted.

"Get a cab and come to my studio," I said, giving him the address.

"But don't we have to rehearse at noon?" he asked.

"Just get a cab, Nick, and come to my place."

He arrived, heard my tale of woe, and was crestfallen. He'd packed his tails, his white tie, and his hopes of conducting a world premiere with the DSO (Detroit Symphony Orchestra) at a gala event. "I guess it just wasn't in the cards," I said to him, "but what the hell, have a nice time on the DSO. Come to the rehearsal. You'll learn little of what to do, and a lot about what not to do."

It was a glacial and somewhat subdued Gunther Herbig who accepted my notes after the rehearsal and the performance. He did a competent job. It wasn't exactly the piece of music I'd written, but it wasn't too bad either, considering the circumstances.

The Lady Remembers was received warmly and enthusiastically at its packed premiere, and it got a standing ovation. I walked onto the stage, and Gunther Herbig and I put our arms around each other, acknowledging the roaring response.

Afterward, there was a huge party, and half of official Washington seemed to be there to celebrate the event. But neither Maestro Herbig nor I had a word of conversation for each other, either then, or to this day.

The next day, we recorded *The Lady Remembers* in Constitution Hall, whose acoustics were better for recording than those of the Kennedy Center. Again, it was a good, workmanlike job, but I knew that the best performance, the one that I would want to treasure for its fidelity and spirit would be the one that Nicholas Dodd would conduct in London.

In fact, a week later, I flew to London ahead of Mary, to go through the final week of rehearsals.

Nick did the kind of job I knew he would. It was Charlie Ketcham all over again, but through a different sensibility. What was emerging in rehearsal was true to the music and true to my intent. I was eminently, thoroughly satisfied.

Mary arrived five days before the concert. "Guess who was on the Concorde with me," she said, and then added before I'd had a chance to think, "Shirley."

"Shirley MacLaine?"

She nodded. This was exciting. Shirley hadn't had a chance to hear *The Lady Remembers* yet, though she knew I'd dedicated it to Christopher. What an appropriate coincidence, I thought, that she should be here.

"That's wonderful," I enthused. "Did you tell her about the piece?"

"Oh yes," Mary replied. "I told her when it was being performed, and where it was being performed, and that you were over here rehearsing, and all of that, and she seemed very pleased. She's staying at the Britannia."

I called the Britannia. Shirley wasn't in, but I left a message, inviting her to the concert as my guest, and went off to another rehearsal.

When I returned that evening, there was no confirming reply from Shirley. Nor was there one the next day, nor that evening. Maybe they hadn't delivered the message, I reasoned, and called her hotel again. Yes, the concierge assured me, they'd received my call, and absolutely, it had been delivered to her. Personally.

This was odd. I knew how busy Shirley was these days, but the least she could have done was to call me back. What was going on? I left another message, urging her to call me.

Two more days passed, and still no call. Indignation, then anger began to rise in me. It was understandable that she should be busy; her career was full and demanding; but it was unthinkable that she should absolutely ignore my calls. I sat down and, in something approaching white heat, wrote her a note that ended, "I go to your movies. I watch your television specials. I read your books. All I wanted you to do was to hear a piece that I dedicated to Chris, and of which I'm very proud. Is the memory of Christopher beginning to dim? Are you still dancing in the light—or merely the spotlight?"

I sealed the envelope and had it hand delivered to her hotel. It produced a reply, all right—a long, violently angry, telephoned vituperation in which Shirley read me out from right to left and top to bottom. How dare I say such things to her, how dare I write to her that way? Who *was* I, anyway? it concluded.

And so, apparently, ended a long and lovely friendship. It's a situation with which I'm anything but happy. I know that harbored anger is bad for both body and soul. And now, today, that eruptive fury I once felt, over what I perceived as a breach of faith, has quieted into sadness. And the loss of a profound and precious friendship has left a vacancy in me that's difficult to fill.

The London premiere of *The Lady Remembers* was triumphant, and soon after I returned to New York, the tidegates seemed to open. A flood of commissions cascaded in. The Chicago City Ballet was the first to arrive, with an offer to write a ballet to celebrate the sesquicentennial of Chicago. Hard on the heels of this, my alma mater, the University of North Carolina, commissioned me to write a chorale for the bicentennial of the university. The American Olympic Festival Committee followed, asking for an overture. Finally, Harvard's famous, journalistic Neiman Foundation wrote, requesting a march to celebrate its fiftieth anniversary.

I plunged into the writing of the ballet immediately. It was becoming more and more natural to write instrumental music, and it flowed easily.

By the spring of 1987, it was ready for orchestrating. The Chicago City Ballet was a small company, without a resident orchestra. It was necessary to score the ballet for synthesizer. Gershon Kingsley, Michael Shapiro, and I toiled for six solid weeks, recording the score on the prestigious Kurzweil synthesizer. For eight hours a day, we slaved over it, section by section, measure by measure, painting the instrumental coloration until it precisely corresponded to what I'd heard in my head.

For me, it was an exciting, new method of expression.

The ballet didn't succeed, but the music did. The choreography was viewed as a distraction rather than a complement to the music.

Every luminary on the city's scene seemed to be gathered for the opening performance. The audience cheered lustily, and the next day, the reviews affirmed the cheers. "This enravishing work," wrote Jacqueline Taylor in *Newcity*, "richly captures *Chicago*! . . . Just as Chicago itself has many moods, many contrasts, the music shifts constantly from jazz to blues to swing to Broadway show sound to lovely lyric passages and again to sudden dissonance . . . In the chiaroscuro he presents, Adler has eschewed the standard temptation to play up Chicago's grimy gangster past, its waterfront brawls and mayhem. Few of us have been part of it, so what we know is what we hear—the serenity of early mornings along the lake, blue shadows just before dawn, lonely clarinet wails, and the insistent drum beat of our lively night life . . . This is music that stands by itself, and enhanced by dance, should provide a cultural coup. Adler is a gifted composer."

The following day, the mayor of Chicago presented me with a gold key to the city.

Meanwhile, the urge to write singable music continued to insinuate itself. Midway through 1987, I was working in Fred Harris' recording studio, and noticed a picture, hanging on the wall, of three beautiful girls.

"Who are they?" I asked, naturally.

"My sisters," answered Fred.

"What do they do?"

"They sing."

"Are they any good?" I continued.

"Of course they are," he countered.

"Well then, if they're good, have them call me," I concluded.

The next day, I got a call, and three days later, the Harris Sisters came to my studio. They were young and bright and musically articulate, and had an emotional quality I'd figured had been computerized out of young singers.

I was impressed. Song ideas began to crowd into my mind, and, over the next few weeks, I wrote a couple of new songs for the sisters. When my time permitted, we began recording, at the studio of a gifted young synthesizer musician and arranger, Dean Bailin.

All of this occupied me richly but not absolutely.

Like an insistent, incipient melody, Christopher's *Gideon Starr* rested at the rim of my attention. A partially finished, potentially successful musical, it deserved to be seen.

Five years before, I'd been particularly impressed by a young playwright and friend of Christopher's, Bill C. Davis. His play *Mass Appeal* was, I felt, a stunning theatrical treat. I got in touch with him.

He turned out to be an enormously intelligent, vital man, bursting with ideas and talent. We talked of *Gideon Starr* for a while, but then, our conversation turned to a partially completed idea he'd had for a musical. It was based upon a wholly unique and yet pervasive contemporary subject—the mentally retarded. Years ago, no one in their right mind would have thought of this as a subject for a musical, but now, I was intrigued by Bill's concept.

He'd spent some time in a country village for retarded and emotionally disturbed adults as a "house parent." What came back to him most strongly, he said, were laughter, violence—and music.

I knew it was right, and suggested that we collaborate. He agreed, and we began to work together,

The wasteland of the past decade seemed to be bursting into flower. New projects were being born, each of them fairly tumbling over each other as they begged to be realized. It was all beginning again, and nothing, I felt, was going to prevent me from working with absolute dedication and vigor.

And yet, that was exactly what was about to happen, and its resolution would form the basis for the most profound, important, monumental transformation of my life.

20.

F O R years, I'd been having regular readings from Pamela Austin, an astrologer and friend. For several of these years, she'd been urging me to go beyond this, and meet a person she called a "Great Being," a "Perfected Master," a "True Saint." This Great Being's name was Gurumayi Chidvilasananda, and she was, according to Pamela, the new Guru of the Siddha Lineage, the oldest Yogic tradition in the world. For years, this meant little or nothing to me. But finally, in May of 1985, partly to pacify Pamela, and partly because I remembered that Christopher had seemed to gain some comfort from Andrew's involvement with Tibetan Yoga, I acceded to Pamela's latest urging to meet this Being, this Guru that Pamela seemed to feel was so special.

Gurumayi was holding programs at the Manhattan Center, on West 34th Street. And so, I grudgingly joined two thousand people one evening in this West Side meeting hall.

The program consisted of a talk by Gurumayi, and a long, and to me boring chant of a mantra, sung in a language that seemed absolutely unintelligible. I tried to join in. But very quickly, I began to ask myself what in hell was I doing there, surrounded by these swaying people, sitting cross-legged on the floor while a dark-skinned, very beautiful woman dressed in orange robes spoke admittedly eloquent words to them, and led them in song in a strange language.

Finally, the chant ended, and an enormous line of people, approximately ten across, formed before the orange-clad woman's chair. The crowd snaked all the way to the back of the enormous hall. I certainly wasn't going to take part in this, I thought, and I turned to leave. But before I'd taken two steps, Pamela appeared, grabbed my hand, and led me to the front of the line.

"Come on," she whispered, "You're about to have *darshan* with Gurumayi."

"*Darshan?* What's *darshan?*" I asked.

"This is a *darshan* line," she explained. "It's a sanskrit word, and it means 'being in the presence of a holy being.' "

"Sanskrit?" I whispered back. "Is that what we've been singing for the past two hours?"

We approached the guru.

If there had been a peacefulness in the hall, it was deepened around the chair occupied by Gurumayi. She was the most exquisitely beautiful person I'd ever seen. And there was a kind of serene assurance about her that I'd never encountered in anyone before.

Pamela motioned for me to sit next to Gurumayi, and I did so, chastened and respectful.

Gurumayi turned, and began to discuss music. We talked easily for a minute or so. And then, as Gurumayi was turning her attention back to the long line of devotees who were now kneeling before her, I asked her to bless the memory of my late son, Christopher.

She nodded, silently, and I left with Pamela. "Glad you came?" she asked.

"Glad it's over," I said, "I'm tired."

Two years passed. In mid-June of 1987, I found myself in a state of disturbing inner turmoil. The first flush of energy I'd felt with the beginning of the Chicago City Ballet commission was scattering itself. Although I was working hard, I was deriving very little joy from it. Although I was still married, and I felt an enormous devotion and responsibility to Mary and her lovely and blossoming daughter Laura, the marriage had turned into a loving friendship, and Mary and I had decided to separate. Although I was healthy, I had a malaise that apparently went deeper than my body. My mind was racing at an unbearable speed. I knew I needed to slow down, but I seemed to be powerless to bring this about.

And then, I remembered Christopher's meditations in the hospital. I called Andrew in Paris. He'd been the one who'd instructed Christopher in meditation, and it had brought Chris immense peace at a time when he was in dire need of it. Maybe it would do the same for me, I thought, and I asked Andrew for some specific instructions.

He started me with deep breathing exercises. "Start small," he said. "Don't push it. Begin with two-minute sessions."

I tried. I did everything he told me, and in less than a minute, my eyes would snap open, and I would be fidgeting. I simply couldn't sit still, even for a few moments.

I called Pamela Austin for help. "The best way to begin meditation is to go up to the Siddha Meditation Ashram in South Fallsburg, New York," she said.

"In the Catskills?" I asked, remembering Grossinger's and Eddie Fisher.

"Yes," she said. "Take the beginner's intensive in August."

So, on August 1, I drove to South Fallsburg. When I arrived, I suddenly had a revisitation of the feeling of two years ago, at the Manhattan Center. What the devil was I doing here, I thought. How did I let Pamela talk me into this? I felt foolish, and my lodgings in an old hotel, renamed Atma Nidhi, did nothing to help me. The room was spartan, spare, uninteresting, a tunnel of a place with a television set that didn't work. Oh, it was clean enough. Everything about the place was spotless, and there seemed to be no end of people dusting and polishing and rearranging. But it was all still strange and uncomfortable to me.

I attended an orientation meeting on Friday night; I dutifully reported to the large and beautiful meditation hall early the next morning, and went through the agenda—some teachings, some chanting, and two agonizingly long meditations, which seemed like time on the torture rack for me. By noon, I was kicking myself for being there at all. It wasn't the money I'd spent that bothered me; it was the fact that I was ungovernably bored and nervous, and I'd come here for enlightenment and peace. It just wasn't working.

That evening, Peter Hayes, a writer and longtime devotee who was the master of ceremonies, told us that we'd be receiving *Shaktipat.*

Shaktipat, I muttered to myself. What is *Shaktipat,* anyway? A lesson? A present? A piece of cake?

We were told to assume the meditative posture, with our backs straight, our eyes closed, our bodies relaxed. I assumed it. For a little while. Then, I of course opened my eyes, defiantly, and on the far side of the hall, I could see Gurumayi. She was passing slowly from one person to another, holding some sort of fanlike object at the end of a pole. She seemed to be hitting people on the head with it. I later found out this was a wand of peacock feathers.

Great, I thought. Is that what *Shaktipat* is? Being hit on the head? What am I doing here? And the longer the ritual went on, the more discomfort I felt. It took Gurumayi an eternity to wend her slow way to the section of the hall in which I sat, asking myself questions, squirming in my seat, filling myself with as much doubt as I could muster.

As the rustle of her gown drew near, I closed my eyes tightly.

Suddenly, I was bopped in the face with the fan. It felt strangely comforting, unusually soft and caressing. Immediately after this, a pair of hands pressed firmly on my temple, and then, a current of electricity shot through my body. It felt as if I'd been struck by a bolt of lightning. I'd never experienced anything like it. I was almost catapulted out of my chair. It was the most exhilarating feeling I'd ever had in my life. And I knew then that *Shaktipat* was no mere piece of cake. It was something remarkable, something divine.

What had happened to me, I was later told, was an awakening of the primordial power that resides in every human being. This is called the *kundalini*, and it lies, coiled, at the base of the spine. The bolt of lightning that had coursed through me was the transmission of spiritual energy from Gurumayi, allowing her grace to awaken the dormant *kundalini*, or God, in me, releasing it to begin its journey upward, as I developed spiritually, through my own efforts at loving and perfecting my soul and the souls of others.

It was a lot to take in, an immense amount of feeling and knowledge, all fused together in one blinding moment of revelation. My mind tried to contain it, and couldn't. It was all whirling like a tornado within me.

And then, gradually, as I drove back to New York, it faded.

But not entirely. A seed had been planted, and later that winter, I went to another intensive, held at the Manhattan Siddha Yoga Ashram, a converted brownstone on the Upper West Side of New York City. The room was enormously crowded; I was immensely uncomfortable and restless, and before the intensive had ended, I'd departed.

But I took one priceless experience with me. Partway through the proceedings, a gentle, genial, and powerful Black man got up to speak. I was spellbound by his words, his demeanor, his thoughts. His name was Eugene Callender, and I later learned that he was the president of the Siddha Yoga Foundation, an ordained Presbyterian minister, and a man with an extensive and respected background in government.

I phoned Pamela Austin and asked her to set up a luncheon date for the three of us, which she did. And from that moment forward, Eugene Callender and I became fast and loving friends.

But thus far, Siddha Yoga was still a minor, almost forgettable part of my life. "It won't be that way forever," said Eugene Callender, with a knowing twinkle in his eye, on the afternoon of our luncheon. But I only half listened to him. I'd been around.

That spring, I departed for my annual stint at Chapel Hill. For two years, I'd been asked by the University to spend time as composer-in-residence, going from class to class, on an informal basis, discussing with students the world of music and drama beyond the University.

In early April, I noticed a faint uncomfortableness in my throat. It felt muscular. There was no pain, only a slight twinge, and I thought nothing of it. But when it didn't go away for two weeks, I asked a friend of mine, Susan Ivory, to bring a flashlight, and look in my throat. She did, and saw nothing unusual.

I was still concerned. I was aware of my body, and I knew when something wasn't entirely right. I aimed the flashlight down my throat and looked for myself. And there, on the left side, was a small, pink nipple. On the right side, there was nothing.

I called Chancellor Fordham immediately and asked him to set up an appointment for me at Memorial Hospital in Chapel Hill. He did, and I reported to the Ear, Nose, and Throat Department.

The doctor who examined me acknowledged what I had found. "I think it's just a piece of tonsilar scar tissue, left over from when you had your tonsils removed. Why don't you just watch it for a few weeks, and see if it changes."

"Should you biopsy it?" I asked.

"We could," he answered. "But I don't think it's anything at all."

"I'd like it to be done," I said.

He removed part of the nipple, and sent it off to the lab. "It's nothing to worry about," he said, as I left the office. "Just relax and have a good time."

The next day, a message was waiting at the desk of my hotel to call the doctor. I did, immediately.

"Mr. Adler," he said, "I'm afraid I have some bad news for you."

"Do I have—?"

"I'm afraid so," he said. "A squamous cell carcinoma. Maybe you'd better come over here and—"

But I didn't hear much more. There was a roaring in my ears. I felt like I'd been hit by a truck. Cancer! It just couldn't be! This was something that happened to other people. This was something you read about; you didn't experience it. And why me, God, why me, when my life was finally settling into comparative peace, when my career was beginning to move again?

Two years before, when I'd begun my stint as composer-in-residence at Chapel Hill, I'd met Susan in a parking lot. She was a professional photographer, and a lovely, bright young lady. Two weeks before the discovery of my tumor, we'd met again, and had become good friends, having dinner and going to movies together. She came to me when she heard the results of the biopsy, and she stayed closely by my side through almost every moment of the unfolding nightmare that was to come.

Mary was aghast when I phoned her and told her the news. "What can I do?" she asked, without a second's hesitation.

"Call Sloan-Kettering Memorial Cancer Center," I said, "and find out the best person for me to see. I'll be back in a couple of days."

And she did. She called me and told me that the doctor I should see was a Dr. Elliot Strong, who was Chief Surgeon for Head and Neck at the hospital. But Dr. Strong was out of town for a week. I could see him the following Wednesday.

In the interim, she suggested that I go to the Mayo Clinic, in Rochester, Minnesota. A mutual friend, Dr. William Manger, a Mayo fellow to whom she'd also talked, was eager to set up an appointment.

So, I went to the Mayo Clinic, and Susan, after arranging for the care of her two children, joined me a day later. Dr. Brian Neal, the Chief Surgeon for Ear, Nose, and Throat, examined me.

"Mm-hm," he said, as he probed the tumor with his fingers, "Sneaky little bastard. Gotta come out. Gotta come out."

And with all the casualness of a weatherman explaining an approaching front, he described a ghastly, disfiguring operation. It involved sawing the jaw in two, extracting a tooth, and going into the tonsilar pillar to excise not only the tumor but all of the lymph glands on the left side of the neck and possibly even some of the tongue—which might mean having a speech impediment for the rest of my life. In addition to this, the nerve to the lower lip would be severed, numbing the lip. A plate would be placed, he continued, in the roof of the mouth, and the plate might have to be replaced surgically from time to time.

Stunned, I was then shuffled, day by day, from member to member of his team, and each of them confirmed and embroidered Dr. Neal's diagnosis and suggestions. It was like descending into Dante's seven rings of Inferno. Each doctor's words were like devils' pitchforks, prodding me, depressing me, discouraging me, until I was reduced to a quivering tangle of raw nerves.

I did manage to choke out one question: "What about radiation?"

The doctors shook their heads negatively. "Not in this case," they concluded.

I walked over to the highly polished windows of that floor of the Mayo Clinic, and looked out on a lovely, calming vista of green, rolling hills and abundant trees. It was an exquisite and familiar scene, the nature I loved so much surrounding, almost cradling me. I thought about Sloan-Kettering, where Chris had died, in the middle of the turmoil of the city, and concluded that it would feel better to recuperate in the midst of the nature I'd always needed, rather than in the middle of New York City. I booked surgery for two weeks later, and gave some blood, in case it might be needed for my operation.

I went back to the hotel a broken man. I stretched out on the bed, and closed my eyes. It was too much to absorb all at once. I tried to sleep. And then, suddenly, from somewhere inside of me, a need began to assert itself. Gurumayi. Gurumayi. Gurumayi. The name and the face and the need grew until they became undeniable.

I'd spoken with Eugene Callender before I'd left for Chapel Hill, and he'd told me that Gurumayi was coming to the United States from India that month. She would be at the ashram in Oakland, California, he'd said. I got up and phoned Eugene in New York.

"Gene," I said. "I'm in trouble." And I poured out my experiences of the past few days, urging him to arrange a *darshan* with Gurumayi in Oakland, immediately.

He agreed, and an hour later, called back. "Gurumayi says you should stay in the hospital, and not tire yourself," he said.

I apparently hadn't made myself clear to him. "I'm not in the hospital," I explained. "I'm fine, physically. I have no symptoms. Just this damned tumor. Please explain that to her. I can easily make the trip."

"Okay," he said, "I'll have Gurumayi's appointment secretary, Claire James, call you."

Another hour passed, and the phone rang again. The soft, British voice of Claire James asked, "What can I do for you, Richard?"

"Claire," I said, "It's urgent. I must see Gurumayi. Please explain to her how important, how crucially important it is for me to see her."

"Stay there," said Claire, reassuringly. "I'll speak to Gurumayi and call you back."

Within a half hour, she was back on the line. "Gurumayi says to come to Oakland next week," she said.

I felt pounds lighter, years younger. It was the first good news I'd had in days.

The next morning, Susan went back to Chapel Hill, and I went to New York, to keep my appointment with Dr. Strong at Memorial Sloan-Kettering. The waiting room of his office was a terrible, depressing location, populated by frightened, mutilated victims of this vicious disease that kills without mercy.

Finally, I was led into Dr. Strong's office. He'd examined the CAT scan, and his face was not at all as settled in its analysis as Dr. Neal's had been. "I don't know, Mr. Adler," he said, "The CAT scan shows nothing. I'm not quite sure. Let me call in my associate in Radiation."

Dr. Strong was a distinguished looking man in his late fifties or early sixties. I automatically assumed that his associate would be around that age. But when the door opened, I was startled. A boy stood there. A fresh faced, handsome, smiling boy. He looked as if he couldn't have been older than twenty-five.

"This is Dr. Harrison," said Dr. Strong. "I want him to examine you."

Dr. Harrison held out a hand. I was wearing a UNC sweater. He looked at it, then at me. "You went to Carolina?" he asked.

"Yes," I answered.

"I went to Duke," he said, smiling, and there was something in his voice that reached out warmly and flooded me with assurance. But still, I thought, as he prepared to examine me, he's a kid. And how can a kid be the head of Head and Neck Radiation Oncology for Memorial Sloan-Kettering, one of the most distinguished cancer centers in the world? How could that be?

Dr. Harrison began to probe, as the other doctors had. Nothing different about that. And then I looked up at his eyes. They'd become one unified laser beam of concentration, boring into my throat. I'd never seen anything like this before—except perhaps, years ago, in a meeting hall in Manhattan, with a woman in an orange robe. I relaxed. I knew I was in the presence of brilliance.

Dr. Harrison finished his examination, and the two doctors retired from the examining room. Ten minutes later, they returned. "We think you should have an exploratory," Dr. Strong said, "under a general anesthetic, so we can really get in there and see what's what."

"Fine," I said, with the sort of relief that a condemned man finds in a reprieve. "When?"

"Ten days to two weeks," Dr. Harrison said.

It was working well. I'd be able to get to Oakland and back in time for the exploratory.

Friday morning, I left, with Susan, for California. We were met at the airport by a driver, who took us directly to the ashram. There was a message waiting for me, to call Mary.

I called her immediately.

"You have to come home, right away," she said.

"Why?" I asked.

"The exploratory operation has been scheduled for this coming Monday, and you have to report to the hospital before noon on Sunday, for tests."

It was a shock. I'd planned on spending three or four days at the Oakland ashram, extending and deepening and exploring my experience in Siddha Yoga.

That night, Susan and I went to the evening program. There were close to two thousand people in the meditation hall. Gurumayi spoke, eloquently and simply. There was a chant, and a meditation, and then, again, the long *darshan* line formed. This time, Claire James came and gathered up Susan and me, ushering us to a spot in front of Gurumayi.

I knelt, and as succinctly as I could, considering the hordes of people behind me, outlined my problem. She listened carefully, and then said, "Would you care to sit to the right of me?"

This, I knew, was a great honor, and I of course nodded yes. And so, for half an hour, we watched, fascinated, the faces of the devoted, coming up, one by one, to Gurumayi, communicating with her, each in his or her own way, each held for a moment in that loving gaze that seemed to plunge directly and personally to one and all.

About a half-hour later, Gurumayi leaned over and asked us, "Are you hungry?"

We were.

"Claire will take you to the *Amrit* for dinner. Eat and come back," she said, softly.

And so we ate, and returned, and sat for another two hours, until eleven o'clock, when the *darshan* line finally ended.

Gurumayi rose from her chair, said, "Good night," and left.

"We'd better get some sleep," I said to Susan. "We have to get to the airport early in the morning."

As we were turning to go, a tall, young, dark man, in a gray suit, came up to us. "Mr. Adler," he said, "would you please follow me?" And Susan and I followed him down a long corridor, through a door, and into a vestibule.

There sat Gurumayi Chidvilasananda.

And there, in that quiet, small, contained room, the floodgates opened, and I poured out my fear, my depression, my anxiety, my despondency.

Gurumayi said nothing. She merely nodded her head, up and down, without expression.

When I was drained of all I had to communicate to her, I got up, thanked her for her blessing, and started to leave. I walked to the door, and suddenly, Gurumayi spoke her first word. "Richard," she said.

I turned around. She was standing now. She walked over to me. She was wearing a long, peach-colored, hand-painted, silk meditation shawl around her shoulders. Gently but affirmatively, she removed it, and, wrapping it around my throat, she said, "Wear this before the operation and have someone put it on you after, and I'll see you in Manhattan." Tears leaped to my eyes. And at that moment, at that instant, the fears, the anxiety, the despondency disappeared forever, and I knew I had it licked. All of the negativity was replaced by abundant joy.

Dr. Strong and Dr. Harrison stood at the end of my bed after the exploratory operation. I had a choice, they told me. I could either have surgery or radiation.

"What's your recommendation?" I asked them.

They preferred, by a slight edge, radiation, because the borders of the tumor weren't clearly defined, and radiation could cover the more general area, including the microscopic cells of cancer.

I breathed a sigh of deep relief, for two reasons. First, an escape from surgery is always an escape from unknown horrors. And second, this choice would make Louis Harrison the doctor who would be medically in charge of me. The confidence and comfort I'd felt with him that first day of examination had grown in the ensuing days. He was now more than a respected doctor; he was the most important man in my life, the physician who could *save* my life, a friend that I determined would become a best friend, and a member of the team that would, I now knew, bring about my recovery.

The most important and vital change that any cancer patient can undergo had occurred. I was no longer a victim. I was part of a recovery team that was composed of myself, my guru, my care nurse Cindy, my wife Mary, my loving Susan, and my doctor, Lou Harrison.

Shortly before the radiation therapy was to begin, I asked Dr. Harrison what to expect. "Lou, give me the bottom line on side effects," I said.

"Well," he sighed, "You'll have the worst pain in your throat you've ever had; so bad, in fact, that you may not be able to talk or swallow. And in that case, you'll have to be fed through tubes in your nose. Your sense of taste will be warped, but you'll get over that, as you will the pain."

I thought for a moment. I'd been booked for two performances, three weeks hence: one for ASCAP's Diamond Jubilee Anniversary with some of the world's greatest songwriters at the Marriott Marquis Theatre on Broadway and 45th Street, and the other, a fundraiser for the Democratic Senate. My longtime friend, Senator Terry Sanford had asked me to organize the program. I was to be the emcee and perform, and I'd already booked my fellow songwriters Charlie Strouse, Sheldon Harnick, George David Weiss, and Leiber and Stoller to do their great medleys.

"Will I be able to keep these dates?" I asked Dr. Harrison.

"No," he said, emphatically. "Not a chance. You won't be able to sing. You might not even be able to talk."

It was discouraging, but somehow I waited to cancel.

On June 2nd I began radiation therapy, seven weeks of it, five days a week, two hundred RAD a day. The maximum. A plaster of paris cup had to be molded to hold my head in a precise position, and I had already experienced radiation simulation to correctly line up the target area, and to focus the tumor in the crosshairs of the radiation gun. The "gun" was an immense monster that loomed over me like some creation in the laboratory of a mad scientist.

Three minutes of three different positions were my doses each day, pumped into me in isolation—just the monster and me in a lead-lined room.

My sense of taste got scrambled right away. Sweet tasted salty. Salt tasted bitter. But during all of those seven weeks of treatments, I never felt a thing. No pain. No swelling. No redness. Nothing. Zero side effects.

One week, a blast of radiation did bounce off the gold crowns on my teeth, badly burning the edge of my tongue. But that was all.

I never had to cancel my appearances. I did both shows, in perfect voice (no ego intended). I invited Dr. Harrison. He was astonished, amazed, and certainly more speechless than I.

At the end of the fourth week, Lou shook his head in bewilderment. "I don't understand this," he said. "I just don't understand this. You're going through radiation—the full amount, two hundred RADs a day, as much as a body can take. And you've had no side effects at all. Not even a scratchy throat. You know what? If I didn't have the X-rays, if I didn't see the tumor disappearing, I'd swear the machines hadn't been turned on."

I nodded, secretly and affirmatively. This had become a joyous routine, and as Lou would marvel, I'd say, "Gurumayi. Siddha Yoga. Gurumayi. Siddha Yoga." He'd ask me questions, and I'd explain this spiritual awakening that I knew was responsible for my miraculous recovery. And he would never challenge it. He would just listen, and nod, and marvel.

If I'd been a skeptic about Siddha Yoga before, I'd gone to the opposite perception now. I was a full-fledged, dedicated devotee, doing the practices, meditating, chanting, repeating the mantras, reading the teachings of Gurumayi and her guru, Baba Muktananda, and conducting introductory programs at my studio to share my joy with my friends—to try to help them see the way. To this day, it hasn't changed. It's compounded. As time progresses, I go more deeply within, closer to my inner self. I increase my *Sadhana,* or devotion to daily practices, and my love grows for Gurumayi, who not only saved, but transformed my life.

As the treatment neared its end, I resolved to express my gratitude to Dr. Harrison by giving him and his lovely wife Ilene a fine present. Maybe a trip to Europe for two weeks, with all expenses paid, I thought. Or a cruise in the Caribbean.

And then, on the next to last day of the treatment, a third possibility presented itself to me. I walked into Lou Harrison's office. "Look, Lou," I said, "out of the deepest gratitude in my heart, I'd like to give you a real gift. And please don't be embarrassed. I'd be hurt if you didn't accept it. Here are three possibilities: A trip to Europe. A cruise on the Caribbean. Or," and I paused, "the beginners' intensive at the Siddha Yoga ashram in South Fallsburg this August."

Lou didn't hesitate for a moment. "The intensive at South Fallsburg," he said, smiling.

And he and his wife Ilene went. And today, both of them are devotees of Siddha Yoga.

The treatment ended on July 21, 1988. I was completely and totally cured of throat cancer. And I remain, to this day, completely and totally cured. And my gratitude—to God, to Gurumayi, to Lou, and for the blessings I've received, are boundless and endless. They, like my love and devotion to Gurumayi, merely grow, every minute I live and give thanks to her.

But, I learned something special as I climbed over this huge road-block to the flow of my life, called cancer. I learned who my real friends are. And I learned there are many who I counted as friends—who are not. There are many who knew of my battle with cancer who ignored me and rebuked me by *not* writing, *not* phoning—obviously *not* caring. Oh yes, there are those who cannot deal with a situation like this—who feel too confused—who are too embarrassed to bother to make contact or give any slight signal of sympathetic recognition. I don't want to sound judgmental, but their silence both hurt me and even angered me.

But then there are those steadfast, loyal pals who would call two, three times a week; invite me out to lunch or dinner quite frequently; people like Martin Revson, Patsy and Howard Johnson, Evvie and Steve Owen, Marilyn and Andy Weiss, and Susan and John Weitz. They were there for me, and I shall always remember how their love and caring and friendship helped me through one of the most difficult periods of my life.

The therapy did take its toll, in a draining of energy, and Lou told me that this would be inevitable. "Your body's been bombarded by cancer and radiation," he said. "It's going to take a while for you to get your strength back."

Ordinarily, I would have gone to Southampton, to spend some time in my pool, in the sun, on a tennis court. But even before the treatment had begun, I knew that this would not be the place I would need for my recuperation. Southampton represented a time in my life that had been, in some part, counterproductive, and was now, in totality, behind me. I had little feeling for the near-obligatory social life I once craved. And though I have some good friends I still cherish, and always will, I wanted to be elsewhere. I wanted and needed serenity.

So, before the treatment began, I rented a home on Lake Placid for the month of August, and I looked forward eagerly to retracing some of the steps of my boyhood, while I renewed the newfound energy of my rebirth.

Two years before, I'd accepted an invitation to be the guest of honor at the week-long Lake Placid Festival of the Arts to be held in August, 1988. The Sinfonietta would play some of my "seriouser" music, and I had agreed to do a two-hour "Evening with Adler" at the Lake Placid Center for the Arts.

August and the festival came, and though my tongue hadn't healed from the radiation scatter that had lacerated part of it, and though I was ennervated, almost as soon as I got to Lake Placid, a wellspring of energy began to bubble in me. And, on the appointed date, I did a full two hours of singing, telling anecdotes and general horsing around with no difficulty. And I loved every minute of it.

And, as the summer unfolded, that well of energy grew. Susan and I swam a mile a day; we climbed some of the peaks of the Adirondacks; we waterskied; we walked through the woods and fields I'd known and loved as a boy and now loved again, but with a fresh vision.

I'd been a man on the brink of darkness, and now I was in a brighter, warmer light than I'd ever known.

That spring, *The Pajama Game* was given a true and well-received revival at the New York City Opera at Lincoln Center. Judy Ross and I met in the lobby. Her face was a mixture of elation and pain. "How is it?" I asked her, as we embraced.

"If you don't think this is a tough night for me, for memories—" Her eyes filled with tears. I held her closer, and the connection, the richness that repetition sometimes adds to what we experience so blithely the first time became brightly clear to me. There were connections, I understood—and they were part of the theater piece in which we're all involved, every minute we live—the "play of consciousness," as Baba Muktananda calls it.

Knowing this, I began to see everything that had happened to me in a new perspective. It all seemed to be coming together. I was in my mid-sixties, but I felt younger than I had in years. My body wasn't what it was, but my spirit had grown immensely. I was able to go as deeply within as I was willing to go thoroughly into the world.

Susan and I traveled to India at Christmas to be with Gurumayi at her ashram in Ganeshpuri.

Being in that sweet and serene environment reminded me of my other trips to the Orient: The first had been one of discovery—that time and distance and perspective can take you into another world within the world.

On the first of July, 1986, Mary and her daughter Laura, aged nine, my stepdaughter Ritchey, then aged 21, and I had boarded a plane to Seattle enroute to Bangkok, Thailand. It had been my present to Ritchey for having graduated *cum laude* from Harvard in May. This was going to be, as well as a voyage of exploration, my chance to renew my relationship with Ritchey, whom I hadn't seen very much of since her mother and I had parted.

So, it was a celebratory occasion. My fantasy picture of Thailand had been based upon Dick Rodgers' *The King and I,* and I wouldn't be disappointed. It would be a sweet joy, that first, delicious visit to Asia.

After a dinner party in our honor given by Rosa and Fred Ayer in their exquisite home in Seattle, and after a good night's sleep, we'd boarded Thai International Airlines for the flight to Bangkok, via Tokyo. My first glimpse of Asia had been at Narita Airport in Tokyo. And it had been an astonishing one. I'd never thought of myself as particularly tall, but suddenly as I'd strolled through the corridors of that terminal, I felt like a skyscraper. Or a lighthouse. All around me, that morning, swirled a sea of serene little people, most of them dressed as if they were on their way to some Lilliputian version of Wall Street.

But it was a different sort of exoticism that had awaited me in Bangkok. There, I'd wakened at five o'clock in the morning, too excited to sleep, too full of wonder to stay indoors. The smell of flowers, the freshness of the dawn air, the murmur of activity along the riverbank had drawn me outdoors and thrilled me like only a first experience can.

I'd paid a price: it had been July fourth, and we'd been invited to the American Embassy for a holiday celebration. I'd been unable to eat, or even face food. Too little sleep and an abundance of jet lag had done me in, but the magical experience at dawn along a riverbank my first morning in the Orient had been worth it.

The next day, we'd been invited to the Grand Palace, and that would be the first of many times I would return to that golden city fairyland, that complex of palaces and towers and spires interlaced with exquisite mosaic tiles that soared hundreds of feet into the endless blue of the sky, catching and flinging back the sunlight, glittering in it as if they were fashioned of diamonds.

We'd been escorted by two generals that day, as we would be throughout much of our trip, and we'd experienced an audience with the Crown Princess. It had been a long, cheerful meeting, during which the Princess and I had discussed music, and she'd shown me some examples of the King's compositions. They'd been good, solid amateur songs, and I'd jokingly remarked to her, "I'm a better composer than your father, but he makes a much better king."

I'd come back to the Grand Palace on two subsequent trips. And on that first trip, I'd grown inordinately close to Ritchey, as we'd explored storybook countrysides, strolled through uncommon marketplaces, and climbed ancient pyramids that reawakened the exhilaration and sense of suspension between earth and sky that I'd felt as a boy near Kari-noke.

Of course, as in any rich and faceted experience, my trips to Asia hadn't all been sweet. On my second trip, in 1987, with Mary and Laura, we'd flown to Bhutan, in the lower Himalayas, near Mount Everest. We'd participated in a number of government-sponsored tours and, one rainy morning, as I'd started to enter a van, my foot slipped and a knife edge of jagged steel protruding from the running board ripped my left leg to the bone. Blood poured instantly from the wound, and I was rushed to a nearby hospital. The emergency room, though neat, looked none too clean.

It made me uncomfortable, and the risk of AIDS infection from the needles that would be used for the injections of painkillers had agitated me further.

I'd asked the doctor if the hospital had any disposable needles.

"No, we don't," he'd answered.

I whispered to Mary to get some money out of my wallet. She did this, and I separated three brand new, shiny, fifty-dollar bills from the rest. "Whatever you do," I said to the doctor, "I want to make this contribution to the hospital."

And I'd gotten the only two disposable needles in the hospital, to initiate the stitching of both bone and flesh.

But even that excruciatingly painful experience hadn't dimmed my love for Asia, or the beautiful people of Bhutan. And, in fact, on that very journey, I'd experienced something very close to the flow of fate, the Play of Consciousness of which Baba Muktananda talked.

We'd been in Seattle on October 12th, 1987, and suddenly I'd received an irresistible inner message to sell my considerable Mutual Fund investments. I'd passed it off as a hunch at the time, but I heeded it and phoned in a sell order.

Later, in Bhutan, on October 20th, Mary and Laura and I had had dinner with the Foreign Minister. I'd casually asked him if he'd heard anything about the present state of world markets.

"Haven't you heard?" he'd asked me. "Wall Street crashed yesterday. The market fell 506 points!"

I'd trembled, in fear over what might have been if I hadn't obeyed that inner message.

The following summer, I returned to Lake Placid, and it was like going home, to swimming in the early morning, mountain climbing near sunset, and experiencing the *Shakti* constantly.

In the fall, I returned with a new vigor to work on *Off Key*, which was now the name of the show that Bill Davis and I were writing. Patricia Birch had agreed to direct it, and, in June, before I'd left for

Lake Placid, we'd chanced a reading, in a small, dark studio in lower Manhattan, before a few selected and disciminating friends. The reception had been astonishing. "I was moved," someone said to me, after the reading, "and I don't know how long it's been since I've been moved by a musical."

I sensed this, too. Some other dimension had begun to enter my work. I'd had a premonition of this years ago, but now it was undeniable. It was as if I weren't the creator at all, but a conduit, a passageway into space for something considerably more than I had ever touched before—or that had touched me.

During the two years following my cancer cure and spiritual transformation, two connected events, one unhappy, and the other happy, drew me even more deeply within myself and more closely to Siddha Yoga.

By late June, 1989, my mother was nearly ninety-five years old. In her eighties, she had remained as bright and aware of the world as she had in her youth. But during the last three years, that brightness had begun to dim. I'd made certain that she would be attended twenty-four hours a day.

A principal recollection of my mother is that, no matter what, I cannot remember her ever having complained, not even once, about anything. As 1989 drifted into summer, Mother spent most of her time sleeping, as if her life were slowly and quietly winding down.

I spent the second half of June at the ashram in South Fallsburg, taking courses, chanting, meditating, gathering into myself the spiritually charged energy of this holy place. I called my mother several times a day, every day, and if she wasn't asleep, we would exchange simple, loving words.

At eleven o'clock in the morning of the twenty-seventh of June, I telephoned. Her attendant, Marina, answered.

"How's Mom today?" I asked.

"Not so well," she replied. "Would you like to speak to her?"

"Of course," I answered, and a dark foreboding started to form in me.

She placed the phone by my mother's ear.

"Hello, Mom," I said.

No words, but a few gurgling sounds emerged, and I could hear the extreme labor of my mother's breathing, coming in short gasps.

Things were obviously bad. I said a few more words of loving encouragement, hung up the phone, and went to the Nityananda Temple. It was, as always, a place of deepened peace. I prayed to Gurumayi, harder than I had ever prayed for anything in my life. "Please, Gurumayi," I urged. "Please bring peace to my mother. And soon."

At a few minutes after 4:30 that afternoon, I received a call from our family physician, Dr. Elliott Howard. "Mother has just slipped away, peacefully, in her sleep," he said, quietly.

And though I had expected it, and though I'd asked Gurumayi to make it happen, it was still a crushing blow. My last connection to the past, the person who'd given me positiveness and strength and shelter and encouragement, who had softened the hard times, who had given me the love my father had withheld in my childhood, who was an unfailing beacon of belief in me, was gone, forever.

As Geraldine Fitzgerald wrote, in a letter of sympathy to me, a few days later, I had become "an aging orphan."

I went on to the evening program, and when the *darshan* line formed, I bowed down before Gurumayi, silently. I said nothing as I knelt before her and raised my head.

There was a pause, and then, in a soft, comforting voice, Gurumayi smiled, and asked, "How old *was* she?"

It was her way of telling me that she'd heard my prayer . . . and that my mother was at peace. And that I should be at peace, too.

The other connected event just as thoroughly convinced me that there *is* a flow of fate, an energy that unites us, sometimes causing paths to cross and recross as we slowly grow, spiritually.

One day, I received a call from Lalita Franklin, a disciple of Gurumayi, stating that the guru was sending to New York, from India, a swami who had a massive pituatory tumor. His name was Tyagananda. Gurumayi had directed her to call me because of my miraculous recovery.

"Could you help him?" Lalita asked.

"I'll try," I said, "of course I'll try."

Two days passed, and Lalita called again. "He's here," she said.

I'd already alerted Lou Harrison, who examined Swami Tyagananda at once, and sent him to see Dr. Kalman Post, the foremost surgeon for pituatory tumors in the country.

Dr. Post, after examining the swami, scheduled immediate surgery. But further examination revealed that the pear-sized tumor was the second largest on record; an operation, he intimated would be far too risky at this time. He decided instead to use a certain hormone to try to shrink the tumor till it was operable. After surgery, radiation from Dr. Harrison was indicated.

I went to the Manhattan ashram to meet Swami Tyagananda. One look, and my heart rushed toward him. He was only in his early forties, but he looked gray and wasted. The very life in him seemed crushed, although he maintained a touching, outward cheerfulness. But he was obviously in distress, and going slowly blind from the pressure of the tumor on the optical nerve. He was losing his memory and suffered from dizzy spells and general debilitation. It was a heartrending sight and I stayed for a time, talking with him about the power of grace and the efficacy of hope. But I knew he had a long, torturous time ahead of him.

A few weeks later, I went back to the ashram. Partway through the evening, I ran into Swami Tyagananda. He was a changed man. Color had flooded back to his cheeks. His eyes had cleared. His spirit was high.

"I feel wonderful," he said, shaking my hand. "The symptoms have disappeared. My vision's coming back, my memory's better, I don't feel dizzy anymore—Thank you, Richard, for what you've done."

It was another miracle, and I'd been privileged to be part of it. We chanted together that evening, in celebration and gratitude.

But the miracle wasn't quite over. A few days later, I received a message on my telephone answering machine to call Irwin Steiner, a second cousin on my mother's side, from whom I hadn't heard in at least twenty-five years.

His mother was Virginia Scharff Eisner, a beautiful and charming woman who had not only been close to my mother, but who was also a friend of Julie Wilson, the celebrated cabaret chanteuse. When Julie had taken over the lead in *The Pajama Game*, we would all gather together, and I remembered what a striking and vibrant woman Virginia had been.

But what was I to make of this call, out of the blue and out of the past, asking me to phone my cousin, no matter what time I got in?

It was a peculiar message, because I hadn't talked to Irwin in over a quarter of a century. And to get a call suddenly, asking me to return it, no matter what the hour, piqued my curiosity. So, I called, even though it was nearly midnight.

After exchanging amenities, I asked him, "What's up?"

"I had dinner with Swami Tyagananda tonight," he said.

"Are you a devotee of Siddha Yoga, Irwin?" I asked.

"No," he replied. "The swami is my cousin."

"Your cousin? What kind of cousin?"

"He's my second cousin on mother's side."

"He's *your* second cousin? Then—"

"Right. He's *your second cousin too!*"

And Irwin continued with a genealogical description of exactly how we were related to each other.

So there it was, the converging lines of lives, the nudging of fate. What had brought me to Gurumayi? And what had brought Tyagananda to Gurumayi? And had she known all along that all of this would occur, that in this fateful way, and this joining of two souls, two lost relatives, I could now claim, among my spiritual companions, "My Cousin the Swami"? There are five billion people on this planet and, wonder of wonders, Swami Tyagananda, born John Miller in St. Louis, and Richard Adler of New York should be brought together, by God, and two tumors.

It was December. I was back where I liked to be, back where it felt comfortable: In a bare, tacky rehearsal hall, surrounded by actors and actresses and singers and musicians. A more polished, staged reading of *Off Key* was about to begin. It was a bitterly cold day, in the midst of the worst December imaginable. But the warmth in the room was palpable. *Off Key* had grown over the summer; what had been part of a show in June was nearing completion in December.

The music began; the show began. It was, I knew, like nothing I'd ever written before. It had a substance and a flow to it, turns and colors I'd never seen till now, and it had all come forth without agony, without turmoil. The conduit, once established, once recognized, had seemed to open further as the score progressed. I'd written thirty-five pieces of music, nearly three times the average number for a typical musical.

The story and the score seemed to flow forward together, in one sustained rush of emotion. It unfolded now, reaching out to the small but rapt audience, gathering it in, holding it.

For the moment, I drifted slowly away, back to last summer. Thousands and thousands of us had gathered in South Fallsburg, then, to celebrate Gurumayi's birthday.

I'd written a song especially for her, and had sung it on the Friday of the Birthday Weekend. Then, with Don Smith, my faithful, priceless accompanist, friend, and musical alter ego, I'd joined, that Saturday night, a symphony orchestra, a parade of stars that included John Denver, Lulu, Barbara Carrera, Illinois Jacquet, and Mandy Patinkin, and had sung several of my songs to Gurumayi.

It had been an exquisite evening, a soft, beginning of summer night. It had been raining for days, and the night before, hundreds of devotees had, in a sea of mud, readied the *Shakti Mandap,* an outdoor amphitheater, for the celebration. Now, in the midst of this great gala, Gurumayi had been radiant, laughing and applauding and encouraging the performers, receiving us personally and chatting with us, kidding us, having her disciples place *prasads* of shawls on our shoulders.

I'd gone back to my seat, then, to join Susan, to watch the rest of the program. And suddenly, the lights had dimmed, and several television screens had come alive. Videotapes of devotees in scores of ashrams all over the world were cheerfully singing to Gurumayi, "You gotta have heart / All you really need is heart."

The fact that the program's director had chosen the song without knowing that I'd written it; the fact that the song was first performed almost on the day Gurumayi had been born could be called ironic coincidence, except that I'd learned that there were no ironic coincidences. Everything was part of a giant design.

My eyes had filled then, and they did now, in that stark rehearsal studio in a cold December on the West Side of Manhattan. What Bill and I had written, I knew, had heart, and something more. Everything that I'd done in my life, all of the loving people who had filled my days and my heart were there in what I was doing now: Mother. Dad. Jerry. Marion. Andrew. Christopher. George. Bobby. Gwen. Shirley. Sally Ann. Ritchey. Little Ritchey. Mary. Laura. Susan. Lou. Swami T. And most of all, and encompassing all, Gurumayi.

We were part of this, every one of us, part of one huge heart that beat because of the love we felt for each other and for ourselves. And I knew now, after all of these years, how to pour that love into my life, and into my work.

I looked around at the audience. The music, the words, the story, had reached out and touched them. Many were crying openly and unashamedly.

I breathed easily and well. "It feels like a hit," I said to myself, and I meant the show, and my transformation, and my life as it is and will be now, for as long as it lasts. "Ultimately and finally, it feels like a hit."

INDEX